THE UNSUSPECTING

Like most of us, the men and women who lived side by side at Koptic Court knew little of one another.

Sometimes they knew a name or recognized a face as they passed one another on the stairs in the halls, but that was all. They knew nothing of what went on behind each closed and separate door.

They did not know that

in 3-C the nice, respectable businessman despised his wife and secretly lusted after his son's pretty girl friend

in 2-E a young man was desperately struggling against his unnatural desires for another man

in 4-B a young wife was being driven to strange violence by her nightmarish memories of a concentration camp

in 5-F a bitter and frustrated teen-ager was plotting vengeance against them all

Here is a gripping and intimate novel that plunges you in the turmoil and terror of the forbidden private worlds that lie behind the locked doors of big-city apartments.

7 Keys to Koptic Court

Former title: KOPTIC COURT

By HERBERT D. KASTLE

WILDSIDE PRESS

All characters in this book are
fictional and any resemblance to
persons living or dead is purely
coincidental.

To my wife, Laura

1

THE HOUSE

In 1927, Harold Koptic began building a six-story apartment house in the Boro Park section of Brooklyn. It was a relatively new area then, with two- and four-family houses predominating, with a heavy Italian population and a growing Jewish population. It was a good area, an expensive area, and Koptic drove across the river from his West End Avenue apartment at least twice a week to see how construction was coming along.

"Growing," he'd say to the huge Irish construction boss. "Growing, Delaney, growing. You follow the plans, hear?" He'd clasp his hands behind his back and raise himself up on his toes and puff out his chest—five feet one inch of Russian-Jewish immigrant, 125 pounds of titanic energy, ambition and fear. Mostly fear. Harold Koptic was afraid of poverty and terrified of contempt. He'd lived in an earthen-floored hovel in the Russian Ukraine for sixteen years before coming to the States. He'd eaten black bread, herring and potatoes—when his family had them. He'd been kicked, spat upon, and once almost disemboweled during the gay Russian Christmas festivities when the nobleman who owned the town of Krasilov had drunk too much and led his guests on a Jew-hunt. He'd been bullied and later treated with amused tolerance by Jewish boys his own age who called him Farfel—the kosher equivalent of Shrimp. He had ambition.

5

"Sure it's growing," the massive construction boss would say. "Sure, did you expect it wouldn't?" And he'd tense for what he knew would follow.

Harold Koptic always smiled, and kept his eyes on the scaffolding and the workmen and the rising building. And then struck back at the world. "You keep them going, Delaney. You keep them going fast—faster." He'd turn his narrow, bony face and look up at Delaney with brown eyes grown cold. "I want it should be faster," he'd say, and enjoy the flush moving into the Irishman's pink-white cheeks. "I know your boss very well. I'm going to give him lots of business—lots of houses to build. He will do as I ask."

Each time Delaney wanted to reach out and pound the tiny Yid into the pavement, and each time he nodded, turned on his heel and stamped away. He cursed under his breath and wondered what the hell was driving that little bastard, making him push so hard, making him want to hurt people.

Harold Koptic would smile as he watched the big Irishman. A construction boss named Ivan Ivanovitch would have been better, but who could have everything? A goy was a goy, a black year on them all!

In March of 1928, the house was completed. Harold Koptic was there the day the last workman left—a painter like himself, but a poor fool of a painter, a tall, thin Polish Jew with no brains except to work for others, to work for Harold Koptic.

Koptic had learned the trade from his Uncle Meyer, with whom he'd lived his first two years in the States in a four-room tenement flat off Delancey Street. He worked hard, and soon was able to pick up jobs on his own, undercutting Meyer Koptic's prices on the sly. He worked fast, barely stopping to grab a mouthful of food. He took his pay and stuck it in the savings bank and lived on as little as he could. When he had two hundred dollars, he hired a helper, lowered his rates still more, and worked twice as hard. He had three helpers in one year; they couldn't take the low pay and hard work very long.

He made more money. He worked every day in the week, as late as the customer would allow. He moved from his Uncle Meyer's place into a small room off Houston Street. One Sunday he visited Meyer and met a third cousin—Chava Stern. Chava, or Eva, was his height, chubby and pretty. He looked at her and she smiled and he suddenly wanted to do something—to touch her. His uncle saw and understood, and after Chava and her mother, a monstrously fat woman, had left, he drew Harold aside.

"I could make the match," he said, and roared as Harold Koptic turned white with embarrassment.

Harold Koptic left his uncle's flat without answering. But ten days later he returned and drank a glass of tea and said, "What has she got?"

"You couldn't see?" the uncle replied, and laughed until the tears ran from his eyes. "Ah, you mean what sort of dowry would you get? I don't know, but I could ask. Should I ask?"

Harold Koptic nodded.

"I saw how you looked at her," the uncle said, smiling softly, reminiscently. "You will marry her even if the dowry is small."

Harold Koptic said, "No. A man must live." Then he shook hands and went home.

"A cold fish, that Harold," Meyer Koptic said to his wife. "I'm glad we haven't any single daughters."

The dowry was large. Mr. Stern, Chava's father, owned a hand laundry on Riv. igton Street and was a proud man. Despite his wife's couns :l and his son's angry remonstrances, he offered one thousand dollars. Harold Koptic accepted. The marriage was held on a Saturday night. It was both the first and last time Chava Koptic saw her husband get drunk, dance and sing.

Harold took the dowry and his own savings and invested in a four-family house in Brooklyn. It wasn't a sudden decision; it was something he'd been planning for more than a year. With a first and second mortgage, he was able to swing it. But he didn't move himself and his wife to the new, red-bricked house on the quiet Brooklyn street. He stayed in the three-room cold-water flat he'd rented right after the marriage. When his father-in-law criticized him for this, Harold said, "You got money to burn, burn it. You want to put your daughter in fancy apartments, pay for it."

Mr. Stern listened to his wife and son that time and let Harold stay where he was. Harold was disappointed: he'd hoped to get something more from the laundryman.

But it made little difference in the long run. Real estate boomed in Brooklyn: Harold sold his four-family house at a profit, went partners on three Flatbush tenements, sold them at a huge profit, bought more and sold more, and found himself worth over a hundred thousand dollars by 1926. He was then living in one of his Brooklyn two-family houses, and his approach to life changed radically. He had two sons, was respected for his wealth by all the family, and had almost convinced himself he didn't fear life.

He moved to West End Avenue and decided to build the Boro Park apartment house. It would be a tribute to his success. Even if it took all his cash to swing the deal with the bank, it would be worth it. His name would be carved in stone over the front doors and inlaid in colored tile in the lobby floor. *Koptic Court.* And with prosperity in full swing, he was sure to rent every apartment at top rates.

"You," he called to the tall, thin painter who was last to leave the completed house. "Come here a minute."

The tall man ambled over and said, "Mr. Koptic. A fine house."

Harold Koptic nodded. "You think so, eh? I want your advice." He smiled at the flattered expression which crossed the painter's face. "That carving—isn't it too far to the left?"

The man turned and looked up at the ornate, scroll-bedecked marble block set over the iron-and-glass front doors —an item that had cost far too much but which Harold Koptic hadn't been able to resist. "You mean the scrolls, Mr. Koptic?"

"The name," Harold Koptic said, heart pounding with pride. "Koptic Court. Is it too far over?"

The painter squinted in the growing dusk. "I don't think so. I think it's just right. Imagine, to have your name—"

"Yes," Harold Koptic said, unable to restrain himself. "Yes, I was the smallest in Krasilov and now I'm the biggest and when they see it and read it their hearts will burst with—" He stopped then because the painter had begun to move away. He wanted to make the man return, but all he did was mutter, "Stupid, penniless *luksh!*"

The painter left, and soon it was too dark to see the marble block, and Harold Koptic went home.

Within a month, every apartment in Koptic Court was rented—ten on each floor; sixty apartments in all. A blue canopy stretched from the deep entranceway to the street; a doorman in gray uniform and cap stood impressively under it; the self-service elevator hummed as tenants went about the business of living. And Harold Koptic came at least once a week, ostensibly to talk to his superintendent but actually to look at his name over the doors and in the tile of the lobby.

He didn't know it, but his name appeared in one other place—in the basement, in a dark spot between the elevator and the boiler room. It had been placed there the last day of actual construction when Steve Delaney, raging over Harold Koptic's final insult—"With a decent foreman I could've been renting a month ago. Maybe you drink too much, Delaney. Lots of you people drink too much"—went down to the basement and saw the men doing a patch job on the wall and stood there and drank from a pint he carried under his Mackinaw and raged silently, and then, when the workmen left, jabbed his thick, calloused forefinger into the wet cement as if he were jabbing it into the little man who'd tormented him for a year, and printed: "Curse you and your house, Koptic bastard."

Later, after killing the pint, he slapped his big hand over the soft cement, rubbed and walked away.

If anyone had gone to that dark spot between elevator and boiler room and examined the rough, grayish cement wall, he'd have seen the words "curse" and "Koptic."

Harold Koptic was happy, really happy for the first time in his life. But it didn't last long. Nineteen twenty-nine came. The Wall Street crash came. The depression came, and Koptic Court had seventeen vacancies, twenty-three vacancies, thirty-eight vacancies. Rents were lowered, lowered again, and yet again. The bank foreclosed on Harold Koptic's mortgage, and a few days later had to close its own doors when most of its investments hit bottom.

Harold Koptic committed suicide. He didn't shoot himself, hang himself, gas himself, or do anything else quick and relatively painless. He went back to living in an East Side tenement and painting flats. He kept telling his wife he would make all the boys from Krasilov look up to him when he again owned Koptic Court. He couldn't sleep. He wanted to work, to make money, day and night. There was little enough work during the day; he paced the floors and talked to himself at night.

At the age of 51, about seven months after he'd lost his Boro Park apartment house, Harold Koptic dropped dead while climbing the stairs to his fourth-floor flat.

His wife and older son scraped together a few dollars and opened a candy store in East New York. They never thought of visiting Koptic Court. The younger son rode out there one day with a friend who owned a Model-T Ford. He found the scene of his father's past glory depressing.

After that, no Koptic set foot inside the Fifteenth Avenue building. The doorman disappeared, to be followed by the canopy. The neighborhood deteriorated, but not too much, and was later built up during the 1938 to 1941 boom. World War II came and Koptic Court was fully rented for the first time since the depression.

At the end of the war, the house passed through the hands of half a dozen speculators who refused to expend money on anything but legally required maintenance. In 1953, Ralph Gorman, a non-speculator, took over. He made some needed repairs, and later hired a good superintendent—a middle-aged man named Luke Brown, the first Negro ever to live in Koptic Court. The house was now middle-class in rents, ninety per cent Jewish in tenants, just short of shabby in appearance. It stayed that way. It had reached its level.

2

ELI WEINER 3-C

It seemed that his life had become an endless chain of mornings—gray mornings or bright mornings, but uniform in their lack of promise. He wanted something—something more than he had. Not money. Not possessions. Something really exciting, really important.

The alarm would go off in Dick's room, ring for about the count of ten, and then stop. Rose would sit up and clear her throat and wait and then clear her throat again. "Eli," she'd say. "Eli, that boy will drive me out of my mind."

He'd keep his eyes closed, making her think he was asleep. But he'd have been awake a good hour. He always woke about six and stared up at the ceiling and tried to think his way around the woman lying beside him—the forty-year-old woman who looked so old and meant so little to him. But she was terribly big. She loomed like some gigantic monster under the covers—a small, thin woman really, but so big in the path of his being happy, so big in the path of his reaching out to taste the love of women, pretty women, women he'd never been able to impress as a youth.

"Richard," Rose would call. "Richard! You'll be late for

class!" And then she'd get up and walk out of the master bedroom and into the foyer and past the bathroom and the small bedroom where twelve-year-old Teddy lay curled into a tight knot of solid sleep. She'd turn off the foyer into the bedroom nearest the living room and disappear. He would hear her voice rise and pause and rise and pause, and then Dick's surprisingly deep voice (surprising because it seemed only days ago that it had been a sweet though unpredictable alto tenor) would say, "Aw, for the love of Mike! I said I was getting up!"

Rose would go on to the kitchen, Dick would go into the bathroom, and sounds would begin to fill the five-room apartment—water running, pots and dishware clattering, footsteps padding and clicking. He would look toward the windows where day would be waiting, and feel weak and old and afraid. But it wouldn't be too long before he'd begin to come alive—rub his stubble of beard and move his shoulders and feel the firmness of his arms and the not-too-soft flesh of his chest and stomach. He'd sit up, and Dick would come out of the bathroom and say, "Morning, Dad."

He'd nod and smile. "Morning, Dick." He'd marvel at the way the boy had grown. Nineteen years old and so tall. Wide-shouldered and lean-hipped and graceful. Basketball and baseball at N.Y.U.; handball and touch-tackle with his neighborhood friends. Always moving, eating, dating, playing. Always laughing and living . . .

At this point certain sick memories, certain unhappy comparisons with his own youth would rise up to plague him, and he'd feel he had to get out of bed and leave the house. He'd feel he had to see Miss Lowen, touch Miss Lowen. And yet it wasn't the chubby, middle-aged secretary he wanted. It wasn't the thick legs under his hands, the heavy breasts pressing his chest, the acidy old-maidish voice giggling, saying, "Mr. Weiner, pulease!" in that irritating mixture of excitement, resentment and guilt. It was love he wanted—love pure, love complete, love that ached in the chest as well as in the groin. A young woman's love, a pretty woman's love, an intelligent and desirable woman's love. And couldn't he have it? Wasn't he young enough? Forty-three was young enough. And wasn't there enough imagination, enough convincing words in him to touch the right woman? But a man had to be free to speak the magic words, to weave the beautiful spell for himself and his love.

He could never ask Rose for a divorce. They rarely quarreled; they had two sons; they had friends and relatives and possessions and a history of twenty-one years together. Chains. Chains of the strongest material. . . .

On a Friday morning in March, a gray, rainy morning, Eli Weiner left Koptic Court and walked to the subway and rode to downtown Manhattan. He walked across Broadway and into the huge building and took the elevator to the third floor. The office with *Swan-Style Ladies' Wear* on the door was full of busy, efficient people. He said hello and good morning and entered his own little office and sat down at the old desk and got right on the phone to Louis Bromler, the button manufacturer who was stalling on that special price for next winter's line.

"Listen, Lou, you promised me and I promised my firm. Don't forget, we can always turn someplace else for buttons—"

"A little outfit like yours don't give me enough profit," the voice on the phone yelled.

"Maybe you'd rather I looked someplace else, huh?"

"Sure. Look. But you won't get cloth-covered lower no matter—"

"Listen, will you deliver or not?"

"Sure. Sure. Only an extra forty cents on the hundred—"

"So I look someplace else."

"Go on. Go on. Look someplace else."

It took twenty minutes for Eli Weiner to get his way. Then he listened to one of Bromler's shaggy-dog stories, laughed dutifully, and hung up. He went next door to Stan Ettinger, a short, thin, balding man with a perpetual frown.

"So you got the buttons, Eli. Good. So what about running down a nice line of plastic belts for the Junior Miss series?"

Eli returned to his office and got on the phone. He made eleven calls and six appointments to interview salesmen. It kept him busy until almost noon, and then Miss Lowen came into his office, closed the door and said, "You got any dictation for me, Eli?"

She came closer and he looked at her short, curved body, at the round fleshy face and tinted reddish hair. She wasn't anything he wanted today. But he smiled and said, "Maybe I could dictate something besides a letter, eh?"

She giggled, showing uneven teeth, and started around the desk. He snapped his fingers and said, "Hey, forgot I have to run over to Markel's! My God, if I'm not there by twelve-fifteen we'll be stuck without zippers!"

"Yeah," she said, and shrugged. "Lately it's always buttons or zippers at the last minute. Big rush. Always a big rush."

"All right," he said, his voice sharper than he'd meant it to be.

She pressed her lips together, then made a little palms-up gesture. "I'm sorry, Eli. Want I should check back later? I got letters to type for Ettinger until at least three."

"I've nothing in correspondence today," he said, and waited for her to leave.

She went to the door, then turned. "Eli, my sister's going to Washington again next Wednesday. She won't be home until Friday. Remember—"

He nodded quickly. "Yes, well, I really don't think—"

She turned on her heel, but not before he'd seen her go white with anger. She stomped out, slamming the door behind her.

He leaned back in his chair, sorry it had happened, sorry he'd ever touched her, yet knowing he might want to touch her again tomorrow, or the day after, or the week after. Of course, it had only been that one time when he'd taken her to dinner and then to her sister's apartment and they'd been alone and the year of sly hugs and squeezes and kisses had borne fruit. He'd been disgusted immediately afterward, and yet even then had suspected he might want her again.

That was because he had nothing else, he told himself. Love pure, love complete, love that ached in the chest. . . .

When he got home at six-thirty that evening, Rose told him Dick had called from school to say he was going to a party and wouldn't be in until ten. He was going to bring a few friends home at that time and wanted to use the car afterward. "Okay," Eli said, and sat down with Rose and Teddy at the kitchen table. He was pleased. Dick's friends were tall, athletic boys and girls. They came up and said hello and sometimes they were interesting. They were always good to look at.

"You mind if I play mah-jongg tonight?" Rose asked.

He didn't look up from his grapefruit. " 'Course not."

"Well, you'll have to be host to Dick's friends. I'll make a few sandwiches and there's plenty of milk and soda in the refrigerator."

"Dick's his own host. Don't worry."

"Tell him to drive careful. I think he drank liquor two weeks ago at a house-plan party—"

"I've heard it a dozen times. He wasn't drunk, and anyways, he didn't use the car that night."

"Well, be sure he doesn't drink anything tonight."

He nodded and ate and she asked him about the office and he answered and Teddy asked about going to a basketball game and he answered and kept eating. Once, when Rose went to the stove, he suddenly raised his head and looked at her. His face paled and his eyes closed and he said to himself, "Dear God, I can't live with this person any longer. There's so much I'm missing, so much more I want from a woman."

She said, "How's the chicken?"

He said, "You know it's wonderful. Your chicken is always wonderful."

Teddy said, "I like steak better."

It was then Eli Weiner realized there was only one way he would ever be free of his wife.

He ate a little faster. He tried to block the thought, and yet it came through strong. *He would be free of her only when she died.*

He had skirted that thought many times, but tonight it was clear and tonight he accepted it. And yet, Rose was his friend, Rose loved him, and he didn't want her to die.

Still, men killed wives for love of other women. There was that movie with Joan Crawford—

But he didn't love another woman, and he laughed at himself and finished his tea. Then he went into the living room with Teddy to watch television. . . .

He put Teddy to bed at nine-thirty, tussling with the tall, thin boy and enjoying himself—and yet wondering that he was the father.

"Daddy," Teddy called as Eli closed the door and started toward the living room. "Daddy, can't I stay up a little longer?"

"No," he answered firmly. "If you want to grow, to gain weight so you can play football when you start high school, then you've got to sleep."

"All right, Daddy."

He lowered the sound on the TV and took a cigar from his jacket draped over an armchair. He sat on the couch and smoked and told himself he was a solid, respectable, successful man. Well, maybe a hundred-fifty a week average wasn't exactly successful, but he might better himself in time—work into a partnership when old Ettinger retired, or Frank Silesi finally succumbed to his bad kidneys. Anyway, he was raising a family, supporting them nicely, sending his older son through college, saving for Teddy's education too. The boys always had good summer vacations, and so did he and Rose. They dressed well and ate well and if they saved on rent here it was only being practical. Well, maybe they'd move when an extra twenty, twenty-five dollars a week was coming in.

So he was a father, a businessman, a provider. It meant a lot. Sure it did.

He went into the kitchen and got the bottle of Scotch from the closet. He poured himself a stiff shot and mixed it with cold tap water and went back to the couch. He drank fast, and wanted another, and refused to give in to himself.

He was a father, a businessman, a provider—*and it meant nothing.*

It meant nothing because he didn't believe in it.

Teddy called him Daddy and Dick called him Dad and Rose called him Eli, and he wasn't any of those things. Certainly not the Eli his wife thought he was. He was a boy looking for love pure, love complete, love that ached in the chest.

He laughed and said aloud, "Eli, you're nuts."

It didn't help much. He began thinking of Lily Weinstein, the way he often did when he was feeling shaky and insecure and uncertain about things.

"Christ," he said, and stood up. "What the hell's wrong with you?"

But then he sat down again and remembered Lily and winced. He wished he could go back in time and live it all over. He'd show that silly little bitch . . .

He'd been sixteen when he met her at a dance in a Flatbush Avenue ballroom—one of those places where you paid half a dollar entrance fee and went inside and picked up a girl and then paid thirty cents for a Coke and eighty cents for a malt and a dollar for a sandwich. He'd seen the medium-sized, dark-haired girl walk in alone, and he'd moved toward her immediately because she was pretty and neatly dressed and looked kind. Especially because she looked kind. He was much too thin then, and his face was large-featured and plain. But he liked girls, needed their company and friendship, and was beginning what would be a long struggle to gain their approval.

She'd danced with him, given him her address and the

telephone number of a candy store where (if the proprietor could find a kid to use as a messenger) she could be reached, and told him she "wouldn't mind seeing a movie some night." He'd been ecstatic. He'd taken her home and walked her to the second-floor apartment and been invited in. He'd been appalled by the obvious poverty, and touched on learning she had no mother. When she led him to the door, he'd screwed up his courage and said, "I sure like you, Lily. You're . . . you're nice." She'd stared at him and he'd fled.

He'd dated her the next week. They went to the Loew's Pitkin. On the way, some guys standing in front of a candy store whistled at Lily and made dirty cracks. Eli wanted to do something, but the boys were big and tough and he was no fighter. "Don't let them bother you," Lily said, and tugged his arm. She didn't seem concerned, or even annoyed. "They always talk that way. They never have any money to date a girl."

Somehow, that last remark bothered him, but he didn't know why.

In the movie, he stared at the screen and didn't really see the picture and tried to work up the courage to take her hand. When he finally did, she pulled free and said, "Eli, please," in a voice full of annoyance.

The blood rushed to his face. He turned to her and whispered, "I'm sorry. Don't be mad."

She sighed and looked at him. "I'm not mad." She put her hand in his and left it there for the rest of the show.

He was happy for a while, but then the happiness went away and he felt humiliated somehow. He squeezed her hand to reassure himself, but she didn't answer the pressure and a presentiment of disaster, of pain to come, was born.

When they walked up the street on which she lived, a group of boys and girls was sitting on the steps of a brownstone house. Lily seemed to stiffen, and then she moved close to him and took his hand and laughed and said, "That's a good one, Eli!"

He suspected what it was all about right away. And when the tall, good-looking boy with his arm around a blonde girl called, "Hi, Lil," he knew for sure.

Lily gave a toss of her head, said, "Hi, George," and then turned to Eli as if they'd been deep in private conversation. "That Dixieland jazz show's gonna be fun. We'll go early and get good seats—"

He didn't say anything. He felt insulted, crushed, used.

He continued to see Lily, taking her places on the money his parents gave him, buying her an expensive compact for her birthday and receiving a kiss in return—the first, the only kiss she ever gave him. He kept taking her out, though by now he knew she cared nothing for him, suspected she was actually repelled by his lack of manly qualities. He was tied to her by a compulsion to win out, and by a steady growth of sexual desire. He learned she was seeing George, the tall boy who'd been sitting on the stoop with the blonde, but he didn't dare question her about him.

The relationship ended in crushing humiliation and horror. In a desperate attempt to win some sign of affection, he took her to a Manhattan night club, the first for either of them. The waiter was kind—or hoped for a large tip—and served them pre-dinner cocktails. (Eli's parents drank an occasional martini, so he ordered them with a degree of urbanity.) The potent gin-wine mixture hit them hard, and when they danced Eli found the courage to hold Lily's soft body tight against his own. More than that, he didn't draw away when fire raced through his veins.

For an instant, she seemed about to let herself go with him, but then she pulled back, stopped dancing and said, "Eli, I'm hungry." They ate, and she wouldn't dance with him again, and he took her home after the floor show. It was one-thirty in the morning when they stopped in the hall outside her door. Following what had become standard procedure, she gave him her hand and said, "I had a wonderful time, Eli. Thank you."

This night it wasn't enough. He remembered the wonderful moment on the dance floor when he'd held her tight. He reached for her and crushed her against him and tried to kiss her on the lips. She twisted her head aside and his lips found her ear. Then she was shoving at his chest with both hands.

"Stop it! I don't like you that way, Eli! You know I never meant you should think I like you that way."

He let her go. He was ready to cry, but he said, "Yeah? What way do you like me?"

She was already opening her door. "As a friend. You're a friend."

He couldn't look at her because he was sure he'd see revulsion. He looked down at the grimy tenement floor and said, "I'm sorry." He was going to ask for another date, but she stopped him.

"I think we'd better not see each other any more, Eli."

He loved her, and she despised him. He began to turn away and was suddenly overwhelmed by the long months of frustration and misery. Before he could control himself, a sob tore from his throat and tears filled his eyes.

Horrified, he tried to run down the stairs, but the tears blinded him and he fell headlong. He was lucky, merely scraping his chin and bruising his knees.

When he got up, she was there to help him. "Oh," she said, wincing at his tears and bloodied chin. "Oh, I'm sorry."

He read pity in her eyes, and seized upon it fiercely. He sensed that pity could be used, that it might prolong the relationship.

"Lily," he said. "Lily, please let me see you. I . . . I love—"

But she was too young, too uneducated and uncivilized to be trapped by pity. She said, "Don't be a jerk! I told you! Anyway, George and I are gonna go steady." She ran back up the stairs to her door, opened it, then turned and said the words he would hate for the rest of his life: "You're sweet, Eli."

He didn't see her again. He began using bar bells to build up his body. He dated other girls, and had a degree of success. He met Rose, and married, and never even heard of Lily.

But he often thought of that terrible evening, that humiliating evening, and wished he could go back, relive it, change it, erase it. . . .

The doorbell rang at a few minutes past ten, cutting short his thoughts. He got into his jacket, straightened his tie, went to the door and opened it. Dick said, "Hi, Dad. We're here because we're here because we're here. That's why we're here." He belched and giggled. He was drunk. A husky boy named Walter held his right arm and another athletic-looking boy named Steven held his left. They tried to suppress laughter and failed. Behind them were three girls and they laughed too. At least he thought the three girls were laughing. Later, he realized one of them was merely stretching her lips and making laughing sounds.

He looked at them and felt the stern expression moving into his face and wondered at that because he didn't feel stern at all. They'd been to a party and had liquor and his son had drunk more than the others. So what?

"I'm surprised at you," he said, letting his eyes run over the six of them. "Janet, Ruthie—" And then he examined the third girl and realized he didn't know her and understood that she wasn't really laughing. Her laughter was like his sternness. Her eyes were like his own when he heard his children call him Dad.

She was so beautiful she made his chest ache.

"Irene," she said as he stared at her. "I'm Dick's date."

"Well," he said, "this isn't a very nice way to come home, is it?" And he stood in the doorway and kept staring at her and knew she was the only one who wasn't drunk. Maybe she'd been drinking, but her eyes were watching and waiting and wondering.

"I'm sorry," she said, and now she was staring back at him. "It was a very wild party. It's my fault really. It was in my home."

"The *pater familias*," Dick said, and tried to stand at attention, and succeeded in pulling his two friends off balance. All three staggered and laughed and Dick said, "The grand old man of craptic court."

"Okay, okay," Eli said. "Come on in. And don't make any noise—Teddy's sleeping."

"Wake him up and give him a drink," Dick stage-whispered.

"Enough of that," Eli snapped, and stepped aside, waving them in brusquely. But he was enjoying himself. He couldn't get his eyes off the girl—Irene.

She wasn't like any of the other girls Dick had brought to the apartment. For one thing, she wasn't tall and athletic. She was a dark little girl—dark eyes, hair and complexion. Her face was delicate and heart-shaped; the eyes enormous, the hair silky, the lips wide and full of movement in the corners. She seemed about to crinkle up those corners in a smile one second, and to push them down a childish wail the next. She was almost sickly-looking, and when she walked past him her gait was slow, lazy—fantastically seductive, he felt.

Dick was led down the foyer to the living room by his two friends. The girls followed, Irene last, and Eli closed the door and moved behind her and said, "Since you're his date, I feel I should apologize."

She stopped short just before the archway to the living room. He bumped into her. She was wearing a pale-blue cotton dress and dark-blue shortie topcoat, and through them he felt the softness of her hip and side. He jumped back as if he'd been burned.

"Why should you apologize?" she asked. Her voice was

high-pitched, weak, sweet and lazy. It excited him, and at the same time tugged at his heart. He felt his eyes moving down her body, and couldn't stop them. He saw the maturity of bust and hip, the slimness everywhere else. Then he jerked his gaze to her face.

He'd been startled by bumping into her, startled by his reaction to her voice, but that was nothing compared to the feeling he got when she smiled.

He muttered something about being Dick's father and so feeling responsible for the boy's actions. She maintained her smile and said, "Oh, I see," and it was as if she were telling him not to be an idiot, as if she were laughing at the idea that he could really be Dick's father.

He tried to think of something else to say, and couldn't. He was stunned by that smile.

It was a marvelous thing. The corners of her mouth pulled upward and crinkled; her eyes grew narrow and shiny. The gamin effect was so touching, so beautiful—so intimate. He couldn't shake that feeling of intimacy as they stood in the foyer and the others talked and laughed in the living room.

He looked into her eyes and forgot the nonsense of his being husband and father. He saw himself as she must see him—five-eight, one hundred and seventy pounds, plenty of light-brown hair graying at the temples, a longish, even-featured, kind-looking face and all his own teeth. He kept looking into her eyes, and felt young and handsome and adventurous. He answered her smile.

"Not a very good reason, is it?" he said.

She shook her head, and her boyish-cut black hair moved. "I wouldn't think so, Mr. Weiner."

That "Mr. Weiner" snapped him out of it. He motioned toward the living room and she moved ahead.

Walter and his steady date, Janet, shared the wide black armchair. Steven and Ruthie lolled on the couch. Dick sat in the red bouclé armchair, head back, staring up at the ceiling, grinning foolishly. Irene walked toward Dick, and then continued past him to the television-radio-phonograph combination. She leaned against the big console. She looked very much alone there, very much apart from the other youngsters.

Eli stood under the arch, cleared his throat and said, "I certainly hope you kids didn't drive here."

"Subway," Dick said, still staring up at the ceiling. "But I got to keep my promise, Dad."

"What was that?"

Dick laughed and turned his head and looked at Irene. "Bet your folks are mad—especially at me. They come home to find all their good bourbon gone. Jack Daniels yet." He laughed again. "Some party, huh?"

She smiled, and Eli felt sure it was another muscular display, like the one in the hall. "Oh, well," she said, "I can handle them." She let the smile drift away, and her air of quiet waiting was immensely appealing to Eli.

"Why did you come here anyway?" Eli asked her, and then remembered to swing his eyes to include the others. "Not that I'm inhospitable, but you must have realized—" He glanced at Dick.

"Dick insisted," Irene said in her high, sweet, lazy voice— her exciting voice. She smiled at Eli, and this time he was sure it was real; the sudden, gamin brightness was impossible to fake. "He said he'd made arrangements. We were going to use your car and drive to Coney Island, or someplace."

Eli told himself to stop being a fool. The girl was eighteen, or nineteen—though she seemed older. She smiled the same for everyone.

It didn't work. He knew the smiles differed—the ones she gave her friends were false, the ones she gave him, real. And when he looked at her she met his eyes, and there was a waiting in hers, a kind of passive expectancy, as if she were saying, "I'm here, Mr. Weiner. If you want to reach out for me, I won't run."

He knew one thing for sure: she wasn't happy with her friends. But she was beautiful, whether or not the boys in her own age group could see it.

"Yeah," Dick said. "I insisted. So I got to fulfill my obligations and take 'em out, right?" He stood up, weaving on his feet, grinning. Everyone grinned back but Irene and Eli. Dick turned and looked at his date. "Hey, Little Miss Black Plague—"

"Dick!" Eli said angrily, and then was annoyed with himself. He had no right to interfere.

"I call her that all the time," Dick said, a defensive note entering his voice. "Five dates and I call her—"

"That's right," Irene said, and smiled—a real smile. "It's because he thinks I'm grim, somber, whatever you care to call it."

The others laughed and talked to each other, and Eli had to raise his voice to be heard. "I'm afraid Dick won't be driving anyone to Coney Island tonight."

"Aw, Dad—" Dick began, but his friends cut him short.
"Your dad's right," the husky Walter said.

"Sure, man," the athletic Steven said. "I didn't drink nearly as much as you, and I wouldn't drive tonight."

Janet and Ruthie nodded their pretty heads and agreed in their sweet voices, and only Irene said nothing. She stood leaning against the TV console, staring down at the rug. Again Eli found himself marveling at her beauty—so different from the tall, quick-moving, quick-talking girls sitting beside their dates; so different from any girl, any woman, he'd ever met. Or so it seemed.

"You're nuts," Dick said to all of them. "I'm as good as ever. I'll drive—"

"You're going to bed," Eli said sharply. "The rest of you are going home."

They dropped their eyes, all except Irene, who raised hers and looked at him and seemed about to smile. It was impossible, but he felt sure she was saying, "You're convincing in the role of indignant father, Mr. Weiner. I'll bet they all believe you. But we know better, don't we?"

He was perspiring, tense and excited, and he tried to shake the feeling, to bring himself back to normal.

"I'll drive you," he said.

Irene smiled. Dick flopped back in his chair and looked surly. The other two couples made happy sounds.

Eli got his topcoat, told Dick not to dare waken his brother, and ushered the five kids out of the apartment. When they entered the elevator, he had a sudden feeling of shame, of embarrassment. Someone had scratched a dirty word into the paint of the sliding door. He didn't want Irene to see things like that—ugly little things like that. It made the house so—so cheap. But that was one of the penalties for living in a down-graded, low-rent Brooklyn neighborhood.

No one else, however, seemed to notice. They rode down, Irene standing close to him, eyes lowered, the other kids laughing and horsing around.

On Fifteenth Avenue, they piled into the Buick—and Irene was in front, sitting beside him. He asked her where she lived.

"I'm afraid I'm a problem," she murmured, still not looking at him. "I live in Manhattan." She gave a Washington Heights address.

His heart leaped. He knew he would try to take her home

last, and now it was made easy for him. The other kids lived
in Brooklyn. . . .

At eleven-fifteen, he was driving along the Belt Parkway
toward the Brooklyn Battery Tunnel, averaging thirty miles
an hour, which was much slower than he usually drove. Irene
sat beside him. They were alone. He glanced at her, and she
was looking at him. She smiled her beautiful smile. He was
filled with wild longings, insane excitement.

"Dick is a very lucky boy," he said. "You're the prettiest
girl I've ever seen."

She didn't answer, and he glanced at her again. She was
turned away, looking out her window.

His heart leaped painfully. He'd embarrassed her! He'd
dreamed up promising smiles and mysterious glances for himself, and said something that showed he was a middle-aged
fool, and she'd turned away from him.

He forced a laugh. "It seems you're not used to your boy-
friends' fathers complimenting you." He laughed again, and
it sounded terribly false.

She still didn't answer, and he snarled under his breath in
an agony of shame, raging at himself for flirting with his
son's date, for putting himself in this horribly untenable
position.

He drove faster. It was a clear, cool night. The Narrows
on his left glistened under a sky full of stars; the ferry cross-
ing from Jersey hooted at a freighter anchored near the New
York shore; the smell of sand and water came through the
car's open windows.

The agony passed. He still wanted her. That look in her
eyes; those smiles—

"Would you do something for me?" she asked.

"Anything."

There was a moment of deep silence. He kept his eyes on
the road, refusing to backtrack with laughter.

"Would you tell me your first name?"

"Eli," he said, and felt as if someone had put on the radio,
filling the car with wild, triumphant music. "I wish it were
something nicer now." He looked at her, and she was turned
to him again, and he read her eyes and her smile.

"It couldn't be nicer," she said, and then stared at the
floor.

He was sure now! She was afraid, as he had been. She
wanted to reach out to him—

But in the next moment he was unsure again, warning himself to be careful, preparing himself for coldness or blunt rejection.

"Want to stop for a bite to eat?" he asked.

"Oh, yes," she said, and a truly radiant smile illuminated her face. She drew her legs up on the seat and hugged herself and glanced away in what looked like sudden embarrassment. And then smiled again. "Isn't it a lovely evening? Cold and clear and lovely."

And still he wasn't sure.

He had to be sure!

He laughed and said, "Hope my wife doesn't get suspicious of my staying out late—" He couldn't finish. It sounded so cheap and ugly. The blood rushed to his face and he jerked his head around to look at her. She'd stiffened, her smile gone, her face pale.

"I didn't mean that," he said.

He could just about hear her whispered answer. "Of course not."

He stopped to pay the toll at the Battery Tunnel, and as he pulled away from the booth she moved closer to him. They entered fluorescent-and-tile brightness.

When they emerged in Manhattan and turned onto the West Side Highway, she said, "Would you close your window, Eli? It's getting cold."

He rolled up the window, then said, "Body heat's the best way to lick the cold." He laughed briefly, and waited.

A moment later, she slid right up against him, her head going down to his shoulder. "You're right," she said, and he heard the way her voice shook. As for himself, he didn't trust his voice at all; he merely nodded.

They had sandwiches and coffee in a Tenth Avenue diner, sitting in one of the long row of booths against the chrome-and-glass wall. He finished quickly, then leaned back and watched her. She glanced up at him a few times, and finally put down her unfinished sandwich.

"I can't eat while you're watching," she murmured.

"Sorry." He glanced out the window, and heard her laugh, and laughed too.

"You can look now," she said. "I'm not going to finish anyhow."

"Thank you." He turned to her. "Looking at you is really quite a privilege."

Her lips turned up in that crinkling gamin smile, and he

felt as if she were drawing him across the table. He leaned forward, took her hand and raised it to his lips. He kissed it.

"Eli," she whispered, and pulled her hand away. She glanced around the diner. "Someone—someone you know might have seen—"

"No one I know is here. And I wouldn't have cared."

"Please," she said, eyes down. "It's late and I'd like to start for home."

It seemed a reversal of all the warmth that had been building up between them, and he was suddenly angry.

"All right," he said sharply, and placed some change on the table. He picked up the check and started to rise.

"Eli."

He looked at her.

"I—I don't want to like you," she said. "Not this much."

He sat down again, the anger dying in a burst of exultation.

"I can't like you this much, Eli. We can't like each other."

His heart was hammering at his ribs; his mouth was dry and the palms of his hands wet. "Yes we can," he said thickly. "Yes we can."

They looked at each other, and he reached out and took her hand. She shook her head, but it was a weak, uncertain gesture.

They left the diner and drove to the Washington Heights apartment house in which she lived with her mother and father. He parked on a dark side street and turned to her.

"I've got to go now," she said quickly. "My parents will worry."

He took her in his arms. He did it slowly, giving her ample time to draw away if she wanted to.

She didn't want to.

He kissed her, and though her hands stayed in her lap and her body remained passive, her lips pushed up against his. Then she freed herself, opened the door and stepped out.

"I've got to see you again," he said.

She hesitated, then reached into her purse. She scribbled something on a piece of paper torn from an envelope and handed it to him.

He didn't look at it until she'd walked around the corner and out of sight.

It was a telephone number.

He drove back to Koptic Court, parked the Buick and entered the lobby. As he pressed the button for the elevator, a tall, slender man came in from the street and walked with a delicate, mincing step toward the staircase. They glanced at each other, and Eli recognized Mr. and Mrs. Baer's nephew, Elliot. Elliot Wycoff.

They exchanged nods, and Eli suddenly felt embarrassed. He turned away, then hoped he hadn't been obvious. He didn't want to insult the man in any way, especially since Rose was friendly with Minnie Baer.

He turned back to Elliot Wycoff as the tall man reached the staircase. "Say, you wouldn't happen to know the City College score, would you?"

"City College?" the deep, rich voice questioned.

There, Eli told himself. How can he be queer with a voice like that? And would he be living with relatives?

"Basketball," Eli said.

"Oh. No, I'm sorry. I don't follow basketball."

"Yeah, well, thanks anyway."

"Certainly. Good night."

"Good night," Eli said, and watched him climb the stairs with a smooth, athletic stride. No, he couldn't be queer.

The elevator arrived and Eli got in.

When he entered the apartment, Rose was in bed, asleep. He lay down as quietly as he could, but she woke up.

"Eli?"

"Yes."

"You got the kids home all right?"

"Yes."

"Good. Dick told me he drank too much. He got sick. You'll have to put your foot down."

"I will. Good night."

"Good night."

She rolled over, moving closer to him. He shrank away, upset at the thought of touching her. . . .

3

ELLIOT WYCOFF 2-E

During the two years he'd lived with them, Elliot wondered whether his Aunt Minnie and Uncle Phil were aware of his problem. And then, on a Friday night in March, he found out. The childless couple was sitting in the living room of the four-room apartment, watching a television show, and he joined them, thinking he'd smoke a cigarette before driving to Sylvia Chrysler's place. Sylvia certainly was fortunate to make enough money to maintain a comfortable Manhattan apartment and indulge her tastes in food, drink, clothes and entertainment. If only he could earn eighty-six hundred a year . . .

He shrugged mentally. He had Sylvia for a friend, and also the Derrings and Slocums, parents of boys he'd roomed with at Columbia. The Derrings and Slocums treated him well, and they could easily afford it. Ivar Derring owned and operated a business that had been in his family for three generations—Coronation House, "manufacturers of fine period furniture." Roger Slocum was an investment counselor who had inherited a great many wise investments from his paternal grandmother. Both men were worth well over a hundred thousand a year.

Elliot puffed his cigarette and looked at the television screen and continued to see nothing but his thoughts. Next Friday he was going to a concert with the Derrings—father, mother, teen-aged son. And next Saturday was the dinner party at the Slocums'—mother, father, twenty-year-old daughter. He would stay overnight and all day Sunday.

He smiled to himself. Life wasn't bad at times like that; one could see the value in it, the culture and beauty in it. And life was even better during the summers. He got invited up to the Derrings' farm (called The Hatchery, it was a farm only in a historical sense, and in that the caretaker and his wife raised a few squabs and fine turkeys for the Derrings' table) for weekends of tennis. He was an excellent tennis player and earned his keep, so to speak, by always being available for a game with any member of the family or their guests. He did the same for the Slocums at their year-round estate-home on Long Island's North Shore. He was built for tennis—six feet two and a willowy, supple, one hundred sixty-three pounds. He was always in demand for singles, doubles, a fourth at bridge, or to direct a spirited discussion of the arts.

He was brought out of his thoughts by a shrill peal of laughter from his aunt, and looked at the tiny, birdlike woman. She laughed again, high and shrill, and there was an element of pain and embarrassment about it.

His uncle, short and stout and balding, said, "Stupid stuff," in his deep, gruff voice. "I don't know why people bother to watch it." He didn't look at Elliot, and neither did his wife.

Elliot got a sudden tight sensation in his chest. He turned to the TV screen and understood immediately. A low comic was saying, "Oooh, I'll *thlap* you, you nathty thing!" smoothing his eybrows with one hand, making effeminate slapping motions with the other. Then, as the audience roared, he put both hands on his hips and said, "I'll have you know I played left end for Notre Dame!" He stressed the word "end" and the audience shrieked.

Elliot reacted with automatic, mechanic precision. He laughed, loud and deep. "Coarse, all right, but I must admit he's funny." He laughed again, fighting a fear, a sickness. His aunt and uncle mustn't ever think him—queer. Because he wasn't. Certainly not! He'd never tried anything like that in all his life. He'd never touched a man in any way except the socially acceptable handshake or a hail-fellow-well-met slap on the shoulder. (There *was* that time when he was a kid . . . but that didn't count.) Just because he had feelings for beauty, for things of taste and refinement, people thought he was—effeminate. Well, that certainly indicated a flaw in American *mores*, relegating appreciation of beauty to women! Of course, not all people looked on him with suspicion.

"Mind if I change the channel?" Uncle Phil asked, rising from the couch where he was sitting beside his wife. He rubbed his jowly face and kept his eyes down. "There must be something better on."

Minnie nodded vigorously. "Go ahead, Phil."

"Gee, I hope you folks don't mind," Elliot said, "but I'd like to see the end of this guy's act." Now he was overdoing it —the "gee" and "folks" and "guy" weren't like him. He had to make it more natural. "I'm leaving for my friend Sylvia's place in five minutes and then you change the show if it annoys you. Okay?"

His uncle sat down, nodding, and then smiled—almost in relief, Elliot thought. His aunt reacted exactly the same way. "Of course," she said. "If you like him, Elliot."

"Thanks," he said, and laughed as the comic lisped, "Oooh, you make me tho *mad!*"

He felt fear and rage. They'd given up ridiculing hunchbacks and cripples, but homosexuals were still fair game. As if homosexuality wasn't as great a misfortune, a sickness, as a malformed spine.

But why should it bother *him?* He wasn't—

"That woman," his aunt said, "she must like you, Elliot. You've been visiting her almost as long as you've lived with us."

"Yes," he said, and laughed again, more naturally this time, as the comic switched to another line of humor.

His aunt pursed her small mouth disapprovingly. "You once told me she was over forty."

The comic finished and a commercial flashed on. Elliot stood up. "Don't worry, Aunt Minnie," he said, and chuckled. "I'm not going to marry her."

"Then why do you visit—"

"Minnie!" Uncle Phil interrupted in an unusual show of annoyance with his petite wife. She generally had him wrapped around her little finger.

"I'm sorry, Elliot," Aunt Minnie murmured. "I didn't mean to pry. It just slipped out. Natural curiosity, I guess. Have a nice time."

Elliot forced another chuckle, but now he was raging at her. Silly woman; how could she understand the joys of sharing entertainment with a friend, a real friend and not just a receptacle for a penis? "You have a right to know what I do evenings, Aunt Minnie. You treat me like a son, so you have the rights of a mother."

"Well," she said, a pleased look entering her sharp, black eyes, "as long as Reba is in California and you're here, I do feel that as her sister I should—"

"Of course," Elliot said.

Uncle Phil cleared his throat. "I hope you realize, Minnie, that Elliot is very understanding. It's not every man of thirty-three who would be so glad to answer questions on his personal life."

Glad! Elliot thought. Then he controlled the anger, reminding himself that they'd been good to him—very good to him. Of course, he was living in this contemptible middle-class environment, this ghetto world with its dull apartments, dull tenants, and troops of shrieking, ill-mannered children. It wasn't *his* world in any way—but then again, neither would the kind of Manhattan furnished room he could afford be his world. Besides, he paid only fifteen dollars a week for room and board here—token payment which he himself insisted on —and that left him with enough money to live up to his friends' standards and maintain his Porsche sports car.

"We're good friends, Aunt Minnie. That's all. She has a fine collection of popular and classical music—" he stopped and smiled. "Well, I'd better be going." He'd suddenly realized the impossibility of explaining it to her.

It reminded him of the time—a few weeks before he'd gone into the Marines—that he'd tried to make his mother understand why he wanted to change his name from Wycoffsky to Wycoff. She'd said, "Ah, you're afraid of the prejudice."

He hadn't been able to make her see how much more it was than that. He hadn't wanted a label—a false label. He felt he'd have changed his name from O'Brien, Basconi, Rodrignez, or anything else that implied passions or beliefs, attractive or otherwise, alien to what he was. And what he was —or thought he was—couldn't be explained to Mother. He was a man of culture, sensitivity, intelligence; and he wanted no identifying characteristics that would limit his ability to grow in these directions. Wycoffsky was just such a "characteristic." Of course, an Anglo-Saxon name and background could have been left unaltered because, justly or not, it would have put him in the position he desired.

He didn't bother examining the ethics involved. He felt no resentment of society, nor did he feel the slightest touch of guilt or shame. He wasn't a Jew. That was all. So why carry a Jewish label?

Mother hadn't understood. He'd changed his name regardless, and made her change hers so as to reduce the possibility of any future embarrassing denouements. But she had never understood.

And neither would Minnie, when it came to Sylvia Chrysler.

As he moved toward the closet to get his coat and hat, his uncle winked at him.

At least he'd convinced Phil that he was a man. He wished he could convince himself. . . .

He walked around the corner and halfway up the dark side street to where two identical four-family houses stood parallel to each other. Between them was an alley which broadened out into a back yard and four separate garages. He rented the one on the far right for his tiny Porsche convertible.

He turned into the alley, feeling a little chilly in his herringbone topcoat, anxious to drive the beautiful two-seater. It was his pride and joy; he gloried in its clean lines and quick response. He also gloried in its unorthodoxy, though this was something he rarely admitted to himself.

About two-thirds along the alley, light from a window on the left caught his eye. Automatically, he glanced there. The

shade was drawn to within three or four inches of the sill,
enough to shield anyone inside from eyes in the house across
the alley—but not from someone walking in the alley itself.
A young woman was standing before a mirror. She wore
panties and nothing else. Then she pulled the panties down,
turned and examined her backside.

He jerked his eyes away, face flushing hot.

"Bitch!" he whispered. "Dirty—"

He stopped walking, frightened by his reaction.

But she is a dirty bitch, or at least a foolish one, he told
himself. She should know better than to play with herself in
front of an open shade. And what sort of person goes through
that kind of self-examination—

But she was a young woman, and he'd seen her nude, and
he should have enjoyed the glimpse even if he hadn't stayed
to see more.

"Bastard," he said, and walked swiftly to the garage.

He didn't know whom he meant. He knew only he hadn't
wanted to see that nude woman. He didn't want to be forced
to think of women, and the fact that outside of Sylvia
Chrysler he had no social contact with them.

He drove the Porsche much too quickly, but it failed to
help. He'd begun to think of Tokyo, the dock, the woman
calling from the dark corner near the warehouse, the smell of
water and fish and oil. What was it she'd said? A strange
phrase, showing she knew nothing of American military
groups—

Yes. "Sailor san. Sailor san."

The other two marines guarding the dock had laughed, and
one had said, "Okay, Elliot san, you can go first. But don't
take too long. And show her the difference between us and
sailors—stand up for the Corps, gyrene!"

He'd wanted to say no, but they'd both been looking at him
and the woman had called her ridiculous little phrase again
and he'd had to walk over there.

He drove even faster, and managed to fight the thought.

When he reached the Village and Sylvia's place on Elev-
enth Street, he brought back one part of that wartime memory
to help himself.

"I made love to her. I did. And to Lois Gardner at the
cocktail party. I made love to two women. I was capable."

I hated it!

"Only because I cared nothing for them and I'm the kind of
man who has to love a woman—"

He heard the voice and realized he was talking aloud, and clamped his lips tightly together.

The hell with it! He didn't go for sluts—that was all.

But what about Alex Fernol? And the two dreams?

He saw the parking space only fifteen or twenty feet from Sylvia's brownstone and quickly maneuvered into it.

"The hell with it," he said aloud.

Sylvia had a cool bottle of vin rosé on the ameba table in her studio room. She stood up—short, dumpy, with a round, plain face—a caustic, unemotional, detached woman who'd tried marriage and frankly admitted it hadn't agreed with her.

"To be vulgar about it," she'd once said, "I felt it was a mingling of toilet habits. So love went out the window, never to return."

A sexless woman, Elliot knew. They'd been good friends since he first came to work for the Lester Publishing Company.

"The hi-fi's tuned up and the wine is perfect," she said as they touched hands.

"And the program?" he asked, sinking into an armchair and lighting a cigarette.

She walked to the simple, almost severe, blond-wood console and reached under the open top. "Jazz, dear boy. Dave Brubeck. And afterwards, if you have no objections, I'll satisfy my middle-class tastes with yet another hearing of Tchaikovsky's Sixth."

He nodded, the music began, he leaned back. Soon he was sipping the delicate French rose wine and relaxing completely.

Between albums, she asked how his family was.

"Deadly, sweet Sylvia. Deadly as always. But they can't help it and I'm fond of them."

"And the mother in California?"

"Mother sticks to the new Garden of Eden, thank Gawd."

"Lucky boy. Mine is on a farm in Ohio. She visits twice a year. And she speaks German. Gutteral German. Perhaps I can keep her away this summer by going out there. It's far better than having her live here for almost a month and introducing her to all my friends."

Elliot laughed, and thought of *his* mother meeting *his* friends! Impossible to introduce Mother to Sylvia, the Derrings and the Slocums. She was loud, coarse and rather stupid. Also, she had an accent, having spent her first eighteen years of life in a small Ukrainian town. Unlike Aunt Minnie, who was nine years younger and had come over here at the age of six to gain eleven years of education, his mother had never gone to school. Of course, he loved her, worried if he didn't hear from her at least once a week (she lived with a friend who wrote letters for her and read his aloud), and he'd flown out to California every summer during his two-week vacations. She knew all about his wealthy, erudite friends even if she couldn't understand how vastly their lives, and his, differed from hers.

"Some day I'll come to New York, Elliot, and you'll take me to see all those rich, educated friends and I'll thank them for being so nice to you."

He'd nod, if the remark was made on one of his visits, or write an affirmative answer if it came in one of her letters. But he knew she would never visit New York; she was sixty-one years old and terrified of change and travel. And even if she did work up the nerve to suggest visiting him, he would be able to talk her out of it.

"She's really an attractive person," he said to Sylvia, feeling a little ashamed of himself. "Just unpolished."

Sylvia chuckled. "You needn't explain to me, sweetie. I explain it to myself all the time. And it still doesn't make our dear mothers any more acceptable in our milieu."

He finished his wine and poured another glass. The Brubeck quartet beat out exciting music. Sylvia began comparing creative jazz with other types of music. He disagreed with her contention that jazz would survive as an active art form in the same way as great classical music had.

"But what are Stravinsky and Bartók," she said, "if not jazz composers? Basically, I mean?"

"Oh, well, if you're going to get sloppy in your classifications—"

They enjoyed a heated discussion. . . .

He returned to Koptic Court at half-past one, humming sections of Bartók's Concerto for Violin and Orchestra, which Sylvia had played in an attempt to prove part of her argument. In the lobby, he exchanged a few words with another tenant, then went up to the four-room apartment. He moved softly so as not to awaken his aunt and uncle and, after undressing and washing, got into bed. The vibrant, uninhibited music coursed through his mind, and he felt happy. He closed his eyes and lay there, relaxed, sure he would soon drift into a restful sleep.

But then he heard the sounds from next door. Two in the morning and they were at it!

He twisted over on his side, trying to shut his ears to the creak of springs, gruntings and occasional giggles. Four months ago a young couple had moved into the neighboring three-room apartment, and their bedroom adjoined his. The walls were thin, and when the rest of the house was quiet he could hear them much too clearly.

The mailbox listed them as Mr. and Mrs. Gerald Glaif. They both worked, and so he'd seen them in the hall, separately and together, several times at about 8:00 A.M. and 6:00 P.M. Gerald Glaif was a medium-sized young man, not more than twenty-five, with dark, heavy face and a thick shock of black hair. Mrs. Glaif was about twenty, short, chubby, with large breasts and surprisingly slim legs.

Whenever the sounds began, he visualized them clutching at each other, squirming, sweating and groaning, a dark man and chubby woman, doing coarse, ugly, smelly things.

The sounds finally stopped. Elliot found he was trembling. He sat up and rubbed his face with both hands, trying to laugh it off. Of course, it was annoying to have your rest interrupted, especially by such revolting sounds.

Well, not really revolting, though listening to anything so personal would disgust almost anyone.

Or would it?

Hadn't men in the Corps talked—snickering and leering and almost smacking their lips—about overhearing lovers, or getting a peek at them? Hadn't they been excited, titillated? Hadn't they gained pleasure from seeing and hearing those things? Didn't they pass around pornographic photographs and fight to get first look at them? Didn't they tell long, filthy sex stories with practically no point except for the erotic detail itself?

And hadn't he hated it all?

He lay down again. He wouldn't allow himself to become upset over such things. One of these days he'd meet a girl with beauty, brains and an appreciation of the finer things in life. He'd go after that girl. He'd marry her. He'd have a normal life then, and children.

He didn't really believe it; only just enough to fall asleep.

He had one of his two recurrent dreams—the obscure one. He was walking down a dark, deserted street which was vaguely familiar. He was unhappy because he was going somewhere he didn't want to go. As he approached the corner, he sensed rather than saw that there was movement behind the window of a shop on the right. He paused, afraid, and decided to cross the street and avoid passing that shop. But when he started to walk, his legs took him straight toward the corner. He strained and shouted and cried, but his legs wouldn't obey him; they had a will all their own. With each step his fear grew, and with each step the window grew brighter and he was able to see more clearly what was going on behind the glass.

By the time he reached the corner, he knew a number of things. He was back in his old Philadelphia neighborhood, and the shop was a drugstore he passed on the way home from his friend Ben's house. He didn't want to go home because Father was gone and he was afraid Mother would be entertaining one of her men-friends and he might see something like he had two or three times before.

He also knew what was going on in the window. He didn't want to look; it sickened and frightened him. But his eyes, like his legs, refused to obey him and he was forced to watch.

There were two dogs in the brightly lit drugstore window —a male and a female. The male was a huge white spitz; the female a tiny brown Pekingese. The spitz was in heat; the Pekingese was not. The spitz growled threateningly, mounted the tiny, trembling Peke and began forcing its way into her. The Peke looked at Elliot with pleading, pain-filled eyes. Elliot wanted to help her, but he couldn't move. He could only stand and watch. Finally, with a vicious, jolting snap of its loins, the spitz completed the coupling. The Pekingese screamed and burst into bloody fragments—

Elliot came awake then, trembling, sweating, almost crying. After a moment or two, the terror and disgust slipped away and he was able to congratulate himself on not having had the other dream—the explicit one. . . .

He arrived at the office at nine Monday morning. The Lester Publishing Company occupied three floors of one of Fifth Avenue's less imposing edifices, an eighteen-story building five minutes' walk from St. Patrick's Cathedral. The fourteenth floor held the advertising, accounting, employment and sales departments. The fifteenth, where Elliot worked, held the editorial offices of the company's regular line of hard-cover books—a good-sized list of fiction, a smaller list of nonfiction, and an occasional religious volume (done mainly to please Maurice Lester, now retired, a devout Christian Scientist). The sixteenth floor held the editorial offices of the new but extremely successful soft-cover line, Lester Pocket Library, and the juvenile section, The Child's

Garden of Adventure and Learning, which masqueraded as a book club but rarely (twice in the past three years) used a competitor's title.

Elliot walked past the fifteenth-floor reception desk, getting a cool nod from Lois Gardner. As usual, he wondered why men ever bothered with her. Of course, she dressed well and had a pretty face, if you overlooked the vacuity of her expression. He'd even taken her out himself, but it wasn't exactly by choice. About two years ago, a few weeks after he'd started as an editor here, Lois had invited him to a friend's party. He'd felt that as a new employee it wouldn't hurt to go, especially since she mentioned that many other editors would be there. But the next day she came to his desk and said, "My friend had to cancel that party, Elliot. Guess we'll have to go somewhere else." He felt annoyed, put upon, yet what could he do but nod? They went to dinner and a show, and he found her range of conversation so limited as to be almost nonexistent. At the end of the evening, she said, "I hope we'll do this again, Elliot. Only next time don't be so shy." She arched her body toward him, practically begging for a petting session, but he wasn't going to stand in a darkened lobby and mash a silly prep-school graduate. He said good night and left.

It hadn't discouraged her. She was obviously unable to believe any man could resist her charms, and invited him to five or six more parties before finally admitting defeat. Then, justifying his opinion that her kind of person was vicious when thwarted, she'd begun smirking in a decidedly unpleasant fashion whenever he passed her desk, and whispering to whatever other female happened to be around. It didn't take long for him to deduce that she was spreading rumors about his manhood, or lack of it. He decided he would never again have social dealings with business acquaintances and leave himself open for this kind of thing. (Sylvia Chrysler was the one exception, but he'd felt absolutely safe with her from the very beginning.) He also decided he would have to stop Lois Gardner from talking about him if he was to stay on at the Lester Publishing Company.

He gave the problem considerable thought, and came to the reluctant conclusion that there was only one solution—a highly distasteful one and not easily accomplished. The very next day he asked Lois for a date. She stared at him and said no. He acted hurt, and asked three more times before she finally accepted. She was a sorely puzzled girl when he drove her home in his Porsche from an evening of drinking and dancing in a roadside tavern up along the Taconic Parkway. He'd been as physical as he'd dared be in a public place, and he continued the act—for it was an act with that silly, vicious girl—when he parked near her Queens apartment house. He almost made the grade that night, but she wouldn't invite him in and the Porsche was much too confining. Two dates later, at a cocktail party held in Stewart Miles's home (Miles was head of the sales department), he managed to pour six Martinis down her gullet and lead her into an empty bedroom which had the added convenience of an inside lock. He knew that several people had seen them and would talk about it at the office—and that was exactly what he wanted.

It hadn't been easy for him. He'd had to fight his dislike, almost hatred, of the vacuous receptionist, and at the same time convince her that he was mad for her. He also had to work up sufficient passion to carry it off. He was glad he'd had the foresight to pick up a bottle of Scotch from the buffet table. He drank most of it as he petted and undressed her. Then, somehow, the thing was done. She sobered quickly afterward, and said, "God, all the people outside! We were crazy, Elliot!"

He laughed wildly, drunkenly. "Too bad, honey. If they ask me, I'll say you were very, very good."

She'd never quite understood. But there was no more vicious gossip out of her—not about him, anyway. And even though Sylvia might get an occasional questioning look in her eye when he discussed some stupid woman, he felt sure no one else in the office made the mistake of thinking his high standards meant he was—queer.

Remembering how he'd fought and won that tough battle, Elliot nodded back at the receptionist and smiled knowingly. Her eyes dropped swiftly. She had suffered a great deal of humiliation in the weeks following the cocktail party, both from the looks she got from other employees and the absolute brush she got from Elliot. But it was no more than she deserved.

He went through the back door and past three offices with frosted glass doors. He paused in front of the fourth, heart beginning to hammer, and had asked himself what the hell he was doing. If he wanted to go in and say good morning to a twenty-three-year-old proofreader named Alex Fernol, he could. Alex was new, and had asked Elliot's advice on several matters, and they'd lunched together half a dozen times. They got along well. Elliot liked the slender, soft-spoken boy. He found him good company. Was it a crime to realize that a boy was more attractive—judging by the absolutes of physical beauty which the Greeks had proven did exist—than any other person, male or female, in the publishing firm? Did it make Elliot a degenerate because he wanted to see—

He shook his head and walked on to the fifth office. He entered. As usual, he was there before Sylvia. He sat down at the first desk, the one near the door, and glanced at the manuscript lying in the open paper-box. He'd read it Friday, but hadn't written a comment slip yet. He wasn't sure what to say about the historical romance. It was set in Persia at the time of Alexander the Great's invasion, and concerned the adventures—on battlefield and bed—of a Persian youth who joined the Greek conqueror. Elliot had actually found it distasteful—the gore and sex were so graphic—but he'd seen other books of the same type accepted and published (and do well, saleswise) during his two years at Lester.

Sylvia came in at nine-forty, grim and grumpy. He started a new manuscript, deciding to wait until she'd got over her morning depression before speaking to her about the historical. At ten-thirty he said, "Got a blood-and-sex job here —Persian empire."

"So?" she muttered, looking up from a manuscript she was editing. She did a great deal of rewriting and was paid accordingly.

"So I don't like it, but—" He shrugged. "It might sell."

"Then recommend it. I'll try to glance through it by Friday."

He nodded and got to work, typing out his comment slip. He felt much better now that she'd made the decision for him. He was always that way. He could be enthusiastically convincing about a good book, and caustically humorous about a bad one, but when it came to borderline decisions he was lost. And it was probably because of that, he realized, that he still earned eighty dollars a week, his starting salary, and two newer men had been jumped over his head to better-paying jobs.

He sometimes felt he should have stayed with the Mark Streiker Literary Agency, where he'd been earning the same salary. He might have been raised to a hundred by now; certainly ninety. But then again, he'd begun resenting the people at Streiker, feeling they were gossiping about him—

about his refusing to date Janie Sloan when she'd made a big play for him. Maybe it was his imagination, but he'd felt it was time to move on.

He hoped he would never have to move on from Lester. He liked it here. He especially liked working with Sylvia. He didn't care if his salary stayed at eighty; he could live on it.

At eleven, his phone rang.

"This is Alex Fernol, Elliot," the voice said hesitantly. "I—I wonder if you're free for lunch today?"

Elliot's pulse quickened. He noticed it, and was angry at himself. "Sure, Alex," he replied, and somehow his voice came out gruffer, heartier, manlier than was normal for him. "Twelve-thirty okay?"

"Yes, thank you," Fernol's voice seemed even softer than usual, and he was a very soft-spoken boy. "I appreciate your taking the time and trouble—"

"Nonsense," Elliot said, and now he was sweating in the cool office. "I'll come to your desk at twelve-thirty sharp."

"All right. Goodbye."

Elliot hung up, and felt Sylvia's eyes on him. He turned his head; she was reading a manuscript. But he was sure she'd been looking at him a second before.

"That was Alex Fernol," he said, feeling he had to make it right somehow, then raging at himself for being so idiotic. What the devil was wrong with two men eating together?

"Lunching with him?" Sylvia asked.

"Yes. The kid feels lost here."

She didn't answer for a while. "I think he might feel lost anywhere. He's—just another unfortunate."

He didn't ask her what she meant by that. He didn't want to hear insinuations, especially from Sylvia.

He laughed lightly. "Now, now, dear. Remember Tea and Sympathy."

She shrugged.

They went to the Copperdome, a quiet restaurant with a good view of St. Patrick's from the window tables. Alex Fernol excused himself and walked across the small, crowded place to the men's room. Elliot watched him, admiring the six-footer's erect carriage. He was even slimmer than Elliot, with short-cropped blond hair and a small, perfect face. Girls gave him sidelong glances from almost every table along the way. But there was something . . .

Now he was doing it—forgetting how he'd hated certain

people for their vile suspicions, their ready sneers and quick insinuations.

But it might be valid in Alex's case.

Was it also valid in his own?

He called the waiter and ordered a double Scotch on the rocks. Alex didn't drink.

Later, after coffee, and after they'd discussed several books Elliot had read and Alex proofed, Alex rubbed his strong, slender hands together. "There's—there's something I've been wanting to talk about for a long time. It's . . . well . . ." He laughed rather shrilly. "Let's say a matter of some delicacy. That always implies a lot without saying a damn thing."

Elliot's heart began to hammer. The youth looked so helpless, so vulnerable. He wanted to reach out and touch him, comfort him, stroke his smooth cheeks and strong hands, and say, "Yes. I understand. They're starting to look at you and sneer. They're beginning to make you unhappy—ashamed and unhappy."

He said, "Really? Don't tell me you've impregnated some girl-friend." He laughed loud and heavy, and hated himself as the youth's eyes jumped and then slid away.

Alex laughed unconvincingly. "No, it's something—well, the opposite, you could say." He shook his head suddenly, violently, and whispered, "Listen, can you come over to my place some evening this week? I can't discuss it here."

Elliot wanted to ask, "Why me?" He wanted to say, "Sorry, no, I'm busy the rest of this week, and the week after, and the week after that."

He said, "Maybe. What's it all about?"

"There are some cruel, stupid people in our organization," Fernol blurted; and then his manner changed, seemed to grow calm and sure. He raised his eyes and looked at Elliot, and Elliot felt himself stripped of protection, stripped down to his naked fears, his naked desires.

"Yes, well, it's time we got back," Elliot said. He caught the waiter's eye.

After paying the bill, he stood up. But Alex remained seated.

"You didn't answer me, Elliot. Can you drop over to my place?"

"Yes," Elliot said. "I don't know exactly when—"

"Tomorrow night?"

Elliot nodded.

Back in the office, Sylvia said, "What's the matter, Elliot? You look green around the gills."

"Really? I feel fine."

"Here's my mirror. Take a look."

"I'm not that much of a narcissist!"

"Whew. Aren't we touchy today!"

He didn't answer. Later he said, "Sorry, Sylvia."

"Sure. Anyway, you're starting to look better. . . ."

That night he went to a neighborhood movie just so he could get out of the apartment and not have to talk to his aunt and uncle. He came home after they'd gone to bed, had a glass of milk and sat down in the living room with a last cigarette. He refused to think about anything. It was nonsense. Life was nonsense. The hell with all this worrying and thinking!

He fell asleep as soon as he got into bed.

He had the second of his two recurrent dreams—the obvious one.

He was in a richly carpeted hotel corridor, walking quickly, eagerly, toward a room up ahead. Something good was in that room; something that would make him happy. He reached a door, knocked, and a sweet voice said, "Come in, Elliot." He opened the door and entered a huge, softly lighted room. There were shadows everywhere, but he knew it was magnificently furnished. He also knew that a loved one waited for him in the large double bed near a picture window in which were framed the myriad lights of nighttime Manhattan. He walked slowly toward the bed, savoring the anticipation building up within him. "Elliot, Elliot," the soft voice crooned, and then he could see her—a beautiful woman, the woman of his life, the one he'd always dreamed of. She was going to make him happy; she was going to end all the doubts and worries, all the long years of torment. He reached the bed, and his clothing fell away. He slid in beside her, took her in his arms and kissed her, gently yet passionately, with all the love that had been bottled up in him since he'd lost his father. She responded, murmuring in his ears the terms of endearment he longed to hear. There were no doubts about his ability to make love to this woman! The doubts were finished forever! He was burning for her, his hands running over her body, his lips pressing feverishly into her neck. A moment later he began to consummate his grand passion.

But he couldn't!

He rolled away from her, eyes peering through the suddenly intensified darkness. "What is it, Elliot?" she asked. *Or was it a she?* The voice was so deep; the hand caressing him so large and strong; the face pressing his chest so rough, as if a stubble of beard—

And then he knew it was a man, had been a man from the very beginning, and he began to shout, "No, no, no, no—" But he had no strength to move and the strong hands gripped him intimately and his desire blazed higher as the rough-skinned face moved down over his body—

He awoke and lay absolutely still, repeating to himself the words of his dream. "No, no, no, no—"

Later, he rolled over on his face and gave in to the bitter tears. Silently, he wept into his pillow. . . .

The first thing he did on arriving at the office Tuesday morning was to call Alex Fernol on the phone. The young proofreader wasn't in yet. Elliot tried again ten minutes later. Fernol answered.

"I won't be able to make it tonight," Elliot said quickly. "Something came up."

The soft voice showed deep disappointment. "Tomorrow night then?"

"I'm afraid I'm tied up the rest of this week."

"Can we make a definite appointment for next week?"

"I—I'm not sure of my schedule—"

"Please, Elliot," Fernol said, voice dropping to a pleading whisper, "I just have to talk this out."

"Why me?" Elliot almost shouted. "Why does it have to be me?"

"Oh. I didn't mean to annoy—"

Unaccountably, Elliot felt frightened. He didn't want to lose Fernol's friendship. "I'm sorry. I've . . . had a rough time at home. My aunt is ill and I haven't been getting my sleep."

"Of course," Fernol said softly. "You must think I'm an awful fool, and a selfish one to boot. You'll inform me when you have a free evening?"

"I will." He tried to think of something else to say, wanting to prolong the conversation.

"Goodbye," Fernol said, and hung up.

Elliot leaned back in his chair, and the door opened. Sylvia came in, looked at him, said, "Don't get mad, sweetie, but you're green around the chops again."

He nodded. "Yes, I feel lousy." He got to work.

Mrs. Slocum called at ten-thirty. "Elliot dear, Losh Savarina, the exciting new coloratura I was telling you about, is giving a concert Thursday night. Roger picked up five tickets and I wonder if you could join us?" She paused a moment, but before he could answer she rushed on. "I know it's an imposition, what with your other appointment Friday and our dinner party Saturday, but—well, please come, dear. Dorothy's going with her new beau—the athlete from Yale. A dreadful bore, but she's dating the physical ones now. Please come and save our evening from degenerating into a soccer match after the concert!"

He laughed smoothly, deeply, richly. "I'll be glad to help. And thanks. Heard from Jerry?"

"Oh, he's still getting along famously. Loves Chicago, and the wheat exchange, and his wife. He sent you his regards, and did it in a very cute way. 'Give my best to the most civilized roommate I ever had,' he wrote. I think that just about sums you up, Elliot."

He laughed.

"By the way, as long as I'm piling obligations on you—I'm planning a combination bridge and dinner party the second Saturday in May. Please try and keep it open for me, dear. I'll need a good player, and an escort for a young lady. A very attractive young lady, I might add. Only trouble is she lives in deepest Jersey."

"My car will manage the trek."

Mrs. Slocum laughed. "She'll be fascinated with that Porsche. Didn't you once say your parents always insisted on foreign cars when you lived in Chicago?"

"Philadelphia," he corrected. He didn't remember making that statement, but then again he tossed off many little white lies about his background during the course of an evening with the Slocums or Derrings.

"How stupid of me. Philadelphia. But your mother is in California now, isn't she?"

"Yes. The climate suits her if the society doesn't."

"Really, Elliot, she must come to New York soon. I'm so looking forward to meeting her—"

They talked a few minutes more and said goodbye. Elliot felt better, much better now. Life was good again. All one had to do was stay away from emotion, from everything not completely under control of the brain.

He lunched in the office, sending out for a sandwich and

coffee. When Sylvia left at one-thirty, he called Mrs. Derring. "Isn't it strange," the sharp-voiced woman said, "I was about to dial your number. Ivar's got one of his bad backaches and we'll have to cancel that concert date this Friday. The doctor says he needs a complete rest, and so we're retiring from the world for at least ten days. I've been able to get a refund on the tickets and we'll make it another time."

They chatted a while longer, with Elliot being very sympathetic. "How's David?" he asked, preparing to end the conversation.

"Fine. He's not only an engineer but a gentleman farmer! That West Virginia place of his is beginning to take up all his spare time, what with planting a truck garden and looking after that plum orchard I told you about. And Louise is only three months away from making me a grandmother for the second time." She paused. "I do believe you should take a hint from your old roommate, Elliot. He said he was going to send you a snapshot of a girl who works at his plant. He says she's beautiful, intelligent—"

When he hung up, Elliot felt glum. He'd been looking forward to Friday night and the concert.

Without really thinking about it, he picked up the phone and asked for Alex Fernol. "Just learned I'll be free Friday night," he said, and still couldn't understand why he was doing this.

"Ah," Fernol murmured. "I can't tell you how grateful I am."

"Yes, well, an unexpected—"

"I really do appreciate it, Elliot."

The voice was so soft, so—friendly. Elliot's blood pulsed thick and heavy in his temples. "Well, see you."

He worked very hard that afternoon, barely raising his eyes from his reading. Before taking the subway to Brooklyn, he had a double Martini—a vodka Martini so his aunt and uncle wouldn't know he'd been drinking. At dinner that night, he entertained them with humorous anecdotes of editors and writers. He kept them laughing until almost nine o'clock. Then his aunt said, "Oh, you've been so much fun I forgot about the letter! From your mother."

He opened the envelope and read the single sheet of paper covered with Mrs. Lowenson's painstaking scrawl. It was the same as always—weather nice except for some rain and fog; visited a beach or park or museum; saw a movie star on the street and isn't it thrilling. But there was a P.S. at the very bottom, and it made Elliot's lips tighten.

"My friend and roommate, Mrs. Lowenson, is going away for the whole month of September to stay with her daughter in Denver. We talked about it, and she thinks it would be the right time for me to visit you. I could stay with Minnie and Phil like they've asked me to a dozen times. I could sleep on the couch, or take your bed for the visit. So write me and tell me what you think. I would love to see you, my darling son, and am dying to meet those wonderful friends you and Minnie told me about. Wouldn't it be just grand? Of course, it's a long trip and I'm not sure how I'd take all the excitement. But write and let me know what you think. Also, what Minnie and Phil think."

"Anything new?" Minnie asked.

"She all right?" Phil chimed in.

He read them the letter—but not the P.S. Then he went to his room and pulled his small typing table and portable out of the closet. He typed quickly, knowing exactly what to say:

New York would tire her too much. He didn't want to contradict Minnie and Phil, but there was barely room for three people in their tiny apartment, not to say four, and hotels were awful places, what with noisy conventions and wild parties. He would take a late vacation this year and spend two weeks of September with her so she wouldn't be alone more than twelve or thirteen days. "Really, Mother, I don't think you should endanger your health on such a long trip, especially since you refuse to fly."

He stamped and addressed an envelope and went downstairs. As he reached the corner mailbox, that strange couple from the sixth floor passed him, heading for the lobby. Automatically, he began to nod, but when he realized who they were and that they would look the other way, he did the same. Then he turned to glance after them, remembering what Uncle Phil had said.

"Those kids—the Mastons—are heading for trouble. Mind you, people got a right to stick to themselves if they want to, but those two are afraid of people. That's right, afraid. Why? You got me."

Elliot wondered briefly if Phil was right. The Mastons certainly acted as if they were afraid of *something*.

When they disappeared from sight, his own problems move back into his mind. He decided to take a long, brisk walk.

By the time he returned to Fifteenth Avenue, it was ten-thirty. But he still wasn't ready for sleep. He got his Porsche out of the garage and went for a ride on the Belt Parkway.

It was almost one A.M. before he climbed into bed. He still hadn't been able to stop thinking of Alex Fernol's soft, soft, voice. . . .

4

CHARLES AND CLARA MASTON 6-B

She finished her coffee, then spoke to her husband, sitting across the table. They were at the end of a long foyer, at the point where it broadened out before the living room. This was where they kept their table and chairs, the kitchenette of the two-and-a-half-room apartment being barely large enough to hold a utility table and stool.

"Charles," she said.

The tall, sandy-haired man made a mumbling sound and continued to read the *Times*.

"Charles, put down the paper and finish your breakfast. We have first-period classes and it's seven-twenty."

He nodded, but didn't lower the paper. "Terrific reviews for that new play—the one about a Southern high school in the process of integration."

"First-period class," Clara Maston said in a loud clear voice.

"Yes," he mumbled.

"I know teaching high-school English isn't extravagantly profitable, but we do manage to eat rather well and I'd hate to give up food."

He lowered the paper and smiled—a brief smile, but it transformed his long, thin, serious face; made him look far younger than his thirty-four years; gave him a boyish, almost childish touch, especially around the gray eyes and wide-stretching thin lips; also gave him a sardonic touch by exposing his small, white, uneven teeth. "Okay," he said. "I believe you've made your point. It's just that I hate—" He shrugged. "You know. Leaving and going down in the elevator and meeting people and having them look at me like I was some sort of freak. The *goy* of Koptic Court."

"Oh, it's not quite *that* bad."

He shrugged again.

"I don't mean that you're wrong, Charles. They probably do a lot of talking about your not being Jewish, just as the teachers at school probably do a lot of talking about my not being gentile. What I mean is—why worry about it?"

"I don't worry. I just can't help despising them—both the idiots here and the imbeciles at school. They're so damned narrow—" His voice had been rising, and he stopped himself. "What's the password, honey?"

"Screw 'em all," she replied briskly.

"Right," he said, and laughed.

A handsome man, Clara thought proudly, happily. And when he stood up, towering over her, she saw in his wasp-waisted, lean-hipped, slope-shouldered body the stringy, tensile strength of his New England farmer ancestors, saw in his face and figure all the qualities apposite his character; qualities that, even after fourteen months of marriage (and six months of courtship), were fresh and different to her—so lacking in the Jewish boys of her old neighborhood; so lacking in most New York City men. And even while feeling that way, she laughed at herself, knowing that all who were in love thought their sweethearts "different."

She looked at him, and he winked. The quick heat of desire came, making her knees weak, making her eyelids heavy. She marveled, as she had so many times in the past fourteen months, at fate giving this wonderful man to Clara Cohen— a fate which had seemed determined to keep her frustrated and unmarried forever.

But desire brought another, less happy thought to mind. She had already missed two menstrual periods and was twelve days past her third. She hadn't told Charles, and he hadn't noticed. She was afraid to tell him; she hoped desperately, despite the obvious signs, that she would never have to tell him. (Once before, after they'd been married about six months, she'd skipped two menstrual periods. And all through her adult life she'd skipped occasional monthlies. This time, however, she felt *different*.) They were very happy together, but the one thing they didn't want was a child.

They'd discussed it thoroughly, and decided against ever having children. This world of stupid, violent, religiously and racially prejudiced people—enough of them, anyway, to dominate every major society—wasn't the place for their child. As Charles had put it: "Let the Hollywood philosophers and moralists make their saccharine judgments against planned childlessness; we've defied older and more complex taboos simply by marrying—"

She turned from his smile, from her desire and her fear of pregnancy, and moved through the living room, past the bathroom, into the large, airy bedroom. Charles followed, walking slowly so he could watch the way her chunky yet softly rounded figure undulated gracefully. She had nice shoulders, a narrow waist, legs that just missed being heavy—but the little they missed by made quite a difference, made them shapely and strong.

Suddenly, he forgot his irritation at the people in this house, at the teachers in school. It was March, cold and gray outside, but he felt like spring. Whenever he looked at Clara, he felt like spring. He needed nothing else for his happiness!

She opened the closet and took out her coat, and he looked at her face. It thrilled him. It was the most beautiful face in the world, with its generous features—large eyes, strong nose, round cheeks, full lips—an oval face narrowing suddenly to a sharp, fragile chin. A face he knew would always hold him, even when the warm-toned skin lost its youth, its unwrinkled freshness.

How lucky he was, he thought, that this beautiful, brilliant girl had taken him, a string bean as his brother Lester used to call him, with all his fears and weaknesses.

He moved to the closet, helped her into her coat, brushed her thick black hair, cut boyishly short, with his lips.

She turned then, gripped him about the waist, hugged him so hard he gasped. He took her face between his hands and tilted it upward. They stared into each other's eyes. They trembled, and didn't say anything, and after a moment moved back from each other.

When they left the sixth-floor apartment and walked into the elevator, they were holding hands and smiling. But Charles's face tightened, and so did Clara's, when the two middle-aged men and elderly woman got on at the fourth floor. The men glanced at Charles and nodded briefly. Charles responded with a barely perceptible head movement. The woman smiled at Clara and spoke in Yiddish.

"You're still teaching high school?"

Clara answered in English. "Yes."

Charles looked at her, eyes narrow.

"She asked if I was still teaching," Clara explained.

Charles nodded.

The woman spoke again in Yiddish. "If you don't have your own children, it's good to work as a teacher. But there's nothing for a woman like having—"

They were at the lobby. Charles opened the door and stalked out, dragging Clara with him.

"I wish I could move so fast—" one of the men began to say.

Charles and Clara were out on the street by then, heading for their car. Behind them, they heard soft laughter.

"What did that woman say the second time?" Charles asked, face angry.

"Something about teaching being fine if you haven't children of your own."

"I'll bet she meant that we'll never have children; that mixed marriages shouldn't reproduce. Well, she's right!" He took a deep breath of cold air. "And those men—"

They heard laughter again. Clara glanced over her shoulder. The two men and old woman were walking together in the direction of the subway, talking animatedly, laughing frequently. She felt a sudden anger, a sudden desire to say something cruel about them.

"The password?" Charles murmured as he opened the door of the 1950 Ford sedan.

She gave it to him, with gusto.

When they were both seated in the car, she shook her head. "Sometimes I wonder—well, maybe some of them don't even know you're a gentile."

"They know, all right," Charles said, revving up the Ford's cold engine. "Just like Fred Bailer knows you're Jewish."

"Ah, yes," she said with a brittle smile. "The brilliant math teacher, Frederick Bailer. That pained expression suits his face, don't you think? I mean the expression he wears when he sees us together."

"It does, it does. Suits his entire personality. Because pain is the dominant emotion in his life—pain every time he has to think."

"When he meets you alone, I'll bet he's more at ease."

Charles nodded. "I believe so. He can't understand how a good New England Protestant could possibly leave the fold. He's asked me a dozen times to attend—with my wife— Sunday services at his church. Episcopalian, no less."

"And what do you say?"

"That Laurel Park is where I work, not where I live. That it's much too far to travel to for anything as asinine as church services. That my wife wouldn't ask me to sit in a synagogue and listen to gibberish, and I wouldn't ask her to sit in a church and listen to gobbledegook."

She turned and looked at him and laughed. "Charles, you didn't!"

"Well, perhaps not in such specific terms. But I implied as much. He probably understood no more than that I wouldn't travel out to Nassau County on Sunday."

They reached the Belt Parkway, and he drove faster, and she sat very close to him. They discussed other teachers at Laurel Park High—narrow-minded, prejudiced, stupid people; or so the Mastons preferred to classify them. They laughed at those people, and touched each other every so often, and were in a world unto themselves, protected from real or imagined snub, insult and condescension.

They turned off the three-lane highway, onto the narrower macadam road, dreading the separation this cold, gray day would bring, already looking forward to four o'clock when they could get back in their car and reassemble their world and return to their two-room planet, third-and-a-half from the sun. . . .

Clara gave exams to all five of her classes. They'd been warned Friday that come Monday they would be tested on whatever reading had been assigned to them during the first part of the term, but when she handed out paper and began writing questions on the board for the first-period class (third termers), there was a long, unified groan. She smiled and said, "Now, it's not *that* bad," but inwardly she agreed with them. She disliked testing—at least this way. If she could have talked privately with every student, asking them the type of questions she felt suited their individual intelligences and abilities to study, it would have been different. But the school made the rules, not the teachers. And the state Regents examinations loomed ahead for every child who wished to get college-accredited courses listed on his record.

Once the class settled down to work, Clara had nothing to do. In fact, it was a *necessity* that she do nothing. She had either to sit behind her desk, or stroll around the room, eyes constantly on her class. Otherwise, they would exchange answers ("cheat" was the word used by Mr. Darnell, head of the English department), destroying whatever value the exam might have in helping her to judge which students had earned good grades, which bad, and which (though she had not so classified any student in her two terms at Laurel) must be made to take the term over again.

The inactivity allowed her thoughts to turn to that evening, almost three months ago, when she'd suspected she hadn't inserted the diaphragm correctly. She'd wanted to make sure, but Charles had taken her in his arms and the lethargy of love, and later its urgency, had robbed her of will-power. Now something was growing inside—

"Don't be a fool," she told herself, fighting the panic. "You've skipped before, and it was nothing. You'll go to a doctor and asked for a rabbit test."

But if the result was positive, what then?

"Injections," she murmured.

It was a comforting word—injections. It was clean and held promise of quick, painless elimination of the problem.

There had to be some kind of injections.

"Yes," she promised herself. "Tonight I'll go to a doctor."

She got up from her desk and walked slowly around the room, eyes on her fourteen- and fifteen-year-old students. She examined their faces, their expressions, remembering, as she always did, how she too had sat in a similar classroom.

This time, contrary to habit, the memories went beyond the brief flash-of-feeling stage. This time they tried to take her all the way back to full remembrance.

She walked a little faster. She didn't want the sharp memories. They were painful. They were of a time before she'd known Charles, and she preferred to think of her life as having begun with Charles.

But there was that feeling of something alive inside her, and the comfort of the word "injection" had fled, and there was nothing to do but sit behind her desk or walk around.

The first period ended then, and she had a few minutes of activity as one group of boys and girls filed out and another group (apprehensive about what was to come) filed in. But after she'd handed out paper and writtern their questions on the blackboard, the room grew silent, empty (for her) of mind-filling tasks.

She got up from her desk and moved slowly along the north side of the rectangular room, the window side. She glanced out, two flights down to the concrete yard, and beyond it to the sports field—still set up for football. But her mind was turned inward.

Again she fought against memories. Life was good now; life was a happy thing now, with Charles. Damn everything that had come before!

She turned back to the class, and saw Margaret DiGiconda, a small, dark, intense girl of fifteen—pretty, really, but either unaware or uncaring of that fact so important to most high-school girls—who sat crouched over her paper, lips pressed tightly together, large, black eyes blinking nervously, writing in frantic, spastic bursts. She was a child who rarely smiled, never laughed; who seemed perpetually on the defensive even when attractive boys tried to approach her—to "kid around" with her, as they would put it.

That was the type of child she had been, Clara thought, and her heart went out to the dark little girl. Yes, she too had always been on the defensive (inwardly, at least) because she'd learned early that the world was brutal, stupid and indifferent to the needs of the sensitive. Her own mother had been the prime example. Wonderful, wonderful Moms. . . .

They'd lived in a lot of different places—three apartments in Manhattan and four or five in Brooklyn. The first that stood out clearly in Clara's memory was the most expensive home they'd ever had—a large duplex in a four-story reconverted brownstone close to Washington Square. She was in grammar school at the time—1-A or 1-B—and between six and seven years old. Pop was doing well; she remembered him showing her sheets of paper with his name on top—*Irwin Cohen, Certified Public Accountant, Tax Consultant.* It was his tax-season business (doing corporate returns for downtown Manhattan soft-goods and import-export outfits) that had made the duplex possible. Pop was happy, being successful and having friends over to the duplex (Clara would get up some nights for a drink of water and Pop would take her down to the living room and show her to men and women and they'd all laugh and tell her how pretty she was). But it was about this time that she realized there was something wrong between Pop and Moms. Moms wasn't happy.

There were the arguments; quiet arguments since neither Irwin nor Gloria Cohen were loud people. But that didn't make them any less intense. Irwin was happy with his life as it was, and he couldn't understand his wife's strong feelings about art, education and religion. If she wanted to go to Washington Square College at night, that was her business. If she wanted to read books about nihilism, agnosticism, atheism and God knows what else, he couldn't stop her. But when she questioned his going to *shool* on the High Holy Days, asked why he bothered with synagogue then when he didn't all year round, he grew angry, belligerent.

"God's God, Gloria! Don't be a fool. Who questions God? If you want to read nonsense, go ahead. But please don't bring it into your conversation in our own home. Think of the child!" (He never really answered Moms' questions.)

"If you're so much the believer," she'd say, "why don't you *act* the part? Why don't you conduct yourself as a holy man? Employ a Negro once in a while, or at least a non-Jew."

"But what has one thing got to do with the other? I hire whom I like. Does that make me irreligious? You're a fool!"

Moms would open her mouth, searching for words, but she didn't have them. She went to evening classes, and mixed with all sorts of people in school, and read books in which the liberal wisdom of the world was presented. But she herself did not have quick answers—not those that would convince her husband.

"But—can't you understand?" she'd say, voice trembling. "Can't you see how narrow a life you're living? And as for the child, it's her I'm thinking of. I don't want her making the same mistakes I did."

And then the hurt would flash across Pop's face, and Moms would shake her head and leave the room.

Clara didn't understand it, then, but the strange part was that she sided with Moms all the time, even though she saw it was Moms who made the trouble by trying to change things.

Later, whenever she asked why about something Moms said, Moms had an answer. "I don't believe in God, honey, because I've never had proof he exists. Actually, there's pretty good proof he doesn't exist in our religion—Judaism— and all the other big ones. For each religion is different, and one God, it seems to me wouldn't allow such divisions. nor would he allow the wars and murders and each religion hates and distrusts the others. Oh, you'll hear a lot about them working together, but all through history you'll find people killing each other because they have different religions. And they don't do nearly enough to help persecuted racial minorities—" She'd sigh and spread her hands and say, "Baby, you'll have to make up your own mind when you grow up. But just keep your eyes on the religious people of this world—see if among them aren't most of the bigots, most of the violent fanatics, most of those that will try to stop you from doing the things you'll want to do—"

Clara had gone to Pop and asked him about God, and Pop had bought her a children's version of the Old Testment and read her sections every night. The stories had been interesting —how Adam and Eve lived in a beautiful garden but were naughty so they had to leave; how Moses took the children of Israel away from wicked Egypt and into a land of milk and honey; how Moses went up on a mountain and heard God speak and got the Ten Commandments; how little David slew (she asked what "slew" meant and Pop said it meant "beat") the bad giant Goliath. She liked the stories, but somehow they didn't have anything to do with people and the duplex and grammar school, the way the things Moms talked about did. Clara asked Pop if she could go to a mountain top and hear God talk, and Pop laughed uncomfortably and said, "Don't be silly." Moms never said, "Don't be silly." Moms always tried to answer Clara's questions.

They moved to Brooklyn; a Kings Highway apartment. That was after Pop had bad luck with the tax-season business and sold his list and took a job with a Brooklyn firm. He wasn't nearly so busy any more, and Moms asked him to come with her to night classes and learn about painting and music and great books. (She went to a lot of classes now, and she and Pop didn't argue so much, but then again they didn't talk so much either.) Pop said he would if she'd come with him to a new club he'd joined—a Zionist club dedicated to gaining a national homeland for the Jews. Moms agreed, but then Pop kept skipping classes at Brooklyn College, saying he was tired and it was a lot of nonsense because it didn't teach a trade or how to increase income, and so one night Moms told him his Zionist club, with its exclusion of all things not Jewish, was as bad in its way as that Nazi maniac Hitler was in his. Pop slapped her. Clara remembered because it was at the table when they were eating dinner. Clara cried out and ran to her mother and hugged her and couldn't look at her father. And Moms said, loud and clear, "That's the way of bigotry, of ignorance and prejudice. When ignorance can find no answer to logic, it uses its claws."

Later, Moms admitted she'd made her comparison too strong in the heat of argument, and Pop begged her to forgive him for the slap, but from then on they didn't get along at all. And Clara had begun to see that no matter how kind Pop was to his daughter, he wasn't kind to other people. Sure, he liked his family and friends, but he sometimes used the word "nigger," and lots of times he said, ". . . that lousy goy," and he never read anything but the Daily News even though he was always talking about being a "professional man."

Moms got her degree from Brooklyn College when Clara was in her second term of high school, and Clara and Pop went to the graduation. Pop was proud, all right, but by this time things had gotten real bad between him and Moms.

They moved to another apartment house near Eastern Parkway.

There was the terrible night, just a week or so before Clara's world fell apart, when Moms didn't come home from a discussion club meeting at N.Y.U. (where she'd begun taking graduate courses) until almost two-thirty in the morning. Pop had shouted for the first time that Clara could remember—really shouted, using terrible words. "What are you, a Jewish wife and mother or a dirty tramp? You have liquor on your breath and you tell me you were dancing with niggers and chinks—"

"I said I was doing folk dances with fellow students—and among them were colored men and women, Chinese and Indian men and women. I told you they were going to serve cocktails and that I might be late—"

"Maybe you let them kiss you, those fine fellow students, eh? Maybe you dropped your pants—"

Moms had laughed shrilly and walked out of the bedroom. Clara had called to her from her own room, but Moms hadn't heard. Moms had stopped laughing and sat down in the living room and cried. Then she and Pop went into the kitchen and closed the door. Clara slipped out of bed and tiptoed to the kitchen door and listened. Moms talked very calmly, but the things she said frightened Clara more than shouting and tears—and yet they also made sense.

"No, Irwin, I didn't cry because of what you said. If you want the truth, I wish I were single so I could, as you put it, drop my pants for some of the men I know."

Pop made a thick, choking sound, but Moms went on.

"Yes, I'm probably a bad woman by your standards. I don't know when it happened, but my life with you has become nothing. You aren't the man I want, the man I need. You never were. Of course, when I married you I wasn't the woman I am now. I didn't allow myself to think, and I had no equipment to think with—no education, no choice of various sets of values—"

Pop must have made a gesture, a face, or something else

that showed Moms he was losing track of her argument, or had lost patience with it.

"All right, Irwin. I'll do whatever you want. Separation, divorce—"

"What *I* want?" he said. "What is it *you* want? What in the name of God do you want of me, of life?"

She didn't answer right away, and Clara, trembling outside the closed door, held her breath.

"I want *thought*, Irwin. That isn't too clear, and it doesn't really explain my feelings, but it'll have to do. I want thought —intelligence in my daily life, beauty in my own home, true liberalism in my dealings with people. I want to be able to have Negro friends—"

Again the choking sound from Pop.

"Well, I feel I need it," Moms said. "I also want—" Here she paused for a long time. "I also want to break away from my Jewish background. I have a fourteen-year-old daughter, but I'm only thirty-six. There's plenty of time for me to do the things I want to do, with the people I respect and admire. They're a small minority, Irwin, and not normal in the sense that you'd use the word—"

Pop interrupted harshly. "You didn't explain that breaking-away-from-Jewish-background crack. You never acted like a Jew, religiously or in any other way, so why—"

"I'm a little ashamed of that feeling," Moms said, and cleared her throat nervously. "I'm not sure if it fits in with all the other things I've come to believe in. But I thought I'd tell you the whole truth tonight. I want to break away from my Jewish background—living in a neighborhood where only Jews live; living in apartment houses where the only non-Jews are the superintendents; taking sides in arguments on the basis of whether or not something is good, or safe, for me as a Jew. I—I want to forget the Jewish label because, as you said, I've never really been a Jew."

"Sure, sure," Pop sneered, and he sounded so righteous that Clara felt a surge of fear for her mother's wonderful logic. "So maybe you'll become a Catholic now!"

"No. I—I hate the religious person!" And now Moms' voice was climbing, growing emotional. "He's Joshua ordering his soldiers to kill everyone in Jericho, even the babies in the cribs, because they resisted Israel and dared have erotic sex practices. He's the Holy Council of the Inquisition imprisoning, torturing, killing all those who aren't what the council defines as true believers in Christ—and it makes no difference that Christ was gentle. He's the Catholics killing Protestants, and Protestants killing Catholics, and both killing Jews who are too weak in numbers to continue their Old Testament warfare. He's Mohammedans butchering Christians, and Hindus butchering Mohammedans, and the other way around—every conceivable way around! He's all religious groups killing their competitors." Her chair scraped the floor, indicating she was rising, and Clara darted back to her room.

"Yeah, yeah," Pop shouted. "Like the loonys say, 'The whole world's crazy—only I'm sane.' Like that, eh, genius?"

"Something like that," Moms said in a tired voice.

Pop slept on the couch that night. The next morning Clara went to school, and began to look around—to see and hear things—in a different way. Understanding of what Moms had said, had been saying for years, grew quickly. There was so much hate, violence and stupidity in the world. It bothered her a little, but after all, she still had her wonderful, wonderful Moms—

A week later, her wonderful Moms was dead.

It made no sense. Moms went shopping, and she must have been thinking of what she and Pop were going to do (they'd talked about divorce twice since the night of the big discussion), and she was hit by a delivery truck—a small, dry-cleaning delivery truck. They took her to the hospital and called Pop and he rushed there from work. They said she had a broken back and was hemorrhaging internally. Pop called the principal at school and a teacher drove Clara to the hospital. She and Pop went into the room, and Moms was lying there, very pale. But outside of that, and a bruise on her cheek, she seemed all right. She opened her eyes and looked at Clara—right at her—and said, "Put the dishes in the closet, Ma. I'll put the pots—" And then she stopped and made a throat-clearing sound like she did when she was nervous or about to say something she considered important. But she said nothing. She kept making the sound and her eyes rolled around and it frightened Clara. Pop kept asking the doctor if anything could be done, and the doctor kept shrugging. They waited a long time. They went outside and had something to eat and came back to the room. Moms was paler now—almost a grayish-green. Clara wanted to run to her, to kiss her and beg her to say something important, but Pop made her sit quietly. They sat and sat and sat. Clara was tired, terribly tired, and she wanted to ask how long it would be before Moms would come home with them.

Moms died a few minutes later. She made the throat-clearing sound, and it turned into a terrible, dry rattle, and she jumped a little and then stopped.

Clara and Pop went home. Clara made some coffee for Pop and poured milk for herself and they sat in the kitchen, drinking. They looked at the table and the walls, and finally Pop said, "It—it must have been God's will. The things she said—"

Clara began to cry. Pop tried to comfort her, not understanding she was crying from rage—rage at the terrible thing he'd said, the stupid and vicious thing he'd said.

She and Pop moved to a smaller apartment in a house just down the street, and she became a good cook and house-keeper. She missed Moms terribly, and her understanding of the world's stupidity, ignorance and brutality grew each day. She made up her mind to get as much education as she could, and to meet the kind of people Moms had met during the last few years of her life—the intelligent, liberal, artistic men and women who were different from most people. And (though she wasn't aware of it) she began moving away from Jewish people as much as she could.

Her father married about fifteen months after Moms died. Clara disliked the blond, buxom, cheerful woman who said, "You call me Mother, darling. I'll be as good to you as if you were my own flesh and blood." She began to despise her after an hour-long "heart to heart" talk in which Lena (the stepmother) warned Clara of the dangers of "being a wild girl."

At the age of fifteen, Clara went to a cellar-club party with a group of boys and girls from high school. One of the boys, Johnny Elisando, was short and broad and handsome. She found herself attracted to him physically, and there was no problem mentally because he rarely ventured an opinion on anything (hardly spoke at all), smiled a great deal, and was forever trying to kiss and fondle her. The others in the group she cordially detested since they were neither fish nor fowl—neither bright enough to interest her, nor dumb enough (and attractive enough, like Johnny) to be acceptable on a purely emotional level.

The basement room was long and dark (a few blue bulbs sufficing as lighting) and furnished with old couches and armchairs. She danced with Johnny, looked at his strong teeth and clear gray eyes, remembered what her stepmother had said about being a "wild" girl, and began rubbing up against her seventeen-year-old partner. They had to wait until after midnight, when the other couples left, before they could lock the clubroom door and get on one of the couches.

Clara was prepared for pain, shame and a bitter sense of consummated rebellion. What she experienced was a great deal of pleasure capped by an orgasm of impressive proportions—it left the exhausted Johnny with a torn shirt and a number of deep scratches on his back and shoulders. After that, Clara could hardly wait for their next meeting—this time in her own home, while her father and stepmother were out at a movie. Five more satisfactory meetings followed in the next three weeks, and then she ceased to want Johnny; suddenly had her fill of him. The bewildered boy couldn't understand the abrupt ending of what he'd begun to consider a blessing bestowed upon him by heaven; due, probably, to his attending Mass every Sunday morning for the past eight months. When Clara ignored his dramatic appeal for sympathy ("Aw, gee, Sugar, it's got so I can't sleep good—"), he began to pay serious attention to toothpaste and deodorant ads (Men, are you offending without knowing it?).

Clara graduated from high school with the highest scholastic average in her class, but she didn't make Arista, the honor society, because of her complete lack of social credits —she belonged to no clubs, took no part in war work, kept to herself except when she felt some male might possibly provide her with an evening's entertainment or excitement.

(After Johnny was convinced he'd lost her, he bragged that Clara had "put out" for him. This made her extremely popular, but she disappointed all the high school hopefuls. Not that she wasn't willing to gratify her appetites; it was just that no boy since Johnny had been able to trigger her desire. No boy, but quite a few men.)

Clara attended concerts, lectures on any subject that held promise of interest, and visited all the art galleries and museums she could find. Being a pretty girl with a mature figure, she naturally met members of the opposite sex—men of all ages. She learned a great deal from them, but she didn't find love. And it wasn't long before sex for sex's sake became more trouble than it was worth.

By the time she graduated from Brooklyn College (as a fully matriculated, nonpaying student), she was twenty, dating very little, and dying to get out of her father's home into a place of her own. With a major in English and a minor in pyschology, she was in a good position to go for her master's in education and prepare herself for teaching high school English.

She got a part-time job in a textbook publishing house and entered N.Y.U.'s graduate school of education. At the same time, her father and stepmother began attempting to introduce her to several "solid, respectable Jewish businessmen" in the hope that she would choose a husband from among them, but this served only to precipitate an argument, the result of which was that she packed her things and went to live with a girl from her Psychology of Education class who'd been begging her to share a Greenwich Village studio apartment.

Clara worked and went to school and had occasional dates. She was busy all the time, and yet felt as if she were sitting still, waiting for something to happen, something important, something her mother hadn't had—and she hadn't had.

She was waiting to fall in love.

She got her master's degree in one year (including a 12-credit summer session), took a job as a substitute teacher at the school where she'd student-taught (Tilden High in Brooklyn) and met many new men among the bachelors there.

After sixteen months of subbing (a reasonably profitable state of affairs since she managed to get quite a bit of work), she was appointed a full-time teacher. She continued to live in the Village with her ex-classmate; continued to date men, new men, and wait for lightning to strike.

Two years later, she came home from a dinner-show date to find the apartment looking as if it had been ransacked by thieves. There was a note from her roommate stating that she'd eloped to Florida with a boy-friend, that she wasn't coming back, that the four bottles of vodka in the kitchen closet were all Clara's.

Clara tidied things up, and then sat down on the couch and looked around She was alone. A very nice young man had escorted her tonight, but she'd been alone then too. *She'd always been alone.*

Panic welled up in her, sudden and complete. She went to the kitchen and forced herself to drink some of the vodka. She thought of all the men she'd dated in the past three-four years. And couldn't remember what one of them looked like. Shadows. Pale shadows with nondescript faces who spoke in nondescript male voices. She'd been with them, and been alone. *She would always be alone.*

The panic became too much. She gasped and bit her lip and clenched her hands into trembling, white-knuckled fists. Alone. Alone. Alone—forever.

She drank half a bottle of vodka in order to fall asleep. The next evening, she visited her father for the first time in ten months; and it was a mistake. He was the same—conventional, narrow-minded and opinionated. Added to that was a simmering resentment over the way she was living ("A nice Jewish girl doesn't stay all alone in Greenwich Village!") and an outspoken anger at her having failed to visit him in so long a time. The stepmother was casual and friendly, but her "And when are you going to bring a bridegroom around?" enraged Clara. She left early, realizing they couldn't help being what they were; also realizing she couldn't help her reaction to them.

She came home and sat in the living room of her apartment and played classical records—Stravinsky, Lalo, Rachmaninoff. The panic she'd felt last night returned. She smoked cigarette after cigarette (though she didn't inhale; used them as something to do), and waited for the panic to go. It didn't go. It grew. After a while, she turned off the phonograph and looked around with glazed eyes and began to tremble.

She didn't sleep that night. She paced the floor, smoked, and tried the vodka again. But this time she gagged on the colorless liquid. Shortly before dawn, she thought of killing herself—thought of it seriously, as a means of ending the night's terrible agony—but she finally shook it off.

That same week, she made arrangements for her summer vacation. She would spend all ten weeks on a European trip; tourist-class passage on a Cunard liner, hike-and-bike tour of England, France and Italy. Planning the route she would travel took up her spare time until June arrived; kept her occupied and sane.

No one came to see her off when the *Ivernia* sailed. (She'd informed her father of her plans, and he'd begged her not to go alone. He was sure she'd be raped or murdered in those "crazy foreign places." To prevent any last-minute repetition of his arguments, she refused to tell him which ship she was taking.) She spent most of the first morning on deck, and then, after unpacking and introducing herself to her three cabin-mates (all middle-aged maidens—friends going to Paris together), she went to the dining room and found herself sitting next to a tall, thin man. He smiled at her. She smiled back, and with a tremendous excitement realized she meant the smile. They talked, and strolled about the deck, and later had dinner. They went back on deck and resumed their strolling and chatting, and before either of them knew it the ship's bells tolled one A.M. It wasn't until he said good night that he remembered to give her his last name. "Maston," he said, and their hands brushed and she wanted to stay there in the passageway and talk all night. "Charles Maston. . . ."

Life had begun right then, Clara thought, coming around the south side of the classroom and mounting the low, wide podium to her desk. They'd seen Europe together; made love for the first time a few days before they were to return to the States. It was in a grim hotel room in Liverpool, and from then on there wasn't the slightest doubt (if any had existed) that they belonged together. The were married six months later by a New York justice of the peace; their guest list numbered two—a married couple Charles knew from his Columbia University days who were necessary as witnesses. (Clara had invited her father, but he refused to attend, heartbroken that his daughter was marrying a goy. Charles didn't bother notifying his family—father, mother and older brother Lester—until a month or two afterward.)

Fourteen months of perfect happiness had followed; right up until the present.

She felt a return of fear, a budding of the old panic. Maybe the fourteen months had been too perfect. Even working in the same school (Charles had been teaching at Laurel for a year and had helped place her there as soon as old Mrs. Groworthy had left).

Maybe such happiness isn't allowed.

She laughed at herself, but the ancient fear of a curse, of being envied by the gods for good fortune, was upon her.

The bell rang, ending the test and the period. She took the sheets of paper collected by monitors, stacked them, bound them with rubber bands and put them in her brief case. As she did this, she watched her hands. They trembled.

A child would change things. She had happiness now, so change was an evil to be avoided at all costs. She would fight, do anything, to keep her happiness unchanged!

The day was terribly long. When it finally ended and she was sitting beside Charles in the car, she found she could barely keep her eyes open. She sat quietly, making an occasional comment as Charles told her about Steven Cochrane's latest attempt to convert someone to Catholicism. "One of these days he's going to run into trouble with a parent, and then there'll be a hush-hush board meeting and we'll have a new gym instructor. I hope it happens soon! That's one imbecile I can't tolerate—"

Clara said, "Me, too," leaned back and closed her eyes. Catholics and Protestants and Jews. Moslems and Hindus and pagans. Orthodox and Reformist splitting these divisions into yet more divisions. Sects and offshoots and super-purists and revolutionaries flaking away into dozens of separate, competing units. And all proclaiming *they* had the Word, they alone knew the correct way to gain entrance to heaven; all others were unbelievers and probably doomed to the lower regions. Amen.

This was modern man; this the inheritor of the atom; this the main component of a society into which she was supposed to deliver a child—

"No," she said.

"What?" Charles asked.

She straightened and smiled. "Just clearing my throat."

He went on about Cochrane. . . .

It was ten to five when they parked the car and walked toward Koptic Court.

"You—you *spitting* thing!" a blond little girl shouted, and burst into tears. She was looking down the street to where a boy, slightly older and bigger than she, was dancing around and daring her to chase him. "I'd *catch* you, Gary, you bad boy," the child wailed, "except I got to go in and have supper. I'd catch—" She wept bitterly.

Clara felt a sudden rush of pity, a sudden surge of sympathy. She wanted to kneel beside the pretty little girl—the child's name was Bonnie Allan—and ask her what was wrong and comfort her and kiss away the tears—

She did none of those things. She immediately recognized the feeling for what it was: an attempt by her subconscious to make possible pregnancy more palatable.

"I'll catch you tomorrow!" the blond four-year-old sobbed. "I'll punch you back, Gary, you bad boy you!"

The "bad boy" stuck out his tongue, made horrible faces; then chanted, "Baby, baby, stick your head in gravy."

Mrs. Allan appeared from the deep lobby entrance and Bonnie ran to her, sobbing her little tale of woe.

"Attractive children they raise here," Charles murmured. "Nice, quiet little tykes."

"Oh, they're not so bad," Clara said, and then asked herself why the hell she was defending the brats.

"I guess not," Charles said, and took her arm. "Children are never really unattractive. But oh, those parents!"

She agreed with a sharp laugh. . . .

After dinner, she said she had to run down to Fourth Avenue. Charles was surprised; they rarely went out during the evening—and never without each other.

"I'll come along—" he began.

"No," she interrupted smoothly. "I don't want you to see what I'm buying. Understand?"

He thought a moment; then smiled. "Don't spend a lot. Birthdays aren't too important to me."

She kissed him and left. Birthdays weren't too important to her, either, but she was going to make sure that no new one was added to their little family!

5

BONNIE ALLAN 1-J

In the mornings, it was nice. Bonnie got up and played in her room. Mommy and Daddy didn't get up until much later—seven-thirty, Mommy called it. Bonnie didn't know what that was on the clock, though she was sure she soon would. She learned things every day. But she was only four years old and telling time wasn't one of her accomplishments. She had many others, though.

She knew lots of songs Mommy and Gramma and the television had taught her. Daddy loved to hear them. He was a big, big man and she would lean against his knee and sing, a little embarrassed, but feeling good when he rubbed her head and laughed softly and said, "How about 'Sing a Song of Sixpence'?"

She knew it all the way through to "—and pecked on her nose!" She also knew the songs Daddy had taught her, laughing while he made her shake her little hips.

"I wish that I could shimmy like my sister Kate—"

And Mommy taught her to count to twenty. And sometimes she counted to thirty, but she had trouble remembering that it was all the same after twenty—you just added the one, two, three and four and so on. But it wouldn't be long before she remembered that too. As well as she remembered the alphabet.

"Well it's me and I'm in love again," she sang. "Had no lovin' since you know when. Hooey, baby, hooey! Baby, don't you let your dog bite me!" Another song Daddy had taught her. Another one that made him laugh and rub her head.

She sat on the floor beside her big bed and played with the three plastic dollies Gramma had bought her—Gramma Allan who lived with them right here; right across the foyer in the third bedroom of the large apartment. Bonnie would have liked to go across the foyer and kiss Gramma, but she wasn't allowed to. Gramma worked in New York, like Daddy, only she went later and came home earlier. Half-day, Mommy called it. Gramma made wigs—and she needed her sleep.

"You're a bad girl," Bonnie said sternly, and turned one of the three little dolls over on its stomach and spanked it. "Don't you dare throw your cereal on the floor again!"

Mommy had once spanked Bonnie for that. It hurt. Bonnie didn't forget, and she never threw cereal on the floor again.

She picked up her dollies and went into the bathroom alongside Gramma's room and got her little stool from under the sink. She stepped up on it and turned on the water and washed her babies—Irene, Imogene and Sally. She could reach the water taps from the floor now because she was growing tall, but it was easier with the stool.

"You're a bad boy!" she suddenly said, remembering how that bad boy Gary had pushed her off her tricycle and she'd hurt her finger and Mommy had to put Bactine on it.

Her slim, lovely little face grew red as she thought of Gary. Oh, she'd show him the next time he'd tried that! She'd punch him, with her fists, like Daddy showed her. And she'd make him cry even though he was five. She'd make him cry by singing, "Baby, baby, stick your head in gravy!"

And she wouldn't let him scare her any more. No!

She turned off the water, but forgot to take the dolls. She looked into Gramma's room, and Gramma's eyes were open. "Come here," Gramma said in her soft voice. "Come here, beautiful angel."

"I'm not an angel," Bonnie said, and shook her head so that her medium-length, ash-blond hair swished back and forth. She laughed, and heard Gramma laugh, and said, "I'm not a beautiful angel. I'm a girl."

Gramma sat up and said, "Then come here, little girl."

"I'm not a little girl," Bonnie said, shaking her head and

laughing and getting dizzy and seeing the room jump and shake and Gramma jump and shake. "I'm a big girl."

"Bonnie, don't do that. You'll get dizzy."

Bonnie stopped shaking her head and ran to the bed. Gramma's lips were cool and dry on her cheek and then on her neck and then on her arm.

"Angel," Gramma crooned. "Sweet, sweet angel."

Bonnie loved her Gramma. Bonnie loved the kisses and soft voice. But only for a while. Then she got tired and pulled away and ran into the living room. She turned on the television, even though she knew it wasn't Saturday or Sunday and there were no kiddie shows right now. Captain Kangaroo and Tinker's Workshop came on at eight, and it wasn't eight because Daddy wasn't in the bathroom, shaving. She saw Dave Garroway and watched awhile, and then turned the set off.

She went back to Gramma. Gramma was sleeping again.

She went into her room and played with her coloring book and crayons.

Later, she heard Daddy clearing his throat and Mommy saying something, and then heard them both laughing.

The desire to be with them was so strong it made her slip and almost fall in her haste to get to her feet and run to the main bedroom.

"Daddy! Mommy!" she shouted. "I want to laugh too!"

She ran down the foyer and into the main bedroom and jumped up on the bed and crawled between her mother and father. They grabbed her and smothered her with kisses. Then Mommy got up and left the room, and Bonnie was being squeezed by Daddy.

"Here she is," Daddy said. "Here she is. Here's my girl. Here's my baby. Here's the sex machine—Miss Monroe of 1957. Here she is." It was like a song, and she loved it, and she loved Daddy.

But then Daddy said, "I've got to get washed and shaved, kitten. It's after eight. I overslept. So let me up."

She didn't want to. "Let's wrestle," she said.

"I just told you—"

"Just once! Please! Just one wrestle!"

He lay back on the pillow and she climbed astride his chest and put both hands on his forehead. He grunted and picked up his head, and she shoved it back. They did it a few times, and she laughed so hard her breath caught and she choked a little.

"Okay," Daddy said. "That was five times; not once."

"Just once more, Daddy! Just once more!"

"Now you said once before and I gave you five—"

"Just once more, for real!"

He sat up and picked her up and put her down on the floor. His face wasn't smiling. She knew he was angry.

She felt like crying. "Yipes," she said, and made believe she was falling down dead. "Yipes."

It didn't make Daddy laugh.

"I'm sorry I cheated," she said, the tears welling up in her gray eyes. "I'm sorry, Daddy."

He came around the bed and patted her head and said, "That wasn't cheating, baby. That was being a pest. Now go have your juice."

Bonnie suddenly remembered it was time for her television programs.

"Yipes!" she said, and made believe she was falling down dead. "I almost forgot. Tinker's on!" She ran.

This time Daddy laughed.

She dragged her rocking chair across the carpeting until it was directly in front of the TV set. She turned the knob and sat down and waited. But it was the wrong channel, and the sound wasn't right.

"Mommy! Come fix the television! Hurry! Tinker's on!"

"Yes, master," Mommy said. She came in and got the right channel and fixed the sound. Then she gave Bonnie a glass of juice. Bonnie drank it—even though she didn't like orange juice. She watched television while eating bacon and a piece of toast. She finished it all, even though she didn't really like to eat anything but frankfurters and olives. Mommy gave her frankfurters and olives when she was very, very good, but that was only once in a very long while.

Daddy came in dressed and smelling from shaving, and kissed her. She kissed him back quickly, perfunctorily, and said, "See you later, alligator."

"After a while, crocodile," he answered, and waited.

But she couldn't look at him because Tinker had a white rabbit and was feeding it lettuce and yipes, it had such big ears and such a funny nose and she didn't want to miss it.

Afterwards, there was another kiddy show, and Gramma was there, trying to pick her up.

"Goway, Gramma!" she shouted. "I'm watching!"

Gramma said, "Boo hoo. I'm crying, angel. I'm going away and never come back."

Bonnie didn't look at her because there was this cartoon about Farmer Gray and his cat. But after the cartoon she looked around and Gramma was gone and she worried that Gramma was really crying, even though she knew Gramma didn't cry. Except for the time Grampa Allan went to heaven, and then Gramma cried and cried and cried. But that was a long time ago, in the smaller apartment on the other block, and Gramma didn't live with them then.

"Gramma, are you in the kitchen?"

"Yes, angel."

She ran to the kitchen and kissed Gramma and said, "Were you fooling? Were you crying?"

"I was fooling," Gramma said, drinking coffee.

Bonnie went back to watch television.

Later, Gramma left. Then Bonnie went outside, wearing her coat and leggings because it was March and still cold. She rode her tricycle and that bad boy Gary pushed her off again and scared her and she cried. But after that she ran up to him and punched him with her fists like Daddy had showed her. She hit him right in the stomach. He cried, and she chanted, "Baby, baby, stick your head in gravy," and Beverly joined in, and even that baby, Michael, three years old, tried to sing it. And Gary went crying to his mother.

Yipes, they were playing house!

Yipes, they were playing hide 'n seek!

Then she fell and scraped her knee and ooh, it hurt! Mommy took her inside and sat her on the kitchen table and got out the stinging medicine. Bonnie began to scream.

"If you're a good girl," Mommy said, "I'll let you play in the lobby tonight when Big Stevie, Wallace, Sandra and the others go there. You'll be playing with big boys and girls—"

"All right," Bonnie said, and sobbed fitfully as Mommy came closer with the medicine. . . .

That night after supper Mommy brought her out to the lobby and left her there, and she played school with the five- and six-year-olds. It was fun! But she slipped and fell on her knee—the one with the bandage. It hurt and she cried, and then a man was picking her up, just like Daddy. Only it wasn't Daddy—it was the man Mommy called Mr. Theck. He wasn't as high as Daddy, but he was fatter. He had real fat arms—only maybe it wasn't right to say fat because they were hard and Daddy called them something else. Muscles.

"Hiyo, Silver!" Mr. Theck said, and swung Bonnie way up

so that she gasped and laughed, both at the same time. "How's that for stopping tears, Bonnie?"

"Swing me up," Big Stevie shouted. "C'mon, Mr. Theck."

"Well, I don't know," Mr. Theck said, and looked Big Stevie up and down. "You must weigh almost fifty pounds and I'm not sure I can lift such a big guy."

Big Stevie grinned. "Aw, you got muscles bigger than anyone's. You can lift me easy."

And Mr. Theck did lift him easy. And the other kids too.

He was a nice man, Bonnie thought. He liked children.

He was looking at them, smiling, when Bonnie asked him a question.

"Are you a daddy?"

His smile went away fast. "No," he said, and walked to the elevator.

"Aren't you married?" Bonnie asked, following him.

"Yes," he said, and punched the button three times.

"That don't make the elevator come faster," Bonnie told him. "I know 'cause I heard the colored man—"

The elevator came and Mr. Theck got inside and let the door close. Bonnie wondered why he'd looked so sad all of a sudden. But then she forgot the whole thing because a new game was starting!

When Daddy came to get her, she tried to run away. "Yipes, we're playing clowns and stuff!"

"Yipes, it's time for bed," Daddy said, and caught her.

She had a bath, and Daddy helped, and he kissed her all over, and she liked it. Mommy was talking about the rain and cold. "Terrible weather, Arny."

"Terrible weather," Bonnie said, mimicking Mommy's tone of voice. "Terrible weather, Arny."

Mommy and Daddy laughed and laughed. . . .

6

JOE AND PAULA THECK 4-B

On a rainy day in February, Paula took the BMT at the Fifty-fifth Street elevated station and rode to Canal Street. There she got off, took the downtown local one stop, and stepped onto the platform. She headed for the staircase.

This was normal. This was what she had been doing for the last four years—ever since she'd become secretary to Mr. Dennison of Dennison & Carrol, Import-Export, Inc.

What happened next, however, was not normal.

She was passing one of the metal girders that were spaced every twenty feet or so along the station, and turned her head, and saw something scrawled in red. It was a thick, heavy scrawl. It looked like blood. It was probably lipstick.

It said, "Destroy the dirty Jew bastards."

She stopped and stared and read it again. People brushed past her, a few bumped into her, and finally she went on, up the stairs, into the narrow, crowded Manhattan street. She walked one block and entered the twelve-story building and took the old-fashioned cage elevator to the eighth floor. The operator said something to her, but she didn't hear it. "What was that, Pete?"

"Nice day for fish," the short, thin, curly-haired youth repeated, and laughed. "Nice wet day for fish, eh?"

"Yes," she said.

Pete was surprised; Paula always laughed at his jokes.

She left the elevator and walked down the hall and used her key to open the office door. It was eight-fifty. The rest of the staff would drift in from nine to ten-thirty, depending upon their individual positions.

She took off her raincoat and unbound her plastic headscarf and sat down behind her desk, facing the little wooden fence which separated a small anteroom from the one large room that held nine employees. Mr. Dennison had his private office way in back. Mr. Carrol was dead and his office was now a stockroom—also in back.

She lit a cigarette and inhaled deeply and then got up. She went out to the hall and about fifteen feet to a corner and around the corner to a lavatory. She moved to the sinks and the long mirror backing them. She looked at herself. She looked a long time, and then touched her face with a trembling hand.

She couldn't seem to see anything. She couldn't seem to remember anything.

Only that thick, red scrawl.

"Destroy the dirty Jew bastards."

She heard the voice and gasped—and then realized it was her own voice.

She shrugged in the mirror and laughed in the mirror. "Why, what nonsense," she murmured, and nodded at herself and smiled at herself.

She went back to the office.

It was a busy day. She had cables to decode and they concerned the vital South African market. If the Johannesburg contact came through on that order for cotton goods (and the Durban agent gave his usual order), they'd be in wonderful shape. If not—well, Mr. Dennison would be a hard man to work with for the next few months!

But, somehow, she was bored with it.

Bored with it.

She caught herself thinking this at three o'clock, and it didn't make sense. She liked her job.

At least she *had* liked it.

But then again, she'd been here over four years and that was a long time and maybe a new position—

Mr. Dennison called her into his office.

"What's this?" he said irritably. He thrust a typewritten sheet across his desk. "What's this word on the third line?"

She took the sheet and looked and saw she'd made a typo— a complete nonsense word.

"It's supposed to be 'recorded,' Mr. Dennison."

"And the one on the last line?" the tall, heavy-set, gray-haired man snapped. "What's that supposed to be?"

She looked, but suddenly her eyes were full of liquid—not tears but a steamy result of quick rage, quick hate. She stood there and trembled.

"Well?" he shouted.

She dropped the sheet and walked out of the office. She went to the ladies' room. She stepped into one of the booths and closed the door and stood with fists clenched. "Freilich," she said. "Dirty, filthy, swinish Freilich—"

She caught herself then; it was the first time she'd said that name in years!

She shook her head and the liquid in her eyes turned to tears and the rage was gone. She wept because she'd acted like a fool.

Ten minutes later, she returned to her desk. Mr. Dennison must have been standing at his door, waiting, because he came out as soon as she sat down.

They both said the same thing at the same time.

"I'm sorry—"

He shook his head and laughed uncomfortably. "That damn South African thing is making me irritable, Paula. You've always understood before—"

"Yes. And I do now. And my mistakes were bad—"

"No. What the devil—everyone makes mistakes—"

"I'll retype it right now."

He cleared his throat as she hurriedly got paper from her desk and turned to her typewriter. "Uh—I'll bring the letter to—"

She jumped up. "No. I—dropped it on the floor in your office, didn't I." It was no question, and she ran to his office without waiting for an answer. The letter was still there, on the floor. She picked it up and straightened and almost bumped into him.

They both smiled weakly.

They were very polite to each other the rest of the week, and Paula told herself she was happy again. But Joe asked her if anything was wrong at least five times Thursday and Friday nights.

Going home the next Monday, she was lucky enough to grab a seat on the West End Express. She sighed, settled herself and folded her paper. (She'd been reading while standing on the platform—both at her local stop and Canal Street. She didn't want her eyes straying to billboards—or girders.)

She examined the people around her; and there were plenty. The car was jam-packed—every seat taken, every inch of standing room covered.

She saw the lean, narrow-faced, brown-haired teen-age boy. He was sitting just across the way from her, near the opposite doors, talking to a girl. Paula could just make out his face, and the girl's legs, through the standees. He looked mean somehow—

Paula looked at other people, and the train came to a station and stopped. One voice rose above the hubbub—a man speaking with a heavy Yiddish accent. "So vat you vant me to do—argue mitt him, maybe? I gave him a real good price—"

As the train started again, drowning out the voice, Paula's eyes were drawn to the boy who sat across the way—the mean, hard-looking boy. She saw his face twist—the lips sneering, the eyes narrowing. He murmured something to the girl, and then brought up his hand. He made a clenched fist at the end of his nose; created an extension.

She felt sick.

She'd seen that before—in Germany.

The big nose. The cruel and vicious symbol of a Jew.

She began to perspire, and wanted to get off the train. But she stayed where she was, stayed until her stop, telling herself she'd imagined the whole thing.

That night after supper, she and Joe sat on the couch in the living room of their two-room apartment. Paula told Joe she was bored stiff with her job.

"Then quit," he said. "I never wanted—"

She ground out a cigarette, hands trembling slightly. "The same letters to type. The same cables to decode. The same fools—"

"Hey," Joe interrupted. "Take it easy, honey. It's not that important."

She got up from the couch and stalked around the room, her voice continuing to rise. "That imbecile Dennison. That idiot Hutchins. That slow-talking, slow-thinking fool Loder. I can't stand them any more. I can't take that pack of—of goys!"

Joe's eyes blinked. "I've never heard you say anything like that before."

Her voice grew shrill. " 'Type this letter please, Mrs. Theck. Decode this cablegram please, Paula.' And all the time they look at me with those cold eyes, thinking I don't count because—" She tried to stop herself then, shaking her head.

"Baby," Joe said, rising. "This isn't like you—"

She had to go on. "Thinking I don't count because I'm a Jew!"

Joe stared at her.

She turned and ran to the bathroom and was sick. Later, she went to bed and Joe comforted her—but she wouldn't let the comfort grow into anything else.

That was the beginning. Or rather the resumption of something that had begun when she was just a child.

She worked another week, and then quit. She needed a rest. Anyway, Joe insisted she stay home.

But she was still unable to find herself. She was jumpy, irritable, and she began to have the dream—the nightmare that was factual.

She also met the bread man. . . .

Before the subway incidents, Paula was a reasonably happy human being—or seemed to be. Sixteen full years of normalcy lay behind her—the years since she'd arrived in the

United States. On the dock, she'd stood pale-faced and trembling, a fourteen-year-old orphan shocked into tearless grief by horrors no American could yet understand. But when her aunt and uncle rushed toward her, hugged and kissed her, she wept and was on her way to becoming a normal child.

For a while, there were the terrible memories, the nights when she shrieked for help; but constant love, and the knowledge that she was free, soon had her surging through a teenage world.

The dream was a dim thing then—a vague recollection of Nazi horrors that would touch the back of her mind with miasmic fingers only when she was sick and feverish.

Paula grew into an attractive woman, with healthy desires and a solid capacity for pleasure.

At the age of thirty, married several months to Joe Theck, she overheard a conversation between her mother- and father-in-law in which she was the principal topic. She and Joe were visiting, sitting in the living room and watching TV. Her in-laws were having tea in the kitchen. They spoke loud and clear—quite normal for them. They didn't worry that she might overhear them. Perhaps they even hoped she would.

"—liveliest girl Joe ever dated," the mother said.

"You're absolutely right," the father said, slapping his thigh. "I'll bet that's why he married her. I'll bet he looked for the strongest, happiest girl he could find, and then said to himself, 'That one will give me lots of kids and make me laugh all the time.' "

They both choked back laughter.

"You're crazy," the mother said. "Who picks a wife that way? He was in love. He went for her looks. But Paula's certainly a live one." (More laughter.) "I wonder how long it'll take them to give us a grandchild. A year, you think?"

"Not them," the father answered. "I'll bet they've got one started right now—"

Paula glanced at Joe; he was absorbed in the TV show. She tried to hear more of her in-laws' conversation, but they were wheezing, chuckling and giggling now.

Finally, the father said, "A year at the longest. And then we'll be bouncing a little Joe or Paula on our knees—"

He was wrong; though Joe wanted children right from the start. And Paula was willing too, except that she felt they should wait. She had logical reasons for this feeling; financial reasons. They were both working. It was wise to continue that way for a few years. They would purchase the furnishings they wanted and still be able to build up a bank account. It was only being practical.

Or so she told Joe and herself and anyone else who asked.

But behind it all lay the dream, waiting to be born. And it made children impossible, for who would bring a child into a world in which lurked such horror, vague though it was?

Their first New Year's Eve as husband and wife, Joe and Paula threw a party in their two-room apartment. Present were some people from the city garage where Joe worked, Joe's two brothers and sister and their respective mates, and Paula's best friend Sybil and her husband. Paula got slightly loaded, danced with everyone and sang with everyone. She also kissed everyone—or *nearly* everyone. There was a mechanic named Steiner whom Paula danced with, sang with, but forgot to kiss. Steiner was tall, blond, blue-eyed, and jovially referred to himself as a "thick-headed Kraut."

No one noticed he was the one exception to her kissing spree. Not even Paula; at least not consciously.

"Girl, you're the belle of the ball!" another mechanic had shouted, swinging her out in a wide break to a Lindy Hop, and immediately earning a cold look from his own wife.

But that was almost three years ago. And life had changed radically for the Thecks in the past few weeks—the weeks since Paula had quit her job. Now the dream hung like a stifling blanket of smoke over their every waking moment.

And over many sleeping moments too. . . .

It was a night in early March.

Joe slept soundly.

Paula slept heavily, but without peace. The dream was with her:

It was a flat, gray, barren expanse of plain; a grim, limitless vista with no barbed wire or towers or barracks, without any of the actual physical properties of what she had known as Concentration Camp Three. And yet she knew it was Camp Three. She stood alone, fear and horror growing, and tried desperately to convince herself that this wasn't reality, that this was only a dream.

It didn't work. It never worked. The fear and horror grew, and she began to turn her head, swinging her eyes in a complete circle. The plain was empty.

"See?" she told herself. "There is no one to hurt you." But she couldn't move.

She heard it!

She expected to hear it, and yet her heart slammed against her ribs as if trying to burst and end the misery forever. She looked down at herself and saw the ragged, childish dress drop away and saw her young breasts, sparse pubic hair and long, mature legs.

She heard it again, and tried to cover herself with trembling hands. But it was impossible. Her figure grew more voluptuous—the breasts and buttocks swelling, the belly rounding, the pubic hair thickening. (Only her legs remained the same, but that was no comfort; that was the link with reality that made her terror so sharp. At thirteen, in the concentration camp, her legs had given her womanhood away; had finally brought S. S. Lieutenant Freilich.)

She heard it a third time, louder now, constant now, and the screams began to push up in her throat.

It was the sound of breathing amplified a hundred times, as when Freilich had panted into her ear; the heavy bellows-sound of a male in erotic, aggressive heat.

It came closer, and then she could see him—tall, straight, enormous in his black boots and black uniform; terribly blond; terribly fair-skinned (a pink, quick-to-redden, almost-transparent skin that she'd always identified with young swine). He loomed above the horizon, his thin-lipped mouth loose, his gray-blue eyes narrow and glittering.

Suddenly she could move, and she tried to run. But it was too late. Now she was backed into a corner of a tiny room—the medical-supply room at Camp Three—and his hands were at her body, pinching and squeezing so that she screamed in pain. He pushed her onto the brown-leather couch that smelled, strangely, of violets. His black breeches dropped and his long, muscular thighs emerged. Now the rampant, bestial, carnal maleness was ripping into her; the vile, degrading maleness.

"German!" she shrieked. "German!" But she despaired of his understanding. How could he know the insult she was conveying? How could he know that "German" was the ultimate curse-word in the language of seven million dead and two to three million near-dead?

"GERMAAAAAAAN!"

And she awoke to the firm pressure of Joe's hands on her shoulders.

"All right," he said in his steady voice. "You're home, baby."

She sat up and drew back from his attempt to put his arms around her.

"Please give me a cigarette," she said, her speech holding only the minutest trace of an accent; less an accent than a slightly off-beat timing in her delivery.

He put on the lamp, got out of bed and went to the dresser. He lit a cigarette from a pack lying there and brought it to her, along with an ash tray. She sucked in smoke and said, "Thank you. Go back to sleep now. I'm sorry I woke you. Go on—I'll be all right."

"Sure you'll be all right. You are all right." But he rubbed his big, calloused hands together nervously. "Same thing, eh?"

She nodded.

"Forgive and forget, baby," he murmured. "You got to—"

"Forgive and forget!" she said, voice shaking. "Seven million helpless Jews destroyed! And is the conscience of this wonderful western civilization bothered? Certainly not! Now the Germans are our trusted allies. And we weep and wail about the poor Poles under the heel of the Russians, but those poor Poles helped the Nazis kill Jews whenever they could—and did a pretty good job by themselves even before there were Nazis! But Jews don't count. Only Germans and Poles and Romanians and Hungarians and others count. Oh, don't tell me! I know how that rabble loved to butcher helpless Jews. But Germans are the worst. Are, not were! Why should we believe they've changed? It isn't as if they stopped killing on their own. They were beaten to their knees, and then they decided to change—or England, America and Russia decided to change them. They're rotten inside. And so are the Germans here. Wasn't Yorkville full of anti-Semites, Nazi Bundists, Fritz Kuhns? Didn't you yourself tell me how they filled Madison Square Garden for their rallies? Everywhere you go you see them—the Germans. Everywhere! And do you care? Not you, and not all the other fools like you. But Germany will get powerful again, and then you'll have to care—"

He listened and nodded once in a while, face set in pained patient lines, until she ran out of breath.

"All right, Paula, Even if it's as bad as you say, what can we do? Hating so strong is no good; you get eaten up by it. Anyway, some of the guys down at the garage are of German and Polish descent and they don't give me any trouble. We get along okay. Listen, even with some people hating Jews and Negroes, we gotta live. I know you've been through a lot, honey, but you gotta forget. You were okay for so long—right up until a couple of weeks ago. Why can't you forget now—"

She couldn't forget.

Germans! Germans living all around her, unpunished!

Strange that at first she hadn't seen it that way. At first she done everything to forget. All those years of school, and then work, and then meeting Joe and getting married and living here. Why, the tough time they'd had getting rid of cockroaches in the kitchen had been more important—more trouble—to her than memories of Germany!

But then she'd quit her job. After that, she began to remember—to allow herself to remember—the concentration camp and the Germans. Her hate didn't develop; it had been there since Camp Three and sprang full-grown into the forefront of her mind.

About a week ago she first saw the Hogan's Bread man. He came around every day, ringing doorbells and calling out, "Hogaaaan's. Hogaaaan's." He was tall and blond and wore a gray uniform. He had grayish-blue eyes and a thin-lipped mouth. He looked like S. S. Lieutenant Freilich.

She'd found out that his name was Walter Smith. She was sure it had once been Schmidt.

From the first time she'd opened her door and seen him standing there, carrying a large basket filled with bread, rolls and pastries, she'd hated him. He was so obviously a German. He was representative of all the Germans she feared, hated and despised. If not for them, she would have peace and Joe wouldn't be starting to go out to poker nights and lodge nights and bowling nights; she would remember how to enjoy love and make her husband a whole man, a happy man again.

If she could just strike back at the Germans—at even one of them! If she could somehow destroy that bread man, that Walter Smith, that Herr Schmidt—

"Put out the cigarette," Joe was saying.

"What?"

"It'll burn your fingers."

She felt the heat and saw that she was holding a tiny butt. She ground it into the ash tray, and looked up. Joe's eyes were moving over her.

"I think I'll make myself some tea," she said, and began to walk past him toward the doorway. He got up, put his arms around her, pressed his lips into her neck. "Honey," he whispered fervently. "Honey, I love you—"

She stiffened, began to shove him away, and then told herself she had to stop acting like that. She loved him, wanted him as much as he wanted her, had to show him she did.

She put her head against his shoulder, fighting the feeling of revulsion as he caressed her body. Standing barefoot that way, she was three inches shorter than he, but when she wore high heels they were the same height—about five foot nine. She was a tall, well-built woman of thirty-three with high, firm breasts, full thighs and narrow waist. Despite her hatred for what she considered Germanic coloring, she herself was pink-skinned, blond and blue-eyed.

Joe looked shorter than he actually was because of his broadness; a hundred eighty-five pounds of firm flesh and muscle. At thirty-seven, he had black, curly hair which was thinning at the back and receding in front. His face was full cheeked, perpetually darkened by a heavy beard that needed shaving twice a day, brightened by very white teeth and light brown eyes. He was a healthy, normally happy man. During the ten months of their courtship and the three years of their marriage, he had continually laughed, continually sung and whistled the popular songs they'd both liked, continually kidded her, kissed her, gone places with her. And they'd made love as often as they could, and enjoyed it immensely. But it had all began to change since she quit her job a few weeks ago.

Still, Joe was a cheerful person, always ready to see hope in the future. He was also a healthy, lusty male, always ready to take her.

"Paula, honey," he muttered thickly. "Baby, I've needed you so bad these last few weeks. And you must need me. We go so well together—"

He suddenly picked her up and carried her to the bed. He set her down, and fumbled at the waist-strings of his pajamas. She wanted to beg him to stop. She had too much fear and hate to be able to love. Why couldn't he understand that? Why couldn't he be patient until she somehow rid herself of the hate?

But he had been patient—three or four months. How long could she expect him to wait? How long before he began to reach for other women?

He was pressing her down, drawing her tight, breathing harshly into her ear. She closed her eyes and made herself say, "Joe, sweetie, I love you." Then she tried hard to keep Lieutenant Freilich out of her mind.

She succeeded too, but it was a qualified success; she thought of the bread man, Walter Smith.

Later, she dozed off, and again dreamed of Concentration Camp Three. But this time she awoke before Freilich could shove her onto the leather couch.

"German pig," she whispered, wanting to cry but afraid of waking Joe. Tomorrow was Monday and he needed his sleep.

If a Freilich ever tried to touch her again—

She blinked into the darkness, mind still fogged with sleep and dream-terror, but beginning to function.

This was America. If a Freilich ever tried to touch her again, she would scream and people would come running and the Freilich would be taken away and charged with rape. They sent men to jail for rape. Ten or fifteen or twenty years wasn't much for a clear-cut case of sexual assault. Even life, sometimes!

If Walter Smith ever tried to touch her—

She turned onto her side and told herself to go to sleep. What she was thinking was nonsense. . . .

She awakened the next morning when Joe kissed her on the forehead. " 'Bye, honey," he said. "I—it was wonderful last night; like it was before you got sick. Like it should always be."

She smiled and started to sit up, but he gently pushed her back. "Sleep."

"But your breakfast—"

"I'll get eggs and coffee at a greasy spoon. You rest up—get back to normal fast." He turned away, then stopped. "You know, I been thinking that a little girl who looked like you would sure be fun."

"We've got plenty of time for that," she said. "Years." She rolled over, pressing her face into her pillow. A moment later, she heard him walk out, and then the front door closed. She fell asleep again.

She got out of bed at eleven o'clock, washed, had two cups of coffee and two cigarettes, then returned to the bedroom to dress. The phone rang before she could start, and she ran back to the foyer of the two-room apartment. The phone was on the wall near the utility kitchen.

It was Joe's mother. She wanted to know how Paula was feeling, if Joe was all right, and if they would come over Sunday afternoon for dinner.

"Well," Paula began, not wanting to go. Joe's brothers, Sid and Seymour, and his sister, Shirley, would be there and there was always so much laughing and shouting what with the brothers' wives and the sister's husband and the four kids —Sid, the eldest, had two boys; the others had a girl each. While they were all nice people and she really liked them, she just couldn't see herself in that situation now. "Well, Mom, I don't know. My friend Sybil said she wanted to come over—"

"Ah, Paula," Elsa Theck said softly, "why don't you like us no more, hah? In the last month you haven't been to dinner once—not once. Was it something I said or did? You know Solly and I love you—"

Paula heard a voice call out in the hall; a man's voice. "Hogaaaan's! Hogaaaan's!"

The doorbell rang briefly, and so did the one next door. Walter Smith rang four or five bells in succession and then sold to whoever answered. Generally, he stayed in the hall.

"Okay, Mom," she said, knowing it was the only way to cut the conversation short. "We'll be there."

"'Fine, fine. I'll count on it. Remember now—"

"Yes, Mom. I gotta answer the door. 'Bye." She hung up and started down the foyer; then turned and ran to the bedroom and examined herself in the mirror. Breathing quickly, she put on lipstick and began combing her hair back. But then she stopped. She didn't have time to make herself look the way she wanted to look.

As soon as she decided not to answer the door, her heart stopped racing. But she didn't leave the mirror. She stepped back to view herself full-length, and shook her head at the terry-cloth robe and faded flannel nightgown showing from her calves down. The pink silk dressing gown Joe had bought her last anniversary would be perfect. And she'd wear her spike heels with the ankle straps; they always excited Joe; he said they made her legs sexy as hell. She'd put her hair back and use make-up and perfume. Then she'd get Herr Schmidt into the apartment. . . .

She was ready by ten-thirty the next morning. She sat in the living room, dressed exactly as she'd planned.

When she heard the voice in the hall, she stood up. She patted her hair and smoothed the heavy pink silk against her legs and walked down the foyer on her spike heels. She stopped and waited. As soon as the bell rang, she opened the peephole and said, "Hogan's?"

He was moving away, toward the next door, but he stopped. "Yes, ma'am. Raisin loaf special today—"

"I want some sweet rolls, but I can't come out in the hall. When you're finished with the others, please come in. The door will be unlocked."

"Yes, ma'am." And then Mrs. Dolberger in 4-G came out, and he turned to serve her.

Paula snapped open the Yale lock and walked back to the living room, looking down at herself, watching the way her left leg came through the opening in the dressing gown— a long, white leg showing clear to the knee, unhindered by nightgown or pajamas. Under the robe she wore panties and uplift brassiere; nothing special because she wouldn't allow him to get that far the first time. He would look, and she would make him desire, and that desire would grow during the weeks and months to come, and when she felt he was ready she would spring her trap.

Maybe it wasn't as final as being burned in an oven, but it would have to do.

She sat down in the armchair—the one clearly visible from the end of the foyer, the spot where it broadened out and where they had their kitchen table. He would put his basket on the table and look at her—

She crossed her legs, and the robe parted to reveal a large portion of thigh. She drew the silk back together, leaving only a few inches of ankle and calf exposed.

Not too fast, she thought. He must wait and hunger and finally lose all caution.

She glanced down at her neckline. That could stand more exposure. She adjusted it.

The door opened and Walter Smith said, "Hogan's! Got only two more raisin loaves left." He strode briskly down the foyer, set his basket on the table, raised his head. His eyes blinked several times before returning to his basket. "Oh, yes, you wanted rolls. One box or two?"

"One, please," she said, and was annoyed that her voice sounded so stiff and cold. "The raisin loaf really good?"

"Yes, ma'am!" He drew out a box of rolls and a loaf of bread, and looked at her again. "That'll be—" his eyes went over her swiftly—"sixty cents."

"Oh, my," she said, and this time congratulated herself on the softness of her voice. "Things are certainly climbing in price. I remember when I was able to get a good deal more than that for half a dollar."

He nodded and flashed his toothy smile, and the rage leaped up in her heart. German! Healthy and happy while other Schmidts had killed seven million helpless Jews—men, women and children. Look at him there, with his crew-cut blond hair and glittering gray-blue eyes and pink swinish skin! Dirty German . . .

She cleared her mind, afraid he'd be able to read the hate in her glance. She stood up and walked toward him, rolling her hips, giving him a good look at her leg. His eyes flicked down and up and he turned back to his basket. "Nice outside," he said, and cleared his throat. "Sunny."

She came up close, much closer than she normally would, and bent over as if to peer into his basket. With sidelong glances, she saw that his eyes had darted to her neckline, to the cleavage between her breasts.

But she'd overplayed her hand. He realized she'd seen him peeping. He stepped back, reddening, eyes dropping to the table and staying there.

"Just a moment," she murmured. "My purse is in the bedroom." She walked away from him, swaying seductively. She got her purse from the dresser and started back, feeling unaccountably tired. She wanted him out of here—

But then she stopped. She hadn't accomplished a thing yet. He entered dozens of apartments, and there were bound to be housewives who, consciously or otherwise, exposed a great deal more of themselves than she had, who flirted a great deal more with him than she had.

She would have to indicate that what he saw in her was attainable, was something to be aimed at and planned for.

She loosened the robe a little, and returned to the foyer table. She didn't dare look down at her legs, but she knew that the heavy pink silk was flaring open with each step. And when he glanced up at her, she knew he'd seen something that excited him. His eyes hung at the level of her thighs for a long second or two, and then she was inches from him, handing him a dollar bill.

His breath came quickly as he spoke. "Sixty from a dollar. That's forty cents change. Here you are, ma'am."

Their fingers touched as he gave her the coins. "Do you call everyone ma'am?" she asked, smiling.

His eyes jerked to hers. "Oh, well, sure, most of them—my customers, I mean. A few I call Mrs. So-and-so, like Mrs. Dolberger next door. And Mrs. Weiner in Three-C."

"Don't you ever call them by their first names?"

He glanced at his basket, as if wanting to pick it up and leave, but she was right alongside it and he was a few paces back along the foyer. He would have to move her to reach it.

"Just one; maybe two," he said, and cleared his throat several times in succession: short, harsh, nervous, barking sounds. His breath was coming faster and faster; his eyes took abortive, quickly controlled little trips down her body; his face was pink and slightly shiny with perspiration.

God! He was the exact image of Freilich! His *doppelgänger!*

She smiled and said, "When people do business together, they should know each other. I'm Paula Theck, and I know you're Walter Schmidt."

"Smith," he said.

It was a slip, and she was angry at herself. "That's right." She put out her hand. "Hello, Walt."

He took her hand, then withdrew quickly, almost as if the contact had burned him.

Can he be so naïve? she wondered. Is he really so slow to see a good deal? He was in his late twenties, as Freilich had been, and must surely know enough about women. But then again, he earned his living selling door-to-door for a very respectable company, and would naturally have become more cautious. One complaint would certainly mean his job.

"Guess I'll be going," he said, and took a half-step forward.

She didn't move. "You said it was nice outside. Still as cold as yesterday?"

He glanced at his basket before answering. "No, ma'am."

"Paula," she corrected, smiling.

This time he returned the smile, and the first touch of intimacy entered his eyes, his face, his voice. "Paula. Little warmer. Got a feel of spring coming."

"Really? Now we'll start missing winter. But then again, when I think of sleet and snow and those nights—" She batted her eyelashes. "Cold, cold nights."

He cleared his throat and their eyes met and he seemed to be thinking hard. Then he said, "Well, you got a husband, but a single person really gets cold—" He grinned.

She would have loved to slap his face and throw him out. But that would be such minor punishment. No, what she had in mind was screaming for help and having people burst in to find her fighting him wildly. What she had in mind was jail, the destruction of his life.

So she smiled and leaned toward him and murmured, "Some husbands aren't much for cold nights, Walt. Nor hot nights either."

He was about to reach for her. She could read it in his part-ing lips and trembling hands.

She stepped back and sighed. "But here I am bothering you with my personal problems. And holding you back from your work."

"I don't have to rush," he said thickly.

He was hooked. Now let him think about it. Now let him begin to hunger. When he was wild for her, she'd show Herr Schmidt that a Jewess could fight back.

"Goodbye, Walt, I'm expecting a friend."

"Oh." He reached for his basket. "Well, so long, Paula."

She kept smiling at him, and he smiled back, and his hand fumbled blindly for the basket as he looked at her face and breasts and down along her body. Finally, she turned away, saying, "Please close the door on the snap-lock, Walt." She walked through the living room. This time she knew he was watching her hips roll; she could almost feel the heat of his eyes.

She stopped in the bedroom, hearing his footsteps sound down the foyer. But he stopped at the door without opening it. She waited, thinking of his glittering eyes and feverish breath, thinking of Freilich, hating Freilich and all of them, the dirty Germans!

Suddenly, she saw her mother's terrible smile as they took her away—

"No, don't think," she murmured aloud, afraid of that memory. "Please don't think."

She started back toward the foyer, anxious now to con-tinue speaking to Schmidt, to give him a final bit of teasing and in so doing drive away the image of her mother, *shaine, zisse Momma*—beautiful, sweet Mother.

But the bread man had decided against whatever stalling tactic he'd had in mind. The door opened and shut in an instant. She went swiftly down the foyer and looked through the peephole and heard the elevator hum into motion. She went back to the bedroom.

"I'll dress and go over to Sybil's," she said in a loud voice. "I'll play with Michael—"

She dressed quickly, left the apartment and caught the Sixteenth Avenue bus. She sat directly behind the driver. He was wearing a dark-blue shirt, the collar firm and stiff and tight against his thick, tanned, reddish neck. The combination of near-black collar and reddish neck reminded her of the S.S. guards, of the one who had pulled her mother from the barracks after laughing at Paula and saying, "*Du bist schön, fraülein*—"

"You are pretty, miss. You are lucky. The Lieutenant is going to save you from the ovens, where you really belong. He is going to save you from the medical laboratories with their injections. You'll get different kinds of injections."

And the laughter from the other guards.

"But oh so good for a young Jewess!"

"When Freilich is finished with her, I want what's left."

"When Freilich is finished with her, there won't be anything left. He eats them—skin, bones and all."

"Ah, but will he be able to swallow that plump Jewish ass?"

And while her mother kept herself from screaming in fear and horror as they dragged her off to the gas chambers or ovens or medical laboratories or death vans, while she forced herself to smile back at her thirteen-year-old daughter and heard what was in store for the beloved flesh of her flesh, and knew she herself was going to die—while the assortment of horrors ripped at the mother, a short, stout guard paused a moment to pinch the daughter.

"Yah, on this Jewish ass he will choke. Then we will all share in enjoying it." And out through the rough wood doors they went, the guards laughing, into the yard where other men and women were being lined up.

This was Paula's farewell scene with her mother, standing near her filthy, vermin-infested pallet, listening to the screams of fear and anguish, hearing the big trucks drive up—like moving vans, only the exhaust pipes were many and all led inside and the passengers (packed so tight that most went mad in the darkness) rode away to a quiet field where the German drivers got out and smoked cigarettes and listened to the death-vans' motors running, running . . .

Paula got off the bus eight blocks before her Fortieth Street stop. She walked quickly, looking not at people but at cars and buildings and sidewalks and trees. No, not at people. Because one might be a German and she would think and remember and she refused to think and remember.

She lit a cigarette, and saw the way her hands trembled. She was afraid; afraid of losing her mind. What she was doing with the bread man wasn't really right, wasn't even sane.

She strode on and reached her friend's home. The short brunette was standing in front of the two-family house, watching her little boy dig around the base of a sycamore tree.

"Paula," she said. "You know, you're not looking too well lately—"

Paula changed the subject. But, somehow, she wasn't able to enjoy the talk of movies and magazines and friends and cooking and everything else the way she usually did with Sybil. She didn't even enjoy playing with three-year-old Michael. Still, she stayed. They had lunch and watched television and talked a lot.

Finally, she had to ask. "Sybil, you—you don't hate them any more?"

The dark girl's eyes came away from the TV screen. "The Germans?"

"Yes. And—and other goyim. Poles. Others. Those who killed us."

Sybil's eyes widened. "You shouldn't sound that way, Paula. It's not—healthy. This is America—"

"Tell me. Don't you hate them?"

Sybil nodded, but then said, "Only those who did it. The Nazis. Only the Nazis."

"But they were all Nazis. And they all live—or most of them live. And those here who marched in the Bunds. And the other anti-Semites—"

Sybil was shaking her head now, shaking it steadily. "That's not right. That can't be right. I don't feel that way. I hate those at Buchenwald. They killed my parents and my brother and my friends and so many others. But they were punished—most of them, anyway. And—" She shrugged uncomfortably. "It's over. It was a madness, a sickness, and it's over. Look, let me make some more coffee."

Paula stood up. "I'm late. Joe'll be home soon. I got to go." She was raging, and yet felt sick and ashamed. "It's —it's impossible that you've forgotten. You who went through the same things I did. You who lost everyone, everyone! It's impossible! You're just holding back because you want to be comfortable; because Wallace wouldn't understand and you want to make him happy. It's impossible!" She walked to the door.

"But I don't feel that way any more," Sybil said quietly. "Honest. What's the use of feeling that way? How—what good can it do?"

"That's not the point!" Paula shouted, and then lowered her voice. "I'm sorry. I have to go. Goodbye."

Sybil was staring at her as she walked out. . . .

She got home only a half-hour before Joe. And even then she couldn't seem to start preparing supper right away. As a result, she had to warm up the left-over meat loaf from Sunday's lunch; something she'd intended to make into sandwiches for herself during the week. Joe didn't say anything when she served it, but she knew he'd expected something better.

After they'd finished the dishes, he tried to take her on his lap, but she said she had to shower. After the shower, he tried to kiss her, but she said she thought she was getting a cold. A few minutes later, as they sat watching television, he mentioned that he'd had a very unusual repair job at the garage—one of the buses had dropped its entire drive shaft in the middle of Utica Avenue.

"The driver, a guy named Korowski, said he thought he'd hit a landmine! I tell you, it was the funniest—"

"Certainly," she said, repeating the Polish name to herself, remembering how the Polish Jews had told stories of their fellow-countrymen, their Christian comrades, helping the Germans hunt and round up and even kill Jews. "A Pole always likes to make extra work for a Jew. Do you know that Poles volunteered to serve in the German army? A man named Morris Chopik, a Polish Jew, told me his two sisters were raped and strangled in a Warsaw back yard the week after the Germans came. Five *Polish* did it; they said they might as well get the best out of the pretty Jewesses before the Germans grabbed everything. They killed the two teen-aged girls because they screamed and fought. 'This'll teach you,' one Pole said, 'to have more respect for good Christians.' And the poor brother, Morris, watching all the time from a cellar, not able to do anything because two more women were with him and the Poles would have got them too. Later, at Camp Three, he went insane and the Germans used to make him tell the story over and over and laugh at him as if it were a funny joke—"

"Yeah," Joe said, standing up. "Forgot to tell you—I got a poker game tonight."

"Tonight? But you played Friday."

"Well, they asked me and I said maybe. I'd like to go. Unless you mind?"

She hesitated and then shook her head. "No, it's all right."

He pecked her on the cheek and left. She heard him begin whistling as soon as he got to the elevator.

She shut off the TV and set her hair. She got into bed, read a historical novel and hoped that Joe would come home early. At eleven-thirty, she turned out her night-table lamp and went to sleep. . . .

She had a nightmare. She was being taken away from Camp Three by a tall, thin man in dark clothes. His face was a blur, but she knew it was gaunt and worn. Whenever a sob tore through her lips, he'd murmur, "Nein, nein, Paula."

"No, no, Paula. You are going to be all right now. I am taking you to my home."

They drove off in a small sedan, the Bavarian farmland rich and fertile on both sides of the road. But she continued to sob because she knew she was doomed. This man was a German and no German would help her. Anyway, she wanted to die and be with Momma.

They drove on and on, and it became dark, and even though it was summer and warm she shivered in her gray dress, wanting more clothing, afraid that this German, like Freilich, would look at her legs and then do terrible things to her.

The dream ended as the car pulled off the road and stopped in front of a large, dark house. The tall, gaunt man turned to her, arms outstretched, and she began to shriek. . . .

She jerked upright in bed, and saw that the lamp was on and Joe was sitting beside her, wearing pajamas. "Two nights in a row," he said, taking her hand and holding on tight even though she tried to pull it away—a reflex action after nightmares of Germany. "I think it's time for a doctor, baby. I think you should see a specialist—a nerve man, or psychiatrist, or someone like that. You're getting sick."

She shook her head impatiently. "Can I have a cigarette, Joe?"

He got out of bed, got two cigarettes from the dresser and lit both. He sat down beside her and they smoked in silence. Then she said, "I dreamed about the man who took me out of Camp Three. We were driving and it got dark and we stopped in front of a house and he turned to me and I knew he was going to rape me." She shuddered. "It was horrible!"

"Now, that's proof positive that you need a doctor," Joe said, taking her hand again. "You know damn well he was the minister who'd been friends with your mother; the man who spent a lot of money to buy you out of that camp. He saved your life and yet you dream that he wanted to hurt you. And he was a German too, so how can you hate—"

She knew he was right. She'd told him about Reverend Saurbach herself, when they were first dating and she seemed to be able to think well of some Germans. And Saurbach *had* saved her life—brought her out of the concentration camp, kept her in his home the two weeks it had taken to arrange to ship her to France and then to the United States where her mother's sister lived in Brooklyn. But now she was sure Saurbach had done it for some evil purpose—to get his hands on her—only he'd been thwarted by the fact that his wife or daughter always seemed to be around, or by Paula's state of shock which had lasted from the time her mother had been taken away (a day before Freilich raped her) to the day she'd been taken into her Aunt Ruth's plump arms and hugged and told, "Cry, little Paula, cry. Don't keep it in that way. Cry and forget. You're home. This is where you belong now, where you'll be safe now."

"He got money from my aunt," Paula said, grinding out her cigarette. "She sent him a thousand dollars for getting me out."

"But he didn't know she was going to!"

"He did it for the money, or because he thought he'd get to use me."

"But you didn't say that when you first told me about him, Paula. You said you couldn't remember much because you were sorta shocked, but you felt he must've been a kind, wonderful man."

"Are you arguing with me about something *I* lived through?" she flared, not wanting to hear him say those things. "While you had peace and comfort, I was seeing my mother destroyed and—"

He leaned forward and shouted, "For the love of Mike, can't you shut up already?"

She was stunned. He'd never raised his voice like that to her before. She stared, afraid of this angry stranger.

He got up and walked out of the room.

She lay down and felt the tears pushing into her eyes and fought them. He was blind, like all the rest of American Jewry. Yet she loved him—

"I'm sorry," he said, coming back into the room.

"It's nothing," she said, voice thick.

He went to the closet and began to dress.

"Where are you going?" she whispered.

"Down."

She raised her head and looked at the clock on the night table. "But—but it's not even five o'clock. Five in the morning."

"Yeah." He was tying his shoelaces. "Well, I just want to walk a few blocks. I'll be back in ten, fifteen minutes." He got into his lumberjacket and fumbled with the zipper. "Damn," he muttered.

She saw that his hands were trembling.

He got the zipper up and walked from the room. "Ten, fifteen minutes," he called.

"Yes, Joe," she said, and now the tears ran hot down her cheeks. The hall door opened and closed. She wept. She didn't know what was going to happen. . . .

Joe went out through the lobby onto Fifteenth Avenue. He walked in the darkness, breathing in lungfuls of sharp March air. He was very unhappy. He wanted to stop being unhappy.

God, how happy he'd been back with the folks when he was a kid. Laughing all the time. And now—

He turned up Fifty-sixth Street. When he reached Sixteenth Avenue, he looked at the big grammar school across the street and to his right. He didn't like the building; it was grim, depressing in his eyes. The school in the old neighborhood was much nicer, though it must have been built even before this one—

They'd lived in the two-family house on Sheffield Avenue, near P. S. 190. It was a wide, pleasant street, and if you didn't mind the sounds of children—thousands of children—it was one of the nicest places to live in all Brooklyn.

Joe had thought it the nicest place to live in all the world. And so had his two brothers, and his sister, and his parents. They were a happy family. Joe couldn't remember Mom and Dad ever having a serious fight.

It was good to grow up in a home like that—a home free of fear and tensions; a home full of love and laughter. He didn't realize it until later, when he heard guys talk about the rough times they'd had as kids; when he was able to think back to Blacky Shein and the way his father and mother would yell so loud at each other that the whole neighborhood heard, and Blacky had no brothers or sisters and was a real nervous kid and was afraid of lots of things. He realized it most of all when he met Paula and little by little drew from her the terrible story of her childhood.

So he was a lucky guy. So what the hell could he do about Paula?

How could he help her?

He didn't know. He felt beaten, helpless. He also felt very tired.

He turned and walked back toward Koptic Court, slowing when he approached the big building, examining it carefully, wondering why it looked so run-down and shabby tonight. And the way their floor—the fourth—smelled of cooking. Cabbage, maybe, or other vegetables being boiled.

Funny he hadn't noticed it before. Funny it had seemed okay up until just a few weeks ago.

When he entered the lobby, he saw the superintendent, on hands and knees, scrubbing away at the tile floor near the elevator with a stiff brush which he dipped into a pail of steaming, sudsy water.

Joe glanced at his wrist-watch. Five-twenty!

"Mornin'," the colored man said, raising his head and smiling.

"Morning, Mr. Brown," Joe answered. "You sure take care of this house, don't you?"

"Well, it's lots easier washin' the floor now than when folks start goin' to work. Guess I'm only bein' lazy." He laughed and began scrubbing again.

"Yeah," Joe said, and hesitated a few feet from the elevator door. "Real lazy."

The super glanced up, and said quickly, "Here now—you just go on and ring for that car. Don't worry about steppin'—"

"I don't want to ruin your work," Joe said, and turned toward the staircase.

"No, Mr. Theck," the super called, getting up. "That's four floors you got to walk!"

Joe smiled over his shoulder. "Not me. I'll catch it on the second floor."

He was still smiling when he got into the elevator, thinking what a lucky son-of-a-gun Luke Brown was. Had a job and loved it. Not only that, was good at it. And always laughing.

And his wife looked so calm and happy.

Joe's smile disappeared. He hoped Paula was asleep. . . .

7

LUKE BROWN 1-A

The two colored men, father and son, sat in the kitchen.
"I just can't have you hangin' round here, Sammy," Luke
said, his broad, deeply lined face reflecting weary irritation.
"You know that. I done explained it to you lots of times."

Sammy smiled his sweet, good-natured, white-toothed
smile, and Luke could understand what a slew of light-
skinned beauties had seen in his alcoholic son. Sammy had
the lure of the devil. He had his mother's face, and God
knew Imogene had been a woman to set the world to burning.

"Aw, c'mon, Daddy," Sammy said, voice deep and soft and
pleading. He had the red around his eyes and the dry around
his lips. He'd been drinking heavy again. He'd been on mus-
catel for almost a month. His good blue suit (that Luke had
bought him) was wrinkled, dirty, the jacket torn at the left
elbow. His left eye was swollen and his forehead scratched.
He'd been fighting, sleeping in hallways, and finally gone
broke and come to his father.

"You give up your job again," Luke said, voice dull. "You
gone on wine again. You been cattin' around and fightin',
and after you promised—"

"Sure, sure, Daddy. You know me. But all I want's a place
to sleep in the basement. It's a big basement." He jerked his
head toward the doorway behind him, which led to the living
room of the three-room apartment. "She's still got it in for
me, huh? Sure. But I ain't asking to sleep here. Go on, tell
her to come in and listen. I'll bet it's her that's stopping you
from letting me—"

"It ain't her," Luke said.

Sammy laughed, but there was a touch of desperation in
the sound. "She's a wicked stepma, just like in the movies.
Wicked stepma beating up on the poor stepson."

A woman's voice said, "Lord!" Heels clicked angrily across
the living-room floor; the bedroom door opened and slammed
shut.

93

Sammy laughed. "She hates me. I'll bet she wouldn't hate me if I'd been able to go through with—"

"Shut up," Luke said, eyes narrowing. "Shut up right now, Sammy, or you'll crawl out of here."

"Okay, okay," Sammy Brown said, and now his smile was weak and pathetic, his voice beginning to quaver. "Listen, I just want to sleep in that bin near the furnace. Hell, no one'll see me. I won't use the elevator—I'll use the alley entrance. And I won't go down until twelve, twelve-thirty tonight. And I'll get out before eight in the morning. I could sleep in a basement anywhere, but I don't want to take a chance of being picked up for vagrancy right after a drunk-and-disorderly rap's been suspended."

Luke shook his head. It hurt like hell to have your own son beg to sleep in the basement, and hurt even worse to have to say no. (They both knew he couldn't sleep in the apartment any more because of what he'd tried to do with Cora, his stepmother.)

"Aw, be right, Daddy! I'll spend a few nights in that bin, and no one'll see me." He shoved back his chair and stood up, as if he'd received an affirmative reply. "Give me an old blanket, huh?"

"No," Luke said. He got up too, shorter and heavier than Sammy. He was fifty-four and Sammy was thirty-five. They didn't look at all alike.

Luke was broad, black, somber, with a big, lined face, small eyes, tight-curled hair receding rapidly at the forehead and whitening gradually at the temples. His features were strong in what has been called Negroid characteristics—broad, flat nose; wide, full lips. He was a big man, not a tall man. He was big-boned, big-handed. He was a big, black man.

Sammy was different. Sammy was a tall, lean, brown man with a long, smooth, handsome face—the eyes large and golden brown; the nose small and thin; the lips pouting full, rosebud full. He was a truly beautiful human being; or had been not too long ago. Now the beauty was being destroyed. Sammy Brown had a·wildness and a sickness in him.

Each and every time Luke saw Sammy, he couldn't help thinking of Imogene. Not that it bothered him now. A man can forget anything in twenty years, even a runaway wife.

He wondered where Imogene was. Probably shackin' up with some hophead musician, if she was still alive, still able to get a man.

"No blanket, no nothin'," Luke said. "I can't. Just can't. I got three complaints the last time I let you sleep down there. You bound to get drunk again and make trouble."

"I won't, so help me sweet Jesus."

"Don't use the name of the Lord in vain!" Luke bellowed, raising his thick, powerful arm.

Sammy ducked away and shook his head, laughing easily again. "Okay, okay, Daddy. You're a hard man. But why the hell you worry so much about the ofays beats me."

Luke didn't like the word "ofay." He didn't like thinking of the people in his house that way. Regular white people, in the South especially, were ofays—a pig-Latin term using "foe" as its base, coined by Negro musicians. But lots of whites in New York were friends, and this house was full of nice people who liked him, respected him. He'd earned their respect by hard work—keeping the lobby and halls spotless, the steam high, the water hot, the apartments in good repair—and by never once allowing the tenants to see him drunk during the years he'd been super of Koptic Court. Sure, white folks lost respect for a Negro who got himself drunk in public. Luke liked a drink as well as the next man, maybe even better, but he had a good house and the respect of good white folks and he wasn't going to mess it up for anything. Not anything in the world!

"That ain't it, Sammy," he said. "I got this house to take care of. You understand? I got this good job and good pay and good apartment to live in. It's my duty to keep things right and I'm not allowed to let anyone sleep in the basement. My duty, Sammy. Understand? Every man's got a duty in his job. You had a duty in your job—"

"Sure, pushing a wagon full of clothes through the streets so some fat-assed white bastard could make a pot of dough. Sure, I understand your duty, Daddy. You're an old Southern darky who's scared shitless of whites."

"That ain't so!" Luke said, growing angry. "I'm just doin'—"

"Just doin' what comes naturally," Sammy interjected swiftly, backing toward the doorway. His smile was gone now. His eyes burned, his hands shook, his speech grew thick and Southern. "Kissin' white ass comes naturally to you, Daddy. Born and bred a hundred miles from nowhere in dear old Alabam-bam-bam! Bendin' your head to every fuckin' cracker and sayin', 'Yassah, boss. Yassah, cunnel suh. Yassah, Missie Susie Belle Cracker. Yassah, I sho won't pick up mah ole black head when you-all's around. Yassah, I sho gonna make like Stepin Fetchit so's you all kin enjoy a good laugh. Yuk, yuk, yuk!' "

He backed through the section of the living room and into the foyer, and Luke followed.

"It's you who makes like Stepin Fetchit!" Luke shouted, trying to stop his son's tirade. But he'd never seen him like this before. Sammy's face was twisted with a terrible hate and the torrent of words continued. It seemed to paralyze Luke.

" 'Yassah, ma'am, I be sho', ma'am, to keep my eyes down, ma'am, when you swings yore sacred white ass, ma'am, down the street, ma'am. I be sho' to jump aside when you gets on a bus or trolley, ma'am, because I'm shit, ma'am, and yore the spirit of the magnificent South, ma'am! Yassah! Yassah! Yassah!' "

He was almost incoherent now, and Luke was afraid that someone next door, or in the lobby, would hear him. "Sammy, that's no way—"

But there was no stopping Sammy.

"You're *afraid* of the white folks in this house; not doing any duty to them! Don't tell me, Daddy, I know. I remember how you always worked so hard at the lousy jobs those white folks you're so damn afraid of gave you. I remember you worked as a porter, Daddy, and then you worked in that big hotel barbershop, shining shoes, and then you got your big break—" he threw back his head and laughed like a loon— "a white landlord made you janitor in a Harlem tenement, a rat-trap house where you scrubbed spit and piss off the floors."

He was halfway down the foyer now. The bedroom door opened and a short, stout woman poked her head out. "Luke, make him quiet down!" she said, face frightened. "People'll hear."

"Ah, the other darky am a singin'," Sammy yelled. "Ole black Cora. And ole black Luke. And the plantation owners upstairs saying, 'My, my, don't the niggers act nice? We should always have nigger janitors—' "

"I'm a *superintendent*," Luke said, and the quiet rage in his voice stopped Sammy. "Maybe I'm afraid—I don't know. Maybe I bend my head. But I work, and I earn my bread, and I never been in a jail in all my life, 'cept once down in Bam which it don't count since they ain't no law for us there. I'm a respected citizen—"

"Hah!" Sammy yelled. "Respected citizen! There's not one of us ever been a respected citizen!"

"Booker T. Washington—" Luke began.

"Booker T. Washington!" Sammy shrieked, and laughed and laughed. "Shit! And Joe Louis, and Louis Armstrong, and Ralph Bunche, and a few thousand others. Shit! Shit! You you're—" He couldn't get his words out fast enough and raised clenched fists and shook them at the ceiling and yelled, "Why do you think I drink, you stupid bastard you? Why do you think I can't do a fuckin' thing right? Why?" He held himself back, giving his father a chance to answer.

"You gotta leave now, Sammy," Luke said, his son's words confusing and disturbing him. "I let you call me names—"

"So you can't answer?" Sammy yelled. "Well, I'll tell you. I can't do a fuckin' thing right because I know it's no use. I'm black and this here's a white man's world and I'm screwed to start with and so why the fuck should I try to do anything since I can't get nowhere anyway? Why? Why work like a bastard—" He made a choking sound and suddenly sat down on the floor. He shook his head, mumbling, "Christ, I'm sick."

"Give him a dollar and send him away," Cora said, coming into the living room. "I just hope no one next door or up-stairs heard him yelling."

Luke helped his son up. He took a bill from his wallet and shoved it into Sammy's handkerchief pocket. It was a five, but Cora didn't see.

"Go on, Sammy," Luke said. "You done had your say. But it's all wrong, boy. If'n people thought like you, why we'd all be runnin' around drunk and crazy and gettin' ourselves beat up. If'n people thought like you, there'd be no colored man doing an honest day's work." He'd started very unsure of him-self, but as the argument took hold, he smiled. "You're a hound dog, Sammy, and that's the plain truth of it. You're all talk."

Sammy pulled away and shuffled down the foyer. "Plenty truth in what I said, Daddy." His voice was soft and deep again. "Plenty, only it's mixed up with me being what you said—a hound dog." He turned, grinning. "But Daddy, you're sure afraid of the whites."

Luke suddenly had enough of that. "I'll tell you what I'm afraid of," he said, fighting to hold his voice down. "I'm afraid to be like you. I'm afraid there's lots of us like you." He could have said more, but he was getting too close to the driving center of his existence. He took a deep breath. "Lem-me know how you get along, Sammy."

"Sure, Daddy. Thanks for the money." He winked. "Cora, you ever gonna forgive me for being too slow?"

"Get out!" Cora shrieked; then turned and dropped her head, weeping.

Sammy giggled and left.

Luke walked to the door and opened it to make sure his son departed without saying anything to a tenant. Sammy glanced back. "Yassah," he said, and ambled into the street, laughing.

Luke locked the door and went back to the living room. His wife was still crying. He patted her shoulder. "Now, you can't let that loony get you, Cora."

"That loony," she sobbed, "is your son, my stepson. Lord, Lord, the things he said! It—it makes everything so—so dirty and useless. And I know things aren't that way. They can't be!"

" 'Course not," Luke murmured, and led her to the couch. They sat down. "He just givin' himself excuses for bein' what he is."

"Yes," she said, drying her eyes. "But—but how can he laugh about what he tried to do to me!"

Luke rubbed his face. "It was three years ago. I reckon he feels it's nothin' any more."

"Nothing! I don't care if ten years, or a hundred, go by! He tried to rape me, his own stepmother!"

"He was drunk, Cora. He was crazy drunk and didn't know you and since you ain't really his ma—"

She jerked away and stood up. "You're not defending him against me?"

"No, no, lady. Take it easy, huh?" He smiled and tugged her hand and she sat down again. "He's a loony, like I said. Let's make out he never came here."

She snorted. "That'd be a trick!" She blew her nose and patted her hair. He waited. Finally, she sighed and said, "Well, he's gone."

He nodded. "Makes a man feel low to have a son like that. And yet, he ain't all bad. He's just the laziest, drinkinest—"

"We going to the movies?" Cora asked.

"Well, I don't know. I'd like to stay close to home because that hot-water boiler's been actin' kinda funny."

"Luke, you promised me! It's Sunday, and we been to church, and no one expects you to stay around all day Sunday!"

"Yeah, sure, but that boiler." He rubbed his face again. "What if it goes out and there ain't no hot water?"

"It won't happen. You know it won't happen. Let's go. They got a musical—"

The doorbell rang. Cora threw up her hands. Luke went swiftly down the foyer and opened the door. He smiled. "Yes, Mrs. Schimler? That faucet ain't been drippin' again, has it?" He spoke carefully, trying to pronounce every word clearly.

"No," the woman said. She was about forty-five and dressed in a tight skirt and sweater which played up her plump curves. "I wanta ask you a favor. I'm expecting a package tomorrow—"

"Sure," Luke said. "Sure, just tell them to leave it with the super. Be glad to help, Mrs. Schimler." He spoke to her and smiled at her, and yet his eyes never really touched her. They flicked to her face once or twice, but most of the time they were off on the side.

She smiled. "Thanks. I'll have to ask my Irving to buy you a bottle of something good one of these days."

He chuckled and raised his hand and said, "No, thanks, Mrs. Schimler. Not that I'm against drinking, mind you. It's just that I buy my two, three bottles a year—for company and such—and don't need—"

"Yeah, well, thanks anyway," she said, and walked back to the elevator on the other side of the lobby.

Luke shut the door.

"That was right, Luke," Cora said. "Turning down the liquor. Not that she'd remember and buy it for you. But come Christmas she might give cash instead of that cheap whisky she gave last year."

"They think we all drink like fish," Luke muttered. "Sure, lots of us—" He sighed and sat down on the couch. "Let's watch television. Ed Sullivan's on."

"But what about the movies?"

"I'm afraid of that boiler, Cora. I won't enjoy the show, sittin' and worryin' about the boiler. Don't make me go."

She shook her head sadly, then smiled and kissed his cheek. "That Imogene must have been crazy to run off and leave a man like you. If I ever meet her, I'll thank her kindly. 'Thankee, ma'am,' I'll say."

They both laughed. "So will I," said Luke.

They hugged each other. "What about Ed Sullivan?" he asked.

She got up and turned on the set. "I'll make some sandwiches. I'll also make some highballs."

"Well, it's a little early for highballs. What if I have to go to someone's apartment and they smell liquor?"

"I guess you're right."

Luke suddenly remembered what Sammy had said about his being scared. "I'll have a beer," he called out. "Maybe two."

The TV screen came alive and he began to watch. . . .

At nine o'clock, Mrs. Rotola from the third floor came to the door and said, "Gee, I'm sorry to bother you on a Sunday night, Mr. Brown, but that damned toilet got stopped up again and its backing all over—"

He went up with her. The bathroom was a mess. Mr. Rotola, a short, heavy man in his early fifties, said grumpily, "When're you gonna make that landlord give us new piping? This is the third time it's flooded this year."

Luke said, "I'll tell him about it, Mr. Rotola. You can be sure of that. But now let me take a look—"

It didn't take long to find the trouble. A wadded clump of cardboard was blocking the point where bowl narrowed to pipe. He fished it out with wire from his tool bag, and showed it to them.

Mr. Rotola's face got red. He muttered, "Must've been our nephew, Robbie. The kid's sorta wild. He visited us this afternoon—"

Luke nodded, but he didn't buy the story.

"Well, thanks, Mr. Brown," Mrs. Rotola said, glaring at her husband. She tipped Luke half a dollar, and that made Luke positive that her husband was to blame.

Luke talked with them a while, and then left. Nice folks. Just a little careless. Mr. Rotola was hot-tempered too. But nice folks—like most everyone in the house.

When he got into the hall, Luke brushed at his damp and dirty work clothes. Then he got an idea. As long as he was already dirty, he might as well start the plastering job on the Gordons' bedroom instead of waiting for tomorrow. The Gordons had gone to Florida for two weeks, so he wouldn't be disturbing anyone.

He got what he needed from the supply bin in the basement, and rode the elevator to the sixth floor. He worked until eleven, left everything right there so he could pick it up again tomorrow, and returned to the basement to check the boiler.

The pressure was up, for now, but he'd have to keep his eye on it all week. If it showed a drop, he'd call the landlord,

Mr. Gorman, and ask for a repairman. He didn't want the house suddenly without hot water. If anything riled up the tenants, that was it. He remembered the hard looks he'd gotten three years ago when the boiler failed.

He went up in the elevator. It stopped at the lobby. Mr. and Mrs. Maston were there. Luke stepped out and said, "Good evenin'. Kinda cold for March, ain't it?"

"Very," Mr. Maston said. "But it won't be long before we're complaining of the heat."

Luke laughed hard, slapping his thigh. "That's right!"

Mrs. Maston said, "Good night, Mr. Brown."

Luke nodded and smiled as he held the elevator door for them. "Night." He let the door close.

They were real nice folks, even if they seemed a little uppity with the other tenants; sorta shied away from everyone. But not from him. He *felt* they were nice. They respected him. More than that, they belonged to the small group that treated him as an equal. But it always made him feel uncomfortable. He didn't want them thinking he was their equal. Well, at least not their *complete* equal. That was a hard thing for a colored man to live up to.

He lit a cigarette and glanced around the lobby. Neat, clean, but he'd have to polish the copper-plated mailboxes and wash the glass doors again. Damn wind-driven rain they'd had a few days ago sure messed up the glass.

He dropped ashes into the palm of his left hand and rang for the elevator. He was going to check the lights on all six floors before going to bed. Just in case any had blown. He'd known he was going to do this even when he'd been in the elevator and it stopped at the lobby and he'd seen the Mastons. But he'd gotten out and let them ride up by themselves.

He'd wanted to look around the lobby.

Sure.

The elevator arrived and he got inside and rode to the second floor. He checked the lights and then glanced down the staircase and checked the two bulbs there. Everything fine.

He took his cigarette to the incinerator and dropped it down the chute, along with the ashes in his left hand. He walked back into the hall.

This was a good house; big, beautiful, built to last. And man, man, what a difference from those Harlem tenements! Here the halls smelled nice—from good broiling meat sometimes, or steaming vegetables, or the strong disinfectant Mr.

Gorman bought for washing the floors and walls. Nice smells. Smells that made Luke feel hungry, or clean. Smells that a man could walk through with a smile 'stead of wrinkling up his nose and having his stomach twist. Like the sour stink of piss back in that tenement.

Yeah, this was a real good house. Not many colored men became superintendents of houses like this. He had to make sure that everything was neat, clean, operating correctly. He had a duty to his tenants.

It worried him a lot. He'd been on the job over four years now, but it still worried him. A man could lose his job fast if he let things slide. What looked neat today could be a sloppy mess at the end of the week. Didn't he know it! The time he'd had the flu and stayed in bed two days— Lord, everything had gone to hell. Of course, that was because he'd relied upon Sammy to help out. He knew better now.

But it worried him, the responsibility. He had to keep things just so. This was a big job for a colored man.

In his heart of hearts, Luke Brown was sure there wasn't a white man alive who couldn't do the job better with half the effort. He used to try and tell himself this wasn't so, but lately he'd given up. He just knew it was. He knew a colored man was slower-thinking than a white, and lazier, and just naturally a drinking fool if he let himself go. A colored man had to fight all these things, and make white folks think he was going along smooth and easy. A colored man had to work twice as hard to make up for what God had forgotten to give him. He was certain that applied even to men like Booker T. Washington and Ralph Bunche.

Yeah, sure, he knew what the NAACP said, and what the politicians in Harlem said, and what they said in church. Yeah, but that was just talk. In his heart, he knew it was just talk. And he figured every colored man and woman knew the same thing, only they kept it hidden because it wasn't something you ran off at the mouth about. Besides, white folks shouldn't know about it if they believed otherwise.

Sometimes he felt ashamed of feeling the way he did. Like when Cora would say she was as good as any white because the Lord created free and equal. He'd agree, and feel ashamed, but then he'd convince himself she was just talking to make herself feel good. She must know, the same as he did, that the Bible was full of whites. Christ was a white, wasn't he?

A Jew, maybe, but that was white—like most of the tenants here.

They were all white in the Bible.

Sure, the Queen of Sheba was black, but what did she do anyway 'cept lay for Solomon?

A colored man had to fight to keep a good job like this. Sammy must know it too, when his brain wasn't mixed up from drinkin', only he couldn't accept it. Yeah, that must be it. Sammy couldn't accept the position the good Lord had given colored people.

Well, anyway, that's how Luke Brown felt about it. He'd never say it out loud because all the colored folks would jump down his throat. He figured out that was the way things were—a man admitted certain things only to himself. Also, you could see what happened when the white folks knew about it and talked about it right out in the open all the time. That was the South. And down in Bam, life was pretty bad. Of course, it was because the whites there were real ofays; they didn't have to step so hard on colored folks even if they were smarter and better workers. And then again, come to think of it, some of those crackers were pretty damn stupid and lazy and boozed up on corn liquor—

But mostly, a colored man wasn't up to a white. Luke knew it. And that's why he had to keep on his toes and work real hard. This house was a tremendous responsibility. He had to give it everything he had.

He checked all six floors, and then double-checked by walking down the staircase. He worried a bit about Sammy, but then shrugged it off. After all these years of drinkin', Sammy couldn't be helped. Must be Imogene's bad blood.

On the fifth floor, he saw Mrs. Schimler's boy going to the incinerator with a can of garbage. Luke had a smile all ready, but the skinny teen-ager dropped his eyes and chewed his lip and muttered something that could have been hello. Luke went down half a flight and waited. Sometimes that kid worried him. Sometimes that kid reminded him of Sammy.

He shrugged. The Schimler boy and Sammy weren't at all alike. Naw. The boy wasn't wild or anything like that. But once in a while he got sort of mean-looking and did something. Like the time he'd come out of the elevator and Luke had walked in and there was a dirty word scratched into the paint of the door. Fresh scratched. And the kid had looked tight and mean. And another time he'd come out of the fifth-floor incinerator just as Luke was heading for it, and Luke had found garbage all over the floor.

But most everyone thought he was a good kid, a quiet kid. Luke thought so himself, most of the time.

When he heard the boy go back to his apartment, Luke went up again and checked the incinerator.

Damn kid! Half the garbage was on the floor! And Luke knew he'd done it on purpose. Sure. He'd had that tight, mean look again. Like he hated everyone. Like he wanted to hurt people.

Luke sighed and began to clean it up. . . .

By the time he got to bed it was twelve.

It was Sunday, and he hadn't really worked hard, so he wasn't too tired. He twisted around a little, and Cora said, "You feeling jumpy, Luke?"

"Yeah, sort of."

She got out of bed. "You had a bad day, what with Sammy. Lie still. I'm going to make you a big highball. You ain't going into tenants' apartments now, unless you got yourself a girl-friend."

He laughed and sat up. She brought him the drink, and one for herself. It tasted good and loosened him up. He wanted another, and figured it couldn't hurt none since he was already in bed.

They had two more apiece, and then he put his arms around her and said, "I don't know how I'd pull the load without you, Cora. You're the best woman alive, as God's my witness."

She sighed contentedly and he kissed her and she sighed again. He tightened his arms. . . .

8

LOUIS SCHIMLER 5-F

"Hey, sourpuss," Myra said, coming into his room, "think you can crack a smile if I tell you some good news?"

Lou hurriedly folded the magazine so his sister wouldn't be able to see what it was. "Listen," he said, sitting up on the bed, "don't you know enough to knock when you—"

"All right, honey," Myra said, and the way she said it made Lou mad. Just because she was nineteen she acted as if she were his mother! By God, it was time he told her off! A guy of seventeen didn't have to take guff from anyone!

"Lemme alone," he said. "I don't want your good news and I don't want you busting into my room. I'm reading."

She smiled that sad smile, that knowing smile—and it made Lou want to belt her. She never shouted at him like Mom and Pop. What she did was worse; much worse. What she did made him go nuts, made his head fill with screaming rage.

She pitied him. She read all sorts of junk about teen-agers and took psychology courses at Brooklyn College and figured she knew exactly what made him tick. "Repressed," he'd heard her telling Mom one night. "And that skin condition doesn't help. He needs to find self-confidence; needs to get out more with boys and girls. Honest, Mom, he's going through a very painful process and we have to be understanding—"

God, he didn't want her lousy pity! He had friends. Well, maybe he didn't spend much time with them, but didn't he know guys at school? And girls—

That made him tighten up inside. Girls were a pack of stupid nothings. At least the girls he knew. The girls at New Utrecht High. Stupid nothings who thought that rock-'n-roll and dancing and varsity sports and all that sort of junk was really important.

'Course, he could dance. Myra had taught him. And he liked music, popular music. But heck, he didn't want to bother, that's all.

Before he could stop it, the assortment of memories flooded his mind, warning him, telling him to stay away from girls because they would hurt him. Like the time he'd asked that nice-looking Fran Lauche from his history class for a date and she'd said she had another date and then Saturday night he'd almost bumped into her and her girlfriend coming out of a movie, by themselves. And then the one in his English class who'd said no so fast and wouldn't even talk to him afterwards. And when Myra got him blind dates—maybe six or seven times—and he couldn't seem to make any of them like him and not even one who would see him again.

Hell, girls were—were stupid!

So he had a few pimples on his face. So what!

Anyway, he wasn't going to bother with stupid girls. Later,

maybe, when he changed and looked different he would date Elaine Turner who lived downstairs on the second floor. She seemed nice and intelligent, and even though she dated a lot of guys who played basketball and stuff like that, she always smiled at Lou whenever they met. And that time he'd helped her she'd said thanks so warm—

He got a choked-up feeling when he pictured Elaine. The way she swayed so—so *nice* in a skirt and sweater, and the way her black hair moved around her small, pretty face, and the way her lips were so red and full and kinda damp that you wanted to touch them and tell her you would do anything for her and wanted to talk to her and maybe hold her hand and buy her presents. Like that locket he'd seen at Abraham & Straus. A gold locket, small and perfect. It seemed made for Elaine 'cause she was small and perfect too. He'd wanted to buy it right then and keep it until he could give it to her at her sweet-sixteen party which was coming up sometime this summer. (He knew because he'd heard her mother telling Mom how excited Elaine was. Mom and Mrs. Turner talked a lot.) But he hadn't bought it because he didn't figure on going to Elaine's party. Naw, he didn't know her well enough and he wouldn't change enough by then. But gee, that was a girl he knew he could get along with—later—when he looked different—

"Well," Myra said, "can I tell you what I came in for? Or do I have to go out and knock on your door before you'll let me—"

"For the love of Pete!" he shouted, and slammed the magazine on the bed. It turned over and the cover flipped shut. He grabbed it, but Myra got that soft, sad look on her pretty face. He knew she'd seen he was reading love stories.

He felt the blood rush to his head. "Some guy loaned it to me," he muttered thickly, and threw the magazine across the room. "Said it was good reading. Heck, I didn't know it was all that love and mush. Honest, I just—"

She sat down quickly beside him, that sympathy-laden look he hated getting stronger. "Reading love stories is nothing to be ashamed of, Lou. Why, I used to—"

"So what is it you wanted to tell me?" he interrupted fiercely.

She put her arm around his shoulders. "Please, Lou, don't feel bad. I didn't mean to—annoy you. I never mean to hurt or annoy you. I'm your sister—"

"Yeah, yeah," he muttered, but he relaxed, thinking she

wasn't so bad. It was just that she was always *bothering* him. Heck, he liked to be left alone.

"Got a date for you," she said. "Saturday after next. Sister of a new boy I'm dating. We can go out together in this boy Georgie's car. Wouldn't that be fun?"

He tightened up again. Heck, he didn't want to go out on another blind date. He wanted to wait until he changed and could get his own dates—with Elaine Turner.

"Aw," he said, and got up and walked to his dresser and looked at the model ship he'd made. It was Old Ironsides and he'd done a good job. Even Pop had said nice things about it, and Pop was always getting on him for not doing enough. "Aw, I don't want—"

"I'm sure you'll get along with *this* girl, honey. I met her last week. She's sweet, Lou and—she'd like to meet a nice boy. She's—not like—" She paused, as if struggling to find the right words. He turned to face her.

"She's not like what?"

"Well, not the snippy, turn-up-your-nose-at-everyone type. She's—just nice, that's all, and I'm sure you'll get along with her. Please come. Georgie's got four tickets to a Broadway show, and then we'll go to a place where we can eat and perhaps dance. It'll be fun, Lou. You won't have to pay for the tickets. Please?"

She was so intense about wanting him to go, so sincere about wanting him along on her date, that he felt a sudden, overwhelming rush of affection. "Okay," he said.

She jumped up and clapped her hands together. "Fine, Lou! I'll tell Mom. She'll be so glad!" And she ran from the room.

Lou went to the door.

". . . going out together Saturday after next . . ." Myra was gushing to Mom.

Lou felt sorry he'd said yes. He thought of how he'd have to dress up, and wait with Myra for her boy-friend to arrive, and then go to this guy's house and meet the strange girl. Or would the girl come with her brother in the car? Anyway, he'd meet her—and then it would be like all the other times.

He began to sweat. God, he wished he hadn't said yes!

Maybe he could go in and tell Myra he'd changed his mind.

But she was babbling on to Mom. And soon Pop would come home from work and she'd tell him too and he'd nod and say, "Good. That kid sits around too much. Gotta get him out in the world. Now, if he'd only play a little basketball, or baseball. Too skinny for football, but he should try some sport." He'd slam his calloused hand against his thick chest. "I used to play hours of handball and touch-tackle and stickball and anything else a kid could play on the East Side. Made me strong, confident. Maybe I wasn't a brain in school, but I got by and now—"

He would brag about how well he was doing as foreman for the Speirst-Deveney Construction Company. "Only Jewish foreman they got," he would say, and Lou would hate him a little.

Well, not really hate him. But Pop was so big and thick and strong and nice-looking. Lou had Pop's light hair and gray eyes and even his facial characteristics. But on Pop they were right, and on Lou they were wrong. Myra looked like Mom, except she was taller and slimmer. Everyone in the family was nice-looking—except him.

He closed the bedroom door. He walked back to his dresser and fingered the model ship and then raised his eyes to the mirror. Ears and nose too big. Teeth too big in front. Skinny. Pimples all over his face—

He swung away from the mirror. God, he didn't want to go on that date! But Myra had told Mom, and she'd tell Pop, and how could he back out? They'd say he was afraid —or what was worse, they'd say nothing and look at him like he was a dying puppy.

He picked up the pulp magazine and lay down on the bed and found his place. It wasn't very good writing. Hell, even he could tell that. But it was a pretty interesting story. Yeah. And—and the girl was something like Elaine Turner. Not in looks, since she had blond hair and blue eyes and Elaine was a brunette with brown eyes. But still, the way she acted— so sweet to the shy hero, a poor sap who got tongue-tied talking to a pretty girl and who didn't have money and who had to compete with a flashy musician with a big car and a smooth line. She was like Elaine because she was *nice*, and Lou could see that she liked the shy guy better than the hep character.

He kept reading, and sure enough the girl fell in love with the shy guy. But then the shy guy let the hep character make a fool of him, and wouldn't fight back when the hep character slapped him contemptuously, and the blond girl walked away with the hep character, disgusted with the shy guy.

Lou's heart ached and he felt tears stinging his eyes. Gee, that poor shy guy, stammering and not knowing how to use his fists and having no way to win the blond girl. Lou could understand a guy like that. Yeah, even though he felt he'd fight a mob for Elaine, by God, and beat the hell out of them too—if it meant she'd love him.

On the last page of the story, the shy guy finally beat up the hep character and kissed the girl. She said, "Rod, I've waited so long for this," and he said, "Angela, I've been a fool," and they went off in his shrimp boat to live a simple, natural life with lots of children.

Lou closed the magazine and looked up at the ceiling and blinked damp eyes. "Hell," he muttered, ashamed of being so touched by a crummy love story. "Hell, what gunk."

Pop came home, and Lou hurriedly stuck the magazine in a dresser drawer. Then he went inside to eat.

After supper, Pop lit a cigarette, and Lou said, "I'm going down for a while, okay?"

Pop shifted his big, hairy arm and looked at his watch. "It's six-thirty, Lou. When you gonna do your homework?"

"Did it already," Lou said, eyes down. He couldn't look at Pop's big arms tonight. He couldn't look at Pop, period. He was getting one of his blue feelings, his tight, unhappy, to-hell-with-it-all feelings. "Did history and French and math. There wasn't much."

"Yeah? How come you never get more than seventies and seventy-fives if you do your work so fast and all the time?"

"Pop," Myra said. "Leave him alone."

"What's wrong? The TV says a father should show interest in his son. Otherwise the kid might become a juvenile delinquent and go on dope and knock over gas stations."

Mom leaned back and laughed. "Lou on dope and robbing gas stations!"

Myra grinned.

Pop cracked a smile himself.

Lou got up and walked out of the apartment, making believe he was laughing with them. But he was burning. They treated him like some—like some sort of queer! Well, they were all wrong—especially Pop. So he didn't play basketball or football. He still took care of himself. So he hadn't made out so well with the stupid girls he'd dated, and tried to date. That didn't mean he wasn't able to handle any wise guy who bothered him. There was that jerk who'd been kidding around with Elaine for a whole month, always holding her hand in the hall and walking her home and even taking her to movies. Then the jerk had stopped seeing Elaine, and one day he'd tried giving Lou a hard time by saying, "Watch it, Tarzan," when they were both pushing through the gym doors at the same time. Lou had waited until they came into the schoolyard. Then he'd jumped the jerk. He'd given him a good lacing, by God! The jerk had been surprised. Lou had stood off and belted him for ten minutes with his bony fists. The jerk hadn't been able to touch him; not with Lou having arms almost a third longer than his!

Later, Lou had wondered that he'd gotten so mad and belted the guy around. Because most of the time he didn't want to fight or hurt anyone or even bother with anyone. Heck, he just wanted to be left alone, do his schoolwork as best he could and build model ships and airplanes once in a while. And read. He liked to read.

He couldn't understand why he didn't get better marks in school. Mrs. Frank had once said that a student who reads is bound to gain verbal skills and do better in school. But Lou just about managed to pass his subjects; no more.

He guessed he wasn't very smart. But he didn't want to be smart. He just wanted to get rid of those damned pimples and fill out a little and—well, look nice to girls.

He used the staircase. He didn't want to stand in the elevator, close to people—maybe girls. The pimples were really out today. He'd have to use hot towels and his salve again, but it did so damned little good. None of the doctors Mom had taken him to had been able to help. He'd outgrow it, they said. *Maybe.*

Elaine Turner was in the lobby, talking to a boy who lived on Eighteenth Avenue. Lou knew him from school. The guy said hello, and Elaine smiled and said, "Hi, Lou. Studying for mid-terms?"

The guy, who was in Lou's French class, laughed. "Lou doesn't bother. He never flunks, and he never gets a good mark. He's in."

Lou could've killed him. Just like that, he felt he wanted to put his hands around that jerk's neck and squeeze and squeeze and see the smooth, good-looking face go purple and the eyes bug out and hear the assured voice beg—

"That's more than I can say for most boys," Elaine said quickly, staring at Lou.

Lou realized some of his crazy hate must be showing and forced himself to grin at the guy. "Yeah," he said, and then looked at Elaine and wondered if he oughta keep walking toward the street, or maybe say something else. Gee, he wanted to say something clever and see her smile again. She was wearing a shorty coat and a green crinolined dress and saddle shoes. Her dark hair was caught back at the sides with simple silver barrettes. She—she looked so lovely it hurt his chest.

"As I was saying," the guy said, and winked at Lou and waited.

Lou got it. He was supposed to leave them alone. But maybe Elaine would say something—

Elaine got a little pink and looked down at the floor, but she said nothing. Lou felt he'd been pushed in the face. He had to fight back somehow. "Hey," he said to the guy, "you can do me a favor. I'm taking a girl to a Broadway show and then dancing the Saturday after this. I don't know much about Manhattan night spots. Can you recommend a place? You know—not too steep."

The guy shrugged. "There's the big spots—the Latin Quarter and places like that. I always stick to Brooklyn."

Elaine smiled at Lou. "Girls like a quiet place with soft music, Lou. At least I do."

Lou would have given anything to be able to say the right thing then, but it was the guy from Eighteenth Avenue who did.

"Yeah? Well, what about coming down to the club my friends and I have? Real quiet and plenty of records for the machine."

"That's a cellar club, isn't it, Steve?"

"Yeah," Steve said. "But we get a chaperone every time girls come down. Next Saturday my friend Eddie's folks are gonna sit in. You know them, don't you? Ask your mother if you can come, huh?"

Elaine nodded, smiling warmly. "Okay."

Lou said so long and left. He felt tight and blue and ugly. He—he wanted to do *something!* He remembered the time Elaine had dropped the bottle of milk in the lobby and he'd come in and told her to leave the mess alone. She'd asked him what he meant, and he'd blurted that he would clean it up for her. She'd stared at him, and then smiled that same warm smile she'd just given the guy from Eighteenth Avenue. It had made him feel so good, so—alive and happy. And it had only been four, five months ago. He was sure he could date her, if only the damn pimples would disappear.

God, why did he have to have those rotten things all over his face!

He was out in the street now, and an elderly woman gave him a funny look.

He realized that he had his hand up to his face, the fingers curled like he was going to claw himself.

He dropped his hand and walked past her. It was getting dark. He crossed the broad avenue and went by the old, frame, one-family house with the big backyard. Sounds reached him—music and voices; laughter and stamping of feet.

Damned Italians! Always slugging down the wine and making noise. Sometimes during the summer he'd hear them from way up in his room and get mad as they kept laughing out in their backyard; kept laughing and having fun while he lay in his bed and tossed and turned . . .

Damned neighborhood! Full of jerks. Full of crums who made plenty of noise and didn't even know a damn thing and—

He saw the four guys coming toward him, and tried to relax, tried to affect an easy, casual air. But then they began to laugh and he felt they were laughing at him and he crossed the street so he wouldn't have to squeeze by them.

Crums! Neighborhood full of crums!

He passed the run-down, three-story mansion, its five massive porch pillars badly in need of fresh white paint. A neat, hand-lettered sign tacked to one of the pillars read, "RABBI E. Z. ZUERICH—HEBREW CLASSES FOR CHILDREN."

The windows were full of light; he heard voices and saw people moving about inside.

"Jabber, jabber, jabber," he muttered. "Stupid moishie-oishies—" But then he cut himself short, afraid he'd committed some sort of sin.

He kept walking, faster and faster, but he couldn't get rid of the tightness.

There was a brand-new Plymouth parked at the corner of Forty-eighth. He glanced around and saw he was alone. He went up to the shiny car and took out his penknife and gouged at the fender's smooth paint. He wanted to hack right through it!

Someone coughed around the corner. Lou walked quickly away.

Later, he was ashamed of himself.

9

ELI WEINER 3-C

Eli tried calling Irene from his office the Wednesday following the Friday he'd met her, but a woman—her mother, he figured—answered and said Irene had a late class at school. She asked if he cared to leave a meassage. He said no, he'd call again, and hung up before she could ask any more questions.

It chilled him somehow, that contact with her family. He didn't work up the nerve to call again until Saturday morning, when he went down for a newspaper. He walked to a candy store on Thirteenth Avenue instead of the one he usually patronized on Sixteenth, stepped into the phone booth and dialed. His heart began to pound, his hands to tremble, and he was afraid.

What if Friday night meant nothing to her? What if she refused to talk to him? What if she talked to him but refused to see him again? What if she laughed at him?

The phone at the other end rang six times before a woman said, "Yes?" It was her mother again.

He made his voice dull, bland. "Irene, please."

"Just a minute."

He heard Irene being called, and then she was on the wire. "Yes?"

"Eli," he said, the blood pounding in his ears.

Her voice changed, came alive, made him certain she was smiling. "Oh! I was just thinking of you!"

There was a split second when he felt a strange disappointment, when he realized that it would have been better had she refused to speak to him.

"When can I see you?" he asked.

She hesitated a moment. "Tonight."

He wanted to make the arrangements immediately, but there was Rose. He needed an excuse to get out alone, and he hadn't set it up as yet. "I'll call you back at noon," he said. "I've got to clear up certain—"

113

"I understand," she said, and he knew her smile was gone. "I have something to clear up myself. I'm supposed to see Dick tonight."

It made him feel sick.

"I don't want to see him," she added quickly. "I'm not going to see him again, ever."

"Did he— Has he ever said he liked you? I mean, has he shown special feeling?"

"No. We're only—" Her voice changed suddenly, became brisk and bright and completely impersonal. "Well, that's fine then. I'll expect your call about noon. 'Bye." The line went dead.

He understood. A member of her family had come within hearing range.

When he got back to the apartment, Dick was slouching in a chair near the living-room archway, still in pajamas, yawning into the phone.

"Yeah," Dick said. "Yeah, sure. Maybe we can get together next week. Yeah. So long." He hung up and rubbed his mop of curly black hair and looked at his father. "Guess I won't be using the car after all, Dad."

"I didn't know you were supposed to."

"Well, gee, I asked you last week and you said okay and here you don't—" He grinned. "Heck, I don't need it anyway."

"No date?" Eli asked, a slow hammer starting up behind his eyes.

"That's right. Little Miss Black Death isn't feeling well. Got a toothache."

Eli took off his coat and walked to the short-foyer closet. As he reached for a hanger, he said, "You don't seem bothered. Don't you like the girl?"

"Yeah, sure, I like her. But nothing serious, Dad. I can live without this one date. I'll see her again, I guess."

Just then, Rose came out of the bathroom, leading Teddy by the hand. "He's got such terrible habits!" she said, glaring at the thin twelve-year-old. "He picked his toes and it's a miracle he didn't get an ingrown—"

"Spare me the details," Dick groaned. "I haven't had breakfast yet."

Eli laughed, but Rose said, "Mr. Smart-Aleck. So delicate lately. Why don't you learn to clean up your room if you—"

"Christ!" Dick said, jumping off the chair and walking toward the short foyer leading to his room. He squeezed past his mother, father and brother. "Jesus Q. Christ!"

"And you don't have to mention that name around this house," Rose called after him. "You seem to forget you're a Jew—" The boy's door slammed, cutting her short. "Eli, go in there and give him a talking to!"

"Leave him be," Eli murmured. "Everyone uses the word. It doesn't mean anything."

"So even if it doesn't, and even if he never goes to synagogue, and even if his own father sets the bad example, is it any reason to swear on other people's gods? And he was fresh to me. Go in there—"

"Take it easy," Eli said. He looked down at Teddy and winked. Teddy grinned at him.

"What's this winking and laughing?" Rose said. "Am I a joke in this house?"

"I'll talk to him," Eli said placatingly. He walked away, amazed at how stupid and stubborn she could be. As he reached Dick's door, he heard the sound of a slap.

Teddy cried out; then shouted, "What did I do? I only whispered—"

"You were being a wise guy!" Rose interrupted. "I heard that Holy Moses!"

Eli laughed as he went into Dick's room. The tall boy was standing near the closet, getting dressed. "Your mother's on the warpath," Eli said, and sat down at the edge of the blond-mahogany bed.

"Isn't she though!"

"Say, about that girl," Eli said. "The one who broke the date."

"Irene?"

"Yes, Irene. She looks very nice. I mean pretty."

Dick sat down beside him and began putting on socks. "Yeah." He slipped into a pair of loafers. "She's also kind of —well, she's kind of fast, Dad." He grinned down at the floor.

Eli was shocked. "Fast? She seemed like a sweet kid—" Then he realized he was playing it wrong. "Oho. So be careful, Dick."

Dick glanced at him and then away, still grinning in a combination of male pride and childish embarrassment. "Yeah, I will. She—well, she pets a lot. Sort of treats it casually. She's a funny—a strange—girl."

Eli made his voice brisk, manly, hearty. "You get in yet?"

Dick colored like a ripe tomato. "You got it wrong, Dad. I meant she's fast for a nice girl. You know—she's not a tramp —I don't think she—" He laughed uncomfortably.

Eli stood up, feeling better. "Let's have some breakfast." He opened the door, then stopped. "God! I forgot to tell your mother I have to see someone on business tonight. There's a buyer in town from the Midwest and he's only staying until Sunday night."

When he told Rose, she accepted it with a downward twist of the lips. "I thought we'd see that new Jerry Lewis picture, but business before pleasure." She served her family hot-cakes, bacon and syrup. She didn't have any bacon herself.

At eleven, Dick left to play softball and Teddy went along to watch. Rose left a few minutes later to shop on New Utrecht Avenue. A soon as the door closed behind her, Eli picked up the phone and dialed Irene's number. She answered on the second ring.

"It's Eli," he said. "Can you talk?"

"Yes. I'm alone now."

"So am I. And I can pick you up about eight tonight."

"I'm very glad."

It made him feel wonderful, and slightly ashamed too. But the shame disappeared quickly. "How will we meet?"

"Remember the drugstore at the corner of my house?"

"Yes," he said, and fought to control the excitement, the hammering of heart and pulsing of blood. "Do we meet there?"

"No. Across the street." She paused. "It's a dark spot. I guess you have to be—discreet."

He said nothing. Of course he had to be discreet. He had to be more than that—secretive, back-alley sly, cloak-and-dagger cautious. But it made him uncomfortable to hear her say it.

"Okay," he said. "Goodbye."

"Wait," she said quickly. "I—I want you to say—to say something more. Why are we going to see each other? Why are you—" She stopped, and he could hear the quick, nervous intake of breath.

He understood immediately. And he knew that what he said now would strongly affect their future relationship. And still it was difficult.

"I love you," he murmured.

"Eli," she whispered. "Again!"

"I love you."

"Say it with my name."

"I love you, Irene." It was easier now. "More than anything, Irene."

"More—more than your children?"

It gave him a jolt. He laughed harshly. "That's a different kind of love."

"Yes, yes, I know," she said, voice low and intense. "But just generally—lumping love together—you know what I mean. Just—well, say it, please. Say it so I can understand why we're doing this."

"I love you more than my children."

"Use my name," she whispered.

"I love you more than my children, Irene." He was swept away by affection and sexual anticipation. "I love you more than children and wife and life, Irene."

He would have gone on, but she suddenly said, "I want to believe you, Eli. I—I want to let myself feel that way too. But who knows if it's true?"

"It's true," he said, and he was trembling. "It's true."

"Who knows? Even if you think so, it might be only because you want to—to—"

"That's not so. Of course, I want you. But it's not that which makes me say—"

"How can you be sure?"

He shook his head, forgetting she couldn't see it. "Wait. We're going too fast. We've hardly met."

Suddenly, she laughed—a clear, free, natural thing. "Yes. I'm silly. Please don't think I'm too silly."

The naïveté, the childishness of that statement, touched him and he wanted to hold her and stroke her hair and kiss her cheek. He wanted to show her how much she'd come to mean to him in just a few hours.

He couldn't find a thing to say.

"Goodbye," she said. "We'll talk about it tonight. We'll see. Goodbye, Eli. I—I do want to see you!" She hung up.

He went to the couch and sat down. He was soaked under the armpits. His hand shook violently as he lit a cigar.

Some time later, he thought of himself and wondered what made him—a married man, a father—want not just sex, but love pure, love complete, love that ached in the chest.

There were answers. They lay far back in his mind—back with Lily Weinstein and the other romantic failures of his youth, failures that marriage and parenthood hadn't seemed to touch.

He knew this, but blocked the realization. He stood up and said aloud, "I'll take a shower. Tonight—"

Tonight he'd begin to erase Lily Weinstein; tonight he'd change his history. . . .

He picked Irene up at the darkened spot across the way from the drugstore, drove onto the West Side Highway and headed downtown. They were going to have dinner at a good restaurant, a place where they could dance. But then she slid across the seat, close against him, her breasts pressing his side, her head falling to his shoulder.

He didn't know what exit he took. He left the elevated highway and drove a few minutes and pulled to the curb on a dark side street lined with storage houses and gas stations, all closed. He shut his lights and ignition and turned to her. It was very dark; he could see her face only as a pale blur. He moved toward her, found her lips, touched them gently with his own.

"Eli, don't." But her hand came up and caressed his neck.

This time the kiss was a bruising, crushing thing, and his hands began to move over her fullness and softness.

"I've changed my mind," she said. "I don't want to eat and dance. I want to ride. I want to ride into Westchester, into the country. I want to walk in the dark, on the grass. I want to—" She kissed him. . . .

Later, in the crisp, fragrant darkness of a picnic spot past the second Westchester toll, he experienced something so tremendous that he had to fight to keep from crying afterward.

"It'll always be this way," she said, pressing his head against her breasts. "It'll always be this way, won't it, Eli?"

"Yes," he answered, and was overwhelmed by questions, ugly questions ripping at his mind. "Yes, always."

There was Rose. There were Dick and Teddy. How did one reach over them and find love? Or did one have to dispense with them, get them entirely out of the way?

He felt he'd do anything, everything, to be with this girl.

"I love you, Eli. I've never told that to anyone before."

He answered with a gentle kiss.

They returned to the car and drove back to the city. On the way, they talked. They decided to go away for a weekend together. It was a necessity. They just had to be alone, had to have time to become immersed in each other.

"Two weeks from now," Eli said. "Right?"

"Yes. The last weekend in March. . . ."

He awoke reluctantly, by slow degrees, fighting the process yet wanting to do something about the discomfort in his left arm. Then he was staring up at a light-blue ceiling and trying to understand how his bedroom could change colors overnight.

He heard a high-pitched whimper and turned his head and saw Irene lying beside him, asleep but moving her lips and making frightened, unhappy sounds. He glanced around and saw the strange room and strange furniture, and remembered. He wasn't home. He was in a Jersey motel. It was Saturday morning. He'd had last night with Irene. He would have all day today, tonight, and part of tomorrow with her. Rose thought he was attending a weekend convention of dress manufacturers in Philadelphia. Irene's parents thought she was at an all-year vacation hotel (which she'd left unnamed) in the Catskills. It was their first weekend together, and the most wonderful experience he'd ever had.

He tried to sit up, felt the pain in his left arm, and saw that Irene was lying on it. He moved slowly, pulling it inch by inch from under her until it was free and he could slip out of bed without waking her. Then he walked to the window, rubbing his arm and groaning softly at the pins-and-needles feeling.

The shade was drawn to the sill and he raised it. Bright June sunshine flashed into the room; he saw a man, woman and child walking across a grassy space; he saw cars and trucks traveling the brief stretch of highway visible to his left. He lowered the shade immediately, remembering the need for caution, remembering the look on the manager's face when they had registered as Mr. and Mrs. Turino.

The manager hadn't believed they were married. He was a short, fat man with a round, dark-skinned face. His eyes had narrowed and he'd smiled slyly and said, "A quiet cabin at the end of B row is available, sir. It'll suit you, I believe." He'd begun giving Irene a slow, appreciative once-over.

"All right," Eli had said, and the tone of his voice made the manager jump.

They'd followed the short, fat man through the darkness and thanked him and left him standing outside the one-room cabin. Irene had drawn the shades before allowing Eli to put on the light. She'd looked around, opened the closet door, stepped into the bathroom, and then said, "It's horrible! It's —it's evil-looking. I don't want to stay here!"

He'd felt the same way, but with a difference. He knew his feelings were subjective, based upon the distaste for deceit and following in the footsteps of couples who'd used such methods and places to sneak an evening's lust. He calmed and comforted her, and explained her reaction as best he could. It took almost two hours, but she finally agreed to stay. He then opened his bag and took out the bottle of Scotch and had a drink. She joined him, and from the way she wheezed he knew she wasn't accustomed to liquor. But she stayed with him for a second shot, and a third. Then she began to laugh a lot and rumple his hair, and finally said, "Tell me how much you love me, Eli. Tell me you love me more than your children." He'd told her, and she'd put on a small, bedside radio and danced for him, lifting her skirt and rolling her hips and stooping to plant swift kisses on his face and head.

He'd been amazed and delighted at her grace and dexterity, but ended the performance by drawing her to the bed. She made him turn off the lights before she undressed.

Now it was morning, and he stood near the window and massaged his left arm and tried to rid himself of an undefinable but unpleasant feeling; an unhappy feeling.

He turned and looked at Irene. She lay on her side, drawn up into a tight bundle, knees almost to chin, arms crossed over her breast, covers tangled about her so that she was completely shielded from his eyes as he stood near the window; but when he walked around behind the bed her nudity was exposed from shoulders to calves.

He sat down beside her and looked at her face. It was beautiful, even in the slack, immobile lines of sleep. He ran his hand lightly across her thigh and leg, feeling a quickening of desire. She mumbled unintelligibly and rolled over. He got up and waited, but she didn't awaken. He went to the dresser and looked at his wrist-watch. It was ten after eight.

He went to the bathroom, washed and shaved, returned to the bedroom and dressed. Irene still slept heavily, and he suddenly understood why he felt unhappy. He needed her awake and active beside him as explanation for his being here. He needed to feel his love for her burning high and strong to justify the ugly little lies he'd told Rose, Dick and Teddy.

He looked at Irene, and cleared his throat loudly. She didn't twitch an eyelid. He shrugged, left the cabin and walked toward a diner about two hundred yards east along the highway. When he reached the chrome-and-glass doors, he

stopped, wondering what he would do if he were to meet
someone he knew. But then he shrugged and went inside. The
hell with it. Maybe it would be better if Rose found out. He
wanted to be free to marry Irene—

But the idea embarrassed him somehow. And he felt he
would be free of Rose only when she died. That was the
only way. He liked her too much to hurt her, to destroy her
belief in him as a loving husband and father.

He was the diner's only customer.

When he'd finished his eggs and coffee, he lit a cigar and
strolled back to the cabin. About ten feet from the door, he
heard Irene scream. He stopped, frozen for a second, and she
screamed again. He lunged forward and threw himself
through the door.

She was sitting up in bed, eyes closed, mouth open.

He jerked his head back and forth, trying to find what had
terrified her. He saw nothing.

She opened her eyes and wailed, "I'm not a skeleton! I'm
not!"

He shut the door, grinning in sudden relief. She'd had a
nightmare. "Far from it," he said. "Very far from it."

Her eyes focused on him, cleared, and she looked quickly
around. "Oh, I was sleeping. I was dreaming." But her voice
still held the hollow sound of panic, of horror.

Then he became aware of the picture she presented—bare
to the waist, where blankets were tangled around her middle.
A second later, she became aware of it too and flung herself
backward, drawing up the covers.

"It was lovely," he said, voice thickening. "Why did you—"

"Don't talk about it," she said quickly. "Don't, Eli. I—I
know you thought I was—thin—skinny."

For a moment he thought she must be kidding. She was
slender, certainly, but far from unattractively so; far from
skinny.

Yet her strained, shamed face; her voice—

"That dream," he said, coming to the bed and sitting down.
She shrank away from him. "You said something about being
a skeleton." He laughed, but cut it short as she winced. "What
is it, Irene?"

Suddenly she was shouting. "What is it with you? What
makes you run around with me when you're married and a
father and old enough—"

He felt as if he'd been slugged in the belly.

"No, Eli," she wailed. "No, please try to forget I ever said

it. Please, please!" She rolled over onto her face and cried
into the pillow.

He was too hurt to think clearly. But then he shook it off
and tried to figure out what had happened. It had something
to do with that dream, with her screaming she wasn't a skeleton, with his seeing her—for the first time—nude to the
waist, with his questioning her about the dream.

Suddenly, he didn't want to think about it any more, didn't
want to understand what had happened. It would turn out to
be a weakness, reveal a neurosis, and he didn't want Irene to
have weaknesses. Lily Weinstein had been so perfect—

But it was too late. With the entry of Lily Weinstein into
his mind, a progression of attendant thoughts followed, most
of them too quick to be captured, but all adding to a feeling
of fear and unhappiness.

He was here because of some sick reason, and she was
here because of some sick reason, and so there was no love
in this cabin, only sickness.

Then she rolled over and put her arms up to him, and all
thought slipped away.

Later, she said, "I panicked when you asked me what was
wrong, Eli. Because you'd heard me shouting and because
you'd looked at me. I was afraid you'd think—well, I'm
sometimes afraid of being skinny. But—it's nothing much.
Just something from my childhood; about the only unpleasant
part of it. I was—skinny. I had a cousin who taunted me
about it, a girl my own age who was plump and whom my
parents pointed to as a fine example of what eating could do.
I hated her."

She laughed. He laughed too. He felt neither of them
meant it.

"I still hate her—" She laughed again, and this time he
knew it was real. "I just thought of something, Eli. I told you,
and so it won't ever bother me again!" She hugged herself.
"I'm hungry. Serve me breakfast in bed?"

He nodded.

Walking to the diner, he kept thinking of how she'd shivered in his arms, moaned in his ear. Nothing else mattered.
She loved him. And he loved her.

The next morning, he again woke early and left the cabin
without waking her. He ate at the diner and strolled back to
the cabin, smoking a cigar and enjoying a feeling of well-
being. He was successful with women; extremely successful
because, at forty-three, married and the father of two, he'd

seduced his son's girl-friend—more than that, made her fall in love with him.

It was a fact. There was no getting away from fact. Just as he hadn't been able to get away from failure as a youth, there was no getting away from success as an adult.

He thought of this, and it was wonderful. But then another thought crept into his mind: Failure at sixteen was so much weightier a thing than success at forty-three.

Some of his happiness evaporated, and he threw the cigar away.

When he entered the cabin, the bed was empty. The shower was running in the bathroom. He walked to the door; it wasn't locked. He opened it and stepped into the small, yellow-and-brown, tile-lined room. A dark-brown plastic curtain was drawn across the stall shower and steamy mist sifted out around it.

Desire struck at him. He would look at her. It would be all right after yesterday's confession.

He began to breathe heavily, and moved to the stall. The hiss and roar of water covered his footsteps. He stopped and listened intently, and heard a little voice-sound, a grunt or sigh of tiny clearing of the throat. It heightened his excitement; it meant that she was unaware of his presence, that she was being completely natural. He wanted to see her completely natural. He wanted to see her washing—body unaffectedly revealed, hands rubbing vigorously, intimately.

He whipped the curtain aside. She was bent over, partly turned to him, rubbing at her legs with a washcloth, breasts swinging gently, white skin running water, hair caught tight under a pale-blue cap. For an instant she kept rubbing, for the next instant she merely stood bent over, and for the third instant she had her head twisted and her eyes wide on him. And then she was straightening and clutching at the curtain and saying, "No! Don't look! I won't allow—"

Her voice frightened him. It was high and thin and tight. It was full of fear.

He stepped back, a smile caught on his lips. She pulled the curtain too hard and it opened on the other side.

"Turn around, Eli! Don't look. Please don't look."

He turned his back. "For heaven's sake, Irene. We've been so close. And yesterday you said—"

"Yes, but go out. Right now. Go out."

He went out. He stood in the center of the bedroom and rubbed his face and felt his hand trembling.

He didn't want to think of her as being sick. He wouldn't! It lowered the value of his conquest. He wanted to think of her as a normal girl who'd succumbed to an irresistible hunger—as Lily might have succumbed had he been mature and known how to act.

Irene came out of the bathroom wearing a white towel-robe. "I'm sorry," she whispered, but she still looked frightened. "I—I was startled."

He nodded, trying to believe her, beginning to because he wanted to.

She turned her back on him as she rubbed at her hair with a towel. "You think I'm beautiful, don't you, Eli?"

"I *know* you're beautiful."

She faced him again, smiling.

"But you don't *believe* you're beautiful, do you, Irene?"

Her smile died. "Are we going to play psychiatrist? Because if we are, there are a few questions *I* can ask and a few answers *I* can suggest."

He was suddenly afraid of losing her. "Forget it," he said, and made his tone light, and smiled. "Want me to bring you some breakfast? You must be starved."

She nodded, face somber, and then ran to him and hugged him. "Eli, let's not talk like this any more! It's not important why I don't like to be looked at naked. I just don't." She raised her face and he kissed her and she used one hand to part her robe and press herself against him. "Don't you see enough of me? Don't you have all of me— And I am pretty and you do love me?"

He was on fire now, and yet he felt the fear behind her questions—the deep doubt and insecurity. It made him want to stop and help her, make her whole so she would love him for himself and not out of any weakness, any need for the safe love she received from a middle-aged married man who was too grateful for what he got ever to examine her critically and perhaps tell her disturbing truths . . .

He was horrified at his thoughts.

And at the same time he saw the truth in them.

He began to remove her robe, kissing her fiercely. She slid her lips aside and murmured, "Draw the shades, darling."

"They are drawn," he said, and pulled the robe back over her shoulders. He wanted her, he wanted her, and yet, at the same time, he was waiting for something to happen.

"It's so—so light," she said.

He continued to pull off her robe. She stepped away and

wiggled back into it. She allowed it to remain open, and he gazed at her, and she whispered, "I'm not skinny, am I, Eli? You haven't seen me like this, and like in the shower, before. But now you can tell me—I'm not thin—skinny. I'm not, Eli?"

"You're perfect," he said, but for an instant her fear shook him and he wondered if she wasn't a little too lean—

"Perfect!" he almost shouted, and then took her in his arms and pushed her toward the bed.

Later, he stroked her body and told her how foolish it was to think anything so wonderfully fleshed could be skinny.

"But once it was," she whispered, lips buried where his neck and chest joined. "When I was a little girl, and up until I was thirteen or fourteen. I was so ashamed—" She laughed and hugged him and said, "You can look at me now, if you want to."

He wanted to rest. He wanted to close his eyes and lie there and say nothing. That's the way it would have been with Lily. That's the way it should be after something perfect. But here there was a need to talk, to go over the same things again and again—

He told himself not to be a fool.

He drew the covers aside and looked. Her smile disappeared and she tensed.

"Lovely," he said, bending to kiss her white skin.

But she twisted onto her side and curled up tight and reached for the blanket. She covered herself and said, "I'd like that breakfast now, Eli."

He dressed and went to the door.

"Eli, I'm sorry. I—I just *feel* skinny."

He smiled to show it meant nothing, and opened the door.

"Eli, do you really love me?"

The same things, over and over and over.

He shook his head. "No, I don't love you. I just like to lie to you. It makes me feel good—"

"Please! Please tell me."

"I love you."

"With my name."

"I love you, Irene."

"More than your children?" She smiled in anticipation, sitting up and hugging the blankets to her.

He nodded. "More than my children, Irene."

"But say it from the beginning—you know."

"I love you more than my children, Irene." He smiled

quickly and left. He walked toward the diner and told himself he wasn't annoyed—he couldn't be annoyed with that beautiful, passionate girl.

He loved her. She loved him. It was perfect.

It rained after lunch. They played cards and talked and it was wonderful again. He made love to her at four, and then slept. They drove to a Howard Johnson's at seven and ordered a huge meal. He ate everything and drank two bottles of beer, but she merely picked at her plate. He asked if anything was wrong with the food.

"It's not that," she said, and seemed afraid again. "I—I never eat well. I have to be very relaxed to eat well and I'm never—" She looked at him, eyes bleak. "My childhood again. I could never eat well, gain weight."

He sighed. She was waiting for him to say something comforting. He could tell her how he'd failed with girls as a youngster; that would show her he too had suffered. But he found he couldn't.

"I've been going to a psychiatrist," she said. "I started about six months ago." She looked down at the table. "Does that surprise you?"

"No. And it doesn't bother me either, if you're going to ask."

She smiled and covered his hand with both of hers.

"Has he helped you?" Eli asked.

She shrugged, still smiling. "I don't know. Sometimes I feel it's a lot of bunk. Sometimes I feel he—and the one I had before—are phonies." She picked up a piece of bread, rolled it between her fingers, popped it into her mouth. "In some ways —well, they're witch doctors, medicine men, not always believing their own mumbo-jumbo. Some day they'll have to admit it, too. Some day they'll have to tell people that their wise looks and wise nods and perfect labels—insecurity, agoraphobia, paranoia—don't hold true often enough. Some day a scientist is going to invent a little pill that will supply an unknown vitamin, an unknown element, and cure manic-depressives, or schizophrenics, by the millions. Then the wise looks and nods and labels will have the same medical value as amulets and totem poles." She laughed and clapped her hands together. "I'd love to be around when that happens!"

He laughed too, impressed by her reasoning, her projection of what struck him as a possibility.

"If you feel that way, why bother with a psychiatrist?"

She shrugged. "I cry on his shoulder. I pay him and he lets me cry on his shoulder. That way I don't wear out my parents and friends—and you." She squeezed his hand. "There's only one way I want to wear you out. . . ."

They went to a drive-in movie and returned to the motel at one A.M. He surprised himself by making love to her for the third time within fifteen hours. She called him El Toro and he was proud and kissed her gently, gratefully. He fell asleep, thinking that small irritations were natural in any affair, any human relationship, and that he wanted to be with her always, had to be with her always.

He dreamed Rose was killed in an automobile accident. He felt a pang, a terrible pang, but then went to Irene. Together, they drove away into lush green countryside. . . .

10

ELLIOT WYCOFF 2-E

On a gusty Friday night in March, Elliot and the twenty-three-year-old proofreader, Alex Fernol, had dinner together in the Copperdome Restaurant. They talked very little, and then about books and authors and co-workers. Fernol insisted on paying for a cab to his Third Avenue apartment, and still didn't broach the "delicate subject" which was the reason for Elliot's being with him.

The apartment was one room with a drab, curtained-off stove-refrigerator-sink unit and a tiny bathroom. It was on the third floor of an old, five-story walkup and the neighborhood was near-slum. But Fernol had furnished and decorated nicely, using clean modern pieces—studio couch, two Swedish chairs with black bouclé fabric, blond mahogany coffee table, tall blond bookcases jammed with comfortably worn volumes.

"Most of the books were my brother's," Fernol said, switching on a multiple gooseneck lamp. "He was killed in Korea—one of those fields near the Yalu."

"I'm sorry," Elliot said, and sat down on the studio couch.

"He was a wonderful man. I've never stopped missing him."

Elliot nodded. He hadn't felt comfortable since the evening

began; now he was beginning to grow tense. He crossed his legs, leaned back, sucked on the cigarette he'd lit in the cab. "Very nice place."

"Did the best I could with it, Elliot. In time, I hope to find something in a better neighborhood. Meanwhile, it'll have to do."

Elliot nodded again and cleared his throat and looked around.

"Would you like a drink?" Fernol asked.

"Yes," Elliot said quickly. "Yes, that's an excellent idea."

"I don't care for liquor myself, but I keep it for friends. I've got Scotch, bourbon and the ingredients for Martinis."

"Scotch."

Fernol walked across the room and around the drawn curtain. "Put on the radio," he called. "It's just to your left."

Elliot found the small Emerson standing on an end table, and by the time Fernol returned he'd located WNYC and some good music.

Fernol carried a tray with a fifth of Johnny Walker, a dish of ice-cubes, and a tall glass. Elliot made a drink and took a long pull. Fernol stood over him, rubbing his hands together.

"Okay," Elliot said, and realized he was speaking in a voice deeper than normal, as whenever he was afraid, insecure or on the defensive. "Let's hear whatever's been bothering you."

"Yes," Fernol said, and sat down on the couch, close to Elliot. "Do you know Marge Slower who works on the fourteenth floor in Publicity?"

Elliot thought a moment. "Short, dark-haired, attractive in a very young way?"

"That's her, though I would say pretty rather than attractive. Pretty in an empty-faced, empty-headed—" He rubbed his hands together again, and Elliot was fascinated by them— long, slender fingers, but obviously tight, hard and powerful. "Anyway," Fernol continued, "I talked to her a few times and she asked me to escort her to that cocktail party the company gave for Arthur Lloyd Rieker who wrote *Mountain Boy's Day*. I didn't particularly want to, but, well, I felt it would look strange if I said no—"

Elliot finished his drink and poured another as Fernol continued with his story. He knew what was coming. He'd lived through the same thing two years ago.

". . . went to a show and had dinner and I thought she was completely without charm or intelligence . . ."

Elliot nodded understandingly and finished his second

drink, and a third. He smoked a fresh cigarette and nursed his fourth drink. He'd had enough Scotch, he decided. He was finding it difficult to stop looking at Fernol's hands; those strong, beautiful hands that continued to stroke each other.

". . . day last week I went downstairs to see about my Blue Cross and I passed her department. She looked at me and laughed in a nasty way and said something to a girl sitting nearby. The girl looked up and—and then I knew from the expression on her face that Marge—had been saying things."

Elliot didn't want to ask, but it was the only way. "Things?"

Fernol's eyes came up to his, and they looked at each other, and Elliot felt something breaking inside him—a barrier coming down.

But he didn't want that barrier to come down. He wanted to survive as a social being!

"They were talking about my being—a homosexual," Fernol whispered.

Elliot's head was whirling, but he leaned forward and poured himself another drink and spent a great deal of time dropping in an ice cube. "Screw her," he finally said.

Fernol laughed. "Figuratively or literally?"

"First literally, then figuratively."

"But—"

Elliot waited.

"But I don't want to," Fernol said. "I find her absolutely repulsive now."

Elliot kept his eyes on his glass. "Yes. Of course. She's vicious and you hate her. But it's the only way, and it's a wonderful revenge."

Fernol made a deep-in-the-throat sound of revulsion.

"Of course," Elliot said, "you can let her go on saying those things, and soon people will begin watching the way you walk and the way you talk, and then you'll be labeled a fairy—for good. But if you beat it this once, you'll be safe—" He stopped. He hadn't meant to use the word "safe." He hadn't meant to imply that the gossip about Fernol would be true.

He started, almost spilling his drink, as Fernol's left hand covered his. "I knew you'd understand, Elliot."

Elliot was frozen. He felt as if his hand were burning from the contact, and yet he couldn't seem to move it.

They sat that way for quite a while; then Fernol said, "And what if I am a homosexual?"

"Ah," Elliot said, finding it difficult to breathe. "Ah, well, then you're in trouble."

"Am I?" Fernol murmured. His other hand dropped lightly onto Elliot's thigh. "Maybe I prefer being in trouble, as you put it, to wasting my time with silly little girls, vicious little girls. Maybe I prefer being in trouble to—" he paused for what seemed a long time—"to fooling myself."

Elliot was trembling. The hand on his hand and the hand on his thigh were the most important things in the world right now. A hot, creeping lethargy began invading his body from those two areas, and he didn't want to fight it. He leaned back, slowly, fearfully, unable to stop himself, and closed his eyes. The glass was taken from his right hand, and his excitement pulsed upward.

"I'll try to carry out your advice," the soft voice said. "I don't know if I can. I've had just one sex experience of that sort in all my life, and I was only fourteen at the time. It was a woman counselor at a summer camp. It made me so sick I had to return home before the week was out. But I'll try. I'll certainly try—"

The voice was hypnotic, Elliot realized. Deliberately hypnotic.

And then Fernol's lips touched Elliot's cheek and Fernol's hand moved along Elliot's thigh, and Elliot was living one of his two recurrent dreams—the obvious one. As in the dream, he was both horrified and desirous. As in the dream, he heard himself saying, "No, no, no, no—"

"Elliot, stop fighting it!"

The voice was soft no longer. It was hard and strong, like the hands.

Hands and voice worked on Elliot, draining him of resistance.

"No," he said, and wanted to give in and end the fight, the long fight that meant only pain and loneliness and absence of love. He opened his eyes and looked at Fernol. The blond youth's face was flushed as it came toward him, lips parting. It was a beautiful face, Elliot thought. It was the most beautiful face he'd ever seen.

"No," he said, and gained strength from his own voice. "No! I'm—not a homosexual!"

"Whom are you cheating but yourself? Whom are you hurting but yourself? This is the only way you'll ever find love—"

But Elliot was moving now, and he shoved the boy

away and got up and walked to the door. His strength almost
failed him when Fernol said, "Elliot, don't leave me! I want
you so much!"

"No," he said. "I— can't."

"Thousands of us—"

Elliot shook his head, as he had all his life, and walked
out. . . .

At five o'clock Saturday evening, Elliot left Koptic Court,
dressed in his best flannel suit, gray tweet topcoat and charcoal-gray flattop hat. He carried an Oshkosh leather bag and
pencil-thin Italian umbrella. His light-brown English shoes
were buffed to a dull gloss, his cheeks closely shaven, his
body freshly bathed.

He stopped outside the lobby and turned to view himself in
the glass doors. He smiled, pleased with his image, and then
grinned at the sudden thought. He was worth over six hundred dollars on the hoof, not counting the buck and change
his corporeal self and immortal soul would bring on the
chemist's block.

He walked briskly down the street to where he'd parked
his Porsche at the curb, nodding at an elderly woman who
was moving slowly toward the house. He felt better already.
Tonight and tomorrow at the Slocums' was exactly what he
needed; exactly what would drive away the depression that
had been plaguing him since leaving Alex Fernol's place last
night.

He got into the low-slung sports car, placing his bag in
the extra bucket seat, and pulled away from the curb with a
roar. The feeling of well-being grew stronger and stronger,
and he began to hum a selection he'd heard a coloratura sing
Thursday night.

The Slocums lived in a square, two-story, red-bricked house
that had been built for Roger Slocum's great-grandfather in
1853. Certain modernizing changes had been made indoors
during the last thirty years, a swimming pool had been placed
out back behind the tennis courts and the stables were now
a four-car garage, but the look of solid nineteenth-century
respectability remained, and so did the thirty-one acres of
now invaluable North Shore land.

Elliot drove off the side road and stopped before the fancy
metal-work gate which was the only break in the eight-foot-
high stone wall bordering the entire estate. He pulled the
old-fashioned bell rope, and the green-tinged iron clapper

actually clanked out a sodden call. However, Elliot knew that inside the house, in the kitchen where the maid and butler were usually found, and in the apartment over the garage where the chauffeur lived, an electric buzzer was also sounding.

Blake, the chauffeur, appeared on the left, coming down the road from the garage which wasn't visible from the gate, being partially behind the house and wholly behind a line of old oak trees. The stocky, middle-aged Negro was putting on a dark-blue jacket as he trotted along. He reached the gate and smiled. "Good evening, Mr. Wycoff."

"Good evening," Elliot said in his deep, calm, resonant voice, the voice he would use from now until the moment he drove through this gate Sunday night. "Put the Porsche in the garage for me, will you, Blake? I'd like to walk to the house—it's such a brisk twilight. And have my bag sent to my room."

The chauffeur said, "Yessir," and swung open the gate from both sides. Elliot walked up the pebbled road. A moment later, the Porsche passed him and took the left turn to the garage. Elliot continued toward the wide sweep-around that passed in front of the house's narrow porch and then joined the garage road. He breathed deeply, wondering whether that touch of sweetness in the air was the first sign of approaching spring. Or was it his own sense of pleasure at being here?

No matter. The air was sweet and so was life—at moments like this.

Cooper, the elderly, slouch-shouldered butler, opened the door to Elliot's ring and spoke in the soft voice that always held the suggestion of a deep bow. "Good evening, sir. Mr. and Mrs. Slocum are in the living room."

"Thank you, Cooper," Elliot said, and turned to be helped out of his coat. He then handed the butler his hat and turned to the long mirror beside the umbrella stand. He adjusted his tie while Cooper placed his things in the closet.

Had he been made to think of it, Elliot would probably have decided that this was the part he liked best about his visits to the Slocums, this moment when Cooper, in his old-fashioned black suit, turned to him and intoned, "If you'll come with me, sir."

There was something almost religious in the way the old servant said these words and then paced down the wide foyer to the heavy oak door on the right. The sense of great pride in tradition, great pride in position, was imparted in every syllable, every step. It made Elliot feel part of a wonderfully civilized ceremony.

And while the Derrings also had a butler in their luxurious Sutton Place apartment (he accompanied them to The Hatchery in the summers), the man was much more adept at tending bar than at making guests feel that something very special was happening to them when they entered his domain.

From the moment when Cooper ushered him into the living rooms and the tall, heavy-set man and the tall, slender woman rose to greet him, Elliott was in the world of his choice, the world as he would have it. He smiled and shook hands and talked and then sat down in the deep armchair facing the gray couch. He accepted the Martini Roger Slocum poured for him. He asked about his ex-roommate, Jerry, and paid a small price for being in these wonderful surroundings by having to express interest, amusement, delight and (rarely) sympathy for various minor occurrences in Jerry's life as transmitted by his doting parents. Then beautiful, twenty-year-old Dorothy Slocum came into the room, wearing a pale-blue cocktail dress which seemed composed of a hundred layers of thin lace, and Elliot rose to take her hand. "You look simply perfect," he said.

The tall, willowy redhead arched her eyebrows, narrowed her gray eyes and smiled thinly, coolly. "Now you're just saying that, Elliot."

"I am indeed," he said, and squeezed her hand.

She withdrew it casually, almost contemptuously, Elliot thought. But then he told himself he was getting overly sensitive. He was among friends here. He felt Dorothy was a kid sister, and that's the way the Slocums liked it. That's the way Dorothy liked it—or did she?

She looked him in the eye. "You said it to please Mother and Father. You do everything to please Mother and Father. You're the perfect guest—or rather, the perfect perennial guest."

It was a slap in the face. He felt himself going white, and she laughed and turned away.

"Really, Dorothy!" Mrs. Slocum exclaimed.

"She's developed the strangest sense of humor," Roger Slocum said quickly. "She startles us all lately."

Elliot forced a laugh. "She certainly startled me." He recovered his poise then, and began speaking of a new play opening within the week. But Dorothy Slocum interrupted.

"You must be getting sensitive in your old age, Elliot. You turned absolutely green at my little quip."

He was sure about the coldness in her voice now. He'd sensed a growing estrangement on her part for almost a year, but this was the first time she'd ever been deliberately rude.

"Really?" he said, and wanted to tell her what a little fool she was with her stupid boy-friends, and schoolgirl crushes on the social lions who visited her parents, and the sly drinking she did for kicks. Instead, he smiled and shook his head. "You're getting rapier sharp. I'm afraid some of your supposedly witty friends are in for a rough time when you decide to give them a going over."

The compliment worked, and she giggled. She turned back to him and kissed his cheek. That's when he smelled the alcohol. She'd been nipping again.

"Try using vodka next time," he whispered in her ear. "It's ever so much more discreet."

She glared at him, but he had her now and figured she'd be good. At least for a while.

He was wrong.

She walked to the sideboard where the Martini jug stood and poured herself a drink. She gulped it.

"Hey, Button," Roger Slocum said in a mildly reproving voice. "That's powerful brew. I mixed it myself and—"

"No lectures now, Father," Dorothy said, and dropped into an armchair with a fresh drink. "I'm a big girl, you know. I smoke. I go to dances. I catch boys looking at me, once in a while." She sipped her Martini. "All boys." She sipped again, and her eyes swung to Elliot, and he began to feel cold. "All boys except one."

Mrs. Slocum saw whom her daughter was looking at, and laughed. "Elliot, I do believe your turn has finally come on the crush list."

"Oh, no," Dorothy said calmly. "You're wrong, Mother. We're sister and—" she giggled—"sister. I mean brother."

Elliot dug for cigarettes and lit one and kept a smile on his lips. He smoked urbanely and felt the room beginning to tremble, the house beginning to shake, this whole beautiful weekend world of his beginning to disintegrate.

The bitch! The evil little bitch!

He had to fight, had to maintain his position as a favored guest here. If he didn't do or say something, the Slocums might begin to wonder.

He leaned back in his chair and roared—not just laughed

but roared. He shook his head and kept roaring, and thanked God when Roger Slocum joined in. A moment afterward, Mrs. Slocum also began to laugh. The three of them laughed together, and Dorothy set her glass down on the coffee table, stood up and looked at them. "If you think I'm going to stay here and listen to you people bellow your fool heads—"

"Okay, okay," Elliot gasped, coming to her rescue at what he hoped was the correct psychological moment. "Sorry." He sobered quickly. "If I really thought that you—liked me, I'd be so damned flattered—" He shook his head and laughed again. "Button, you're on top of the world and I'm lucky to get halfway up for quick glimpses."

She flushed, with pleasure this time. He should have been relieved, but the way she smiled at him indicated trouble. The damned girl did seem to have developed a crush on him.

No, not a crush. That smile indicated something else; not quite a crush.

He thought he understood. And if he was right, it meant the beginning of the end of his position with the Slocums.

Dorothy didn't really care for him, wasn't even infatuated with him. But she'd sensed his complete lack of interest in her as a woman and it bothered her, challenged her. Since nothing seemed to work, she'd begun disliking him. And now he'd turned around and complimented her and she was waiting to see what would happen.

It was going to be a rough weekend.

He shook his head slightly, correcting himself.

It was going to be a rough life.

Dinner was scheduled for eight o'clock, but two of the six other guests were late and it was almost nine before they sat down at the massive mahogany table in the long, narrow dining room. Elliot was facing Dorothy, and looked past her to where heavy brocade draperies were arranged around rococo but strangely attractive stained-glass windows. He wished he could forget Dorothy—but he couldn't. She was sitting next to a youth of twenty-two or three, a wide-shouldered, lean-hipped, crew-cut athlete who kept turning to her, saying things like, "We've got a chance to win in the regatta this year," and peering hot-eyed down the front of her dress. There was sufficient motivation for peering, Elliot had to admit. Dorothy was slender, but stacked like a coconut tree. And while she maneuvered so that the college athlete was kept at a steady boil, it was Elliot she spoke to with hungry eyes.

He suddenly remembered the dock in Japan, the woman leaning back on the oil drum and saying, "Sailor *san*, sailor *san*, I love sailor *san* . . ."

They were finished with dessert, a superbly light peach shortcake, and Elliot watched Dorothy drain her glass of Moselle for the fifth or sixth time. She was well on her way to being plastered, but she carried herself well.

And now it was time for Cooper, the butler, to perform another little ceremony which Elliot loved. Elliot's eyes kept flickering to the right, to the archway leading to the small, leather-and-oak library, the magnificent room which he preferred above all others in this fourteen-room house.

The old man finally appeared, moving slowly under the arch, stopping just inside the dining room and dropping his head in an almost imperceptible bow. "Gentlemen, brandy will be served in the library."

"How quaint," the loud woman with the glittering array of diamond earrings, necklace and bracelets shrilled. "I don't believe I've heard a butler say that anyplace—except in the movies." She shrilled again. "Old movies."

"Movies based on books by Charles Dickens," her husband intoned in a deep, impressive voice, and then glanced around to see if he'd said something clever.

"Yes, indeed," Dorothy said softly. "But I prefer movies based on books by Rabelais. Or Huysmans. Or Count de Sade. Or Balzac—"

"Balzac," the college athlete said, leaning over her neckline. "Say, did you ever read those *Droll Stories?* Say, they didn't have censors—"

"But they had standards," Dorothy murmured, staring at Elliot. "Didn't they, brother mine?"

She was bright and sharp and quite sensitive, Elliot thought. Too bad she was a woman—

He stood up quickly then, enraged at himself, at her for making him think those thoughts, at the world for pushing him into corners. Why the hell couldn't a man remain cool and detached? Why the hell did he either have to like women sexually, or else like men the same way? Why couldn't he remain neutral, without passion, totally cerebral?

He stepped toward the library with the other men, looking forward to the fine cognac brandy and Turkish demitasse. But Dorothy called, "Elliot." She'd come around the table and was standing right behind him.

"I'd like to talk to you a moment, brother mine." Her voice

had thickened, her speech become blurred. She took his hand and began walking toward the hall door.

He had no choice but to follow. He glanced around quickly, saw Mr. and Mrs. Slocum watching with passive, slightly unhappy faces. He was a good guest, but when it came to their daughter . . .

He took a chance then. He winked at them, shook his head slightly. It told them he would humor their daughter a little, but there was nothing to worry about.

It worked. They both smiled at the same time, and the old warmth was there. They trusted him, liked him again.

But it would take more than a wink and shake of the head to satisfy Dorothy. She was leading him toward the back of the house, toward the door to the tennis courts and swimming pool. It would be dark out there, private out there.

As soon as they stepped into the chill March air, she turned and looked up at him. "Brother mine, I've known you for seven or eight years now—or is it nine? I've grown from a child to a woman, and you've never said a nice thing to me—"

"I've said *nothing* but nice things to you," he interrupted, hoping to turn the tide somehow, yet knowing it was impossible.

"Not *really* nice things. Not things a woman wants to hear from a man. Not things you should have said long before tonight. Said—and done."

"But I'm a friend of your—"

"Of my brother's and mother's and father's." She pressed against him, touched her lips to his. "Sweet, sweet friend of mine. You appreciate Cooper, don't you? Anyone who appreciates Cooper must be good, must be fine, must be wonderful to kiss." She kissed him again, and he stood with his hands hanging at his sides. She stepped back. "For the love of Christ, Elliot! So you're a friend of the family's and you're not going to seduce me! So you're a poor little editor and you're not going to marry me! So I understand. I *understand*. What the hell has that got to do with taking me in your arms and giving me and yourself some fun? I don't expect to be seduced, or married. I expect some plain old mutually acceptable, mutually pleasurable loving!"

He had to do something positive now. He couldn't stand there, hands at his sides. Another moment and she'd whirl away from him, rejected, humiliated, hating him and ready to look for certain face-saving signs.

He played his part, as he'd played it twice before in his life. He reached out, making a groaning little sound deep in his throat, and pulled her against him and kissed her hard. At least he *thought* it was hard. She obviously didn't because she lunged against him, twisted her arms around his neck, ground her body into his, thrust her tongue between his lips.

As he had noted only a few minutes before, she was bright and sharp and quite sensitive, perhaps even more so in some ways than he had realized. She felt that something was wrong. She moved away from him, said, "No, please," in a thoughtful voice when he tried to pull her back. She stared at him a moment. "Poor baby," she said, and the coolness grew. "I am sorry." She began to turn.

He grabbed her arm. "Sorry? That I just can't catch fire with you?"

He was glad when her lips tightened and her eyes blinked angrily. "I'm not so sure that's—"

"When a man's in love with one woman, does he want to play around with another?"

"You're—in love with—someone else?"

He shrugged, turned away. "I am. It isn't working out, but I am."

"Well," she said flatly. "Well, if that's the case—"

He faced her again. "It *is* the case."

Her eyes fell. "I'm chilly." She went back inside.

He lit a cigarette and took a long drag before following.

The evening went well after that. Dorothy and the crew-cut college athlete disappeared together, and Elliot was able to enjoy a spirited discussion of the dance with a Mr. Senteux, a French national seeking U. S. investors for a projected plastics concern. Mr. Senteux knew his ballet. He insisted the Danish troupe was as fine as any in the world.

"But really," Elliot said. "You don't include Sadler's Wells, do you?"

"Most certainly, my friend, most certainly. Take *Swan Lake*, for example . . ."

At one-thirty in the morning, Elliot went to his room. He'd been given the small, northeast corner cubbyhole because of the full complement of guests, and while that sort of thing had never bothered him before, it did tonight. He shrugged it off and got into bed. But he couldn't sleep.

Sometime later, he heard giggling. It seemed to be coming from the neighborhood of the garage, which was visible from his single window. He got out of the bed, walked to the window and looked out. The bench under the twisted oak was shrouded in black shadows, but he recognized the voices —Dorothy giggling, the college athlete speaking in a penetrating tenor.

"I thought he looked sort of like that," the college athlete said.

Dorothy giggled again, then said, "Shhh. What if someone hears you?"

She sounded stewed, Elliot thought, and his stomach suddenly cramped and he felt like throwing up.

The athlete lowered his voice, and Elliot pressed close to the open window.

". . . guy in my dorm . . . slugged him good . . . put his hand . . . pretty disgusting—"

Dorothy giggled. "I wish you were more like Elliot." She shushed herself. ". . . be good—now, Roy—"

Elliot put his hands over his ears, shook his head. "No," he said. "No, damn you, no!" He dropped his hands and listened again.

". . . just kidding," Dorothy said. ". . . not sure . . . guess he's okay—not nice to talk . . ."

"My trouble's too much of the opposite," the athlete said. His voice dropped and Elliot could make out only an intense word here and there.

". . . baby . . . please . . . Dorothy . . . honey . . ."

Dorothy giggled, but throatily. Then two figures moved from under the tree and made their way toward the pool, and past it into the blackness.

"Fools," Elliot whispered. "Filthy fools. Anyone could hear and see—"

But then he remembered that only the guest in this room could hear and see. And Dorothy had known he was here. She wasn't worried about him. She wasn't sure what he was, but who worried about insulting the perennial guest?

He went back to bed. He lay there and stared up at the ceiling. She'd definitely backed down from classifying him as queer. He was sure she didn't really believe it. Not yet. But what would happen when another six months had passed, another year had passed, and he didn't bring a girl with him and he didn't show interest in any female guest and she once again discussed him with some boy under the oak tree? His world trembled. It was safe for the moment, but still it trembled.

If only there were some way to make Dorothy, to make

them all, stop expecting him to want women. Some way—

But there was no way.

He didn't fall asleep until gray dawn filtered into the room. He kept imagining he heard soft whispers, groans and giggles coming from behind the pool. . . .

Elliot got up at nine-thirty, red-eyed from lack of sleep, and went downstairs for breakfast. He was the only one at the dining-room table, the others sleeping late as usual. He had juice, kidneys and bacon, toast, marmalade, a four-minute egg and two cups of coffee. He wiped his mouth with the soft, heavy, Irish linen napkin, took a plantation cigarette from the antique silver box, and smiled at Cooper who was removing the delicate Wedgwood cup and saucer.

"Thank you, Cooper," he said.

Cooper bowed his head a fraction of an inch. Elliot felt wonderful again, and decided to leave while still in this frame of mind. He packed his things, wrote a note to the Slocums and drove out through the gate in his Porsche.

Dorothy would forget that nonsense before his next visit. Of course she would. Everything would return to normal and he would again gain full pleasure from his stays here. Besides, there was a weekend at the Derrings' coming up soon. That would be fun. He was expected to spend time with someone's daughter, but he'd carry it off all right.

Everything would be fine.

Certainly.

About halfway home, he stopped kidding himself. It wouldn't be long before both the Slocums and the Derrings would stop wanting him around. It wouldn't be long before they began to form certain opinions about his coolness toward women.

He put on the radio. He found classical music and turned up the volume. He turned it still higher, trying to blast the despair from his brain. . . .

Elliot didn't see Alex Fernol for more than a week, but he thought of him constantly. And he dreamed of him. Those dreams left him weak and shaken—and terribly lonely.

On the last Thursday in March, he met Fernol in the hall. The blond youth smiled and stuck out his hand as if nothing had ever happened between them. "Elliot! I've got something to tell you."

Elliot shook the hand, and his knees went weak. "Yes?" he said.

Fernol glanced around to make sure they were alone. "I've already started my campaign against you-know-who. I dated her Sunday and got along pretty well." He laughed. "Also got pretty far. We're going dancing tomorrow night, and maybe Saturday."

"Good," Elliot said, and was horrified at the sudden twinge of jealousy that hit him when he visualized Fernol with Marge Slower.

Fernol looked him straight in the eyes. "Not so good. Revolting, in fact."

Elliot shrugged and stepped past him.

"We'll have to get together some evening," Fernol said blandly.

Elliot nodded and kept walking. When he got to the elevators, he was sweating. He had to stay away from that boy!

"Why?" a little voice asked. "What's the use of kidding yourself?"

He decided to look up some old friends. He hadn't seen Frank Walther in almost a year. Not that he'd really liked the squat photographer with his woman-talk and obscenities, but maybe it would be good for him.

And there was Stanley Ferris from the literary agency, and Carl Adorno who was a public relations man, and Will Stern who lived in Brooklyn with his wife and two kids; all men he'd never thought he'd care to see again.

But he had to break the pattern into which his life had fallen during the past few weeks. He had to stop thinking of Alex Fernol.

He called Frank Walther as soon as he got back from lunch.

"Hey, Elliot!" the photographer bellowed. "Long time no see, hear and smell. We've gotta get together, but soon."

"I agree," Elliot answered, using his ultra-deep voice.

"Tell you what— I've got a stag party next Tuesday night. Friend of mine is getting married and I'm helping organize the last fling. It's going to be at my studio." He laughed. "My studio! Mine and five other shutter-bugs'! Anyway, you haven't seen this place yet. Nice. On Forty-fifth Street between Fifth and Sixth. Jot down the address."

Elliot did.

"Be there at eight-thirty, Elliot. The obsequies won't start till nine or nine-thirty, but you can help me set things up."

"Fine," Elliot said. "Be glad to."

Frank Walther chuckled. "You ain't kidding, mister. Setting things up includes getting the girls ready for their acts."

"Oh? Strippers and stuff?"

"Mostly stuff. You and me and one other guy—Harry Bal-lam—are going to hold that dressing room against a horde of drunken, woman-hungry maniacs. Man, man, won't it be a graaand time! Oh yes, one little item. It'll cost you six bucks. Everyone's chipping in for the liquor and girls, though we did land two strippers for free by promising to get them into *Playboy*. Hah, those bags in *Playboy!* See you, Elliot."

Elliot hung up. He hadn't bargained for a stag party. But then again, Frank Walther and his friends were always in-volved in wild affairs—and it was normal, healthy, just the thing he needed to snap him out of his obsessive interest in Alex Fernol.

"Going to a stag party Tuesday night," he said to Sylvia. "Haven't been to one in years."

She grinned. "From what I've heard, they can be pretty wild. Want me to phone my doctor and have you scheduled for a Wassermann on Wednesday?"

He laughed, but the doubts grew thicker. . . .

Tuesday morning, his aunt called him at the office. "Since you won't be home until late, Elliot, I thought I'd let you know right now that I had a call from your mother."

"Is she—"

"Oh, she's fine. She wanted to talk to me about visiting New York."

"Good grief," Elliot muttered.

"What?"

"Nothing, Aunt Minnie. Of course, you know she'll never actually make the trip. She always backs out—"

"I think I've finally convinced her! I told her how much you miss her, and how we could put her up at the apartment, and I really believe she was convinced. She said something about your being afraid for her health, but I said that was only natural—sons are overprotective when it comes to moth-ers. She said she'd let us know as soon as she made up her mind. Keep your fingers crossed!"

"I will," Elliot said.

After hanging up, he smiled grimly to himself. He'd keep his fingers crossed, all right. But he'd uncross them long enough to write another letter. The last thing in the world he wanted was to have Mother on his hands this September. She'd expect to be taken to the Slocums' and Derrings'.

He could just see the expression on his friends' faces as they met the cultured Mr. Wycoff's mother!

It didn't make any difference that he felt ashamed of himself. It would be pure horror to introduce her around.

He decided to write her immediately.

At a few minutes of five, he asked Sylvia if she'd have dinner with him.

"Sorry, sweetie, I have an appointment. Aren't you going to that stag party tonight?"

He nodded. "It's at eight-thirty. I've got more than three hours to kill."

Sylvia left the office with her soap dish and towel, and Elliot stared at the phone. He hated to eat alone, but whom could he contact at this late hour?

Alex Fernol.

He got up, walked to the window and looked down to Fifth Avenue. He'd have a nice, leisurely dinner at a quiet, little restaurant—maybe that dim, cool Italian place near Lexington, or the German rathskeller on Sixth. He'd buy a newspaper and read as he ate and finish up with a liqueur.

Alex Fernol—perfect face, strong hands, soothing, hypnotic voice.

"Well, why not?" he said aloud, and turned to the phone.

Just then the door opened and Sylvia came in. She glanced around. "Didn't I hear someone speaking?"

He made his eyebrows climb. "It's time to see an analyst when you begin hearing voices."

"I'll be damned," she muttered, and went to her desk. She picked up the phone and asked the switchboard for an out side line. Elliot hesitated. Should he call Fernol while Sylvia was in the office, or wait until she left? It was just about five now, and Fernol might leave at any moment.

He walked out of the office, then stopped, looking at Fernol's door.

"Hello, Elliot," the sharp voice said.

He turned and saw Mr. Lester—Maurice Lester, Jr. the old man's son.

"Hello, Mr. Lester."

"Thought you might be interested in what's happening to Soldier of the Conqueror—that Persian historical you and Sylvia recommended. I read it over the weekend and thought it had real punch. Of course, it's a trifle rough around the edges, but author revision should take care of most of that and good editing will handle the rest. What I have in mind is cutting the introductory sequence to no more than two thousand words. We don't need all that dry description . . ."

He went on talking, and Elliot heard a door open.

"Good night," Alex Fernol's soft voice said.

Elliot couldn't turn because Mr. Lester was still expounding his theory of revision.

As Fernol's footsteps sounded down the hall and out the back door, Elliot silently cursed the short, stout, middle-aged Lester for his garrulous tongue. But immediately after the publisher had finished and walked away, Elliot felt grateful, relieved, happy at having been stopped from making any contact with Fernol.

He bought a newspaper and went to the Italian restaurant near Lexington. He had shrimp cocktail, lasagna, peach pie and coffee, and then checked the time. It was five-fifty.

It wouldn't take him more than ten or fifteen minutes to reach Frank Walther's studio (twenty if he strolled), so he had to waste two and a half hours.

He beckoned to the waiter and ordered a double brandy. The bartender was evidently a man of taste and imagination; the liquor arrived in a medium-sized inhaler glass. Elliot smilled his thanks at the waiter and flipped through his newspaper. But he didn't read. He glanced around the nearly empty restaurant, and out the window into the darkening street, and inhaled the brandy's fragrance. He lit a cigarette, and sipped the brandy, and half closed his eyes.

He thought of his mother.

He'd written a strong letter this time, stating that he just ouldn't allow her to come to New York because the trip vould be too much for her. He stressed the fact that flying vas about the only way a woman in her delicate state of health could travel three thousand miles—and she absolutely refused to fly, was terrified of air travel.

He finished the brandy, feeling the warmth spreading from his stomach throughout his body, and then hoped it wouldn't give him heartburn. He smiled to himself, thinking Mother was probably healthier than he was. But she always worried about her heart, and kidneys, and blood pressure. Not that she'd ever allowed it to stop her from doing whatever she wanted to do.

His smile faded. Yes, she'd lived her life to the hilt.

It had been different when father was alive. They lived in Philadelphia, where Elliot and his older sister Myra had been born, where Father owned a small luncheonette. They had a red-brick house on a quiet street, and from the time he was first aware of himself to the age of eight, life was a wonderful thing for Elliot. He was good in school, had lots of friends, and loved his family—especially Father. Father was tall and slim, with a high forehead and dark hair and a soft, soft voice. He was a calm, easy-going man who'd been in the United States since the age of four. At twenty-seven, he met the beautiful and voluptuous Reba Klein, a greenhorn fresh off the boat, and fell in love with her. When she showed admiration for his American ways, he decided to press his suit, and Reba accepted. They had their first child, Myra, within ten months of the wedding, and their second, Elliot, a year later. Then Reba called a halt to the childbearing, insisting that two was enough.

Morris Wycoffsky was stunned. He'd envisioned a family of six or seven, and his wife's talk of spending their extra money on summer vacations, automobiles and clothing seemed almost lewd. Yet he loved her and felt that in time she would come around to what he considered the "normal" viewpoint.

When Elliot was eight, his sister Myra died of spinal meningitis, and there was nothing but tears in the once happy house. And when the tears ended, the arguments began. Morris Wycoffsky wanted more children. "We're still young enough to have four or five," he said. "Losing Myra must have made you see how foolish it is to have a small family."

"No," Reba Wycoffsky said coldly. "Losing Myra made me see how foolish it is to have a large family. The more you have, the more work and worry and—and maybe agony like with—" She wept, and Morris walked away.

But he returned to the attack many times in the months that followed, and there was a growing anger in his eyes.

"You've got to realize that I have some rights in this partnership too! At least grant me one more child. I want children—"

His wife had lashed back at him, loud and venomous, sharp and cutting, using both Yiddish and heavily-accented English. "Yes, you want children! That's the only reason you married me! Sure, you make love. Sure, like a cow or horse or pig. With you it's all—how you call it?—all breeding. You do it because you're supposed to, not because you want to." She burst into tears and fled to the bedroom.

Morris followed her, and Elliot, sniveling in fright, followed his father. "Well, what is it all for if not children?" Morris asked quietly.

"For *pleasure!*" she shouted. "That's what!"

"If it was meant for pleasure, God would have given us children another way," Morris Wycoffsky said, eyes blinking angrily.

"Oy, *du bist nisht kein man!*"

Morris Wycoffsky's face flamed. "I'm not a man? You mean you're a dirty—" He stopped himself and walked out of the room.

Elliot hadn't really understood, but he'd formed opinions. Of course, he loved his mother, but from what he was able to make of the discussions, it seemed his father was a calm, quiet, clean man, his mother a passionate, violent, dirty woman. The *dirty* was something he'd learned from older boys; they said men and women doing certain things to each other were dirty. And those certain things were all right when people married and had children. So if Mother wanted to do things and not have children, she was dirty, like Father had called her.

He never got the chance to change those opinions.

Morris Wycoffsky caught cold. He went to work with his cold, and at the end of the week had developed aches, pains and a raging fever. Two weeks after that, he died of pneumonia.

Elliot mourned with a depth of pain and misery almost unbearable. Reba Wycoffsky suffered too, mostly from feelings of guilt. She tossed in her bed at night, remembering the arguments, remembering her cruel remarks.

Her guilt, however, soon grew dim and she began to toss in her bed for entirely different reasons. She began dating and bringing her men friends home. She took her pleasure when she wanted it, whether Elliot was expected shortly or not. As a result, Elliot walked in on her and a gentleman friend when he was ten, and it shocked him to the core. But it was only the beginning. Up until his eighteenth birthday (at which time he entered the Marine Corps), he was forever coming home at the wrong time. It got so he was *afraid* to go home. His best friend, Ben, would ask him to sleep over once in a while, and then it was great. They would kid around and talk and laugh and poke each other.

One summer night at Ben's Elliot woke up because he was

thirsty. He went into the bathroom and drank water from the faucet. When he got back into bed, Ben moaned and rolled out of the thin blanket, and Elliot saw that his pajama bottoms had come loose and worked down around his thighs. Suddenly, Elliot's heart was pounding with a terrific excitement. He thought of something, and didn't want to do it because he was sure Ben wouldn't approve, and still felt he had to do it. He moved closer and reached out and stroked his friend's long, firm buttocks. Ben made a throat-clearing sound and flung out an arm. Elliot jerked away. He was ashamed and frightened because he knew it was wrong, knew it was queer. He was fourteen and all his friends, including Ben, were beginning to talk about girls. He wanted to tell them how filthy girls were, but he'd heard of queers, and knew all the guys despised them, and knew he must never let anyone think he was a queer.

He played football and tennis for his high school (overcoming his weight deficiency in football by superior speed and mobility), and made top grades in his studies too. He didn't date much, but attended every big dance, every team social, every affair where people would expect to see him. He didn't sleep over at Ben's any more because that was kid stuff, but he never forgot the tremendous excitement of the moment when he'd touched his friend's body. And yet, he knew he must never go in that direction again.

Shortly before his eighteenth birthday, Elliot convinced his mother it was necessary that he change his name to Wycoff—and that she do the same. A week or so after that, he came home from a movie at 10:00 P.M. He walked out again as soon as he understood what the whispering and rustling of clothing in his mother's bedroom meant. He went around the block about fifteen times, raging inside all the while. And he swore he'd get away from her forever.

Three weeks later, he entered the Marines. His mother came down to the station to see him off, standing on the side while he got into line with twenty-five other boots. He turned to wave to her before boarding the train, and she was gripping her hands together at her breast, crying. For the first time, he saw her as a lonely, aging woman. Pity and love blotted out the rage and revulsion she'd caused him to feel since the death of his father. Pity and love remained from then on, plus a recurrent touch of shame. . . .

"Another drink, sir?" the waiter was saying.

Elliot looked up at the man, and then around the small restaurant. The other tables were empty. "I'm sorry," he said, and reached for his wallet.

He paid the bill and left, walking slowly toward Times Square. He glanced in shop windows, entered a bookstore and browsed, and kept checking his watch. At eight-ten, he started for Forty-fifth Street. He timed himself perfectly and reached the address at eight-thirty on the dot. It was a narrow, three-story building set between two larger buildings. He climbed a long flight of stairs past a door which read, "Mongrim Novelties," and up to the third floor. The door there read, "Do-Right Photography Agency," and six names followed, including Frank Walther's. Elliot opened the door and walked into a huge, bare room with whitewashed walls and a very high ceiling. Frank Walther shouted at him from a corner far to the left, "Hey, boy, me and Harry got everything cleared away. Stow your hat and coat in the dressing room; and you can help us set up chairs and stuff."

Elliot looked to his right and saw the door with center-section of wooden slats. He opened it and stepped into a theatrical-type dressing room with a long, light-bulb-rimmed mirror faced by four chairs, and a Chinese screen cutting off the back third of the room. As he hung his hat and coat on one of several hooks lining the wall just inside the door, a woman's voice said, "That you, Frank, honey?"

He turned to the screen—and a nude woman walked around it. She smiled at him and said, "Oh, you must be Frank's friend Elliot. I'm Marsha Wiley. I do a specialty dance."

Elliot nodded, started and his eyes jumped over her. She was about six four or five and very solidly fleshed. On second look, he realized she wasn't entirely nude; she wore a flesh-colored G-string and cheesecloth bra.

She smiled again. "You'll help me with my costume later, honey."

Elliot said, "Yes," and a sinking feeling invaded his stomach. She—she was just too much woman! And there would be others.

He began to feel ill.

The stripper smiled even wider, misinterpreting his reaction. "Mustn't touch the goods, baby." She turned, twitching her big hips provocatively. "Tell Frank to send me in another Scotch, will you, honey?"

Elliot left the dressing room. "The girl wants another Scotch," he told Frank Walther.

"Sure," Frank said, shoving a washtub full of ice-cubes into the corner. "Grab one of the bottles from the table there and mix her—"

A short, balding man with olive complexion and small, bright eyes came out from behind a partition Elliot had mistaken for the far wall. "I'll handle the chore, men." He introduced himself as Harry Ballam, mixed four drinks (ten-ounce highball glasses three-quarters full of Scotch, and the rest ice), and carried two into the dressing room.

"Hey," Frank Walther bellowed, "Don't you go trying to pinch Marsha's ass, you horny little bastard. She's liable to get insulted and walk out on us. Besides, we got work—" The dressing-room door slammed shut. He shrugged. "She'll toss him out anyway." He raised his glass and Elliot did the same. "Chug-a-lug, man, so we can really throw this party into shape!"

Elliot decided he might as well.

They drank down the six or seven ounces of straight Scotch and wheezed for breath. "Man, man," Frank Walther said, "now I could go in that dressing room and chase Marsha around myself."

Elliot laughed, and found he couldn't stop, and they both laughed for a good five minutes. The room was shifting and changing shape in Elliot's eyes as he began to shove chairs and tables around according to Frank Walther's directions.

The guests began arriving two drinks later, and Frank led Elliot into the overcrowded, overheated dressing room. There were five girls present now, all in various stages of undress. Elliot blinked in the terrific brightness cast by two ceiling fixtures and the mirror's forty-odd bulbs. He finished his fourth huge Scotch and bumped into a woman completely nude except for some sort of sequined fig leaf.

"I'm terribly sorry," he mumbled.

"Now listen, Frank," the girl said, turning to Frank Walther who was sitting on a stool and sipping a highball. "You guys gotta help us get ready. All this drinkin'—"

Walther shoved his glass into her hand. She shrugged.

Elliot next found himself behind the Chinese screen with the huge stripper, Marsha Wiley. "Miss Wiley," he said, bowing gravely. "How do you do. Did I tell you I'm in publishing?"

"No. But just hook up these feathers like I asked you. C'mon, honey, those boys outside are howling for action!"

He was on his knees, his face only inches from her big, powdered buttocks, trying to hook together two ends of a feathered waistpiece. And drunk as he was, revulsion climbed in him.

He didn't want to feel revulsion. All those men out there—hammering on the door, begging to be allowed to help, dying to get in here where they could see and touch the strip teasers and sex entertainers—all of them considered him blessed with extreme good fortune.

But revulsion wouldn't be denied. He couldn't stand the naked bottom so close to his face, the heavy, pink thighs, the smell of damp, powdered flesh which filled the sweltering little room, the women's laughter and shrill commands and casual reprimands—"You got a dozen hands, honey, but I gotta do a show—"

He finally got the hooks together and lurched to his feet. The stripper turned and grabbed him. "Here's something for nothing." She kissed him on the lips. "Publishing, eh?" she murmured, fluffing up her feathers and hooking on a gaudy blouse-thing. "You hear Frank's getting me into *Playboy*? If your company's got any good magazines—"

He was trying to wipe the taste and smell of her from his face with a handkerchief, and began explaining that he dealt with hard-cover books. But then she was gone and he was wrapping a nude little blonde in gauze bandages, starting at her neck. "I'm a mummy," she said, her voice a baby whine. "I get unwrapped by the guest of honor and then I throw my arms around him and try to get him to do it right there in front of everyone." She giggled.

Elliot kept wrapping, his hands numb, his face numb, his brain numb but not numb enough. "Not really?" he mumbled. "You're so young—"

"If he don't do it, I get someone else. If you want, it can be you. I gotta get someone out there, or no payday. How about standing by just in case—"

He kept wrapping, and felt nausea rising in his throat. "Pigs," he muttered. "Lousy, dirty, filthy—"

"What?" the blonde asked.

"Nothing," he said.

"Whad'ya mean, nothing? You say something about me. You said lousy and dirty." Her voice was rising. "Just because I ask you—"

"It wasn't that," he said, trying to clear his mind. He turned her around so he could swathe her buttocks with gauze.

"Yeah? Well I heard you—"

"So you heard me," he said thickly. "So the Whore of Babylon heard me. So shut up."

She made a hissing sound and, bending suddenly, thrust her bottom at his face. He straightened, spun her around, slapped her face. She gasped and twisted away, arms pinned by the gauze. "Frank! This lousy square slapped—"

Frank was there, and another girl, and they were all talking, and Frank's thick face came close, saying, "What kinda guy—"

Elliot couldn't see or hear or think too well, but he was afraid Frank was going to say something, and he had to stop him. There were the lights and smells and people—the naked filthy lecherous women—and the walls curling and the mouth moving, saying "What kinda guy—"

He saw Frank Walther clearly for an instant. He reached out and grabbed him and his voice was deep and his hands were strong and he said, "Listen, Frank, you sonofabitch, you've shot off your fuckin' mouth too damn much!" And he swung and felt his knuckles sting and heard Frank bellow and then he was down on the floor and Frank was under him and he was swinging, swinging, exulting because by-God-no-one-could-call-him-a-queer-by-God-he-was-a-man - and - belting the-hell-out-of-Frank-Welter-by-Jesus-by-God-he-was-a-regular-feller-and-here-eat-another-fist-sandwich-by-Jesus-by-God—

He saw blood on Frank's face, and then hands had him and he was up and he was moving and he was in the long room with all the people and he heard shouts. For one terrible second he saw the sex-act girl whom he'd wrapped as a mummy and whom he'd slapped and she was pointing at him and he thought she was going to make him do it with her in the middle of the studio and all the men would see that he couldn't, just couldn't. He screamed, "No, I can't, I can't, it's ugly, ugly—"

He was out of the long room and being carried down the long flights of stairs. And then he was alone, sitting on the sidewalk in the darkness. He got up and staggered around and then started fighting the alcohol. It took time, but he found a dark doorway and sat down and began slapping his face and pinching his arms and talking to himself. He staggered into the street and threw up and went back to the doorway and did some more slapping, pinching, and talking. Later he was able to step carefully out of the doorway and brace himself against a lamppost and hail a cab. When he fell into the back seat, the driver began to protest. Elliot took out his wallet and found the ten and gave it to him. "It's yours," he said, speaking slowly, very slowly. "That's double, you know. Just take me home."

The cabby took him home.

Elliot got into his room without waking his aunt and uncle. He undressed and fell into bed and the walls began to fold over him. Just before everything went out, he thought of Alex Fernol and mumbled, "Right, Alex. You're right. No use fooling myself—"

There was a sudden flash of fear then, and he wanted to sit up and argue against Alex and Alex's ways. But it was too late. He was deep in alcoholic sleep.

11

CHARLES AND CLARA MASTON 6-B

They'd just entered the apartment, hands and cheeks still red and cold from the brisk twilight air. Charles kissed her and murmured, "I want no music, reading or erudite conversation tonight, woman. I want you—and food."

Clara laughed, but it wasn't real laughter. She was knotted up inside, tense and nervous and unable to think of anything but the phone call she'd make as soon as Charles left her alone for a moment—went to the bathroom, or downstairs for cigarettes, or asked her to come for a walk (which she'd refuse, telling him to go on without her). Dr. Philips had taken a specimen of her urine a week ago, and told her to call tonight for the results of the rabbit test for pregnancy. So her happiness hung in the balance—a positive report meant life would change and perfect happiness necessarily become imperfect. She and Charles together, alone, constituted the only real joy she'd ever known. She didn't want a child. If she'd had any faith whatsoever that a rational God existed, she'd have tried prayer.

She took off her coat, gave it to Charles who was hanging

his in the bedroom closet, and went to the kitchen to prepare dinner.

Charles decided to shower right after finishing his coffee, and Clara had her moment alone. As soon as she heard the water start hissing, she ran to the bedroom and the telephone standing on a night table. She dialed, and then the doctor was on the wire.

"This is Mrs. Maston," she said softly. "I took—"

"Yes, the pregnancy test. The results were clearly positive. Now, while I haven't treated you before and don't know if you're planning on using an obstetrician during the period of . . ."

He continued to talk, and she continued to hold the handset in the proper position, but she was no longer listening. Her mind was filled with a crying, a wailing out against the trick of fate that had been played on her.

". . . wish you and your husband would drop in for a chat," the doctor was saying.

"Yes," she said, and was surprised that her voice was so steady. "I think that would be wise. You see, we don't want a baby. Perhaps you'll be able to suggest some course of action."

The doctor was silent a moment. "I'm afraid there's no course of action open except having the child, Mrs. Maston."

"But surely there must be something? Injections?"

"Those injections are effective only in cases where menstruation difficulty is due to some cause not connected with pregnancy. They bring on a delayed menstruation; don't do away with an organism already in growth."

She'd used the word "injections" all week to allay panic, but his answer didn't surprise her. Actually, she'd known no such simple method of ending pregnancy existed.

"That leaves me only one alternative, doesn't it, Doctor?"

"I hope you mean having your child and enjoying your role as mother."

"I definitely won't have the child!"

He cleared his throat. "Then there's nothing I can do to help. I still suggest that you drop in—"

"I will. With my husband. Can it be tonight?"

"Yes. Make it eight-thirty. I'll be able to spend some time talking to you then." His voice grew hearty. "You'll see, Mrs. Maston. It won't be long before you'll want that child more than—"

"Eight-thirty will be fine, Doctor," she said, panic bubbling inside, fear and hatred of the world coming alive as it hadn't for almost two years. She wouldn't listen to goody-goody nonsense! She wouldn't be dragged into the squat-and-rock sorororarity that met each clear day in front of apartment houses all over New York City. She had no need of a child; wouldn't bring one into this world of curse and crisis; wouldn't destroy the status quo that had brought her happiness. There was always abortion, and when the doctor saw for himself how strongly she and Charles were set against having a child, perhaps he'd tell them where to go for the illegal operation.

She said goodbye and went back to the living room to wait for Charles.

When he came out of the shower, dressed in the gray towel-robe she'd bought him in October, she burst into tears. It shocked him (and her as well) because he hadn't ever seen her cry. Her hastily prepared speech (in which she'd planned to tell him calmly of her pregnancy and then go on to state that she'd decided on abortion) fled her mind and she flung herself into his arms. "Pregnant!" she gasped. "I'm pregnant! We'll have to find someone to do an abortion—" The tears and heavy sobs made further speech impossible, and she just couldn't bring herself under control.

He got her to sip some bourbon, and a few minutes later she was wiping her eyes and blowing her nose. She took her first look at his face, and was unaccountably hurt by its pallor. When he nodded grimly and said, "You're right, of course. I hope we can find a good surgeon for the job," she was even more hurt.

But then she understood her reaction; knew that she'd wanted him to prove his love for her by revealing some momentary flash of delight at the prospect of being father to her child. And that was asking too much of him; he was all the things that most other men were not, so he couldn't be expected to react as they did.

Her hurt disappeared when he stroked her hair and said, "I want one thing understood right now, Clara. While neither of us wants a child—we've discussed it often enough to know each other's minds—the abortion has to be performed by a competent surgeon; at the least a practicing MD with experience in the field. No back-alley butchers!"

"Yes, Charles. But we're bound to find whoever does it rather distasteful. He'll have to be a—a criminal type. After all, it's against the law and they do it for the money and so—"

"You don't have to tell me that," he interrupted sharply, and then shook his head. "Sorry. What I mean is that we're not going to risk your life."

"I'd rather do that than risk our marriage," she said, holding one of his hands in both of hers, looking up into his face. "I've never loved anyone before you, Charles. I think I'm stating a truth when I say I couldn't love anyone else if you went away."

"I know," he said quietly. "Don't I feel the same way? Now, let's map out a plan of operations."

"We're seeing a doctor in about an hour. Philips on Fourteenth Avenue. He ran the pregnancy test on me. Perhaps if we convince him we have mature reasons for not wanting a child, he'll recommend a reliable abortionist."

Charles's face was grim. "There's no doubt that our reasons are mature, but is the doctor?"

The doctor, a medium-sized balding man of fifty, was mature enough in his approach to their problem. He listened as they took turns describing their backgrounds briefly, and their feelings in detail. (Clara even added something she didn't actually believe, but which she felt the doctor might—that a mixed marriage could only bring confusion into a child's life.) He expressed understanding and sympathy—but his maturity didn't extend to breaking the law.

"Under no circumstances would I recommend an abortion —unless it were legal. Besides, you're in your third month— too late for an abortion, which is a relatively simple process of scraping the uterus. You'd have to wait until your fifth or sixth month, then try to induce labor and create a miscarriage. If that didn't work—and it doesn't most of the time— you'd have to undergo a hysterotomy, a type of Caesarean section. It involves opening the wall of the stomach, opening the uterus and removing the fetus." He looked at them. "Now wouldn't it be simpler to have the child?"

"No," Clara said. "That—hysterotomy doesn't sound too bad."

The doctor shrugged. "About as bad as Caesarean birth."

"No organs removed?" Charles asked quietly.

The doctor shook his head. "If you had a medical reason for needing a hysterotomy, any surgeon, or obstetrician, could do it easily enough. But you have no medical reason. And besides, I don't know any doctors doing illegal operations."

Clara leaned forward in her chair, eyes brimming. "Please, Dr. Philips. Please help us!"

Philips hesitated; then shook his head. "Good Lord, woman, what's the tremendous problem you've built up in your mind! You and your husband are obviously very much in love. A child would bring even more happiness into—"

"No," she said. "It would change things."

"She's right," Charles said. "We've no desire to alter our way of living. Nor do we want to subject a child to the vicious mess of contradictions that American society presents. World society, for that matter." He stood up. "But you probably don't recognize those contradictions."

The doctor leaned back in his chair, looked down at the desk. "You've made me angry, and I feel like saying something sharp and insulting. But that's exactly what you want; exactly what you need to bolster your feelings of martyrdom. Though I'm sure you find plenty of that every day." He raised his eyes to them. "It might surprise you, but I too am hurt by the things I see, the things I read—the vicious contradictions, as you put it. I know that a mixed marriage like yours must heighten sensitivity—"

"We're not asking—"

"You're not asking for sympathy or understanding," the doctor interrupted, and his voice grew sharp. "I know that too. But I'll tell you something else you're not looking for—a means of helping *eliminate* the vicious contradictions! Exactly what have you two done in the fight against prejudice, against stupidity and violence?"

Clara rose to stand beside Charles. They both wore the same weary, cynical, superior smiles. "Thank you, Mr. Anthony," Clara murmured. "How much do we owe you?"

"Ten dollars, including the rabbit test," the doctor said, voice losing its anger. "I know you're both intelligent, sensitive people. I wish I could photograph and present you with copies of the cruel, insulting—yes, *violent* smiles you're throwing at me. I think you would see what a vicious contradiction *that* is."

Clara knew it was due to the shock of the evening's events, but she just had to look at Charles's face. She caught his smile, and it shamed her, and her own smile died. Charles put two fives on the desk and took her arm.

"In the movies," he said, "we'd be chastened, run to the nearest church, pray, and then go home to prepare joyously for our blessed event. But since this isn't a movie, we'll walk out and start looking for an abortionist—good or bad. And instead of being the kindly Dr. Christian, you might very well be the cause of misery and pain."

"All right, Mr. Maston. I'll accept that. Now do me the courtesy of accepting this: I honestly believe that you and your wife can't continue alone, with your present attitude, and remain happy together. I honestly believe that a child would bring you into contact with the world you despise, make you find means of coping with it instead of withdrawing from it. And I honestly believe that would be a good thing—for both you and the world."

Charles stared at the medium-sized, balding, unprepossessing man. Then he shrugged. But Clara had the distinct impression that he was startled, as startled as she was by the doctor's obvious sincerity. Charles led her to the door.

"All right," the doctor suddenly said. "There's a surgeon in Jersey—a man I've never met—who might help you. I'll give you his name and address. From what I've heard, he's a fanatic exponent of legalized abortion on the Norwegian plan. He performs hysterotomies, and charges plenty, but he's not an out-and-out criminal and he *is* competent. I can't let you fall into the hands of some murderous quack—"

Clara felt the tears coming, and this time managed to stop them. "Thank you," she whispered thickly.

Charles put his arm around her shoulders. They returned to their chairs and the doctor began to speak. . . .

They didn't get back to the apartment until nine-thirty. By then, Clara had regained her composure and was ready to face the future with hope.

Charles warmed up the hi-fi record player, selected several sides from the collection that had cost them over three hundred dollars, and then went into the kitchenette. When he came back, Clara straightened on the couch, surprised. He was carrying the almost full bottle of bonded bourbon (it had been almost full for a year), two glasses and a dish of ice cubes.

"Feel the need of a little liquid support?" she asked, smiling.

"Yes. And I'd like you to join me."

Her smile faded at his abrupt manner. "Is the reaction finally setting in? Are you going to cordially dislike me for being so stupid as to allow this mess to develop?"

He placed bottle, glasses and dish on the coffee table, crouched at the phonograph, punched the automatic selector button and quickly lowered the volume as the first strident notes of Gaîté Parisienne rang out. He turned to the couch, sat down, put an ice cube in each glass and poured two liberal shots. He handed one glass to Clara, raised his own, said, "Here's nothing." He drank, emptying the glass with one quick gulp, and immediately poured a double strength refill.

"You didn't answer me," she said quietly, and now she was frightened. "Do you blame me for—"

"I don't blame you for anything. I don't blame me for anything." He emptied his glass again, shuddering slightly. "C'mon," he said, and pushed Clara's glass to her lips. "Drink up. Good for the baby."

She sipped and put her glass on the table. "You're acting like the Hollywood stereotype of man-trying-to-drown-sorrows. Would you prefer I go to bed and leave you to your drinking?" Her voice was quiet, but those damned tears sprang to her eyes again and she said, "Hell!" and started to rise.

"No, no, darling," he said, and pulled her down and against him. He kissed her gently. "I just want to feel—happy, I guess. This business of having you go to an abortionist—" He shrugged and looked at her glass. "You going to drink that?"

"No."

"Mind if I do? Mind if I get slightly pickled tonight? I feel like it. For the first time in years, I feel like it."

She began to answer, but he added quickly, "I won't, if it'll bother you."

She was reassured and shook her head. "I don't mind. Want me to go to bed?"

"You stay right here."

She leaned back, listening to the music and watching him, His eyes had grown brighter, his speech thicker. He finished her drink and shook her ice cube into his glass and poured whisky. He lit a cigarette; then remembered to offer her the pack.

"No, thanks, Charles."

Gaîté Parisienne ended. Lalo's Symphonie Espagnole began, Milstein the soloist.

"Lester would have made jokes about this kind of music," Charles said abruptly. "And inside he'd be thinking it was dangerous, immoral, unnatural—because everybody didn't listen to it all the time. Like popular music. Popular music's all right with Lester. Popular books and popular thought and popular religion. Anything else is crazy. That's the word my dear brother always used—crazy. Not going to church on Sunday was crazy. And when I was sixteen and refused to go, and Mother and Dad couldn't convince me, Lester dragged me out behind the barn and—" He shrugged. "Hell, I whipped him good before leaving for the army. And he wasn't taken because of a bad ear. So who came out on top anyway?"

"You," Clara said.

He jerked his eyes to her, startled, as if only now aware that he wasn't alone.

She touched his hand, glad the subject had switched from their problem. "You've told me how you hated your home as you grew older; how narrow and strict your parents were in all ways. And I know your brother Lester was part of it from an occasional word you've dropped here and there. But you've never really talked about him."

"I talked about him for a solid year, to a psychoanalyst." He poured and drank and lit a third cigarette. "The psychoanalyst wasn't nearly finished with me, but I was finished with him. I met you and I was finished with him. And with Lester."

He leaned over, kissed her, then drew back and shook his head. "Goddam classical music's no good tonight. Goddam swing's what I need. Those old Goodman numbers. But Lester loved 'em too—about the only thing we loved in common—so I stopped loving them. I cut them out of my life completely. Well, maybe not *completely* completely. In that army barracks bag of mine, in the back of the closet, you know—that's where I got a few old Goodman records. Bought them in Chicago, last time I really got drunk. In 1946. February of 1946. Was discharged from the army at Camp McCoy, Wisconsin, and caught a train to Chicago and sat around a hotel room a whole day and looked at the walls and kept saying, 'Well, Charlie old boy, it's time to head back for the old turkey-apple-and-pear farm outside old Washington, Connecticut, and start living again with old Mother and old Dad and dear old brother Lester.' I liked the idea so much that I went out of that hotel room and bought a fifth of whisky and went back to that hotel room and drank the fifth of whisky. That was the last time I really got drunk. And it was the last time I thought of going home."

"I'm glad you didn't go—" she began, but he cut her short.

"Can you see me as a farmer? A churchgoing farmer?"

"What about those records?" she asked. "The Goodman records?"

"Oh, yes. I bought them later the same night I got drunk. I forgot I needed a phonograph. So when I got back to the hotel room, I held them up one at a time and sang the numbers."

She laughed.

He got up and picked the phonograph arm off the *Symphonie Espagnole* and went into the bedroom. She heard him shoving things around in the closet, and then he said, "Sonofabitch! Why do we save all this shit!" She tried to remember when she'd heard him use profanity before. Maybe once or twice, when he'd hurt himself, but never like this.

He came back with a large, flat, brown-paper package, and in a moment was holding a dozen ten-inch records. He took the long-plays off the machine, unceremoniously tossing them on top the hi-fi cabinet, and placed the ten-inch records on the turntable. He pressed the automatic selector and stood up.

"Don't forget to make it seventy-eight rpm's," Clara said.

"Yeah." He crouched and lost his balance and sat down. "Yeah man." He fumbled with the knobs, finally got them set, started to get up, and then lay back full length on the floor. He clasped his hands under his head and crossed his ankles.

Loud, throbbing music filled the room. He sat up, pointed at his wife and said, "Know what this is? 'Sing, Sing, Sing.' That's what it is. Harry James on trumpet. Krupa on drums. Urbie Green on trombone. Stan Getz on tenor sax. And Goodman himself on clarinet. It's good, honey. It's not Beethoven, or even Mozart, but it's good." He grinned foolishly. "Now you see the boorish side of friend hubby."

She wanted to run to him and press her lips to that wonderfully foolish grin. "Boorish? Well, maybe not to my taste any more. But you're not the only one in this family who appreciated good jazz, or swing. I leaned more to Stan Kenton—'Eager Beaver,' 'Artistry in Rhythm,' 'Southern Scandal.' "

Charles reached to the coffee table, poured a half-glass of whisky and leaned back on his elbows, sipping. "Tonight," he said gravely, though far from clearly, "I feel destiny catching up with me. My wife has a fetus growing in her womb—" He looked at her. "How's that for dramatic prose? A fetus growing in her womb. Good. My wife has a fetus growing in her womb, and it is my fetus as well as hers, and if allowed to grow and then emerge into the world, it would drag us into horrors such as Parent-Teachers Associations and Kiddylands and—" He was struck by a thought. "Hey, what would our position be in the PTA—parents or teachers?"

"Both," she said, and wanted him to drop the subject. "You were saying that this little problem of ours has created a desire in you for strong drink, and so you're satisfying it."

"Exactly. Couldn't put it better myself. Couldn't put it nearly so good—or is it well?—because I can't talk so well —or is it good? Well, anyway, I was in Chicago, wasn't I?"

She smothered a laugh. "Yes, darling."

"I was drinking there. And later I bought these records. That's 'Jersey Bounce.'" He turned the volume up until it was blasting. "Man, listen to it. That's good!"

"It's also loud," Clara said. "Mrs. Gorelick will soon be knocking up with a broomstick the way she did when you let the *Pathétique* get out of hand."

"Fuck Mrs. Gorelick," he said, and then stood up, weaving on his feet. "I'm sorry. I didn't mean to say that. I haven't said that since the army."

She laughed. She loved seeing this side of him—this totally new side as far as she was concerned—but she wondered, and worried, at its timing.

"'And the Angels Sing,'" he said, unnecessarily since the vocalist was at that moment singing those exact words. "Ziggy Elman. Great." He looked at her. "I wish I wasn't afraid of having a child."

Her mouth opened and she wanted to say something and there wasn't a thing she could say. All their discussions, all their logic and reasoning, were fresh in both their minds. There was no sense in repeating it.

"I'm drunk," he said, and turned up the volume still higher. He staggered; dropped into the room's one armchair. "I love you and you love me and we don't want change. That's the main thing. Isn't it, honey? Isn't it?"

She got up to lower the blasting music, and as she did the doorbell rang.

"Tell 'em to go away," Charles muttered.

Clara shut the phonograph and went down the foyer. She looked through the peephole and opened the door. The short, fat, aging woman said, "Enough is enough, Mrs. Maston! I can't be expected to have music beating down on my head like a bunch of elephants—"

"What a stupid simile," Charles said from the head of the foyer. Clara glanced back to wave him away, but he was already weaving toward them, talking steadily. "Music doesn't beat down on your head like elephants. Footsteps do. Music beats like waves, see?" He made expansive, flowing motions with his arms. "The waves of sound and waves of water. That makes sense. But what you said—"

Clara forced a smile. "I'm sorry, Mrs. Gorelick. I've already turned it off."

"But I'll turn it on again," Charles said pugnaciously, bumping into Clara and then standing behind her. "I'll play it as loud as I want. It'll do you good, Mrs. Gorelick. Make you understand swing."

"Oh," Mrs. Gorelick said, and turned pitying eyes on Clara. "I see. Well, try to keep him quiet, will you? Maybe some black coffee—"

Suddenly, Charles was enraged. He shoved Clara aside and shouted, "So you're giving us that drunken-goy stuff, now, eh? So you're trying to tell my wife I'm a no-good—"

Mrs. Gorelick was gone; she'd fled to the staircase and was halfway down it.

"That wasn't necessary," Clara said, and closed the door.

They walked back to the living room.

"Sorry," he mumbled. "Sorry for this and sorry for that." His eyes blazed momentarily. "But she was giving you that lousy, patronizing look, that married-to-a-drunken-goy look! The whole damned house acts like I had the plague! How the hell can Jews expect equality if they don't give it to others! How the goddam hell—" The anger drained away and he sank into his chair. "Jews and Christians and Moslems and Hindus and crap. That's it. That's why we're going to see an abortionist."

"Yes," she said. "Exactly."

He held out his arms. She went to him and sat in his lap. Then he said, "Go to sleep, Clara. I'm going to take a cold shower."

"I'll wait."

"No. Make me feel guilty, lousy, unhappy. Go to sleep."

She walked into the bathroom and washed. When she came out, he was still sitting there. She kissed him and said good night and went into the bedroom. As soon as she turned off the light, he came to the doorway.

"So the shower won't wake you," he mumbled, and closed the door.

But the shower didn't start. She heard him go back to the living room; a moment later "Sing, Sing, Sing" was being played on the phonograph, very softly.

She rolled over and shut her eyes. He would live out his moment of agony. He would make peace with himself, and then they would do what was necessary to save their happiness.

The hysterotomy. The knife cutting into her—

She shook off the fear, remembering what Dr. Philips had said about it being no more dangerous than an appendectomy when performed by a qualified medic. And the man they were going to see was an expert.

A living thing destroyed—

She rolled onto her stomach, amazed at herself. But then she accepted the fact that one couldn't live all one's life in a society and remain immune to its religious and ethical homilies.

It would be done. She and Charles would drive out to Jersey this Saturday morning. They would make the arrangements and then, in a few months, a minor operation would remove a major problem.

She fell asleep, the faint notes of a climbing clarinet touching her consciousness. It sounded like an infant wailing in a tunnel. . . .

They left the house at seven-thirty Saturday morning and drove up Flatbush Avenue, over the Manhattan Bridge and down Canal Street. It was a cold day, gray and drizzly, and traffic was very light. But they didn't relax and enjoy the ride. They listened to classical music on WQXR and watched the road and thought their private thoughts.

The radio went dead as they entered the Holland Tunnel, and they were oppressed by the sudden lack of civilized sound. There was only the savage humming of wheels and roaring of engines caught within the tube, and they were afraid they would have to fill this vacuum, brief as it was, with speech.

And, for once in their relationship, there was nothing to say.

The doctor's combination home and office was in Union City, a square, two-story, graystone house with lawn area on all four sides. The street was residential, wide and pleasant, with semi-attached one-family houses, and lawns, and trees.

Charles pulled to the curb. Clara read the shingle hanging

on a pole. "Blaise Cormond, M.D." She looked at Charles. "We're here."

He nodded.

They got out and walked up the concrete path to the door. A black plate with white lettering, fastened behind the door's upper panel of glass, announced that Dr. Cormond's office hours on Saturday were 10:00 A.M. to 1:00 P.M. It was now eight-forty, but that was the way they'd planned it, acting on Dr. Philips' suggestion that they try and catch Cormond when no other patients were present.

Charles pressed a doorbell and chimes sounded inside. A moment later, the door opened and a man wearing a bathrobe blinked at them. "I hope this is an emergency," he said, and his voice suited him perfectly—a small, thin, intense voice for a small, thin, intense man.

"Are you Dr. Cormond?" Charles asked, and now that he was here he wondered how to go about revealing the purpose of his visit. Cormond would probably be as cautious as a smuggler, or dope peddler, or any other criminal.

"Yes, yes," the doctor said impatiently. "What is it?"

"My wife is ill," Charles said. "We went to our neighborhood doctor in Brooklyn, but he wasn't able to help us. When he learned how—how desperate we were, he finally mentioned your name."

"Mentioned my name for what?"

"Can we come inside?"

"Mentioned my name for what?" the doctor repeated, eyes swinging to Clara.

"An operation," Charles said. "I—I don't think we should talk outside this way because it's a delicate thing and my wife is—"

"Your wife is very attractive," Cormond said, emphasizing the word "wife." He smiled thinly. "Come in."

Clara found herself disliking the man. There was something ugly about him, dedicated-believer-in-freedom-of-abortion-on-the-Norwegian-plan or not; there was something of the poolroom character, the slick article, the skin-merchant about him. When he stepped aside to usher them into his consulting room, she caught his eyes at her legs.

They sat down on a leather couch and the doctor perched at the edge of a desk, his bathrobe parting to reveal plum-colored pajamas. "Now, just what kind of operation does your neighborhood physician think your wife needs?"

"Let's get something straight right now," Charles said, dull red moving into his cheeks. "She *is* my wife, and has been for fourteen months. We can have this child if we want to; no problems as to legitimacy, legality, money or anything else. We just don't want it—don't want to change our lives—"

"Child?" Cormond said softly, and he watched as Clara opened her coat. "You mean the operation concerns a child?"

Clara wanted the situation out in the open, but she couldn't seem to do it herself, couldn't tell the doctor she wanted a hysterotomy. She found herself despising Cormond, and wondered if it were some sort of psychological trick a pregnant woman's mind played in a subconscious attempt to thwart an abortionist and save an unborn child. She glanced at Charles, and Charles glanced at her.

The doctor laughed. "This is interesting—though I don't know what's going on. From the way you two act, anyone would think I performed abortions."

"And hysterotomies," Charles murmured, trying to smile.

The doctor got off his desk, walked around behind it and looked out a window. "Who is this doctor who recommended me?"

"Dr. Philips," Charlies replied. "But he didn't recommend you. He merely mentioned that he'd heard rumors—"

"What's his first name?"

"Arnold," Clara said.

"Dr. Arnold Philips, Brooklyn, New York," Cormond muttered, and swung around to face them. "I don't perform illegal operations. Do you understand that?"

Clara paled. "I—we're not trying to make trouble—"

"I don't break the law," Cormond interrupted harshly. "However, I'm going to call this Dr. Arnold Philips and find out just what's going on."

"But we don't want to implicate—"

Cormond ignored her. He took a large, leather-bound directory from his desk and opened it.

"I've got his number," Clara said. "As long as you insist upon calling him, I'll give it to you."

"Thanks," Cormond said dryly. "I believe I'll check on my own, and call the number I find here." A moment later he made a small, satisfied sound. "What was that number you were going to give me?"

She told him.

He nodded. "All right. Just sit tight." He picked up his phone, dialed, then gave the operator Dr. Philips' number. He settled into his swivel chair and sucked his teeth. His eyes strayed to Clara. He smiled at her. "Very nice." He winked at Charles. "I congratulate you."

Charles looked at the floor.

The doctor laughed and began to say something; then spoke into the phone. "Dr. Philips? This is Dr. Blaise Cormond in Union City. A young couple—" He glanced inquiringly at Clara, and she quickly gave their names. "Charles and Clara Madison—or Maston—yes, Maston. They came to see me and said you'd recommended my services. They want me to perform a delicate piece of surgery. Now, Doctor, are these people legitimately in need of surgery, and are they in a position to protect themselves—" He stopped and listened. "I see. Married, and solvent, and with intellectual instead of social reasons for wanting surgery. Thank you." He listened again, and then laughed. "Really, Doctor? You shouldn't have recommended me if you feel that way." He listened for quite a while. "Of course—you allowed your sympathetic emotions to override your judgment. But doesn't that speak well for me, since your sympathetic—" He stopped and looked at the phone. "Hung up," he said, replacing the handset on the cradle. "A Victorian mentality, and he sends me patients." He shook his head and laughed and his eyes moved over Clara. And though she tried to sneer at herself, she felt dirtied.

"Will you do it?" she asked.

"Well, now, if you mean will I perform a hysterotomy, that depends on whether you're willing to pay my fee."

"Which is?" Charles asked, and couldn't look at the man, couldn't watch him undressing Clara with his eyes.

Cormond leaned back and murmured, "A thousand. That includes ten days to two weeks convalescence—"

"No," Clara said firmly, and stood up. Dr. Philips had warned that abortionists took all they could get, but he'd also said that between four and seven hundred was the sum to be kept in mind. "Four hundred is all we'll pay."

Cormond laughed, and shook his head admiringly. "Smart. Attractive and smart and knows enough not to get stuck with any man's offspring. Leave yourself free for change and advancement, eh? I approve."

Neither she nor Charles answered. They looked at each other and strengthened each other and remembered that they would only have to see the doctor once more—if he took their case.

"Yes, I approve, but I've never done this kind of a Caesarean section for under six hundred, and I don't intend to do so now, even for so attractive—"

"We were told not to pay above four," Clara interrupted sharply.

"You were told wrong. I'll admit I try for a jackpot, but my basic fee is six hundred. After all, this is no simple scraping of the uterus. This is a full-fledged Caesarean—"

"All right," she said, and sat down again. Charles stood up and came around to stand near her at the end of the couch. Together, they faced the doctor. It didn't stop his darting eyes—his sick, compulsively suggestive eyes.

Ten minutes later, they left. Clara glanced back to see the doctor watching her from his window.

They talked a lot on the way home. They were nervous and irritated and—though they didn't admit it—sickened by the interview. But they'd accomplished their purpose. Clara would come to Cormond's office the third Friday in May. She would be operated on early in the morning and spend a week to ten days convalescing in one of the doctor's upstairs rooms—standard hospital rooms where his many legetimate patients recuperated. Then she would be able to travel home, if not to resume teaching. But that was all right since she had accumulated quite a bit of sick leave. She would rest for another two, three weeks, and then it would be finished. Life would be safe again, perfect again.

The farther they got from Dr. Blaise Cormond's office, the better they felt. By the time they reached Koptic Court, they were chatting cheerfully. But then they parked the car and entered the lobby and saw Mrs. Gorelick waiting for the elevator with her husband—a man as short and fat as she, who wore a battered gray fedora winter and summer, covering, no doubt, a bald head.

"Christ," Charles muttered under his breath.

"Hello," Clara said brightly as they walked up to the elderly couple.

Mrs. Gorelick murmured, "Hello," and her husband nodded and stared at Charles. Charles cleared his throat and dug out cigarettes and lit one. Mrs. Gorelick said something in Yiddish to her husband. Charles pressed his lips together in a tight line; he was sure he'd made out his name somewhere in that stream of guttural. Sounded like "drunken Maston goy." He sucked smoke and jetted it through his nostrils and wanted to say something to them, something insulting, something to show he didn't give a damn if they and the rest of the house resented his being gentile and marrying a Jewish girl.

"Where the devil's that elevator?" he said to Clara.

She looked at him, and took his hand. "Kids probably playing around. It'll be along in a minute."

They stood there, tense and nervous, feeling the world's antagonism directed against them.

Mrs. Gorelick said something else to her husband in Yiddish.

Charles looked at Clara.

Clara shook her head slightly and smiled, as if to say it had nothing to do with him. But he didn't believe her.

He reached out and shook the door violently.

"That'll bring it," Clara said quickly.

"Sometimes it makes them spite us and keep it longer," Mrs. Gorelick said.

Her husband looked down at the floor.

Mrs. Gorelick said something else in Yiddish.

Charles drew in breath with a harsh sound.

The elevator arrived and they filed in. Just as the door closed, someone shouted from the lobby, "Hold it, please!"

Charles, who was the last in, tried to shove the door open again, but it was too late. The inside door had already begun to slide shut.

"Say," the man's voice said from the lobby, "that's real considerate of you! Thanks!"

"What the hell does he want me to do," Charles said, voice rising. "Break down the damned—" He shook his head and dragged on his cigarette.

"Silly man, whoever he was," Clara murmured.

The Gorelicks said nothing. They got out at the fifth floor. As the elevator moved upward, Charles heard Mrs. Gorelick's Yiddish begin again.

"Tell me she wasn't saying anything about me *that* time," he said.

"Well, I couldn't make out—"

"And the other times?"

"Nothing. How could she, with me standing there?"

"She can't know you understand Yiddish. Tell me the truth, Clara. I heard my name once—"

"No you didn't!"

"You needn't shout!"

"If you hadn't shouted that night she came to the door, we wouldn't have to worry about her saying things—"

"Then she *did* say something. I knew it. Old idiot! Not that I give a damn—"

The elevator stopped and Clara got out quickly. Charles followed and stepped past her to open the door to their apartment. They walked inside, and then looked at each other.

"I'm sorry," he said. "But you know how those people talk. And anything, even a contemptuous look, is enough to make me want—" He went into the living room, paced the floor, rubbed his hands together.

She watched him, and tension rose in her, and she was afraid. They were alone, and vulnerable, and no one really accepted them, and the world was a rotten place—

"I'll make something good for lunch," she said.

"I'll help you."

"I've got a duck in the refrigerator."

"Let's use that wine-sauce recipe."

"Yes. And put Beethoven's Ninth on the phonograph—not too loud, but not too low either!"

He nodded. They moved toward each other and kissed. They clung together, and the world's stupidities, crudities and animosities receded.

Charles turned on the phonograph, then headed for the kitchen. "Let's start on that duck!"

"Certainly. But don't you think we should take off our coats first?"

He looked at her, and at himself—and she joined in his laughter.

Later, they ate and talked and enjoyed themselves. They were safe as long as they were together, alone. They would keep it that way.

12

BONNIE ALLAN 1-J

Weekends were best. Bonnie wasn't sure what weekends were, but she'd find out when she remembered to ask Mommy or Daddy or Gramma. Once she asked, they'd tell her and she'd know. Meanwhile, she knew it was when Daddy and

Gramma didn't go to work. It came every week and was one day or two days or three days. It was more fun than anything! She played a lot with Daddy, and Gramma took her downstairs and over to the playground on Eighteenth Avenue. Yipes, she went on the swings and jungle bars!

Not the sliding pond. She didn't like the sliding pond. It scared her. Daddy once tried to make her go on it and she screamed and Mommy said, "That's the worst thing to do, Arny! The child will be terrified." Daddy stopped trying to make her go, and wiped her tears, and said he was sorry. He never did try anything like that again.

She still didn't like the sliding pond. When she got bigger —like Gary, who was her friend now and didn't push her any more—when she got big like him and was five years old, then she'd go on the sliding pond.

She was being very quiet in her room because it was early and it was the weekend and Mommy and Daddy slept late. But not Gramma. She got up the same as when she went to work. Sometimes she got up even earlier, if Bonnie went into her room and made a little noise.

Bonnie got her Daffy Duck from the toy chest and kept thinking how nice it would be if Gramma woke up and played with her. Then, feeling like a real bad girl, she pulled the squawking wooden duck out of her room, across the foyer and up to Gramma's door. She opened the door, hesitated, then ran into the room, the pull-toy making a terrific racket on the wooden floor.

Gramma was lying on her stomach, but she rolled over right away. "Hello, angel," she murmured. "You woke your grandma up because you want to play?"

Bonnie suddenly felt terrible. It wasn't nice to wake Gramma. Mommy said Gramma needed her rest. Mommy said Gramma should be treated best of all because she got tired fast.

Bonnie ran to Gramma, tears welling up in her eyes, and said, "I'm sorry, Gramma. Don't tell Mommy. Go to sleep and don't tell Mommy."

But Gramma laughed and hugged her and kissed her, and Bonnie forgot all about feeling bad.

Later, Daddy woke up and there was more fun in bed, more hugging and kissing and some wrestling. She sang one of Daddy's songs, and he kept laughing and laughing until she saw the tears run from his eyes. She stopped singing—"I got a gal who lives on the hill, she won't do it but her sister will"—and asked Daddy why he was crying. He just shook his head and laughed harder, and Bonnie got annoyed and said, "Are you crying, Daddy? Are you laughing? Are you fooling?"

Daddy finally stopped laughing and wiped his eyes. "Sing another song, baby. Sing 'I Wish That I Could Shimmy Like My Sister Kate.'"

"No!" Bonnie said, still annoyed at Daddy's fooling around with laughing and crying. "I won't! You can't make me! Try and make me! I won't!"

Daddy laughed again, and Bonnie got red in the face and jumped out of the bed and ran toward Gramma's room. "Silly Daddy!" she yelled back. "Silly Milly Daddy!"

He kept laughing. She heard him say to Mommy, "God, I wish I could stay home every day just to see her and play with her. How did we ever live without her?"

Mommy said, "I don't know. I only know we couldn't live without her now. I once had a nightmare about her being hit by a car. Arny, it was so awful and I didn't want to live. . . ."

After breakfast, Gramma and Mommy talked about how cloudy it was and how it looked like rain and how there was always lots of rain this late in March with April only a few days away. "April showers bring May flowers," Gramma said. Bonnie started to whimper.

"But I want to go outside, Gramma. I can wear my raincoat. You said we'd go out, Gramma. You promised me! You did!"

Daddy said, "Go on, Mom. Take the kid out. You both look forward to it all week long. And it isn't raining yet."

Gramma said all right, and Mommy got Bonnie's orange raincoat and put the matching sou'wester hat on her head. Then Bonnie turned around like she always did when she wore the raincoat; modeling, it was called. They all laughed and Daddy said, "Just like an old-time sailor. Sing 'Row, Row, Row Your Boat,' sugar."

"No," Bonnie said, remembering she was angry at Daddy. "You can't make me."

"Hey," Daddy said, not laughing any more. "You've been mean to me all morning. Just for that I won't take you to the Prospect Park zoo."

"Row, row, row your boat," Bonnie sang.

Mommy and Daddy and Gramma laughed all the way to the end. Bonnie laughed too, because she was glad with Daddy again and it was the weekend and she was going to the playground and zoo and maybe for a ride in the car.

Bonnie and Gramma left the apartment and walked past the incinerator and across the lobby. Bonnie was all ready to run into the street, but Gramma said, "Oh, my, it's starting to rain, angel."

Bonnie looked, and her full little lower lip began to tremble and the tears spilled from her eyes. She took a huge, shuddering breath and then wailed her disappointment, her grief at being deprived of fun outside with Gramma. It—it was just so mean and—and *spitting!* (She'd learned to spit from a bad little girl last summer, and Mommy had said spitting was worse than anything. So it became Bonnie's curse word.)

"Ah, don't cry, angel," Gramma said, getting down and hugging her and then wiping her tears with a tissue. "We'll go out anyway. It's just a drizzle. I'll get your daddy's big umbrella and it'll cover both of us and even if it rains harder you'll be fine with your raincoat and that umbrella. All right? Happy?"

Bonnie jumped up and down and yelled, "Yipes! Yipes! Yipes!" And then she fell down and made believe she was dead. Gramma told her to get off the lobby floor, and went back to the apartment for the umbrella.

Just then, Gary came out of his apartment at the other end of the ground floor, over near where the man with the black skin who Mommy said was just-like-you-and-me lived. Gary was bigger than Bonnie, and a year older, and her good friend now that he was afraid to push her because she punched hard. He was wearing his raincoat, like hers only it was blue and had a hood. "I'm going outside," he said, coming to a stop in front of her and putting a finger in a nostril. "I'm going to watch the painters in the house around the corner."

"I'm waiting for my Gramma," Bonnie said, but suddenly she wanted to see the painters in the house around the corner more than anything in the world! "I'm going to the playground."

"Aw, that's crazy. It's raining."

"Well, anyway—"

"C'mon to watch the painters," Gary said, and struggled with the lobby door. "C'mon, they used red yesterday."

"You don't know colors," Bonnie replied haughtily, and followed him out the door. "You say everything's red. I know colors. I'll tell the color."

"I do so know colors!" Gary shouted, and then broke

into a run and left her behind. "Baby, baby, stick your head in gravy!"

"I'll punch you like my daddy showed me!" Bonnie shouted, running after him. "Better not say it, Gary."

Gary took heed of the warning, and slowed down and waited for her. They turned the corner at a more sedate pace and walked toward the apartment house a third of the way down toward Sixteenth Avenue. They discussed television.

"Tinker stinks," Gary snorted. "He's for babies. I like cowboys."

"He is not for babies!" Bonnie countered. "Cowboys shoot people and my Mommy says that's crazy. Tinker's kind, and gentle to animals, and he loves children."

Gary didn't have time to answer. They'd reached the apartment house. They walked to the lobby doors and looked inside. Men in spotted white coveralls were painting the walls.

"Let's go inside," Gary said, and pushed open the door.

Bonnie never thought of Gramma. She followed Gary and they moved to an out-of-the-way corner and stood watching.

"See, Bonnie? Red."

"Silly Milly Gary! That's not red. That's like white, only with something else in it. Brown, maybe. . . ."

Later, she and Gary came outside and it wasn't raining. He said, "Race you," and ran toward Sixteenth Avenue and the big, wonderful school where Mommy said Bonnie would start going soon—when she was five and half. Bonnie kept her eyes on the red-brick building and ran as hard as she could and told herself she was as good a runner as Gary because a girl who was going to start kindergarten in a big, wonderful school had to be a good runner. But she couldn't catch him and she got a stitch in her side and stopped and leaned against a tree.

"Ooh!" she said. "I'm not running any more!"

As Gary went around the corner and disappeared, Bonnie heard a voice. It came from Fifteenth Avenue, and she turned to look. It sounded like Daddy calling her. Only this was yelling loud out on the street, and Daddy never did that.

"Bonnie! Bonnie, where are you? Bonnie! Bonnie!"

And then she saw that it was Daddy. He was running on Fifteenth Avenue, across Fifty-sixth Street. "I'm here," she shouted, loud as she could. But he didn't hear her and kept going and was gone. She started walking toward Fifteenth Avenue, suddenly afraid, suddenly sure she'd done something bad. But she didn't know what.

She began to whimper.

Daddy came back across the intersection. "Bonnie! Bonnie, please answer—"

"I'm here!" she screamed, and began crying. "I'm—here—Daddy—Daddy—"

He turned, and saw her, and ran to her. He swept her up and said, "Thank you, God. Thank you." He hugged her and she kept crying because she saw how funny his face was—white and shiny-looking and his eyes all jumpy. Not like Daddy at all.

He began to carry her to Fifteenth Avenue, talking fast, his voice shaky. "Do you know how long Grandma and Mommy and I have been looking for you? Do you know, baby? An hour and a half! We thought you'd been kidnapped, or hurt, or—we didn't know what. Do you understand what that means? Do you understand how sick we were? God, God!" Suddenly he stopped and held her out at arms' length and shook her, his face white and angry. "Why did you walk away like that when you knew Grandma was coming out with the umbrella? Why?"

Bonnie cried and cried and Daddy shook her again and said, "Why?"

"Because," Bonnie sobbed. "Because. Gary came and we went to the painters and then he ran to the corner—" She sobbed so hard she couldn't talk any more.

Daddy's face lost the white, angry look. He put her down and they walked around the corner toward the house. Mommy came out of an apartment house across the way. Bonnie cried hard all over again when she saw that Mommy was wearing house-slippers and her long nightgown showed under her coat and she had the same white look Daddy'd had. Daddy called, "Sally. Here—" Mommy ran across the street, grabbed Bonnie and began hugging and kissing her.

"You were only lost, weren't you, baby," Mommy said, tears running down her cheeks. "Only lost, and we thought such terrible things—"

Gramma came out of a two-family house across the street and Daddy called her. Gramma saw Bonnie, then went back to the two-family house and sat down fast on the stone steps. Bonnie couldn't do anything but cry. Daddy and Mommy and Gramma—all acting so—so crazy!

Daddy went across the street and Gramma leaned on him as they came back. Gramma didn't take Bonnie, but she reached out and touched her face, once, with a trembling hand, and said, "Ah, angel. I thought I'd finished us all. I'll never leave you alone like that again—"

"Don't say that, Mom!" Daddy yelled. "It wasn't your leaving her. She should know better than to wander off for an hour and a half. Getting lost—"

"I wasn't lost! I was with Gary. You were lost!" She squirmed out of Mommy's arms and started running away. But Daddy caught her and picked her up roughly, hurting her arms.

"So you want to give us more trouble!" he said, and smacked her one, two, three times on the bottom.

She'd never been hit that hard before, and it stunned her, and she threw up whatever was in her stomach.

Then Mommy and Gramma had her and they all went inside.

She cried a long, long time. Mommy and Gramma comforted her, but Daddy stayed away. He kept walking around the apartment, smoking cigarettes and breathing hard.

Later, when she was sitting in her rocking chair, watching TV in the living room, he came over and said, "I'm sorry if I hurt you, Bonnie. But you were a bad girl. You must remember never to walk away without telling us." He kneeled down and rubbed his cheek against hers. She kept watching the cartoons. "Want to kiss and make up?" he asked.

"Sure," she said, and kissed him fast so she wouldn't miss what Crazy Cat was doing with the big fish.

Daddy hugged her and got in the way of the television and she said, "Daddy! I'm watching! Go 'way!"

He laughed, and she wanted to laugh back at him, but yipes, that fish was a whale and Crazy Cat was getting swallowed up!

13

JOE AND PAULA THECK 4-B

Paula didn't see the Hogan's bread man the remainder of that last week in March. She heard him in the hall Wednesday, Thursday and Friday mornings, and he rang her bell each time before leaving the floor (and even returned Friday a half-hour later to ring again), but she was going to let him stew awhile. During the fifteen or twenty minutes he'd be moving around and talking to other customers near her door, she would sit in the armchair facing the foyer, telling herself he was suffering doubt and desire and that she was enjoying it. But her stomach would twist and cold perspiration trickle down her sides. God, she hated him!

Saturday morning was gray, cloudy and rainy, but the weather forecast said it would clear later, and Paula felt she just had to get out of the apartment. Joe suggested they drive out to Montauk Point to stroll around the lighthouse, watch the breakers roll in, and breathe the clean sea air. There were hardly any people out there this time of year, he said, and it would be a pleasant change.

She was finishing her breakfast, and jumped up from the table with childish enthusiasm. "Yes, Joe! What a wonderful idea! Then we can eat out at a nice restaurant. It'll be such fun! How did you ever think of it?"

He grinned and caught her about the waist and lifted her off the floor. "Guess I'm just a genius. Who else could think of driving to Montauk? Now, a plain guy might think of movies, or plays, or bowling, but we geniuses—"

"Shut up, idiot," she said, the laughter rising in her throat.

They grinned at each other, and it was good. He lowered her slowly, gently, and ran his lips across her cheek and down to her neck. She stroked his thick, muscular arms, looked into his soft brown eyes. "Joe, I love you so very much. Please remember that."

He kept his lips against her neck. "Why can't it always be this way," he murmured. "It used to be, remember?"

She nodded, almost sleepily, lulled by the gentleness of his arms and lips and voice.

"I know you've been through a lot, Paula. And I understand how you feel. Honest I do. I've never talked much about it, but I've run into anti-Semitism and—well, I got sick about it and angry—"

"Let's not discuss it any more," she said, pulling away from him. "It'll all work out." She thought of the bread man, Walter Smith, and felt her happiness evaporating, her fear and hate returning. "You'll see. It'll all work out, soon."

They went to Montauk, and the skies cleared. It was surprisingly cold at the Point, and surprisingly free of people. They walked along the deserted beach, picking up multicolored pebbles and skimming them across the crashing surf.

They found a narrow dirt path leading up and around the
steep hill on which the lighthouse stood, and set off to ex-
plore it.

As they turned a corner, they found themselves facing a
group of soldiers from the nearby fort. There were seven of
the eighteen- and nineteen-year-olds, hair clipped almost to
scalps, uniforms rumpled (they'd unbuttoned their coats and
jackets and loosened their ties). Joe and Paula stepped to the
right of the path, pressing against the rising dirt siding as the
soldiers advanced. To the left was a hundred-foot drop to a
boulder-strewn beach.

The soldiers were a noisy bunch. Several were drinking
from quart bottles of beer, one held a pint of whisky, and all
stared openly at Paula. Two Pfc's—the leaders of the single-
file group advancing along the narrow path—paused only a
second before resuming their conversation.

"I say Cleveland will take the fuckin' pennant. Lousy Yanks
got no real pitching—just a lot of lucky, no-stuff farts. Wait'll
the season starts."

"Yeah? You must be the stupidest sonofabitch—"

"Hey," Joe said. "Can't you guys see there's a lady around?
Hold it down, will ya?"

Paula was suddenly terrified. Joe shouldn't have said that!
They were alone with these drunken, uniformed *goyim* (she
had immediately classified them all as non-Jews; probably Germans, Poles, and other violent types), and now Joe
had antagonized them. She pressed close to him, whimpering
under her breath.

But the soldiers quieted. They filed past, glancing at her,
several throwing Joe challenging looks. The last in line, a tall,
slim yardbird, muttered, "I'll say whatever the fuck I want."

Joe laughed, a surprisingly insulting sound. "Sonny, you
sure got lousy upbringing wherever you come from. Back in
forty-three, we made latrine generals out of guys like you.
And if you want to argue the point—"

The yardbird followed his comrades around the turn and
out of sight. Only then did the group answer Joe—with a
series of long, low whistles and shouted quips.

"See the shape on the big blonde?"

"Lucky civilian!"

"Like a brick shithouse!"

"And to think I gotta bunk with you, Jonesy!"

"Now why don't we find a few dames—"

"Yeah, why'n't we hitch a ride—"

Paula glanced up to see that Joe was grinning.

"What's the matter?" he asked, sobering quickly as he saw her face. "You weren't really afraid of those GIs, were you, honey?"

She shook her head. "Can we go now, Joe? I—I'm hungry. Let's eat some place back toward the city. It's getting late anyway. It'll take three or four hours to get home. Let's start now, please, Joe?"

"Sure," he said, and led her back toward the road and the parking lot. "They were a little high and wanted to show off for you. Maybe they overdid the man talk, but hell, I was the same way during the war. Fact is, they were almost gentlemen compared to how we acted in Wisconsin and Texas. And overseas! I'll never forget the night we—"

"All right," she said, wanting to forget the whole thing. She was still afraid. And it was suddenly clear that there wasn't a place in the world where she wouldn't be afraid.

By the time they got back to the car, she was shivering. Joe helped her into a heavy sweater, and then pulled out of the lot.

"Tell you what," he said. "I'll take a week of my vacation right away instead of during August."

She looked at him. "What?"

"A week of my vacation right away."

"But—but we planned two weeks of travel up into Canada—"

He kept his eyes on the road. "We'll do that another summer. I can call the foreman, Hal Sherwood, at his home. I can get the week starting this Monday."

"But why, Joe?"

"You need a complete rest, baby, and you need it now. We'll try a cabin up in Vermont—where my Cousin Adele stayed last October. No people; plenty of fishing, hiking and boating."

"It'll be so cold—"

"The place is heated. And I'll show you how good I can cook."

She laughed briefly, feeling it was expected of her.

"Well, at least breakfasts," he said.

She was silent a moment; then turned to him. "But—but how can going away help me if my sickness is realizing the truth? If I were afraid of riding in cars, or hated my dead father, or wanted to kill you, I could see some good in a rest cure and doctors and anything else you had in mind. But knowing that Germans and people like that hate us, that they killed millions of us, is *fact*."

"Only part of it is fact," he said quickly, as if he'd been preparing his answer for quite a while. "You always mix the truth with your bad dreams. That's what makes it so tough to —to straighten out. The Nazis killed the Jews. That's fact. They also killed Poles and Danes and Swedes and Norwegians and Frenchmen and Russians. They even killed Italians, their allies. They were nuts. They killed everyone who didn't fit in with their ideas. But they're gone. Nazi Germany is gone, right?"

"The leaders are gone—"

"The damned country is gone! Nazi Germany is gone! I oughta know—I helped kick the shit out of it!"

"All right," she said. "Don't shout."

He took a deep breath. "Sorry. But—well, they're gone. I know all the arguments you can give me, but—just this once, let me go on."

"Certainly." And for a second she almost hoped he could come up with some miraculous argument that would convince her. But in the next second she knew he couldn't; no one could.

"Okay," he said. "The Nazis killed Jews. Some Poles, like collaborationists in all the conquered countries, helped them. And some Poles, and other Europeans, had a bad record on their own before the Nazis came—were rough on Jews. But to say that all Germans were and are murderers, and the same for Poles and others, is wrong. And to say that Americans of German and Polish descent—and whatever others you pick—hate Jews and want to kill them, is also wrong."

She was surprised, but not impressed, by his loquacity. "You must have been thinking of this a long time."

"I've been *living* with it a long time."

"All right. I suppose that now the Germans are blameless, and all those in this country—of German descent, if you want to put it that way—are without hate for Jews?"

"I didn't say that. There are Nazis who got away and probably still think like Hitler taught them; and there are others who should have been shot who were given jail sentences; and more released from jail who should've been kept locked up for life. There are people in this country who would like to push us around; maybe some who want to destroy us. But—" here he reached out with one hand and gripped her thigh— "but this is the important point: Most people—Germans or

Poles or Italians or Russians or pick-'em—most people don't
spend their time hating anything or anyone. They're too busy
raising families, working, having fun, solving personal problems—you know, *living*. It's only a small minority that hates
strong, and they hate in lots of directions: Jews, Negroes,
Catholics, Protestants, rich people, poor people—anyone who
is what they're *not*. The only people who hate strong are *sick*
people, fanatics, and there aren't enough of them to worry
about. At least not the way you worry."

"So how do you explain Hitler's Germany?"

He sighed. "Listen, I can't answer everything. There are
books that say Hitler and his group took over because the
Germans were ready to believe anyone who would promise
them jobs and security, and that they didn't know what they
were letting themselves in for, and that by the time they did
see the score it was too late—"

Paula snorted.

Joe shrugged. "Hell, I don't believe that either. But I'd like
to. I'd like to believe anything that would make them look
better. Otherwise, you have to give up on people. I—I just
know that hating is bad—"

"In this case, that's like saying the truth is bad."

He took his hand from her leg and made a little palm-up
gesture of defeat. "Whether you're right or wrong, it makes
no difference, Paula. Hating is sick and I don't want you to be
sick. So I thought we'd go on our vacation—"

"And was the hate Americans felt for the Japanese after
Pearl Harbor a sick thing too? Or was that different—different because it concerns Americans and Americans can do
no wrong?"

He drove a little faster, perspiring as he searched for answers. "It was a sick thing when there was too much of it.
But remember, we were fighting for our lives then. Hate was
just another weapon. We had to hate to win. And it was the
same with our hating the Germans. But that was years and
years ago, and the hate is gone. It's finished, done with, ancient history. Do we hate England for the Revolutionary War,
and Mexico, and Spain? Of course not. The same goes for
the Japs and Germans. Why, we got the Japs into the U.N.
We're friends with them. And you don't ever hear guys who
served in the Pacific talking about the Japs like you talk about
the Germans; not even guys who lost brothers; not even
women who lost husbands and sons."

He turned his head from the road a moment to nod emphatically. "That's what you got to remember, Paula. Normal people don't hold onto hate when it's no use to them. When you got to fight and kill, you hate. When the fighting and killing is over, you got to forget the hate or it'll eat you up. Yeah—"

She leaned back and closed her eyes. She was confused by all the talk, but her hate remained constant. "All right, Joe. Maybe a rest would do me some good right now. I'll admit I haven't been feeling too well."

"Great! It'll be okay with Sherwood, and I'll call the number Adele gave me."

They got home at nine that evening, and within half an hour Joe had arranged to start a week's vacation on Monday and to spend it at the place his Cousin Adele had recommended. Paula called her Aunt Ruth and mother-in-law to say she and Joe were going to leave the next morning, and then they packed. At one o'clock they finished and dragged themselves to bed, exhausted.

Joe fell asleep immediately. Paula began dozing off, and then found herself thanking God that Joe had rushed her into this quick trip. Perhaps by the time they returned she would feel different, stronger, and the plan to destroy Walter Smith would have faded away.

But then she was asleep, and dreaming about her mother, and she screamed, "Germaaan!" She woke up, and sat up, and Joe muttered, "You okay?"

"Yes," she said, and lay down again.

He went back to sleep.

She stared up at the ceiling, wide awake, hating Freilich and those drunken GIs and the bread man and all the world of violent goyim. The hate boiled inside her, and she remembered Joe saying hate was a sickness, and she remembered her own short-lived hope that the vacation would make her forget hate—and it made no difference. She wouldn't change in a week, or a year, or a hundred years! She would never change! She was going to destroy that dirty, grinning, Aryan degenerate, Walter Schmidt. She would!

"On my mother's soul, I swear it," she whispered into the darkness.

After that, she was able to sleep peacefully. . . .

They had a two-room cabin, one of four perched on the side of a hill near a small lake high in the Vermont uplands. The town of Bennington was only twenty minutes away.

The view was breathtaking—thick forest ran from behind their cabin clear to the top of a sizable mountain; and from the nearby highway they could see an entire countryside stretching out—after a precipitous falling away of solid ground—a thousand or more feet below. The tiny lake was the color of lapis-lazuli—a blue so intense toward late afternoon that it didn't seem quite real. The weather was perfect; cold only after sunset. It rained just once in the eight days, and even that took place at night. They had complete privacy—the cabins were more than a hundred feet apart, and the other three were unoccupied.

There was only one thing wrong, and that purely from Paula Theck's point of view. The owners were a tall, heavy, graying man and his wife, a tall, heavy, graying woman. They were named Kurt and Hilda Streiger and lived about three hundred feet from the cabins.

"Germans," Paula had whispered to Joe as soon as they'd left the two-story frame house. "Real back-country Germans. The worst anti-Semites—"

"Why did you let me pay them in advance?" Joe had demanded, stopping. "Do you want me to go back and say we've changed our minds?"

She heard the anger in his voice, and the disappointment, and looked around at the beautiful spot. "No. Of course not. It's lovely, Joe. It's just that I hate the thought of paying Germans for anything."

"Maybe they're Swiss," Joe said. "Maybe they're Austrians. For all we know, they could be Dutch."

"No, I recognized the accent. I'm sure of it."

He turned on his heel and walked toward their cabin, leaving her behind. Then he stopped, waiting for her to catch up. "Can't you understand that this is Vermont, not Prussia or Bavaria? Those people are Americans!"

She forced the smile and nodded. "There's a float in the middle of the lake, Joe. Row me out to it."

Later, as they sat on the float, looking at the fantastic colors of the Vermont sunset, she came to a momentous decision: She wasn't going to speak her mind to Joe any more. If she felt fear or hate, she'd keep it to herself. She didn't want to see the baffled hurt and anger in his eyes; she didn't want to hear him try to argue her out of feelings she knew were logical. Most of all, she didn't want to alienate him any further.

But the decision made her feel terribly alone.

She lay down on the warped wooden slats, threw an arm over her eyes and peeked from behind it at the sunset.

"Beautiful, isn't it?" Joe said. "You forget how nice it is in the country. City people like us get cheated out of a lot of beauty, don't we, Paula?"

"I guess so," she murmured, eyes filled with the dying sun. "But when you're happy, life in the city has beauty too. I remember we used to spend summers near a little town in Bavaria—I don't remember the name but it had the thinnest church steeple you ever saw; like a needle pointing at the sky. And every Sunday a high, almost-tinkling bell would ring from that tower.

"We had a cabin—not like this one; more like a small house—near a deep, deep lake. My father would go down every Sunday morning with his oils and brushes and canvas to paint. Momma would say, 'Don't bother Poppa. He's painting.' She said that word 'painting' like it was some marvelous mystery, and I used to think of Poppa as a kind of Moses on Mount Sinai—talking with God. But I did bother him once in a while because I wanted to be with him. And when I was eight or nine he said something I remembered. He said, 'Paula—'" She stopped, overwhelmed by the sharpness, the poignancy of her memory. She glanced at Joe, embarrassed.

"Go on," he murmured. "You never talk much about your father. It's always your mother. I got to feel that you didn't like him, or that his death was so painful—"

"No, I loved him. And his death was relatively easy. He was shot down in front of our Berlin clothing store for being too slow in obeying a Blackshirt. All the neighborhood Jews were scrubbing the streets on their hands and knees, and my father was slow in wiping some soapsuds off a Blackshirt's boots. So they shot him through the head. My mother saw it all from the shop. I just saw them carry him away."

"Well," Joe said, and cleared his throat. "Well, what about that time down at the Bavarian lake?"

"Yes. We used to go there every June and stay until mid-September. My father came out when he could, but my mother and I lived there about three months each year. We owned the cabin. My mother didn't know what to do after my father was killed, so she packed our things and waited till night and then took a bus to the summer house. We were there when they arrested us and took us to Camp Three. It was 1936. I was thirteen—" Her voice drifted off as the hate surged up. She wasn't going to tell Joe those things any more.

But her mind ranged back to the days and nights of horror.

"What did your father tell you down by the lake?" Joe asked again.

She repeated her father's words, but she was remembering the terrible events following that childhood summer.

" 'Paula,' he said, 'my hobby is painting and I always try to paint beauty. A small talent should always seek great beauty because then it might capture at least a portion of it.' He pointed at the lake. 'That is great beauty—the water and trees and sky; nature's gift to man. So I try to paint it. But the greatest beauty of all, I can't try to paint. Because it's not visible; at least not to my amateurish eye. And it's man's gift to man, something we ourselves create. Do you know what it is?'

"I guessed at trains and cars and wiener-schnitzel dinners. He laughed and shook his head. I said I gave up. 'It's what you and Momma and I have back in our Berlin apartment; what we have here in the summer house; what we have wherever we are. Love and peace and security—that is man's greatest beauty. Love. When that goes, man has nothing though he live in a Garden of Eden.' "

"He was right," Joe said, looking down at her, hoping she'd see the way it applied to her own state of mind. "He must have been a brilliant man."

"He was a kind man," she murmured, eyes turned to the darkening waters but seeing a far darker world of the past. "He talked a lot and wasn't really too good at anything, but he loved us, Momma and me."

"I think we'd better head for shore," Joe said, yawning and stretching.

"Another few minutes," she said, closing her eyes. "So quiet here. . . ."

But she wasn't using the quiet to relax; she was using it as a vacuum into which she could bring all the displaced memories. She remembered the long hours of pure horror following her father's death, when she and her mother had huddled in their apartment above the clothing store, listening to the shouts and laughter of the storm troopers and the screams of friends and neighbors. Toward evening, her mother had begun to pack, not daring to put on a light, weeping softly all the time. Paula had also wept, but something had begun to happen to her then—a sort of dullness began to invade her brain, making it hard for her to see and hear clearly, making it almost impossible for her to remember what had happened to her father.

Somehow, they made their way through the midnight streets to a bus terminal, and her mother paid a uniformed official almost all the money she had, in addition to buying two tickets. Paula remembered the man's wide-mouthed grin and stained teeth. "Yah, now I can see you are a good Aryan, Fraülein. Get aboard!"

They arrived at the summer house about four that morning, unseen, and stayed there three days without once stepping outside. Then Paula's mother was forced to seek food, and walked to the small town. The first person to see her, the Protestant minister named Saurbach (whose church had the needle-like steeple piercing the sky), told her to get back to her cottage because it wasn't safe for Jews in town. Later, he brought food to them.

Paula had feared him at first sight—that tall, cadaverous man with the hollow cheeks and sad eyes who reached out to touch her head. She pulled away, knowing he was a Christian German and so to be feared. She'd learned this lesson very well in the years of her childhood, the years since Hitler first raised his hysterical voice.

Some time later (she had now begun to lose track of time, the dullness protecting her from all sharp edges of reality), a group of boys stoned the cottage, yelling, "*Jude! Jude! Jude!*" Windows smashed as she and her mother huddled in a corner. Her mother wept and trembled, but not Paula—she merely blinked her eyes and waited, the dullness making everything seem far, far away. Poppa's death didn't seem real, and neither did anything that had happened since the children had first started calling her "*Verdammet Jude!*" in school way back when.

The minister came twice more, and then the Blackshirts came. Paula's dullness didn't work too well that day because it was hard not to see one's mother beaten across the breasts by a short, slender sadist with moist eyes, thin lips and delicate hands. The sadist had a weighted rubber blackjack and whipped it in sidelong strokes into Momma's full breasts, mumbling to the two younger, stronger troopers, "Hold her up. Up, I say. Ah, that was a good one! Steady, steady. Ah, that was a good one. . . ."

They rode in a truck, Momma lying unconscious on the floor, Paula kneeling beside her, dull-eyed. Finally they stopped, and it was dark. They got out, two Blackshirts carrying Momma like a sack of potatoes, and Momma began to moan. They moved past guards and an opening in a high, barbed-wire fence and through a yard around which were grouped long barracks. They were shoved at rifle point into one of the barracks. It was pitch-dark, but the guards merely locked the doors and walked away.

Paula dropped to the floor beside her mother and rocked back and forth, back and forth. . . .

The next day they were taken to a different barracks; all women. Momma was treated by a fat man in white shirt and trousers who smeared ointment on her blackened breasts and said, "Will you shut up!" when she cried out through clenched teeth.

Time passed, and Momma got off her pallet and helped Paula survive in the atmosphere of terror, hunger and nightmarish hate. More and more Jews were brought to the camp; and then the prisoners found out the purpose of the new brick building—windowless, square, with two huge metal doors facing the yard and three tall, thick smokestacks. One morning, a list of three hundred names was called. The men and women were lined up in the yard and marched into the brick building. The metal doors clanged shut. The prisoners in the barracks heard screams for quite a while. Then the screams stopped and the tall, thick smokestacks belched blue-gray smoke. That was when Paula's mother began to pray.

"God will save you, my baby," she would say to Paula. "I feel it. I do. I do!"

More time passed, and other prisoners were marched to their deaths, and Paula wondered why she and Momma weren't called. It didn't really make much difference to her now, the protective dullness in her brain was so strong. She didn't really see or hear or feel anything—just shadows of experience, and weak shadows at that.

Perhaps that was why it took her so long to notice the tall Nazi lieutenant who seemed to be around every day when her barracks was allowed out for an hour's walk in the yard. But when she finally did notice him, fear penetrated her dullness. The look in his eyes was terrible, personal, directed at her alone. He would stare at her legs and up along her tall, lissome body and lick his lips and smile to himself and sometimes rub his chin as if wondering about something. Momma began to notice him too, and she prayed ever harder.

But the prayers began to sound frantic, less loving, more hysterical and demanding—and on the day that Freilich tried to drag Paula into one of the offices, Momma cursed God. Paula had broken free of Freilich, and she and Momma ran to the barracks. The Nazi reached for his gun, but then shrugged and said something to a guard. The guard wrote the name, Deborah Stein, on a slip of paper.

A prisoner had seen and heard. When the exercise period was over, he told Deborah Stein to prepare to meet her God. Deborah Stein was Paula's mother; she spat and clenched her fists and raised her face to the ceiling.

"You are not there! I see it now! How can You be there if these things happen! I should have understood this when Hitler first came. And if You are there, then You are cruel and rotten and a maniac—a maniac God of a maniac world! All Jews will begin to see this and soon you will be despised—"

Some men moved forward to try and stop her, but she stopped herself, turning to Paula and clutching her tight and weeping, "No, no, Paula, you mustn't believe that. I am a foolish woman, a selfish woman. There is a God and he is good. All this means something. God will take care of you, I'm certain of it. Believe in Him. Believe in Him. Come, we will pray together. Come, my Paula."

After praying, she began to smile the smile Paula would never forget—a forced, unnatural thing meant to calm her daughter, meant to ease a memory that would soon be formed.

The next morning, Deborah Stein was taken away and destroyed. The afternoon after that, wrapped in numbness approaching a complete withdrawal from the world of reality, Paula was taken to the medical-supply room, hardly larger than a closet, by two grinning guards who patted and pinched her, ran their hands under her dress and across her breasts.

"The lieutenant was right. This one is ready."

"*Gott in Himmel*, if I could be the one to sample the goods—"

"Here he comes across the yard!"

They left and she waited, the world a gray plain. Then the tall, blond man in the black uniform was there, and he penetrated her protective fog, bringing hate and horror into her life. What had happened before—to her mother and father, to her people—suddenly became real and clear, and it was all embodied in this one enemy, this one German, this Lieutenant Freilich. What he did became her symbol of what all Germans had done to all Jews.

He kept her there, pressed down on the couch he'd scented with violet perfume, for what seemed an eternity. When she was allowed to leave, it was dark. "Until tomorrow," he said, and yawned.

But he was disappointed in his plans to use her for an extended period of time. The next morning the commandant himself—a rarely seen, elderly little man with round body and round face who looked completely out of place in his black uniform, but who ran the death camp with exactitude and competence—entered the barracks with a guard and told her to pack her things and come with him.

Paula got off her pallet and picked up a dirty towel in which a few articles were wrapped. They took her to a big, black Mercedes-Benz sedan and told her to get in the back. She obeyed. The guard got behind the wheel. The commandant stood outside and said, "The minister is right. You can see she's Aryan. Those dirty Jews must have kidnaped her when she was a child; taken her from some good German family. Well, the wheels of justice grind slowly, but we Germans don't make mistakes." He didn't look at her once while saying this.

Later, while driving her to the town and the local jail in which she was lodged for two weeks, the guard grinned into the rear-view mirror and said, "He must've got a nice bit of money for springing you. Every time he makes a deal, I have to listen to that speech about the wheels of justice and Jews kidnaping Aryans."

She hadn't understood and hadn't cared. Life was terror, and this was merely another phase of it. Whoever had paid money for her would use her and, sooner or later, destroy her. How else could it be in Germany?

"C'mon, smile a little," the guard said, turning his head briefly. "You're out of it now, kid. I'll buy you a cold soda at the first place—"

She lay down on the seat, curled up her legs, covered her ears with her hands. She didn't know what he was saying. She didn't want to hear his filthy talk. Let him do with her as he pleased. Soon, soon, she would be with Momma.

She stayed in the jail, and then Reverend Saurbach came and took her away. She knew he wanted to do things to her,

but she was lucky and he never got the chance, and somehow she was riding on a train with a strange woman who
showed the conductor papers and said, "My daughter Maria
and I are going to Paris. It's pleasant, but all the red tape
with the French "

The conductor said, "Give the Fuehrer time and you won't
have to bother with the French to visit Paris." He winked
and laughed.

Then she was in Paris where friendly people talked to
her and comforted her. And then she was on a ship.

But it wasn't until she landed in the United States and
was enfolded in her aunt's arms that the tears came and she
was, again, a fully alive individual.

Her Aunt Ruth and Uncle Martin had no children and
were wonderful to her. She went to grammar school, and
Aunt Ruth hired a tutor for evenings and summers, and she
skipped classes rapidly. She went to high school at sixteen
and graduated at twenty. Ruth and Martin would have
sent her to college, but she wanted to work, earn a living,
have some fun. So she went to business school for ten months
and then got a job with a Manhattan dress manufacturer as
secretary-typist. She liked her work, dated many boys, lived
in perfect harmony with her aunt and uncle.

In 1952, at the age of twenty-nine, she met Joe Theck at
a party given by a married friend. He took her home, was
full of fun and confidence, and kissed her in his car a half-
dozen times before she fled upstairs. He called her the next
night, came over and took her for a ride. He talked about
his work as a mechanic for the city bus lines; then suggested
they go to Coney for hot dogs. She said okay, and on the
way back he parked in a deserted spot near Tilden High
School. They petted, and she felt every bit of resistance
flowing out of her. She couldn't believe it; except for the
brutal rape by Freilich, she had never allowed any man to
make love to her, or to get nearly as far as Joe Theck had.
But then again, never had any man seemed so kind and
happy and strong and attractive as Joe Theck.

She begged him to take her home, but when he complied
she couldn't resist inviting him upstairs to the apartment.
Ruth and Martin were in bed, fast asleep, and Paula made
coffee and sandwiches. They ate, and then he got up and
took her in his arms. A moment later, she knew she wouldn't
be able to stop him. An hour later, getting off the couch
and arranging her clothing, she knew she loved him. They

returned to the kitchen and didn't look at each other and he said, "Well, I guess I'll be going."

She nodded. "Good night, Joe."

"Yeah. Good night, Paula."

He left. She went to bed and wondered what would happen.

He didn't call for a week. When he did, he said he was in a candy store just a block from her place and would she please come down. She said all right, and by the time she'd reached the street he was parked at the curb. She got into the car, expecting him to pull away, but he just sat there. Finally, she said, "What's the matter, Joe?"

"I think I—" he began, and then rubbed his big hands together. "Listen, Paula, I want to know something. Do you really like me? I mean, *really*."

She laughed. "Oh, I see. You're trying to find out if I sleep with everyone or just with you."

He was obviously shocked. "I never meant that! And you shouldn't say such things!"

She laughed again, beginning to feel wonderfully happy. He cared for her! She could see it, feel it! "I really like you, Joe. That answers the question you asked. And I never slept with any man before. That answers the question you didn't ask."

They talked a long time, and then he came upstairs and met her relatives and stayed until after twelve. They dated steady from then on, and ten months later were married.

Life had been good. Love had been good. . . .

"We'd better get back to shore," Joe said, standing above her. "Hey, Paula, you listening to me?"

She looked at him; then accepted his hand and stood up. He pulled her close, kissed her ear. "I've got that vacation feeling already—"

She twisted away. "Really, Joe. I'm chilled to the bone."

He turned to the boat—quickly, angrily.

A few days later, they drove into town. Walking past a shop Paula caught a whiff of violet. She thought of the couch in Camp Three, and Freilich, and then of Walter Smith.

That night, sitting outside the cabin, she said, "I'll be glad to get home."

Joe glanced at her. "This is the first time I can remember your wanting a vacation to be over."

"It's not that, exactly. It's just—" She shrugged. How could she tell him? How could she explain wanting to get on with a man's destruction?

They arrived home on a wet, windy afternoon. Paula felt better despite her thoughts of Walter Smith. She decided to try avoiding him, and to try avoiding thoughts of Freilich and her past.

Joe was right.

God, he had to be right!

14

LUKE BROWN 1-A

Luke knew the hot-water boiler was going to fail. He just knew it. Hadn't he told Cora at least a dozen times in the last few months? Hadn't he? "It's gonna go cold just as sure as I'm standin' here," he told her.

She'd shrugged like he was some kind of worry-head old woman. But it failed. The end of March, it failed.

He came up from the basement at seven-thirty that morning and told her about it as he dialed Mr. Gorman's number. "I told you, didn't I?" he said. "Didn't I?"

She laughed. "Yes, you sure did. Six months ago, and ever since."

"Well—" He stopped short as Mr. Gorman's voice, sleepy and irritable answered.

"Sorry to bother you, Mr. Gorman," Luke said, speaking as clearly as he could, " but that hot-water boiler went. Yes, just went cold, so I figured the fuel line—" He stopped and listened. "Thank you, sir. I sure hope that man gets here quicker than the one last time. That one didn't come till almost six and all the tenants—" He listened. "Thank you. Goodbye." He turned to Cora, rubbing his face like he always did when he was worried. "Men gettin' ready for work about now. Watch. Just watch. The calls'll be comin' in any minute. I gotta post a notice on the elevator door. I sure hope no one thinks—" He stopped and rubbed his face again.

Cora didn't say anything. She felt a little guilty for having laughed at him before. But she knew there was nothing she could say to make him feel better. A boiler failure was like a death to Luke Brown. What could a body say or do about a death?

No hot water—period. Nothing Luke Brown could do. No hot water.

The doorbell rang. Luke sighed and walked down the foyer, slower than usual.

"Say, Mr. Brown!" the heavy-set, redheaded man said belligerently. He was wearing trousers, an undershirt and house-slippers. "What's going on? The water's—"

"Yes, Mr. Rosner, I know," Luke said, smiling sadly. "I know. Nothin' I can do for the moment. Nothin'. We're getting a repairman down here real soon."

Mr. Rosner waved his hands. "Yeah, but meanwhile I can't shave and my wife can't wash Gary—" He shrugged, made a snorting sound and muttered, "Hafta boil water—" He turned to his doorway. He was Luke's next-door neighbor on the east (on the west were mailboxes, window and wall).

Luke sighed. Other tenants, from other apartments and other floors, should be coming in a little while. . . .

They came, all right. They came all morning, irritated people making their complaints and expecting Luke to work miracles. By noon, he was so upset he couldn't eat his lunch. He kept working around the basement and lobby, waiting for the repairman.

At two-thirty, he called Mr. Gorman. Mr. Gorman told him to calm down, that the repairman would come as soon as he could. After hanging up, Luke turned to Cora and said, "He ain't doin' this right, Cora. First time in all the years I been here, but he ain't doin' it right! He's hirin' some cheap guy, I bet. That's why we're not gettin' quick service."

Cora was surprised. "He wouldn't do that, Luke."

Luke walked down the foyer. He rubbed his face. "Well, maybe I'm wrong. Sure wish that man would get here. . . ."

The repairman didn't come until four ten. He was a short, stout Negro. Luke stared at him as they went down to the basement. "You work by yourself?" he asked.

The short, stout man nodded. "Yup. Nice house here? Folks treat you good?"

"The best," Luke said. He rubbed his face as they approached the defective boiler. "You sure you can fix it up? It's a bad feed line from the oil supply—"

"Man, that's the simplest job in the world. Ah, here we are. Need more light—" He stopped suddenly as movement in a nearby bin caught his eye. He turned, and Luke turned with him, knowing beforehand what it was.

"Hey, Daddy," Sammy said, staggering out of the bin into

the boiler room. "This place's getting busier than Grand Central." He wore his old army trousers and shirt, and a pair of sneakers. He was filthy and looked like he hadn't shaved for a week. "Hi," he said to the repairman.

The repairman's lips tightened and he turned back to the boiler. "Hold that flashlight for me," he said to Luke. "I gotta fix this thing fast."

Luke held the flashlight, and his temper. He breathed deeply, telling himself it wouldn't help none to tear up the pea patch with Sammy.

"Sammy," he said quietly, "go upstairs, will you?"

"Sure, Daddy. I'll just ask Cora to give me a bite to eat, huh?"

Luke's voice went tight. "No." He glanced at the repairman who had turned to look at them. He smiled meaninglessly. The repairman turned back to his job. "No, Cora isn't —feelin' good. Just—go—up."

Sammy shrugged, but stepped toward the elevator, afraid of his father's anger. "Got a buck or two, Daddy?"

Luke wanted to say no. He was fed up with Sammy. The boy had lost two jobs in the last three weeks, and taken sixty dollars from him. Now this!

But what would Sammy do with no place to sleep and no food to eat?

Luke used his left hand to get his wallet. "Here," he said. Sammy came over.

"Take two dollars," Luke said, holding out the wallet.

Sammy licked his parched lips. "Daddy, I need—"

"Okay, take five," Luke said, glancing at the repairman's back, filled with shame and hurt and rage. "Gowan!"

Sammy took a five and fled.

The repairman worked another ten minutes, then got up, wiped his hands and lit a cigarette. He smoked a moment in silence, and Luke looked down at the floor.

"Your son?" the repairman finally asked.

Luke nodded. "Been sick lately," he muttered. "Can't seem to straighten out since he been sick. You know—" He floundered lamely.

The repairman nodded hastily. "Sure. Well, let's get back on that line. 'Nother ten, fifteen minutes should see the end."

It was, however, almost an hour before he finished. "Hell," he said as he got up. "Hadda replace half the damn pipe." He looked at his hands. "Could I wash up someplace?"

"Sure, use my bathroom," Luke said.

Ordinarily, he'd have brought soap and towel to the sink in the washing-machine room on the other side of the elevator. But he wanted something from this man.

Cora wasn't in. Luke showed the repairman to the bathroom, and a few minutes later offered him a beer.

"No. I'll be getting home to supper," the man said. "Thanks anyway." He picked up his tool case and started down the foyer.

Luke blurted it out all at once, grinning and sweating and rubbing his face. "Listen, you talk much to Mr. Gorman? I mean—I hope you don't mention what happened down in the basement. Okay? My son just—well, Mr. Gorman wouldn't like—"

The repairman's plump face stiffened. "What you think I am, anyway? You think I'd make trouble when we got enough trouble just being what we are?" He stalked out, insulted.

Luke stood there, more ashamed of himself than he'd ever been. Then he sighed and got a beer from the refrigerator and drank it down fast. Man, man, it tasted good!

When Cora walked in a few minutes later, he asked her to make him a couple of sandwiches. She did better than that; she broiled three lamb chops and home-fried a mess of potatoes. He told her about Sammy while he ate. She looked at the table and shook her head. "Luke, that boy'll bring trouble on our heads. . . ."

It didn't take long for her prophecy to come true. Two days later, the phone rang while she and Luke were having breakfast. She answered it; then returned to the kitchen, biting her lip. "It was a policeman, Luke. He says Sammy's been arrested and wants you to come down to the station."

Luke got up slowly. "What he do?"

"Fight."

"Anyone hurt? I mean bad."

She shook her head. "I asked the same thing. Just a fight, but they got Sammy for being drunk and disorderly."

Luke nodded, relieved.

"You going, Luke?"

"Guess I better." He walked past her. "Gonna change clothes. You get the address?"

"Yes. I wrote it down. . . ."

At 9:30 A.M., Luke walked into the Manhattan stationhouse. He wore his good blue suit and new gray hat. His black shoes were polished and his white shirt crisply starched.

He removed his hat, placed one hand on the railing and looked up at the desk sergeant. He smiled apologetically.

"I'm here to see Samuel Brown. I'm his daddy."

The officer had a broad, pasty-white face and small gray eyes. He looked at Luke and grunted. He turned the pages of a newspaper and sucked his teeth and looked at Luke again. "You seem to be a respectable man, Mr. Brown. Why can't you keep your son in line? He's been on drunk and disorderly seven times in the last two years. You know what that means?"

Luke nodded humbly, but said nothing.

"That means he's bound to get into serious trouble sooner or later. That means he'll end up hurting someone in a fight, maybe killing someone . . ."

He went on that way, and his voice grew louder and harsher, as if Luke were the guilty party. Luke continued to nod and smile apologetically, but inside he was raging. Sammy! Always Sammy! Like some sort of curse hanging over his head. And now this—making him come to a police station to be looked at and yelled at!

The desk sergeant finally stopped and had Luke shown to a big room in back. There were two long wooden benches, some straight-backed chairs, and a single grimy window facing an alley. Luke sat down and waited. The dank smell of the room made his flesh crawl, and he remembered the only other station-house he'd ever been in. That was back in Bam, when he was fifteen and had gone to town with his older brother Jeff. He and Jeff and their widowed mother worked hard to make the truck farm and few pigs pay off enough to keep them alive. Luke had dropped out of school the year before, and Jeff hadn't been to school since he was twelve. But they were hard-working boys and well liked by everyone in the area. Even Mr. Higgins down at the crossroads general store (a man who'd ridden with the Klan and bragged about the two sassy niggers he'd whipped half to death with a metal-tipped cat-o'-nine-tails and the white nigger-lover from Boston he'd shot in the leg) said the Browns were "damn fine niggers, by God, who knew their place and earn their bread by the sweat of their brow."

Luke didn't like town much, but Jeff kept talking about the two Amos girls who lived above the barbershop in the colored section, and what with it being summer Luke got all lathered up.

"Lucy's the older one," Jeff said. "She's the one I'm gonna

be with. She's got hands softer than a baby's. She got legs makes you go crawly all over. She knows how. I mean she knows how! Her sister's about fourteen. Nice too. Big gal. Old Amos goes visitin' his brother over Locust Corners every Friday night, so we'll have them gals all to ourselves."

It didn't work out the way Jeff said it would. First of all, old Amos hurt his back and didn't go visiting his kin. When Luke and Jeff came into the four-room flat over the barbershop, old Amos was in the kitchen eating pancakes and drinking coffee. He squinted at the brothers and said, "You wanna see my daughters, you see them in here where I can watch close. I don't aim to have no big bellies lessen I got in-laws."

So Jeff and Luke sat around the kitchen with Lucy and Violet, and old Amos kept his eyes on them every minute. After a half-hour of that, Luke got up and said good night. Jeff followed him out of the door. Luke glared at his brother. "Not only was you wrong about old Amos," he said, "but that Violet's the skinniest gal I ever seen! Brother, you tried to rope me into somethin'! You wanted that Violet outa the way—"

"Stop honkin'," Jeff snapped and stalked into the dark street.

But Luke was angry and kept talking, and Jeff kept telling him to shut up, and finally they both got so mad they began throwing punches. Luke was three years younger than Jeff, but only an inch shorter and a few pounds lighter. He was doing all right for himself when he saw the white man coming on the run. The white man was medium height and thick and wore khaki pants, khaki shirt and a big-brimmed brown hat. That's when Luke realized they were in the middle of the street and pretty close to the white section of town. "Hold it!" he gasped, but Jeff was in mid-swing and connected. Luke sat down from the punch on the cheek, and the white man reached Jeff at the same time.

"It ain't nothin', suh," Luke said, and started to get up.

Jeff turned, an apologetic look flashing across his face as he realized there was a white man behind him. The white man moved his right hand toward his hip pocket.

"Where the hell you niggers think you are?" he roared. "Drinkin' and fightin' like you owned this town! Don't you know white ladies are sittin' on that porch down the street? Don't you know you're disturbin' them with your drunken—"

"We ain't drunk, suh," Luke said, getting to his feet. "We brothers. Just a family fight, suh. We sure sorry. Honest. We heading home right now."

Jeff nodded and kept his eyes down. "That's right, suh. You ask anyone about the Brown brothers. We ain't never been in trouble—"

The white man whipped his hand from his hip pocket. Jeff took a half-step back, but he was too slow. Something struck the top of his head with a dull, heavy, thumping sound and he crumpled to the pavement. "I'll teach you to give a deputy backtalk," the white man shouted, and came toward Luke.

"No-s-sir," Luke said, stammering in fright as he moved away. "We didn't mean—"

"Stand still!" the deputy shouted, and Luke obeyed.

Then he found out what had knocked Jeff unconscious. A blackjack smashed against his left ear, a scraping blow that could have killed him had it landed squarely. He heard a woman scream, "Those niggers are attacking Deputy Romer!" and then a roaring filled his head and he passed out.

He awoke in a cell. Jeff was there too, and they were both sick; damned sick. But it wasn't until some seven hours later that a colored doctor was brought to the cell. He said that Luke had a concussion and would have to go to a hospital.

Luke never did understand exactly what happened next, but it ended up with him and Jeff getting fined five dollars apiece. The doctor loaned them the money and then drove Luke to the colored hospital in town. Luke stayed there three weeks, and by the time he got out he'd made up his mind to one thing—as soon as he was old enough and felt Ma and Jeff could spare him, he was heading for New York to find out if Harlem was as nice as Uncle Barney wrote it was.

At nineteen, he finally made his break with the South. Barney was a porter at Grand Central Sta⁺⁰⁰ and put him up for a while. Luke was sickened by the crowded, dirty tenements, noise, loose living and crime. But one thing made up for all of that—the feeling of being a man free and equal under the law. So he stayed, and worked, and married a wild, beautiful mulatto, and had a son. His wife ran off and left him, so he got a divorce and married Cora and worked harder than ever. The climax of his life came when he landed the job as superintendent in the Brooklyn apartment house.

But he'd never forgotten the smell of that cell in Bam, and now, sitting in the back room of the Manhattan police station, his nostrils sniffed it again—a smell of sweat and pain and fear; a smell of *trouble*. And Sammy had brought him to it.

He made up his mind. He was going to disown Sammy, just like in the Bible. He'd say, "Sammy, you no son of mine any more, hear? No son of mine!" And then he'd walk out and forget that load of trouble forever. He should have done it when Sammy tried messin' with Cora. He should have whupped him good and disowned him right then. A man could take just so much from another man, even if that other man was his own flesh and blood. Just so much!

A policeman came into the room, and then Sammy came in. Sammy looked like he'd been shoved through a mangle.

The policeman sat down near the door and began biting his nails. Sammy shuffled to the bench where Luke was sitting and pulled up a chair and sank into it with a sigh. "Daddy," he said, and his eyes filled with tears. "Daddy, I sure am glad to see you. Help me get outa here, Daddy. Help me and I swear I'll never touch another drop again. I swear to Jesus!" He took Luke's hand and bent over it, and Luke felt the hot tears.

"Aw, Sammy," Luke murmured, and patted the bruised face. "Sammy, stop that cryin'."

"You will help me, won't you, Daddy? I can get another job. And this time I'll stick to it. This time I'll find myself a nice girl and marry and settle down . . ."

Luke listened and nodded, and the hope rose in him that Sammy had finally learned his lesson. "What I gotta do, son?"

Sammy's head came up and that sweet smile transfigured his beaten face. "I need two hundred dollars."

"Two hundred! But you ain't been to court yet. I mean, you got to be tried before they can find you, ain't you, ain't that so?"

Sammy leaned forward, licking his lips nervously. "That's just it, Daddy. If I pay this bartender two hundred bucks he won't press charges and I'll walk out of here in a day or two. But if I don't pay him, I'll get at least ninety days in the workhouse. And maybe more. And I couldn't take time in the workhouse, Daddy! It'd drive me nuts! So just lend me the two hundred to pay this bartender, will you?"

"But what'd you do that you owe him so much?"

Sammy dropped his eyes and cleared his throat. "Well, it was a fight and I threw a few bottles and broke some mirrors and chairs and maybe a front door. I didn't mean to, Daddy. Honest. You just gotta help me!"

Luke sighed and rubbed his face. He and Cora had cut corners to save their four hundred and fifty dollars. They didn't owe anyone a penny; never bought anything on time like so many other people did. They were proud of their nice furniture, nice clothes, and proudest of the fact that they were absolutely free of debt.

It hadn't always been that way. They hadn't gotten out of the red until two years ago. And then they'd begun to save for a good used car. They would have enough in another year, year and a half—

"Two hundred dollars, Sammy," Luke murmured.

Sammy's eyes widened, his mouth began to tremble. "You won't let me down, Daddy? You won't let me go to that workhouse!"

Luke sighed again and stood up. "No," he said. "I won't let you go to the workhouse. I'm leavin' now, Sammy." He walked toward the door, wondering how he was going to tell Cora. She'd been dreaming of a car for years. She'd planned trips to state parks and beaches which weren't crowded like Prospect Park and Coney Island, and she'd even talked of having him take a week off so they could drive up into New England and see some sort of concerts played out in the open.

He could hear her voice, happy and excited, as she explained these things to him. Now he was going to withdraw two hundred dollars, and her dreams would be set back a long time.

The officer got up and opened the door for him. "You're being taken, Pop," he said. "That boy of yours'll never—"

"Thanks," Luke said quickly, and went through the door.

When he got outside, he took a dee , breath of fresh air. Later, he worried that the officer migł : think he'd been disrespectful.

15

LOUIS SCHIMLER 5-F

The Saturday Louis Schimler had been dreading for two weeks arrived. He spent the morning working on a model airplane, and then went downstairs and talked with a few guys in front of the candy store on Sixteenth Avenue. He kept telling himself it was just a silly blind date and meant nothing to him, one way or another, but he got tighter inside as the day wore on.

After dinner, he got up from the table and said, "I'll take a walk—"

"No, you won't," Myra said, finishing her dessert. "It's seven o'clock and you have to start getting ready."

"Heck, just a few minutes—"

She fixed him with her eyes and said softly, "Lou, please don't try to back out. I—I understand certain things, but you've got to face up—" She stopped.

He said, "Who's backing out?" But he didn't ask her what she meant by the "facing up" and other stuff. And he didn't press the issue. He went to his room and laid out his clothes.

He took a long time in the bathroom, coming out only when Myra called, "Lou! I've got to shower too, you know!"

He dressed slowly, getting into his new blue herringbone. He dressed completely—except for tie. But then he had to go to the mirror and put it on.

Carefully, he made a Windsor knot, and ran a comb through his dark-blond hair. He turned away, but then turned back again and looked at himself—*really* looked at himself. The pimples weren't so bad; at least not as bad as they'd been two weeks ago. He'd even been able to shave lightly and get rid of most of the fuzz. Of course, he'd cut himself about eight or nine times where the pimples were worst. But it wasn't too bad. No, not too bad—

He twisted away.

Why the hell had he let Myra talk him into this date! He didn't want to go! He just wanted to be left alone! By God, he'd tell her right now that he'd changed his mind. Sure, a guy could change his mind—

Pop came in. "Sharp, Lou. Real sharp." His small eyes touched Lou's face and quickly slid back to the suit. "Yeah, you'll knock her dead. But what I came in for was to ask if you need some dough."

"I got eight dollars," Lou muttered.

"That might not be enough. Here, better take this ten. You can return what you don't spend."

Lou took the bill. "Thanks, Pop. But this guy Georgie has tickets for a show and all I got to pay for is myself and the girl at a restaurant."

"Yeah, well, you don't want to feel short. You always want

to be a few bucks ahead on a date. It gives you that confident feeling." He looked at Lou's face and away again. "Just— just feel confident, Lou. That's all you need." He rubbed his big hands together. "Yeah. Well. You'll knock her dead." He went out.

Lou wanted to yell after him, "Why all this fuss? What the hell does it mean? Who the hell cares?"

The doorbell rang. High heels clicked down the foyer. "Hi, Georgie," Myra said. "Come on in."

Lou's heart began to hammer. He went to the closet and got his topcoat. He went to the door and then stopped, breathing heavily. "Crap," he muttered. "Pure crap." He opened the door and went into the living room.

A tall, nice-looking guy, about twenty-four or five, was just sitting down on the couch beside Myra. Mom and Pop were in the armchairs facing the couch. The guy got up as Lou approached. So did Myra.

"Lou, this is George Becker. Georgie, this is my brother Lou."

"Hi, Lou," Georgie said, and stuck out his hand.

Lou shook it, and noticed the way Georgie's eyes slid quickly across his face. He figured Myra had told the guy something about him. He wanted to fall through the floor.

But then again, he always felt like this on meeting new people—especially if they had anything to do with a date. So he said, "Hi," and smiled and looked around quickly.

"Georgie's sister, Imogene, is waiting in the car," Myra said, and then looked at Mom and Pop. "'Bye, folks. Don't wait up for us."

"With Lou along as chaperone," Pop said grinning, "you can stay out all night."

Mom said, "Irving!"

Myra smiled thinly, and Lou knew she didn't like the crack. But then again, she was always getting that annoyed look when Pop made jokes in front of her boy-friends. Lou had always thought it kind of funny. But not this time. This time he wished he could kick Pop right in his big mouth. This time he felt as though Pop were telling everyone that his son was a helpless goody-good who'd never be able to get a girl in trouble and was going out only to watch his sister—

"Come on, Lou," Myra was saying. "You'll have plenty of time to stare at your loving father tomorrow."

Lou snapped out of it, felt himself getting red, said good-bye to Mom and Pop. He followed Myra and Georgie down the foyer, and now he was burning at Myra. She didn't have to say that in front of the guy.

God, this evening was really starting off great!

Georgie's car was parked around the corner on Fifty-fifth Street, in a dark spot between lampposts. When Georgie opened the door, the inside light went on and Lou was able to see his date.

She stunned him. He looked at her and mumbled his, "Pleased to meet you," and got in back beside her. They began to drive, and Myra kept chattering about the show they were going to see, and Georgie kept asking questions and trying to make everyone talk. But Lou and Imogene said very little. Lou was trying to pull himself together; trying to understand how he should take this.

Imogene had a nice, round, pleasant face and reddish-blonde hair. She was a little chubby, but her figure wasn't bad. She had a sweet voice, what little he'd heard of it. But she wore a brace on her right leg. It was necessary, Lou could see at a glance, because the leg itself was withered.

He didn't really mind. Not deep inside. She was nice and he could spend the evening with her and maybe even date her again. Sure. Why not? She wasn't Elaine Turner, but then again he wasn't ready for Elaine. And as far as the leg went, he almost wished Elaine had something like it. Then maybe the wise-guys she dated wouldn't be around and Lou could show her how much he really cared.

No, there wasn't anything about Imogene Becker he disliked. But there was something about Myra's not telling him Imogene was crippled that smelled bad. Myra had tricked him. Yeah, that's what bothered him. She'd tricked him! She'd been afraid to tell him about Imogene's leg. And he knew why. He *felt* why. She was afraid he'd think she was pairing off two cripples. And because she was afraid of *his* thinking that, it mean that *she* thought it!

She wanted him to have a girl, and she felt he couldn't hold a normal one, and so she'd found him one who wouldn't be choosy. What was it she'd said about Imogene two weeks ago? "—Not the snippy, turn-up-your-nose-at-everyone type."

Yeah!

Myra was still talking, but she hadn't turned toward the back seat even once.

Lou hated her! She'd done something—*dirty!* Something dirty to both Imogene and himself.

He felt sick inside, and was sure the evening would be a

long, miserable affair for him. It no longer mattered that Imogene was nice and that he could enjoy himself with her. What mattered was that his own sister thought of him as a cripple!

But, by God, Imogene wouldn't know anything was wrong! He wouldn't make her suffer for Myra's mistakes.

He turned to her and smiled. "Gee, it was nice of your brother to treat me to the show."

She nodded and glanced at him and then glanced away. "Uh-huh. Do you go to New Utrecht?"

"Yes."

"I have a friend who goes there—Miriam Cleve. Sixth term."

"I don't think I know her. Don't you go to Utrecht?"

"No. Lincoln. Do you like Broadway plays?"

"Well, I've only seen three—"

He liked her. But he burned when he saw the smug, self-satisfied look that passed between Myra and Georgie. The matchmakers! The cripple-helpers! Sonsofbitches!

It went all right while they were in the car. And when Imogene got out in front of the theater, Lou understood why Georgie had driven his Dodge to Manhattan and was willing to pay a four-buck parking fee. Imogene limped very badly; she'd have had a tough time using the subway.

During the intermission following the first act, when Georgie and Myra went out for a smoke, Imogene told him about it. "Polio. I was just nine years old. At first they thought I was going to die—"

He started to like her more and more. But then a strange thing began to happen—the more he liked her, the more it seemed to him she acted like all the other girls he'd dated. She wasn't looking at his face, as she had in the car. But then again, the car had been kind of dark, and here—

He told himself he was imagining it. Heck, this girl knew she was lucky to have him—

But that was the way Myra had thought—a dirty, rotten way to think—and he cut it short, ashamed and confused.

Still, as the lights dimmed for the second act, the thought returned—and comforted him.

After the show, they went to a restaurant where there was a band and dancing. Imogene surprised him. She danced very well—a lot better than she walked.

"You're terrific," he said to her as they did a rumba. "Really terrific."

She gave him a warm smile and said, "You're not so bad yourself." But then her smile slid away, and so did her eyes, and she was looking past his shoulder.

"You know," she said a little later, "I've got an awful lot of friends in Lincoln."

He wondered why she'd said that. "Sure, Imogene. I'll bet you have."

She was quiet awhile, and the music switched to a fox trot.

"Lots of friends," she said. "Lots of boys as well as girls. But my brother seems to feel I'm—some sort of poor lonely soul."

Something tightened in his chest. Wasn't she showing the same kind of resentment he'd felt earlier in the evening; resentment at being paired off with a cripple?"

That couldn't be!

"He's always getting me blind dates," Imogene continued, voice thin and angry. "He can't seem to get it through his head that I have more than I can handle—" She suddenly glanced up at Lou. "Not that this isn't fun, Lou. It is. I didn't mean—"

"Heck, I understand," he said, and told himself she just *couldn't* be feeling sorry for him!

Imogene pleaded weariness a few minutes later, and they sat down at the table and ate with Myra and Georgie. Afterward, when the older couple went back out on the dance floor, Lou stood up and said, "Shall we?"

Imogene shook her head. "Honest, Lou, I'm so pooped—"

She'd studied late last night and attended a club meeting early this morning and gone swimming at an indoor pool this afternoon ("not only my favorite sport, Lou, but the doctor says it's good for my leg").

He sat down. "Gee, no wonder you're pooped." He smiled and fiddled with a spoon and looked around the night club. He understood. Sure. Anyone would be tired after a full day like that. Sure.

And still the tightness in his chest remained. . . .

When they drove up in front of Koptic Court, Georgie and Myra got out quickly and Georgie looked in the back seat. "You two kids can talk a while. Myra and I want to take a walk." They strolled off around the block.

Lou was holding Imogene's hand, but by now he was feeling all his usual insecurities and fears. Still, he couldn't believe she'd actually turn him down.

"I had a very nice time, Lou," Imogene said suddenly.

"Thanks a lot. You don't have to sit around until they get back. I know it's late—"

"Heck, I like it," Lou mumbled, and squeezed her hand, and got no response. "Say, Imogene, maybe we could see a movie next Saturday night?"

She cleared her throat and drew her hand away.

Lou knew what was coming.

"I'm sorry, Lou. I've got a date."

He carried it to the bitter end. "The week after?"

"My mother doesn't like me to go out too much. She says I'm too young, and I get tired fast—"

He got out of the car and closed the door. He walked toward the lobby.

"But I had a wonderful time," she called after him, and he recognized the new element in her voice. Hell, yes! Hadn't he heard it often enough from other girls, and from Myra, and from Mom, and even from Pop?

Pity.

He carved a dirty word into the paint of the elevator wall. He carved it with the thought that he was carving it into all the people who pitied him.

It was two o'clock, and Mom and Pop were asleep. He undressed quickly and got into bed. Myra came up a few minutes later and tiptoed into his room. "Lou," she whispered.

"What?" he muttered, rolling over to face her.

"Did you like Imogene?"

"No. Lemme sleep, huh? And don't do me any more favors with blind dates." His voice began to rise, and he couldn't seem to control it. "Just lemme alone from now on! Just don't bring me any more cripples—" He stopped then, and fought the tears.

"Oh, Lou," she murmured, and there it was again—pity! "I—I know you didn't mean that. I saw you liked her. Did she—" She shook her head and began to turn away.

Lou sat up and grabbed her arm. He drew back his fist and almost punched her in the face. But she cried out, and his mind cleared, and he let her go. She ran from the room, sobbing. He lay down again and told himself the whole business didn't mean a thing.

Anyway, the only girl he cared for was Elaine Turner. And she hadn't turned him down. No, sir! She wouldn't get the chance! Only when he was ready, when he was changed, would he ask her. And then she'd say yes because she liked him. . . .

The next morning, Myra left early for a friend's house, saying she had to study for exams. Lou was glad. He worked on his new model plane until lunch, and then Mom and Pop asked if he wanted to take in a movie. He said sure, and they went. It was a good double feature—a love story and a mystery. Then they ate in a Chinese restaurant. It was a big place, crowded, and they sat in a booth near the door. They laughed a lot and had a good time—up until Pop began asking Lou how he'd liked his date and whether he was going to see the girl again and why not and on and on and on.

Finally, Lou said, "For crissake! Can't you let a guy alone? I didn't like the damned girl, that's all!"

"What'ya yelling at?" Pop yelled.

"Shhh, Irving," Mom said, glancing around the restaurant. "People will hear."

"So who cares?" Pop said, really angry. "I ask my son a civil question, I expect a civil answer."

"But it's his personal business, Irving," Mom said placatingly. "Really, even a young boy has the right—"

"Whad'ya making it sound like a funeral?" Pop said.

Lou agreed with him there; the pity was really dripping from Mom's voice. Myra had probably filled her in on the whole thing.

"I'm going," Lou said, standing up from the table. "I'll catch the bus. I want to visit a friend—"

"Sit down!" Pop shouted, his face turning red.

"No," Lou said, and stepped away.

Pop half rose, as if to grab him and drag him back, but then he glanced around and saw that people were beginning to look his way. "Okay," he said, voice mean. "Okay, so you can't take it. So you run like a crybaby because the girls don't go for you. So you won't listen to your father who might be able to help—"

"Help?" Lou said, coming back and bending close to his father. "Maybe you can wish my acne away?"

Pop looked down at the table. Lou walked out. . . .

Frank Lombardi, a guy he got along with pretty good, was in front of the Sixteenth Avenue candy store. They talked awhile, and then Frank said, "Ralphie Zimmer ask you about the social club?"

"What social club?" Lou said.

"Oh, nothing," Frank muttered, looking like he was sorry he'd mentioned it.

"So they're forming a social club," Lou said. "So I wouldn't want to join anyway. Tell him that, if he asks you about me. Honest; I'm what my Pop calls a nonjoiner."

He headed home. He didn't understand what he'd done that God should let him get stepped on this way. He went to synagogue on the High Holy Days, and whenever else Pop asked him along. He didn't curse much, and he didn't do things that were sins.

He came into the lobby. While waiting for the elevator, he saw the super go into the incinerator off to the left. The Negro gave him a hard look; maybe 'cause he suspected Lou of carving up the elevator a few times and dropping garbage on the incinerator floor upstairs.

The hell with him! The hell with all of them in this house! He remembered the time—about two years ago on the Fourth of July—when Stan Safardi had carried a whole box of fireworks out to the sixth floor incinerator of his Fourteenth Avenue apartment house. (Lou and two other guys had been there, and Stan's folks were away.) They'd all watched while Stan dropped the box of fire works down the shaft. At first nothing happened and Lou had been about to say, "Told you we wouldn't even hear it." But then there'd been this big *boom!* and a few smaller bangs. Man. Stan had laughed like crazy when people downstairs had run into halls yelling and asking what the hell was going on.

Lou wished he had some fireworks right now. He'd drop them down the shaft here and scare the life out of that super and everyone else. He wished he had a ton of the stuff —fireworks and cherry bombs and rockets and torpedoes. He wished he had enough to knock pieces off the building!

Boy, would that shake up the jerks around here!

But he wouldn't want to scare Elaine Turner. She'd have to be out of the house or he wouldn't do it—

The elevator came and he rode upstairs. Mom and Pop weren't back yet. He went to his room and began working on his model plane. About ten minutes later, he found himself thinking of Imogene and the way she'd pitied him.

He squeezed the plane into tiny fragments of balsa wood. Then he went to the dresser and pounded his model of Old Ironsides until there was nothing left but the hull. He put all the junk into a paper bag and took it out to the incinerator.

That evening, watching television with Mom and Pop, he felt sorry, angry at himself. Now he'd have to build a new three-master and a new P-51. . . .

16

ELI WEINER 3-C

It was the third week in August—a humid Wednesday. Eli left his desk at eleven-thirty and walked to the washroom, carrying a towel. He took off his shirt and undershirt and washed his face, neck and chest. But he still felt sweaty, grimy, pooped out, and he couldn't even look forward to going home at five. He was meeting Rose at a hotel clubroom for an evening of dining and dancing. Not that he really wanted it, but Rose had complained of being stuck in the house so much of the summer—the first summer she and the boys hadn't spent in the country—and he felt guilty. What with work, and seeing Irene, he'd neglected her shamefully.

She was driving into the city and had wanted to pick him up at the office, but he'd talked her out of that. He couldn't have her up at the office, or even in front of it where some of the men he worked with might see her and stop to chat. She might chide old Ettinger, or Frank Silesi, for making her husband attend so many out-of-town conventions, week-end conventions, during the summer. And then they'd either say, "What conventions?" or else nod and look at him with narrowed, amused, contemptuous, knowing eyes.

He couldn't have that. So she was meeting him at the hotel where, he'd convinced her, she'd be able to find a parking space only if she arrived ten or fifteen minutes before he left the office and the five-o'clock jam began.

He returned to his desk and looked over the letters he'd received from six Southern mills concerning delivery schedules on various types of cotton print cloth they'd displayed at a New York showing last month. He decided to write two of them and ask for specific dates.

He picked up the phone and asked the switchboard to get Miss Lowen. A moment later the plump, middle-aged secretary came in. She barely glanced at him—and that an extremely cold glance—before sitting down in the chair alongside his desk. She flipped open her steno pad, poised her pencil, said, "Yes?"

208

He felt uncomfortable. She'd become more and more un-friendly during the past six months. She actually seemed to hate him! And there was nothing he could do about it. The only way to make things right between them was to show interest in her again as a woman, and that was out.

He said, "You know, it's getting close to lunch time, Miss Lowen. Maybe we'll have a bite together and discuss exactly how I'll handle these mill people."

"I'm sorry," she said, voice tight. "I have a luncheon ap-pointment. Besides, I don't like to discuss business while eating—on my own time." She didn't look at him.

"Ah, yes," he murmured, and still felt he should try to make her act a little warmer. "Maybe tomorrow."

She raised her eyes. "I'll tell you, Mr. Weiner. I'm free only one time for the next few weeks, maybe months. I can have dinner—" She stopped and her eyes took on an anxious, pleading look. He backtracked immediately.

"Yes, well, we'll see. Maybe some night when my wife has a club meeting."

"Yes," she said, and the ice was heavy again. "Can we get on with the dictation? I want to leave at twelve-thirty."

He cursed himself for ever having bothered with her, and still felt uncomfortable, and began composing his letter.

"Cantersall Mills, Incorporated—address listed in our files —attention James L. Stowell, Jr. Dear Sir: In your form letter of August 18th, you stated that delivery on the new pastel Lady Diddi and Princess fabrics would be four to six weeks after receipt of order accompanied by one-third pay-ment—"

The phone rang. Mind still formulating words, he picked it up.

"Eli?"

He went rigid. It was Irene. She'd never before called him at the office. "Yes," he said, thinking of the switchboard girl. She could easily listen in—and often did.

"It's Irene, darling."

"Yes. How are you?" He knew his voice sounded stiff and unnatural, and he cast about in his mind for a way to end the conversation quickly without insulting Irene or arousing Miss Lowen's suspicions. He glanced at the secretary, and she was watching him from the corners of her eyes.

"I hope you don't mind my calling you at the office, Eli. These darned summer classes are so terribly drab that I—I just had to change the pattern."

It seemed to Eli that her voice was unnaturally loud and shrill, and that it would certainly carry to Miss Lowen's ears. In fact, he was sure Miss Lowen was already looking at him strangely.

"I'm in the middle of some rather important—"

"Oh," she said, and she was hurt. "I'll say goodbye then." But she held on.

He cleared his throat and said nothing.

"Maybe you'll also be too busy for this weekend?" Irene said pettishly.

"Of course not." The sweat began trickling down his sides. "Uh—just a moment, please."

He covered the mouthpiece and turned what he felt sure must be a red, sweaty face to Miss Lowen. "Since you have an appointment for lunch, we'd better continue after you return."

The plump woman closed her pad, stood up and left the room. She seemed to be hiding a contemptuous smile.

Eli told himself it was only his imagination, and again spoke into the phone. "Hello. Sorry, but I was giving my secretary dictation."

"You sent her away?"

"Yes, but—"

"You know, I'd love to come up and see your office, Eli! I'd love to see where you spend so much of your life! It would—"

"Can I call you back?" he interrupted, wondering whether he'd actually heard a soft click or was imagining it. That switchboard girl was as good as Walter Winchell at spreading gossip! "Our switchboard is rather busy. You understand?"

She didn't. "Call me back? But I'm in a phone booth in school."

"We have a switchboard," he said desperately. "I'll—call you tonight."

"Oh," she said. "Oh, now I see."

And now it might be too late, he thought as he hung up.

He sat there, wincing at the memory of that "darling" she'd used, and at her statement concerning their coming weekend together. God, if anyone found out—

And then he was ashamed of himself. Hadn't he told Irene time and again he'd almost welcome discovery because it would bring matters to a head? Hadn't she been the one to advise caution?

And still he was afraid. And still he winced at what the switchboard girl, or Miss Lowen, might have heard or surmised from that telephone call.

He had lunch sent up from a nearby restaurant. He told himself it had nothing to do with his desire to avoid passing the switchboard. . . .

At five o'clock, he walked out to the elevators, nodding goodnight at the switchboard girl. She smiled and nodded back, and he could find nothing there to sustain his worries. Feeling somewhat better, he stepped into an elevator and turned to face the doors. Miss Lowen just made it, looked at him, and the corners of her lips seemed to come up in a tiny sneer.

Immediately, he was tense and perspiring. Immediately, he felt revealed as something low and rotten.

When they reached the lobby, he walked quickly past the secretary and out into the street. He caught a cab and settled back for the slow trip uptown through rush-hour traffic.

The sick, ugly feelings ripped through him and he clenched his fists and said, "Damn!"

The cabby turned his head. "What's that?"

"Can't you make better time than this?" Eli snapped.

"Just take a look out the window, bud. Could you?"

"Should've used the bus," Eli muttered.

The cabby shrugged.

It was an uncomfortable twenty minutes.

With this sort of a beginning, he was sure the evening was going to be murder. But, to his amazement, it went fine from the moment he entered the hotel lobby and saw Rose sitting in one of the leather armchairs. She smiled and stood up and walked quickly toward him. "This is a lovely place," she said. "They've got four different clubs. Let's go to the Orient Room. I'm starved!"

She tugged his arm, enthusiasm written all over her face, and he found himself admiring her slim figure in the stylish black sheath cocktail dress (something he'd picked up for her at a wholesale showing almost two years ago). Why, she looked almost pretty. No, not almost—definitely pretty!

"You know," she said, "we haven't been out dancing since last New Year's. And we used to be such fox trot and rumba bugs."

"I doubt if we'll get a rumba here," Eli said. "It's all cha-cha and mambo now."

"We'll dance every dance anyway," she murmured as

the waiter led them to a table. "We can rumba to them. I know—I practiced a few times when I was alone in the house—" She grinned and looked at him. "Don't tell the old lady she's nuts."

He laughed, and then they were at the table. They had a good roast beef dinner, and he realized he hadn't been this relaxed, this at ease, in months. No glancing at the door to see if anyone he knew had entered; no constant, nagging, oppressive feeling of shame, fear, or frustration of one kind or another.

They danced, and Rose was right—it was possible to do a rumba to the mambo and cha-cha and not get completely balled up. Then the highly advertised second orchestra came on and there were plenty of fox trots and waltzes.

When they returned to their table, Eli ordered a bottle of imported champagne. After the waiter had left, Rose shook her head and whispered, "That wasn't necessary, Eli. It'll cost seven or eight dollars here. We could have had high-balls." But then she smiled and squeezed his hand. "I love bubbly! I'm going to drink more than you!"

She did too.

It was eleven before they left the Orient Room—and they had started dinner at five-thirty. But it hadn't seemed like five and a half hours to Eli. It had gone quickly, pleasurably.

"Let's take a drive before going home," she said when they pulled away in their Buick. She snuggled up close to him and giggled. "That wonderful, wonderful bubbly. Remember the last time you brought home two bottles—on my birthday? Remember how I drank most of it? That was the night we figured Teddy was made." She giggled again, put her hand on his thigh. "Let's drive out to the country, honey. Westchester, maybe."

Westchester brought Irene to mind; they'd gone there the first time he'd made love to her.

"How about a short trip into Jersey instead?" he asked. "We're near the George Washington Bridge. . . ."

They went over the bridge, and then onto a small, dark side road. Rose got closer and closer to him as they drove, her hands pressing his thighs, her lips touching his cheek and neck every so often. Finally, she whispered. "Eli, remember when we went to Florida the year after our marriage? Remember the night we stopped—"

He remembered. They'd been driving six solid hours, and somehow that feeling got started and they couldn't wait until they reached a motel. They'd pulled off the road and parked in a dark field and made love right there in the car.

"Let's—let's stop now," she whispered.

He wanted to laugh it off, but she was hugging him, breath coming in short gasps, lips parted, face tight with hunger. It had been a long time—months—since he'd touched her. And suddenly he too felt hunger.

He'd make love to her and it would be as good as with Irene and then he could stop the lying, the cheating, the constant fearing. Yes, he'd find out that he was running himself ragged for nothing!

"All right," he said, and put one arm around her for a brief hug. Then he took a curve and his headlights caught an emergency parking area and a flat, grassy picnic spot beyond it. He got onto the grassy spot, parked, and turned to her.

"Eli," she said, "we haven't been close lately. Let's change things tonight. . . ."

It wasn't what he'd hoped for. Rose, however, enjoyed herself immensely; she was full of love, tenderness and passion.

He envied her. As for himself, he didn't know what he'd felt, but he knew it wasn't the tremendous explosion, the cure-all he needed.

He would see Irene again. With Irene it was wild and explosive. At least it *had* been—

He drove back onto the road, his wheels screaming as they left dirt and hit asphalt. He wanted to get home and into bed.

"Eli, Eli," Rose murmured, leaning against him. "It was wonderful, darling, wonderful."

"Yes," he said. "Wonderful. . . ."

It rained Friday morning and afternoon; then the skies cleared and the air became surprisingly cool. By evening, the temperature was down to sixty-five—the lowest reading since mid-June.

Eli left his apartment at 8:00 p.m., carrying a suitcase. Rose walked with him into the hall and over to the elevator.

"You never went to so many conventions before," she said.

For a second he wondered if she suspected anything, but then he remembered how happy she'd been since Wednesday night and told himself to stop jumping at shadows.

"Three this summer, Eli. And all that night work. It's knocking you out—you're looking tired, worn."

"I feel fine," he said.

The elevator arrived. He kissed her, and felt a rush of tenderness—or was it guilt? He kissed her again, suddenly remembering how good supper had been tonight—fresh fruit cup, vegetable soup, breaded veal cutlet, whipped potatoes, iced tea just the right strength.

Good meals were important, he thought. A woman who gave you good meals and kept a clean house and brought up your children in decent fashion and had a healthy, normal approach to life—

"Well," he said. "Goodbye." He kissed her a third time.

She smiled and patted his cheek. "The old man's waking up."

He flushed, and stepped into the elevator to keep her from seeing it. "See you Sunday."

"Early Sunday," she called. "Remember, you promised to be home early—"

He let the door close, and the elevator went down.

As he walked through the lobby, three girls came in from the street. One was Sheila Dergano who lived on the fifth floor. He nodded at her.

"Going on a trip?" she asked.

"Yes." He stopped and looked at her friends. The frail blonde was familiar, but he'd never seen the busty brunette before. She had a sweet, young, small-featured face; a full rosebud mouth. "Want to come along?" he cracked, and couldn't keep his eyes from slipping to the brunette's sweater. Baby face and lush figure—an exciting combination. "Atlantic City's nice late in summer."

"Boy, would I!" Sheila said, laughing. "But I don't think your wife would approve."

He looked into the brunette's eyes. "We wouldn't tell her."

The brunette's smile weakened and she glanced away.

Eli gave them a hearty laugh. "Well, so long." He went into the street. Behind him, he heard whispering and giggling, and he was annoyed with himself. Not that he'd done anything except kid around a little; they'd certainly understood that. But it wasn't smart to flirt with girls so close to home—

Flirt? He wasn't flirting! Just kidding around.

He got into his car, and thought of Irene, and of Rose, and then of the brunette. He found himself building a fantasy around the brunette, and was suddenly confused and frightened.

"What the hell do you want?" he said aloud. "Where will it end?"

But then the fear went away, and he told himself he was going to have another wonderful, love-filled weekend with Irene, and he felt better. . . .

She was waiting for him around the corner from the drugstore. She got in the car and he took her small valise and put it in back. He drove toward the West Side Highway.

"I had trouble with my mother," she said, sliding across the seat and snuggling up against him. "She insisted on coming downstairs with me. She no longer accepts my explanations of why I won't let her and my father drive me to the station."

"What did you tell them this time?"

She shrugged. "Same as always—with variations. That I don't like goodbyes. That I want to go alone because it's the only way I relax. But tonight she walked down with me and I actually had to hail a cab. I stopped the driver after three blocks and got out. I walked back. God, if she ever found out about you!"

Eli felt a tremor of fear. He laughed, a little too loud. "What could she do?"

"What *couldn't* she do! Tell my father. Tell your wife. Make things tough for us in a million ways—"

She went on, and Eli's stomach twisted. A month ago (or was it two?) he'd have said, "So what? So it would force the issue and we could bring it into the open," and almost have meant it. The first month of their relationship, it would have been the absolute truth. But now, he didn't want to lose Rose and the boys. Irene was still exciting and desirable, but he no longer felt he would trade everything for her.

Or was it merely normal fear of being shamed—

What about his yearnings for that brunette a short while ago?

He refused to think of it.

"Where are we going, Eli?"

"Upper New York."

"Where are you supposed to be this time?"

"Atlantic City."

"Convention," she said, and laughed.

He didn't like the laugh, but answered with one of his own, telling himself that all the nonsense running through his mind would disappear as soon as they got into bed. Then his love would come alive, stronger than ever.

He put his right arm around her, cupping her breast.

"Let's stop someplace soon, Eli."

He nodded.

"I missed you so much this week, Eli. That's why I called your office."

"I'd have been happy to talk to you; you know that. But the switchboard is dangerous. Anyone can listen in."

"I understand," she said quietly. "You explained it a number of times."

"A number of times? Just that once on the phone—and now."

"All right." She looked out the window.

He caressed her breast and turned his head for a quick kiss. "I missed you too. Didn't I call twice?"

She sighed and nodded and looked at him. "Yes. And yet, it wasn't enough. I missed you and missed you. Especially at night." She paused. "I wonder if I ought to tell you what I did."

"Go on."

"You might get angry."

He glanced at her. "What was it?"

"As I said, I missed you most at night. I wanted to call you just to say a few words, to tell you how much I loved you. I wanted to do it so badly that I kept picking up the phone—and on Thursday night I dialed your number."

His heart leaped. He remembered that the phone had rung twice last night, but stopped before Rose could pick it up. He wanted to tell Irene never to dare do a thing like that again, but forced a laugh instead. "Sort of dangerous," he said.

"Why? If anyone but you had answered, I'd have asked for Dick. I have a legitimate excuse to talk to him. He called for a date this week, and I said I'd let him know if I could make it. I—I felt so evil stringing him along."

He wanted to ask why she had told him that.

Almost as if she'd read his mind, she said, "I guess I shouldn't have mentioned it, but—well, I like to tell you everything, Eli."

"I wish that were true," he said to change the subject.

"It is true."

"You never talk about yourself as a child. All I really know about you is that you live with your mother and father, attend N.Y.U., will be twenty on September eighth, and have some silly fear of being thin."

"And that I love you."

"Do you?" he asked, half in jest, half in earnest.

She turned to face him. "Do you love me?"

He nodded solemnly, but felt discomfort.

"How'd we ever get on this track?" he said, and laughed.

She relaxed, and laughed with him, and said, "I'll tell about me, and you tell about you. I mean the important things—what shaped us when we were kids. The fears; the defeats. Okay?"

He nodded. But he knew he would never tell her of his childhood failures with girls, of his humiliation with Lily Weinstein. "Sure. But I had a very boring childhood. I can give it to you right now. I was born in Brooklyn, went to Thomas Jefferson High, was a business administration student at City College for a little less than two years, and then went into the business I'm now in—ladies' dresses. Nothing very important happened after that—until I met you. Because of my wife and children, and my mother who was still alive and dependent on me at the time, I wasn't taken for military service. That's it."

"Where did you meet your wife?" she asked softly.

"At the beach," he said, refusing to remember how it had been, refusing to remember how much he had loved the slim, pretty girl so many years ago. "Coney Island. A pickup, you'd call it. I was with friends and she was with friends and we just paired off. I was young and didn't know what I wanted and—"

"You must have loved her," Irene interrupted, voice still soft, but insistent. "You must have had real feeling for her."

He sighed. "At the beginning. Anyway, that's my life's story. Now let's have yours."

She nodded, but just sat there, staring out the window.

He didn't press the point. He lit a cigar and put on the radio, giving her time and silence in which to fight out whatever battle was going on inside her. . . .

About an hour before they reached the tourist court off the Taconic Parkway, she began to talk. She told him of her earliest memories—her public-school days, her high-school days—right up until the present. He got a picture of a somewhat neurotic girl whose major insecurity revolved around the feeling that she wasn't normal when it came to weight, when it came to being well fleshed. And it was with respect to this problem that he sensed she was holding back some memory, some painful incident.

At eleven that night, he was lying stretched out on a wide bed, looking up at the cabin's pink ceiling. Irene lay beside him, propped on an elbow, eyes pointed at his face but glazed, staring through him into the past. She hadn't said anything for about five minutes, and he felt she was working up to something important.

"There's one thing I haven't told you," she finally said. "I find it hard to even *think* of it. It happened a long, long time ago . . ."

As a child, she'd been very thin—and very sensitive. Her mother had forced her to eat, jammed the food down her throat, and raised hell when she threw it up. Meals became battles, and she just couldn't eat. (Meals were still battles, only now she fought herself, fought to eat enough to keep her figure attractive.)

She had a cousin, Lila, a chubby, active child who lived only six blocks away and visited often. Lila teased Irene about being skinny, bullied her, and was pointed to by Irene's parents as a glowing example of what eating could do. So Irene hated Lila, and when she was nine put a match to Lila's long, dark, curly hair. Only the prompt arrival of Irene's mother prevented Lila from being horribly burned. As it was, she carried scars on her ears and neck until plastic surgery, at the age of fifteen, removed them.

Irene had been sent to a child psychiatrist who found her totally uncommunicative. Shortly afterward, she had hysterics on waking up in her darkened bedroom. Her father, shocked by her recent attack on Lila, took this as further evidence of her being "spoiled" and decided to cure her with a terrific spanking. Irene, who had looked upon him as her great protector (since he never took part in her feedings), suffered a traumatic shock, turning so white and rigid that her father called a doctor. By the time the doctor arrived, she had vomited, been put to bed and fallen asleep. The doctor, a general practitioner who regarded children as "tremendously healthy organisms" (a phrase which impressed his wife, his nurse, his patients, and most of all himself), laughed at the father's description of Irene's pallor and rigidity and said that the child had "put one over" on him to prevent the spanking from continuing. Irene's father thought about it, and the next evening, as soon as he walked into the apartment, resumed the spanking where he'd left off. Irene promptly went into a state of shock, once again turning white and rigid. This time she was flung on her bed, the lights turned off and the door locked with a key.

The next morning, her parents looked in on her. She had

undressed, gotten under the covers and was sound asleep. The father was about to tell the worried mother, "I told you so," when he noticed his child's hands. They were gouged, as if by the claws of a wild animal; actually ripped open, blood clotting on palms and backs.

She would never admit it to them (fearing further punishment), but on finding herself locked in a dark room, she'd ripped her hands in an agony of terror—and also, a psychiatrist later guessed, as self-punishment for what she'd done to Lila.

It had, however, ended her father's confidence in the general practitioner and just about eliminated spankings.

"I—I thought I'd die that night," Irene whispered. "I thought I'd scream and go mad and they'd have to put me in a closet or a box and then I'd go even madder. But I fought it—" She grabbed Eli's shoulders and looked into his eyes. "It doesn't make you despise me, does it, Eli? Eli, you mustn't despise me!"

"Silly," he said, and they kissed, and she wouldn't end the kiss, and they began to make love.

But he felt desire slipping, slipping, and hated himself. He was sorry for her, wanted to help her, and yet she was no longer his dream of love—love pure, love complete, love that ached in the chest.

He groaned and buried his face in her hair. She thought it was his passion tearing at him, and said, "Ah, Eli, my darling, I'm so happy—"

And later: "Eli, Eli, how I need you! Tell me you love me. Tell me you love me more than your children."

He told her. But it was with a shame, a sickness and a self-contempt.

He was tired, terribly tired, and couldn't forget that she needed him. Like someone with a stomach-ache needs an enema, or a drunkard needs a bottle, or a cripple needs a crutch, or, or, or—

"Or crap!" he said.

She was lying beside him, and turned sleepily. "What is it?" she mumbled.

"Nothing."

He waited, and soon she was breathing regularly. He felt old, so old, and love was something that had gone forever.

Just before he fell asleep, a thought crept into his mind— a disturbing thought. He wondered if he was damaging his health. . . .

The next day, Saturday, was warm and bright and beautiful. They drove upstate on the Taconic and decided to stop at a large, rustic-cabin restaurant. Eli pulled into the parking lot, began to get out, and then froze. Three people were coming through the restaurant doors on his left. They began walking along the concrete path which ran between the cars parked grill-first and a high wooden fence. They might come as far as his car; might pass it to get to one of the others parked farther along; might see him.

"Get out and go into the restaurant," he said.

Irene looked at him, mouth opening.

"Hurry!" he whispered. "People I know are coming!"

She got out, shut the door, walked away. He kept his eyes on the three people, wondering if they'd seen Irene leave his car. They were still about fifty feet from him and he couldn't tell—

"God," he said, and turned the key in the ignition, wanting to back out and speed off. But then they'd certainly look and recognize him and he'd be in trouble—terrible trouble.

The three people were Mr. and Mrs. Baer and their nephew, Elliot. They lived in Koptic Court. Mrs. Baer was friendly with Rose.

"God," he said again, and shut the ignition, and watched them come closer.

It didn't seem real—more like a corny TV show. And yet, he'd often thought of just this situation, often worried about it. He knew a lot of people, and had been seeing a lot of Irene, and so it was almost inevitable that they run into someone like the Baers sooner or later.

He heard the breath rushing in and out of this throat, and felt sweat sting his eyes, and thought of throwing himself down on the seat.

But he sat absolutely still. He was too frightened to move. Last night, when Irene had spoken of her mother's suspicions, he had felt only minor fear because the threat to his security had been theoretical—something that *might* develop *if* the woman happened to catch them red-handed. And that was a remote possibility. But this was different—

The three people came closer and he heard Mrs. Baer's high cackling laughter, and suddenly visualized that same laughter directed at him and Rose and the boys.

For a second, he hated Irene! If not for her—

The Baers were about twenty feet away now. Only two cars stood between them and his Buick, and he saw that one of the cars was a four-door Chevvy hardtop. Didn't the Baers have a Chevvy hardtop, blue with white roof?

Sudden hope made him hold his breath.

They turned off the concrete path and went to the Chevvy, and he watched them through the windows of the car between. Once again Mrs. Baer's shrill cackle sounded, and Mr. Baer's deep voice said, "So what do you think I told him then, Elliot? I told him maybe you got a better—" A door slammed and the voice dimmed out and the Chevvy's engine coughed into life.

Eli made up hs mind then. He slid across the seat and got out the opposite side and crouched behind his front fender, touching the tire as if examining it. He stayed there, listening to the Chevvy back up and drive toward the highway. He heard it stop, and then pull into traffic with a roar of sudden acceleration and a shriek of spinning tires.

He straightened and walked to the restaurant. Irene was sitting at the far end of the long, rectangular, sun-shot room. She was the only person there. He joined her at the table and said, "I'm sorry."

She was examining a menu. "For what?"

"For—well, for being so short with you. You know—go into the restaurant."

"Oh, that." She was being cynical. Then she looked up. "If you'd apologized for being terrified, I'd feel much better. Whatever happened to that I-don't-care-who-sees-us attitude? Or was it an act?"

He took her hand. It lay in his like a dead thing. "Listen, honey, what good would it do to create a scandal—"

She jerked her hand away. "That's not the point."

"But you yourself used to worry about being seen!"

"I still do. But to be so obvious—to make me feel like a tramp who isn't worth—" She turned to the window with brimming eyes. "Look, a car just drove in. Maybe you'll know the people. Maybe we'd better sneak out the back." She got up. "Order me a rum and Coke." She went to a door marked HERS and disappeared.

He ordered the rum and Coke, and a gin and tonic for himself. The drinks arrived before she did. He'd almost finished his by the time she came out of the ladies' room. He admired the way she walked, but it didn't mean much. He was worried about someone seeing them. . . .

They visited a local museum, and then a drive-in movie, and they didn't do much talking. When they returned to the cabin, Irene went into the bathroom, and he heard the shower start. She stayed in there a long time—almost half an hour. Finally, he knocked on the door. "Irene," he called. "Irene!"

She didn't answer, and the door was locked. He undressed and got into bed.

A car drove into the motor court, headlights flaring across the cabin's windows. He wondered what he would do if it were Rose and the boys and they'd come to check on what Mr. and Mrs. Baer had told them—

The next thing he knew, Irene was kissing his face, wetting his cheeks with her tears, saying, "Never leave me, Eli. Please, darling, I love you so much. I didn't mean those things I said. We love each other. You know we do. Tell me, Eli, please. Tell me how much you love me."

He told her, realizing he must have fallen asleep. He spoke automatically, petting her, soothing her.

"More than your children, Eli?"

"Yes."

"Say it."

"I love you more than my children, Irene."

She covered him with her body. Passion came. He took her, grateful for the end of talk, the end of fear and irritation.

Afterward, he was too tired to bathe. He got under the covers, and she told him of a girl-friend who had a place in Manhattan. "She'll be in Chicago visiting her parents the entire month of September. We can use her apartment, darling! We can have evenings there, listening to good music and drinking cold wine and talking and relaxing and doing whatever we want. It's a beautiful two-room place . . ."

She went on and on, and he wanted to sleep.

"What do you think?" she asked.

"Sounds terrific."

"Yes! Imagine the freedom . . ."

Later, she stopped talking and he fell asleep. He woke once during the night, not knowing why, listening for something. But there was nothing to hear; no shrill laughter. . . .

On Sunday he slept until noon. He might have slept even longer, but Irene was in a playful mood and kissed and tickled him until he was wide awake. She wanted the play to lead to something, but he managed to shunt it aside. He was exhausted. He wanted to have breakfast, and then either sit outside in the sunshine or take a nap.

He told her how knocked out he was, blaming a heavy work schedule and late hours the preceding week. She stroked his head and asked him to tell her how much he loved her —"More than your children, Eli?"

They ate and returned to the cabin. He napped. She washed her hair and set it up in curlers and read a paper-backed novel. They had lunch at five, and he began packing his bag. She knew they were to return to the city early; he'd told her he was expected home about eight. But she began to stall, saying that he could get home at twelve or one and blame it on heavy traffic. He knew that as well as she did, had actually expected to use it as an excuse, but now he wanted to keep his word, wanted to get home and make Rose happy.

Irene continued to stall, and though his irritation grew he was unable to be harsh with her. "Please, Eli," she said later. "Please, please, please let's wait till dark!"

She was a spoiled baby, and he was a tired old man, and he couldn't do anything with her. She removed the curlers, and combed out her hair, and then said, "I'll change to a dress, Eli. It's only seven, but I'll change and we'll go. Okay?"

He nodded, but inside he was straining at the leash. Even if they left right now, and traffic moved quickly, he wouldn't get home before midnight.

He sat down on the edge of the bed. She went to the closet and took out a blue print dress. She draped it across a chair and went to the dresser and looked at herself in the mirror. Then she unbuttoned her toreador pants and dropped them to the floor.

He was surprised. She would allow him to undress her, to a point, but she herself had never undressed in front of him.

She took off her blouse and her brassiere, and stood with her back to him, looking into the mirror, breathing heavily. Then she hooked her thumbs in the elastic band of her white nylon panties and began pushing down.

He wanted to tell her to stop because it was much too late. But he sat and watched.

She removed the panties and turned and walked to the bed and stood directly in front of him, head up, hands on hips, nude except for her low-heeled shoes. "Am I skinny, Eli?" she asked, and it was only through her voice—a shaky, frightened whisper—that he knew she'd done something that took great courage, overcome a terrible fear.

"You're perfect," he said, and reached for her, trapped more by pity than desire. . . .

They didn't leave the cabin until nine. Everything was gone from him now but irritation. She'd made him late. Even in so small a thing as being home when he'd promised, she'd made him break his word. She'd left Rose absolutely nothing.

"I think we're all washed up," Irene said as they passed through the first Westchester toll. "I feel it."

"Damn this traffic," he muttered. "It'll be two in the morning before I get you home."

"I don't think you really love me."

"Of course I do. Please, Irene, let's not discuss it now. I'm jumpy and tired, and so are you, and we can't be objective. We'll talk during the week."

She sat quietly until they passed the second toll; then slid across the seat and snuggled up close and murmured, "I guess I'm silly. I guess you do love me."

"Of course," he said, oppressed by weariness, irritation, confusion.

"Tell me, Eli. Tell me you love me more than your children."

"For the love of God!" he shouted. "Not that nonsense again!"

Her entire body jerked. It was as if he'd smashed her with his fist. She moved away and covered her face with her hands and said, "So there, Irene. So there."

"Listen," he said, turning his head to look at her, frightened and sorry. "Listen, honey, I didn't mean—"

"No, Eli. You were right. We shouldn't talk now. If you want to talk, you'll call me at my home."

"But I want to explain—"

"Please!"

They drove the rest of the way in silence. When he let her off in front of her apartment house, it was a quarter to two. She took her valise and walked away. He waited for her to turn, to wave or at least glance back. But she went straight into the lobby and out of sight.

He sat still a moment, feeling—feeling rejected.

It enraged him. He hated himself! What the hell was he, not wanting her one minute, feeling ill the next because she walked away from him? And what about his desire to see Rose, to be good to her? And what about that chesty brunette in the lobby Friday night?

He churned inside, knowing that he'd lost Irene, feeling

sick about it and glad about it; not knowing how he really
felt about anything any more.

"All screwed up," he said aloud, and drove back toward
the West Side Highway. "All screwed up, by God."

But he would talk to Rose tonight, explain about heavy
traffic, and she would get up and they would have a cup of
tea together like in the old days. . . .

When still ten or twelve blocks from Koptic Court, he
heard the noise and saw the red glow against the sky and
smelled smoke. He picked up speed, wondering, fearing just
a little, still engrossed in the enigma of his personality. He
had to slow down a few blocks later because there were
people running across the street, shouting at each other, and
all sorts of cars, ambulances, police vehicles and fire engines
moving about. He saw where the fire was, and didn't quite
accept it, and pulled to the curb because the street was
blocked by policemen.

He got out and said, "But this can't—" He shook his head
and began to walk toward what had been the lobby, and then
began to run, not believing that this blazing, smoking, gutted
ruin—this smashed, shrunken, flickering rubble—could be
Koptic Court.

The hands grabbed at him and he pushed them away and
one pair grew insistent and stopped him.

"Dad! I thought you too—"

It was Dick, and he was pale and red-eyed. He threw his
arms around Eli and hugged him like when he was a little
boy and wept. "Dad, Daddy, Daddy. I thought you too—"

They stood together and staggered to the curb together
and Eli knew. He knew, and he thought, "So what does it
mean, damn you, Eli Stephen Weiner? Is this some kind of
Old Testament punishment? Is this stupidity real?"

". . . explosion," Dick was sobbing. "I got home from a
date and it was smashed and the fire was just starting and I
couldn't get in. It was a bomb or something. The whole
lobby blew up. No one could get in. The super helped some
people, but Mom isn't out and Teddy isn't out and the fire's
been all over the place so long now, so long now, Daddy—"

They both looked up. Nothing inside those ruins could be
alive.

"Maybe they got out before," Eli said. He shook Dick's
arm. "You didn't look good, you fool! You didn't look all
around. In the ambulances and all around! Before you came,

people got out! You—" He let go and held up both his hands. "Okay. Now we'll look. Together. Come."

"Yes," Dick said, the tears pouring from his eyes. "Yes, I didn't really look. Yes, Dad."

They began walking.

The sirens wailed.

"We'll find them," Eli Weiner said to his son.

17

ELLIOT WYCOFF 2-E

On the second Sunday night in August, Elliot returned from a weekend at the Derrings'. He left the Porsche in the garage and, carrying his bag and tennis racket, walked down the dark alley with quick, bouncy steps. He was suntanned, had gained five solid pounds since March, and felt in top physical condition. (Just that afternoon he had played three sets of tennis up at The Hatchery, and last week at the Slocums' he hadn't lost a set in two full days!) His mental condition, however, was an entirely different matter.

His mother was clinging to her plan of coming to New York on or about September first. And even though he hadn't had any further private meetings with Alex Fernol, the boy was constantly on his mind.

He didn't know what to do about Mother. She'd trumped his ace by making a complete reversal of her previous stand, agreeing that she would have to fly if she was coming to New York. She seemed to be trying to put aside her lifelong fear of aircraft.

With his aunt and uncle now firmly behind the idea, Elliot had no way of defeating it. And yet, he had to! He just couldn't bring Mother to his friends!

As for Alex Fernol, maybe that was no problem at all; maybe he'd created a problem where none existed. If he liked the boy, he should see him. If that meant—other things, well, he'd been drifting in that direction all his life anyway.

He walked even faster, his lips tightening. He didn't want to give in. He didn't want to leave the pale of normalcy.

But what else was there?

He didn't care for women; that was definite now. And what reason could he give people for not dating, for not having anything to do with women?

If he could find no reason to give others, he could find no reason to give himself.

He could see himself staying clear of all sex the rest of his life, but there had to be a reason for staying clear of women, a face to show the world. Otherwise, he would, in time, lose the Slocums and Derrings just as surely as by becoming an active homosexual; and he would also lose Sylvia Chrysler and all future friends.

So why not Alex Fernol, and others like him? He would find love and friendship there to take the place of what he would lose—

He reached the lobby, and winced. What a contrast to the simple, tasteful surroundings of The Hatchery! That garish scroll over the doors—*Koptic Court*—which some coarse, ego-centric, bourgeois builder had inflicted upon the tenants. Not that many of the current crop of tenants knew enough to resent it. And tonight the dominant odor was not food or children but disinfectant; cheap disinfectant with an undertone of kerosene—

Mr. and Mrs. Schimler from the fifth floor were waiting for the elevator. They nodded and said hello, and he did the same as he headed for the staircase.

A thought struck him and he glanced back at the middle-aged couple. They were standing quietly, looking at each other. He'd had no undue effect on them. But that would change once he started going with the Alex Fernols, dropping all attempts at being a normal man, allowing the walk and talk and air of homosexualism to have free rein. Then their eyes would grow contemptuous, their hellos cold—and that's the way it would be with everyone.

He reached the apartment, put the key in the lock and opened the door. "Ah, Elliot!" his uncle said, looking down the foyer from the living room. "Good to see you! Have a nice time?"

"Yes," he said, appreciating the obvious sincerity of the welcome. "Very nice."

His aunt came into view. "Good news, Elliot! Mother reserved a seat on a nonstop, coast-to-coast flight for September fourth! She'll be with us that very evening!"

He answered and smiled, and inside he was shriveling, sickening. It was too damn much!

He went to bed a half-hour later, pleading exhaustion. He tossed and turned and thought of Alex and then of his mother.

Actually, he told himself, *she's an attractive person. Her face and figure are still passable for a woman over sixty. Except for her accent (and a host of famous emigrés have that!) she's socially acceptable. Of course, she isn't up on anything resembling plays, books and music, but be grateful for her lack of interest in men.*

He rolled over on his face. It was no good trying to rationalize the problem away. Just because Mother no longer seduced every man she met didn't mean she wouldn't shame and embarrass him in a million other ways. Maybe it was contemptible for a son to feel like that, but he did.

He fell asleep. He had his obscure dream, the one about two dogs in a drugstore window, and woke up. It was 3:00 A.M., but he felt he couldn't remain in bed. He tiptoed into the kitchen, closed the door and turned on the small, white, plastic radio Aunt Minnie kept on top of the refrigerator. He found music at the end of the dial and sat down at the table.

"I love you, I love you, I *lo-o-o-ve* you," a throaty female vocalist sang. "I love you 'cause you're everything a girl could want—"

It went on that way, on and on that way, like all the other songs about love. Like the songs that had been played in boot camp, and in the Frisco bars, and on the juke box aboard ship. (His particular marine unit had been assigned to an aircraft carrier as permanent personnel, and so he was more a sailor throughout the war than a soldier; more the old-fashioned marine.) Nineteen forty-five, and the carrier had docked in Tokyo harbor early that morning. The war was over; just a few days over. The Japanese waited fearfully for the conquerors, and the Americans waited fearfully for the occupation.

"They'll fight a guerrilla war against us," a corporal named O'Hearn had said to Elliot as they prepared to go on watch. (Due to the sudden end of hostilities, everything was fouled up and the captain had ordered three gyrenes to stand guard on the mysteriously darkened stretch of dock.) "Maybe we'll get a taste of it tonight."

O'Hearn wasn't a friend. Elliot had no friends on board. He repelled all attempts at friendship, had done so since boot training, and for a very good reason. Friends would have insisted he go places with them, and when a marine goes places he's interested primarily in one thing—women. Friends would have wondered about Elliot's lack of interest in women, and wonder would have given way to active opinion, and that would have been disastrous. (Despite all the stories he'd heard about homosexuality aboard U.S. naval vessels, the citizen-sailor and citizen-marine of World War II was as quick to jump on a "fag" as his army counterparts.)

Elliot snorted and said, "You're full of crap, jarhead. They're licked, and licked good. If they don't want another atom bomb dropped down their throats, they've got to act nice, real nice."

That's the way he talked all through his three-year hitch in the Corps, and he was quick to take umbrage and use his fists. It was the surest method he knew to allay any and all suspicions. Like people everywhere, marines and sailors equated homosexuality with feminism. In essence, they were right to do so, but covering up was simple enough for Elliot and, he was sure, for many other men fighting against joining the third sex.

"Well, wait'll we get on that dock," O'Hearn said, strapping on his .45 automatic. "You can relax if you want to, but I'm keeping my hand near this pea-shooter."

Elliot and O'Hearn joined the third guard, an eighteen-year-old boot named Kurtz, and at 10:00 P.M. they were patrolling a darkened, thirty-yard area of dock. At midnight, they were still on the job, with two more hours to go. The ship was quiet, the city beyond the dock seemed dead—and that's when they heard the woman's voice calling from the vicinity of a warehouse about a hundred feet past the ship's bow.

"Sailor san, sailor san, I love sailor san."

Elliot whirled, hand reaching for his gun, but he wasn't really frightened. He felt sure it was a prostitute on the prowl for the conqueror's cash. However, he hoped O'Hearn would mistrust the voice, as per his theory of guerrilla warfare, and that there wouldn't be any decision to line up on the woman.

His hopes were shattered a moment later. O'Hearn and Kurtz joined him, and they whispered excitedly.

"What a break!" Kurtz said. "Twelve weeks at sea and she drops right into our laps. There—there she is! See?"

"Yeah!" O'Hearn said. "Behind a bunch of big barrels. She's waving. We'd better hurry before she gets scared."

"Gee, I don't think we ought to take the chance—" Elliot began.

"Christ, Wycoff, it's the perfect setup!" O'Hearn said. "No one can see us on this dock tonight. You heard Captain Rolls talking about how all the lights along this stretch are out. By tomorrow they'll have them fixed, but tonight is perfect. Even if all three of us went at once, no one on board could see!"

"But what if Lieutenant Hodges makes his rounds—"

"Shit, he was here only twenty minutes ago! C'mon, we'll—"

"Sailor san, sailor san, I love sailor san," the sweet voice called.

O'Hearn pushed Elliot forward. "You can be first, Wycoff, only cut the crap and get moving before someone on board hears her. Then we'll have a riot. And show her the difference between us and sailors—stand up for the Corps, gyrene!"

"No, listen—"

Kurtz shoved his face close to Elliot's, peering through the darkness. "What is it with you, Wycoff? You act so damned—"

"Okay, okay," Elliot said quickly, moving toward the warehouse and what looked like oil barrels. "But don't blame me—"

"Go on, boy, and leave some for us!" O'Hearn interrupted.

Elliot walked ahead, sweating. He'd been in the battle of the Coral Seas and seen action eight other times in the Pacific. He was a corporal and worked a brace of antiaircraft guns— far from the safest job on ship—but he'd always been reasonably calm under fire.

Now he was terrified. Now he knew he would have to do something he'd consciously avoided doing all his adult life. He was a virgin, and wanted to remain so. But O'Hearn and Kurtz would soon be taking their turns with that woman, and she might be able to communicate any failure on his part—

He had to do it.

He reached the barrels stretching in a line three-deep across his path. Behind the barrels he saw the woman. She was a small, shadowy creature with a white face; that was all he could make of her in the darkness.

"Sailor san," she said, and now he heard the way her voice trembled. "Sailor san, I love sailor san."

He felt his way to the right, around the barrels, and slowly moved toward her. As he came closer, he was able to see that her face was oval and small-featured and rather pretty. But she wasn't young—about forty, he guessed. And she wasn't cheap-looking, though he wasn't sure that American standards of "cheap" and "fine" would apply here.

"What do you want?" he whispered, sure now that she wasn't a prostitute.

"Sailor san, sailor san—"

"Yes, yes," he interrupted, not bothering to explain he wasn't a sailor. "You want food?"

"Food?" She shook her head. "I speak. I understand." She raised her arms, spread her lips in what was supposed to be a smile. But he knew she was terrified.

He moved closer, and she half stepped, half fell against him. "Love sailor san," she whispered in her sweet, trembling voice. "Love sailor san. Dōzo. No kill husband. No kill children. I speak. I understand—"

He understood too, but he couldn't stop her. She was fumbling with his clothes, pulling him against her as she herself leaned back against a metal barrel. She was an educated woman, a well-to-do woman if he could judge by the softness of her hands and the quality of her kimono, but she believed that the Americans were going to butcher her people when the occupation swung into high gear. She was here to seduce American servicemen—all of whom were "sailor san" in her limited English vocabulary—thereby purchasing immunity for herself and her family.

"We aren't going to kill—" he began, and knew it was hopeless, and was full of pity, disgust and fear.

"You make love, sailor san. Dōzo. Tell everyone no kill family of Mitsayo—"

"Hey," O'Hearn whispered from the other side of the barrels. "Snap it up, boy! Don't be a hog!"

"Hai!" the woman said, as if acknowledging a command. She pulled Elliot closer.

Elliot kissed her, and felt nothing. He wouldn't be able to go through with it, and in her agony of fear and worry she'd say something to O'Hearn and Kurtz that would set them to thinking and talking . . .

She'd somehow raised her clothing and was lying back on the barrel. *He had to become a man!*

Several fumbling, frantic moments later, he accomplished his task. He used a simple stratagem: he thought back to the night he'd caressed his friend Ben's naked body. It worked, but it left him more revolted, more fearful than ever.

He returned to the dock and made appropriately lewd remarks and kept a sharp lookout while O'Hearn and Kurtz visited the woman behind the oil barrels. Later, he tried to tell himself he was rapidly developing the proper attitude toward women.

In October of 1946, he was honorably discharged from the Corps as a sergeant, and returned to Philadelphia. He hadn't seen his mother since a ten-day leave in 1944, and was shocked at the way she'd deteriorated. Reba Wycoff was only fifty, but she looked ten years older. She'd lost most of her teeth due to a severe attack of pyorrhea, and her dentist was still in the process of fitting her with upper and lower plates. She had a puffy, sallow, sunken look about the face, and had gained considerable weight around her once-trim waistline. But she still retained a strong interest in men, and had finally decided to remarry.

"He's a fine fellow, Elliot," she told her son the day after he'd returned home. "You'll like him. Seymour Eddelman, his name is. He's a professional—a druggist."

Elliot nodded, but he wasn't prepared for the huge man who stomped into the house that night. Seymour Eddelman was over six feet four and weighed close to three hundred pounds. He gave his age as fifty-five, but judging by his ruined, craggy-featured face, he was closer to sixty-five. He was about the ugliest man Elliot had ever seen.

"Well?" his mother asked, after Eddelman had left. "What do you think of him?"

Elliot shrugged. "Big. Old."

"Old? Well, maybe he's older than fifty-five. Fifty-eight, I think. Sixty at the most."

Elliot examined his hands. "Do you really have to, Mother?"

"Have to? Marry him, you mean?"

"Marry him, I mean. Haven't you had enough—"

She burst into tears, sobbing, "How you talk to your mother! You insult me like I was some sort of—of tramp."

He said nothing.

She raised streaming eyes then, and he met them squarely. She turned away quickly from the contempt and pity she read there.

"I wasn't very smart as a young woman," she muttered. "I didn't know it bothered you to have me bring friends—"

"Friends," he intoned, deriving a fierce, bitter satisfaction from the dull red color invading her neck and face.

"Vuss vilst du fon dein mutter?" she wailed.

"I want nothing from my mother," he said, getting up. "I'm —I'm sorry if I said anything to hurt you. If you want to get married, good luck to you. But please understand it has nothing to do with me. I've already applied for entrance to Princeton University—"

"But that's not in Philadelphia, Elliot! You're not going away from home so soon after more than three years in the Marines? You wouldn't—"

"I'm going to a good college, Mother," he said firmly. "I've made up my mind. In any event, I wouldn't—couldn't—live here."

She wept again, accusing herself of being a bad mother. When he maintained silence, refusing to contradict her, she changed tactics and called him an "unnatural son." He accepted this calmly, once again in control of his emotions, and later apologized for being harsh.

He soothed and pampered her a few weeks, and at the same time learned he couldn't get into Princeton. Not that his scholastic average wasn't tops (third highest in his graduating class), or that he wasn't personable, even impressive, but there were just too many applicants waiting for admission, especially those from Princeton's "feeder" schools.

He wanted to try Harvard, Yale or another snob school, but then decided not to since it would probably mean waiting lists similar to Princeton's.

He applied to, and was accepted by, Columbia University, and left for New York City where he landed a job as salesman in an exclusive men's shop. He lived in a dormitory—Hartley Hall—and made himself so useful at the clothing store that he was retained on a part-time basis when the spring term arrived and he began attending classes.

He remained in Hartley Hall until he received a bid from an excellent fraternity, then moved into the frat house which was one of a solid row of similar establishments on the south side of 114th Street. There he roomed with Jerry Slocum, a junior. Jerry was an economics major who had served only eight months in the army before having his right thighbone shattered by a grenade at Salerno. He retained a heavy limp, but was a reasonably cheerful guy and the perfect roommate for Elliot since he was ultra-particular when it came to female companionship—a subsconscious protective device due to the limp, Elliot suspected, but one that operated to make him a more selective personality.

Elliot double-dated with Jerry a few times as part of his plan to make the wealthy army vet accept him completely. Finally, Jerry invited him to his family's Long Island estate for the summer vacation. Elliot said he'd let Jerry know, but that was merely an act meant to show that he had equally attractive opportunities elsewhere. He accepted a week later.

Meanwhile, his mother had been disappointed in her marriage plans. Not that Seymour Eddelman had changed his mind. In fact, he was hurrying to see Reba Wycoff when misfortune visited him in the form of a cerebral hemorrhage. He died immediately. This so unnerved Reba that she entered a local hospital for a complete physical checkup. And from then on, staying alive became her major concern, with a resultant increase in her hypochondria.

Jerry Slocum graduated when Elliot became a junior. Elliot went home for the first time in two years for his between-semesters vacation, and his mother informed him that she could no longer take the "terrible Philadelphia winters." Because of her "delicate health," she was selling the house and furnishings and moving out to California. She had relatives there and they'd promised to put her up until she could find a nice, inexpensive place to live.

Elliot was all for it; the more distance between himself and his mother, the better! But on the night he returned to school, she told him something that made him feel warmer toward her than at any time since he'd been a child.

"It's a sad thing to most women, Elliot," she said, not looking at him, "but I think I'm glad. You know— I mean—" She thought hard, trying to find words, and then said in Yiddish, "I don't need men any more. It's gone, that feeling. Gone. Poof. Like it never was. I'm—sorry if I did things to shame you—"

He stopped her then, and a high wall that had stood between them began to crumble. She accompanied him to the station, and when they said goodbye he had to fight back tears. She was his mother, all that was left of his old life, and she was going far away.

Back at school, he maneuvered the most eligible freshman pledge (most eligible from *his* point of view) into becoming his new roommate. David Cresham Derring was a short, thin, shy, sensitive young man who was grateful to the point of servility for Elliot's friendship. Later, when he adjusted to his new surroundings, he began repaying Elliot's kindnesses with invitations to his home and The Hatchery. Elliot, who continued to see Jerry Slocum and his parents, now had a second wealthy New York family to visit. He enjoyed both families as much for their erudition as for their social position and ability to provide fine surroundings and good entertainment.

By the time graduation came, he had decided to live on in New York and maintain, at all costs, the friendships college had brought him. With a B.A. degree, and honors in English Literature, he moved into his aunt and uncle's Brooklyn apartment, "temporarily."

Finding a good job was a lot more difficult than he had imagined—at least in the field of publishing. Finally, he landed a position with a literary agency, and after four years moved on to the Lester Publishing Company. Meanwhile, both his ex-roommates had married and moved out of town. But Elliot managed to retain, even to solidify, his position with their parents. And he had visited Mother for the past three summers, flying out to California during his two-week vacations. She looked reasonably well for an aging woman, and while he didn't actually enjoy his visits, they lulled a certain sense of guilt and made his return to New York all the more pleasurable.

His life had been going along in this fashion, and he'd been content with it, until the coming of Alex Fernol and his mother's sudden decision to visit New York. . . .

"I love you, I love you, I lo-o-o-o-ve you!" the vocalist concluded. Elliot got up from the kitchen table and shut off the radio. He started back toward his bedroom, wondering what was going to happen to his life now, and he almost walked into his Aunt Minnie.

"I knew I heard sounds," she said. "What's the matter, Elliot, can't you sleep?"

"I was thirsty," he said, looking down at the small, thin woman whose face vaguely resembled his mother's. Suddenly, he was overwhelmed by the desire to unburden himself—to tell her why he couldn't have Mother visit him here; to admit that he was slowly losing the fight against becoming an active homosexual. "I—I was thinking—"

"Yes?"

But he couldn't go on. She would never understand. No one would understand. There was no shoulder for him to weep on in all the world—unless he turned to Alex Fernol and the fraternity of the damned.

"Something's been worrying you the last few months," Minnie Baer said. "Won't you tell me, Elliot? Maybe I can help."

He smiled. "Thanks, Aunt Minnie, but it's nothing, really. I guess I'm a little nervous. We've had a lot of extra work at the office because of vacations and unexpected sick leaves. I need a good rest."

She put her hand on his arm. "Then come with Phil and me this weekend. We're going to a small hotel up in Connecticut. It's not a fancy place, but there's always a few young people around and I'm sure you'll have a good time—"

He was going to shake his head, but she kept talking, pleading with him, and then he asked himself why not. Sure, he'd go along with them and have a good rest. Maybe it would help him think of a way to block Mother's trip, and shove Alex Fernol from his mind. But then again, that would be a miracle, and he didn't believe in miracles. But he'd go along anyway.

"We'll use our Chevvy," Aunt Minnie was saying. "You'll just lean back and let Phil handle the driving and the traffic. You'll leave your tennis racket here, and sleep a lot and sit a lot and calm down. Please, Elliot, I want your mother to see a happy, healthy son when she comes for her visit."

"All right," he said, and bent to kiss her.

She patted his cheek, smiling. "Maybe you'll even meet a nice girl. The last time Phil and I went there, we saw a lovely girl and Phil said, 'Wouldn't she be perfect for Elliot!' Of course, we didn't know if she was smart enough—"

"Hey, I'm a happy bachelor," he said, maintaining the smile but feeling irritation rising. "I'm coming along for a rest, remember?"

She nodded, but he didn't like the gleam in her eye. He went to bed. . . .

He ran into Alex Fernol twice on Monday, and the blond youth looked more attractive than ever. At four-thirty, Alex called him and said, "I'm thinking of renting a cabin up at Cape Cod for the weekend, Elliot, and I'd appreciate someone sharing the cost with me. How about it?"

It sounded wonderful to Elliot. He'd be able to tell Alex of his mother, and of everything else bothering him. Alex would understand. Alex would be the shoulder to weep on; would offer friendship—and love.

But there'd be a price.

To hell with the price! a voice shouted in his brain. *To hell with what people think! They'll all shy away from you sooner or later. You have no valid reason to give them for not wanting women, and they'll damn you for it before too long. To hell with them!*

But Aunt Minnie and Uncle Phil had already made reservations for him at the little Connecticut summer resort. He couldn't back out on them now. Besides, he wanted this last weekend, this last pause-for-breath before taking the long-deferred plunge.

"Sorry," he said. "I've already made other arrangements."

"That's too bad," Fernol said smoothly. "I'd hoped for a congenial—partner. And I'm going home for the Labor Day weekend."

"Well, if we have an Indian summer, there may yet be a weekend or two fit for sunning and bathing. Perhaps we can share a place then."

"Definitely!" Fernol said. He hesitated a moment. "I'm glad you've decided to—to be friendly. I feel we have too much in common to ignore each other."

"Yes," Elliot said, and cleared his throat.

That soft, soft voice pulling at him. And yet, he wasn't ready; didn't really want to give in to the siren call; didn't want—

"I'll be keeping my fingers crossed for good weather," Fernol said. "It would be wonderful if we could—"

"Yes, I'll be speaking to you," Elliot said, and hung up.

After a rainy Friday morning and afternoon, the skies cleared and the air turned cool. Elliot went to a movie with his aunt and uncle that night. They were back in the apartment by ten, and in bed an hour later, bags packed.

They'd hoped to be on the West Side Highway by nine Saturday morning, but Minnie insisted they have a big breakfast, and neither Phil nor Elliot felt any compulsion to rush. So they didn't get into the four-door Chevvy hardtop until almost ten.

It was pleasant. The radio played popular music, and Minnie hummed along with the tunes, and Elliot had the back seat all for himself, stretching out his long legs comfortably. By noon, the sun was hot and they were all thirsty. They stopped at a gas station which had a restaurant around back, but Phil said, "Let's just have a Coke here. Remember that nice place we ate in the last time, Minnie? The big place made to look like an old-fashioned inn—Rustic Something-or-other, I think it was called. Right on the Taconic, about an hour from here."

She nodded, and asked Elliot if he could wait another hour for his lunch. He said, "Certainly; good for my girlish figure," and laughed too loud and too long.

It was one-fifteen when they reached the rustic-style restaurant and parked in the big lot. An hour later, they came out, stuffed with duckling and baked potatoes. Elliot had drunk two bottles of Dutch beer and felt pleasantly sleepy—the way he hoped to feel all during the weekend. (He'd bought a fifth of Paddy's Irish whisky and tucked it away in his bag, vowing there would be no nightmares or sleepless nights this time around!) As they reached the Chevvy, with Uncle Phil telling a story of how he'd bested a competitor in the leather-goods line, Elliot saw a man leave a car and then suddenly disappear, as if he'd crouched down behind it. It looked like someone he knew; someone from Koptic Court. He glanced at the car, a Buick, and recalled that Aunt Minnie's friend, Mrs. Weiner, had one like it. Could the man be Mr. Weiner?

He was going to ask Minnie about it, but Uncle Phil's story was a long one and by the time it ended they were back on the Taconic and Elliot was dozing.

He never did get to ask about Mr. Weiner. His weekend was so bad it drove all trivialities out of his mind.

They arrived at the little hotel at three-ten and were shown to adjoining rooms. Then they strolled around the grounds until six. Elliot didn't like the place; it was shabby, and the couple who ran it were big and loud and had the look of vigorous entertainment planners, the type who never allow anyone to escape a dance or parlor game.

They turned out to be even worse than entertainment planners. They were active matchmakers.

Dinner was served between seven and eight, and when Aunt Minnie knocked on his door at seven sharp to say she and Phil were ready, Elliot told them to go on without him.

"I'm not even washed yet," he said through the door. "It'll take me at least another half hour, so go ahead. I'll meet you in the dining room."

When she said all right and walked away, he went back to the narrow, lumpy bed. He'd showered and gotten into shorts and been lying there for the past forty-five minutes, sipping from a glass of Irish whisky and water. He needed the stimulant; the hotel depressed him.

They were on the second floor, and from all sides came shrill laughter, music, and clanking of utensils from the dining room. He wondered why he'd ever let himself in for a thing like this. These hotels, big and small, were happy hunting grounds. A weekend consisted of a series of introductions, passes, rejections and acceptances. The boys were out to

make the girls; the girls were out to "interest" the boys—
lead them to the altar. This place was as wrong for him as the
stag party had been.

But he had a second drink, and got into slacks and a sports
shirt, and examined himself in the dresser mirror. He looked
fine. He'd eat dinner and relax with Minnie and Phil and get
a long night's sleep. Tomorrow he'd lie around in the sun and,
if he felt like it, try the small pool behind the pathetic tar-
and-pebble tennis courts. They'd be heading back home by
seven or eight that evening, so it wouldn't be bad.

But he underestimated the Graebers, owners and operators
of the hotel. Minnie had evidently mentioned him to them,
stressing the fact that he was a bachelor. That was all the
Graebers needed to know. They had half a dozen eligible fe-
males in the hotel and picked one they considered the intellectual type. Her name was Miriam Dovnik; she'd graduated
from C.C.N.Y. with a major in Primary Education. She
taught in the New York City system, and was proud of her
position and contemptuous of almost everything else in the
world. She did, however, respect editors, mainly because she
had never met one before.

As soon as Elliot reached the entrance to the noisy dining
room, his aunt and uncle waved at him from a table on the
left. The table was large and round and could seat eight people.
At the moment, it seated Minnie, Phil, an excessively healthy-
looking girl with red hair, and an elderly gentleman who was
just rising. The elderly gentleman and Elliot passed each
other; the elderly gentleman marked the passage with a loud
belch. It was, Elliot decided, the keynote to his evening.

The excessively healthy-looking redhead was Miriam Dovnik. Minnie introduced them, and then tugged Phil's arm.
"Oh, yes," Phil said, beaming. "Minnie and I are going to
take a walk in the moonlight. Why don't you young people—"

"Thank you," Elliot said, raising a spoonful of fruit salad
to his mouth. "Do you mind if I eat first?"

"Not at all," Phil said, the irony completely lost on him.

"Let's go," Minnie said.

They left, glancing back frequently. They were met at the
doorway by Mr. and Mrs. Graeber, and all four turned and
beamed at Elliot and Miriam Dovnik. Then they walked out.

"So you're an editor?" Miriam Dovnik said, her ruddy,
pretty face alight with interest. Her eyes flickered over Elliot
for at least the fifth time, and she evidently liked what she
saw. "Tell me about your work."

Elliot chewed his fruit salad, swallowed and looked at her. "Since you've already partaken of nourishment, Miss Dovnik—"

"Oh come now, Elliot. We don't have to be so formal. Call me Miriam."

"Miriam. I think you should be the first to do the talking. At least while I eat."

She giggled. "Of course. Well, I teach the third grade . . ."

She went on, and on, and on. She told stories of "cute" children and "bad" children, and every so often would pause and smile at him and say, "I really could write a book about my experiences. Don't you think plain people would find the adventures of a teacher exciting?"

He'd nod, and keep eating. He finished the eight-course dinner and lit a cigarette. "One thing I never cared for," he said when she paused for breath.

"What's that, Elliot?"

"Dancing. Social dancing, that is."

She blinked her eyes, startled at the sudden change of topic. "Oh—" She recovered quickly. "To tell the truth, neither do I. At least not when nature's beauties compete for honors."

Yoiks, Elliot thought. We're off.

"Would you like to take a stroll, Miriam?"

"Love to!"

They walked out of the dining room, through the lobby and onto the wide porch. Minnie, Phil and the Graebers were sitting in a close, conspiratorial group. They stopped talking as soon as they saw Elliot and Miriam.

"Ah," Phil said. "Going for a walk?"

"Yes," Elliot answered, and could cheerfully have slit his uncle's throat. "I thought you and Minnie were going to do the same?"

"So we are, so we are. In a few minutes."

"Good," Elliot said, and turned to Miriam Dovnik. "We'll wait for them, won't we?"

"Of course." Her eyes blinked in confused, startled fashion.

Phil's mouth opened. Elliot smiled at him. Phil's mouth closed and he glanced at his wife. Minnie couldn't seem to find anything to say; she glanced at the Graebers. The Graebers had plenty to say.

"Hey!" Mr. Graeber bellowed jovially. "What sort of romantic walk in the moonlight would that be! Go on alone, young fellow! Go on and take the girl out on the beautiful grounds! Go on!"

Elliot felt he ought to salute, do a smart about-face, and whisk Miriam off in double-time.

"Young folks like to look at our swimming pool at night," Mrs. Graeber, a greasy woman of close to two hundred pounds, simpered. "The floodlights shine in the water, you know."

Elliot decided anything was better than listening to this. He took Miriam's arm and fled into the darkness. "The swimming pool by floodlight," he murmured. "How romantic."

Miriam laughed, and he was grateful for that. "They aren't the most tactful people, Elliot, but their hearts are in the right places."

"Really?" Elliot murmured, and then felt he was being supercilious. After all, the girl was rather nice, and it wasn't her fault she'd been paired off with him.

They went to the swimming pool. Three or four other couples were already staring at the rectangle of spotlighted green water. Elliot hoped they found something in the view, but he couldn't imagine what the hell it would be.

He was irritable enough to voice the thought. Miriam Dovnik laughed, but it sounded uncomfortable, nervous, rather forced. She seemed confused and unhappy as they walked toward a dirt road.

They said nothing to each other, and then a series of deep-throated barks made Miriam grab his arm. A large collie came out of a field and into the road. Elliot stopped walking and said, "Yes, yes, boy. That's a good boy."

The collie came up to him, barked again so that Miriam gasped, and trotted back to the field.

Elliot found he was holding the schoolteacher's hand. He had no desire to do so, but thought she would be happier if he did. He continued to hold it, and she relaxed and began to talk. She talked about her home in the Bronx, how she had tried an apartment of her own in Manhattan "but men think you're—well, you know—" she stiffened her shoulders and plunged ahead—"an easy mark. So I gave it up and went back to my parents' place." She recalled more teaching experiences, and he felt he gave an excellent performance of a man enthralled.

And all the while he was bored, annoyed, resentful of his aunt and uncle for having pushed him into this senseless business. There was also an element of shame—shame at wasting this girl's time, at allowing her to look at him with interested, hopeful eyes.

"What say we turn back, Miriam?" They'd been walking almost an hour and the road was beginning to climb steeply.

"There's a beautiful view from the top of this hill," she said. She laughed. "Not the swimming pool, really. I've been up here with a few boys in the past eight days and it always affects me—" Her voice died out, and he realized he'd been expected to bolster her with some sort of laughing remark, or at least a word or two of encouragement.

"Then what're we waiting for?" he said—eagerly, he hoped.

Always the actor. Always the need to lie. Always the emptiness.

If only there were a reason to give Minnie and Phil and the Graebers and the Slocums and the Derrings and the world; a reason for his not wanting women; a reason that would satisfy people without alienating them—

There was no such reason for him. If he'd been born a hunchback, he could show bitterness, supersensitivity, rejection of women—and everyone would shake his head and say, "Poor Elliot, he's afraid of being hurt. Maybe it's best he stays away from girls. They'd only hurt him . . ."

If he'd lost a limb during the war. Even Jerry Slocum's limp had been enough to explain his modicum of antisocialness at college.

"There!" Miriam Dovnik said as they reached the top of the hill. "Isn't it beautiful?"

He looked around. The countryside, visible for several miles in three directions, was washed in moonlight, colored a greenish black.

It was nice. It wasn't beautiful in the sense that a Colorado mountain scene is beautiful, or a Vermont copse is beautiful, or a Martha's Vineyard stretch of sand beach is beautiful. It was tilled fields and a few farm buildings and the shabby resort hotel, in moonlight, seen from a height. It was beauty to the eye that is either starved for anything antiurban, or cannot rate beauty.

"Yes," he said, and put his arms around her and kissed her.

"Oh, Elliot," she breathed. "I liked you right away—"

He took her hand and turned and walked back down the hill. There'd be no vicious whispering about him here!

They sang a few popular songs together and she walked very close to him. He was sick. He thought of tomorrow and wondered how he could avoid her, and thought of Alex Fernol and knew there was no way of avoiding him.

With a reason to give the world, he could have survived

without love, without passion. But there was no reason, and he would be destroyed as a social being sooner or later. And so he would speak to Alex this Monday.

With that decision made, another kind of sickness and despair came, dull and aching rather than sharp and unbearable. He would grow accustomed to it. He would learn to live with it. He had no choice.

The next morning, when Minnie and Phil knocked on his door, he asked if they'd have some breakfast sent up to him. "I'm feeling pretty sick," he muttered, looking out at them through a narrow opening.

"But what is it?" Phil asked, face worried.

"Tired, I guess," Elliot answered, and it wasn't entirely a lie. "Overtired."

"Lie down, dear," Minnie said. "Rest."

He stayed in his room all morning. At noon he had three drinks of Irish and went down to face the dining room and Miriam Dovnik. Her pink-skinned face lit up when she saw him. He returned her smile, and hoped he was convincing. Evidently he was; she remained at the table after the elderly gentleman, Mr. Seleg, had belched his way into the lobby and Minnie and Phil had departed with glowing backward glances.

"Your aunt tells me you weren't feeling well," Miriam said.

Elliot wanted to end the farce. "It was nothing." He took out his address book and pen. "Mind giving me your telephone number? I'm going to lie down the rest of this afternoon and I want—"

She flushed and nodded. Her voice was soft as she gave him the information he would never use.

"See you in the city," she said, and touched his hand.

"Yes. Goodbye for now." He went up to his room and lay on the bed and drank quite a bit from the bottle of Irish. He didn't go down for dinner. Minnie brought him two sandwiches. He ate part of one, threw the rest in the wastebasket, and packed his bag. He looked out the window and listened to loud, happy voices. A line from something long forgotten came to his mind.

"Goodbye, lady bird."

He told himself he didn't know what it meant, but it made his chest ache and his throat thicken.

"Goodbye, lady bird."

It was so stupid, it was laughable.

He didn't laugh.

They reached Koptic Court at eleven-ten. Minnie and Phil went right to bed after washing up; Elliot sat in the living room, reading a magazine. He was finishing a short story when the floor seemed to push up under his feet and a terrific roar filled his ears. He cried out as the lights died and plaster fell. Then he blacked out for a while.

Later, he got to his feet and took a step toward the center of the room, and almost fell through a hole in the floor. He staggered and went down on his knees. More plaster fell, and a large piece struck him on the head. He crouched, dazed and trembling.

He heard his Aunt Minnie screaming, his Uncle Phil calling. He smelled the dampness of old plaster and the acridity of an explosive and, some time later, the smoke.

Smoke.

The thought of fire frightened him, made him shake his head and try to think.

"Elliot! Elliot, help us! For the love of God—"

Uncle Phil was still calling, and Aunt Minnie was still screaming.

He stood up. He could think a little now, and he wondered why they didn't leave their bedroom and come in here and go through the living room window and down the fire escape. He felt his way through the darkness, stumbling over lumps and cracks and, once, going knee-deep in a fissure.

A fissure in the foyer outside the bathroom. Funny.

He passed the bathroom and his bedroom, and reached the master bedroom—or a pile of stuff where the bedroom door should have been.

He touched the pile with his hands, and from beyond it heard his uncle.

"Elliot! God, what's happened? Elliot, there's smoke in there! There's fire coming up from downstairs! The door's blocked. Something—the ceiling and part of the bathroom wall—Elliot!"

Minnie screamed, and Phil tried to quiet her, and she screamed again. Phil's voice began to break.

"Fire! Fire's coming up—Don't go near that hole, Minnie! God, Elliot, Elliot—"

Elliot shook his head. The smell of smoke was stronger now, and he began to pull at the pile of rubble in front of the bedroom door. Pieces came away easily and he tossed them over his shoulder.

Light began to filter in from somewhere—reddish light.

"Fire!" Phil screamed. "Fire coming up from the first floor! Help! Help! Get away from the window, Minnie! Help me pull at this junk. You can't jump out. You'll break your neck—"

"I'm coming," Elliot said, and realized he wasn't speaking loud enough to carry over the growing sounds—the shouts and screams and wailings and cracklings which came from upstairs and downstairs and all sides now. The crackling bothered him the most, and that growing light. Fire was coming up through holes and fissures in the floor. Fire that crackled avariciously, eating more and more rapidly into the old walls and floors and ceilings. Fire coming up fast.

He ripped and tore at the stuff blocking the bedroom doorway, and his mind cleared completely, and he shouted, "I'm coming, Phil, Minnie! I'm coming! Just a few more minutes—"

But he wasn't sure how long it would take.

Things kept falling from above—bits of ceiling. The entire house groaned and sagged and chittered as a multitude of fragments dropped. And all the time the crackling grew louder, the reddish light stronger.

He suddenly broke through. "Here!" he shouted, and his groping hands touched another pair of hands.

"Minnie, Elliot's got through!"

They tore at the loose pile of wood and plaster and something else, something big and solid. The reddish light flared inside the bedroom, flames licking up through a hole in a corner near the windows, and Elliot saw an armchair blocking the door. But where could an armchair—

He glanced up, saw the huge hole, heard the voices.

". . . baby over to the fire escape—"

Upstairs. A chair from upstairs! What the hell had hit this house? Was it the atom bomb?

He and Phil worked from opposite sides and got the chair out of the way. Minnie came out first, and Elliot helped her over the debris. Phil stumbled out and led his wife toward the living room and the fire escape. Elliot turned to follow, and heard the creaking, ripping sound. He glanced up.

The whole ceiling was coming down.

He lunged forward, began to call his uncle, felt a sledge-hammer blow high on his right arm. He went down, agony investing his flesh. Then he was on his knees, crawling toward the living room, sobbing in pain.

He crawled a little more, but kept falling over on his right side.

God, he was tired. And his arm burned terribly.

His head swam and the reddish light seemed to be dimming and he had to rest.

"Lie down a second," he muttered, and then said, "No!" The crackling would catch him; the flames from downstairs would consume him. He had to move.

Uncle Phil was suddenly there, and he was leading Elliot to the fire escape. They were outside, and the smoke was heavy, and the heat was unbearable. Screams sounded; screams everywhere.

"Atom bomb?" he asked his uncle. "Radiation?"

Phil didn't answer, and Elliot decided to steady himself as they went down the narrow steel steps. He reached out with his right arm, or tried to. But something was wrong because the arm didn't rise and he toppled and Phil had to catch him.

Funny. Very funny. Reach out and arm doesn't move. Funny.

He was laughing. His head spun wildly and he was laughing. He was in the courtyard and his aunt was saying, ". . . ambulance! My God, my God, he'll bleed to death!"

Funny. He was lying on the pavement and people were looking at him and he saw his uncle cover his eyes with both hands.

"Elliot, Elliot," his uncle said. "You came for us. You came for us, Elliot, and that's why it happened. Elliot—"

Funny. A strange man was tying something around his right arm, high up near the shoulder, and Uncle Phil turned away, and Aunt Minnie's voice wailed from far off.

"Elliot, Elliot—"

He looked at his right arm. It lay motionless, the hand palm up. He blinked his eyes and stared at it and wondered if it was really a part of him. He couldn't feel it; it was gray and lifeless except for the pulsing rivulets of blood which ran down from somewhere near his shoulder. He followed the lines of blood onto the pavement.

So much red. So very much red.

Funny.

He heard a siren wailing, and was suddenly terrified. "Father," he said, and tried to sit up. But he couldn't.

The siren grew louder and his aunt's crying grew louder and his uncle's shaky voice grew louder. Everything grew louder, filling his ears and brain with wailing, mourning, frightening sounds.

He wondered if he was dying.

18

CHARLES AND CLARA MASTON 6-B

From the day that they'd gone to see Dr. Blaise Cormond, time passed slowly for the Mastons. But pass it did, bringing change. Change in the weather: from cold to springtime mild. Change in Clara's physical condition: she carried small, and though others didn't see it, she felt growth. Change in the relationship between her husband and herself: a mass of frightening complexities.

She'd wake one morning, and yesterday's certainties were gone. It would take a day to build a new set of certainties, but then they too would crumble. And it was a *slow* process; a process of incalculable moments of thought and counter-thought within the framework of ten, fifteen or twenty hours, a brief span of time by normal standards, but a terribly long period when jammed full of concentrated thought.

Slow, slow change in her life, her marriage; terrifyingly steady; controlled, it seemed, by the change in her body, by the growth of a doomed life within her; the happening of the very thing they'd thought to avoid by destroying their unborn child.

They went to school together in the mornings, and returned together in the late afternoons; and spent the evenings together, and the weekends, and the precious moments of passion (which should have been even more precious since freed of the mechanical element of contraception)—and it wasn't at all the way it had once been.

She and Charles had never gone out much; just to an occasional concert, play or art exhibition. Once in a very long while, they would see a movie—usually a foreign film that attempted to break some of the taboos erected, or perpetrated, by American mass-media distributors and religious leaders. They'd done this limited stepping out on weekday evenings.

"Why rush with the lemmings?" Charles had said when

they were still dating. "If it were possible, I'd make our weekends on Tuesday and Wednesday, or Wednesday and Thursdays. That way we could drive places on relatively empty roads, see things without having to fight a mob, and best of all be free of the infernal, all-pervading gobbling (he still thought of distasteful or nonconstructive human speech in terms of the turkeys his father raised) that fills this world when people are let out from work!"

She had agreed; it was one of the many points of agreement which made her love him, made her want to marry him. So they'd spent Friday and Saturday nights at home; always. They never saw friends; in fact, didn't have a single one. They read, listened to music, talked, marked papers or prepared lesson plans when necessary, cooked exotic dinners together, and, in general, thoroughly enjoyed each other. However, she'd often wondered if such isolation, such complete intermingling of two personalities to the exclusion of all others, could be successfully maintained; if it wouldn't eventually lead to tension, or boredom; lead to a point where they'd have had a little too much of each other. Charles had obviously worried about the same thing because, just a month before she'd conceived, he'd asked her whether she realized they'd achieved "undiluted companionship."

"It could lead to minor irritations," he'd said.

She'd agreed, and then they'd kissed and gone on cooking their *poulet au Brisson* and listening to Boris Godunov.

The "minor irritations" had finally arrived. Of course, they knew it was due to an outside force (if the fetus growing within Clara could so be classified), and that they could look forward to a return to happiness once it was disposed of. They talked it out and agreed on this.

So there was nothing to worry about.

Except that it became impossible for them to spend a full weekend in the apartment as they always had. And, though they didn't admit it to themselves, they couldn't quite see a complete return to the old magic.

One bright Saturday afternoon in mid-April, Clara came to a terrible conclusion. They were bored with each other, with their "undiluted companionship," and would have reached this point even without the fetus.

She didn't voice this conclusion to Charles. She told herself it wasn't true and that everything would be fine once the hysterotomy was over. But she did suggest that they get out a little more—to help her *physically*. (She doubted whether there was any basis in fact for her statements about needing more movement, more diversion, because of her pregnancy, but Charles seemed more than willing to accept them without question.)

They went to a few weekend-evening movies, found them noisy and (since they chose quickly and without applying their usual standards) generally poor entertainment, and yet enjoyed the simple act of getting out and doing something. They went on Saturday- and Sunday-afternoon drives as the weather grew warmer, and though Charles railed at the jammed highways leading to Montauk or Westchester, and Clara said the stench of gasoline was unbearable, they managed to gain pleasure by going somewhere, looking at other people and—another not-to-be-admitted-to-self point—especially enjoyed watching the actions of very young children.

But then it was the third Thursday in May, and they made arrangements at school to be absent the next day as well as the following Monday. (Charles would resume teaching on Tuesday: Clara would call in ill day-by-day for as long as was necessary.) That night they decided to eat out. They chose a small place on Fourth Avenue that specialized in good stews and low prices. Charles ordered for both of them: beef ragout in wine sauce with Yankee beans, hot peach pie and coffee. Clara was so tense she was sure she wouldn't be able to eat a mouthful, but she surprised herself. As soon as the food was placed before her, she became ravenously hungry. She finished everything, and even had half of Charles's stew.

"I feel like a pig," she murmured, and looked away from him. She was terribly ashamed. He'd sat there, barely touching his food, and she'd devoured everything in sight. In light of the circumstances, of what was to come tomorrow, it was almost unforgivable. "It must be the baby."

He laughed briefly. "Yes," he said, and then asked if she'd like a whisky.

"No, dear. But you have one."

He ordered a double rye and water, lit a cigarette and waited. His drink came, and he gulped it, and then took her hand. "I want you to understand something, Clara. I don't care what I've said before; if you want to back out of our plan and have the child—"

"No," she said quickly. "Of course not. Why should I?"

"I mean—if you're afraid of the hysterotomy."

"I am afraid, but I'd be just as afraid of having my appendix removed."

He smiled and nodded. "Then it'll be okay. In a few weeks, we'll be back to normal. It's been rough on you."

"On both of us."

"Can you imagine us as doting parents?"

"Can you?" she answered, laughing.

He laughed with her, and then they just sat there and looked around the restaurant.

"Charles," she said. "I know what you're thinking—or feeling. It's the same with me. There's a natural reluctance to destroy—" She couldn't go on, couldn't find the right words.

He nodded. "I'm glad you said that. It clears the air. We've got built-in drives to procreate the species, and not only sexual drives. Also, the prejudices of our society against abortion are bound to have some effect; we can't be immune to everything around us." He raised his finger as if about to emphasize another point, but then shrugged and stood up. "Let's take a drive. It's over sixty degrees according to the radio. Let's go to Rockaway."

"Yes," she said. "We'll stroll on the boardwalk. Maybe we'll stop at one of those stands and have hot dogs and custard and—"

He laughed and looked down at her stomach. "He eats like a true Maston."

She began to answer his laugh, and then it seemed wrong, and they both grew quiet.

They didn't go to Rockaway. They went home. They played their records and sat reading. At nine-thirty the doorbell rang. They looked at each other, and Clara went to the door. She looked through the peephole for what seemed a long time.

"Who is it?" Charles called.

"People," Clara said, voice tense. "I'll handle it, dear."

"People?" He got up. As he walked to the foyer, he saw Clara opening the door. Then he stopped dead. The doorway was filled with people—five or six of them. Mrs. Gorelick stood in front, her husband beside her. In back were two elderly men, a middle-aged woman and a young woman—all tenants of Koptic Court.

"Yes?" Clara said, and her voice was cold.

Charles took a deep breath. He knew why Clara wanted him to stay away, why her voice was so cold. She expected the worst—a delegation of tenants come to make some sort of complaint. Maybe they didn't like the fact that he smoked on the Sabbath—Saturday—or played the hi-fi then and other times or maybe they just wanted to show their dislike of the mixed marriage in some abortive form—

But Clara was stepping aside and asking them in.

Asking them in!

Sweating, Charles watched them file past him into the living room. They didn't sit down, even though Clara indicated the couch and armchair. Mrs. Gorelick stood at the head of the group, and looked at Charles, her face stern. She opened her mouth, and Charles stiffened in preparation.

What came was a complete shock to him. It was a slow, solemn speech in Yiddish, interspersed by sober shakes of the head.

"She's right, you know," Mrs. Gorelick interrupted.

"*Der ganze hoise ess*—" Mrs. Gorelick was continuing, when Clara called an end to it.

"My husband doesn't understand Yiddish," she said, and her voice seemed choked. "But we'll certainly consider your appeal."

"It's really a shame, Mr. Maston," Mrs. Gorelick said in English. "Trying to shut down that orphanage after all the years it's taken care of poor children. As a Jew, you should fight to keep it going. Honest, even if you don't go to *school* like so many young people today, you should want to see an orphanage like that—one that gives yeshiva-type training to the kids—"

"I don't bother with synagogue much myself," the young woman interrupted brightly, "and my husband is Reformed, but I still want to help keep that orphanage open. And every ten-dollar donor will be mentioned by the rabbi who holds services for the children there. Your name blessed in services, Mr. Maston! I tell you, even though, like I said, I'm not religious, it gives me a thrill—"

"*A greissur mitzvah*—" Mr. Gorelick began, waving his finger at Charles. Then he remembered, and repeated in English, "A great blessing for any Jew who helps, Mr. Maston. A great blessing."

"Yes," Charles said, stunned. "Yes, I see."

"We'll talk about it," Clara said, voice even more choked than before.

"I'm the chairlady," Mrs. Gorelick said proudly. "We're calling on everyone in the house."

"Then I'll drop in to see you in a day or two," Clara said.

The committee smiled and said thanks and walked down the foyer. "Remember," the other elderly lady said to Charles and Clara, "It's a very important thing for Jews to support. If we don't save it, who will? *Gitten nacht.*"

"Good night," Clara answered.

"Night," Charles muttered.

The door closed. Clara covered her mouth with both hands and shook.

Charles stared at her, and realized she was laughing.

"So they talked about you because you're a goy, a gentile," she wheezed, fighting for breath. "So they gave you contemptuous looks and—" She shook her head and laughed until the tears ran from her eyes.

He turned and walked back to the living room. He sat down and picked up his book and looked at the print. "I'll be damned," he muttered. Mrs. Gorelick thought he was Jewish —accepted him as a Jew!

Then he joined Clara's laughter.

It was funny, all right, but not funny enough to keep them laughing more than a few minutes in the face of what was to come tomorrow. They went to bed early. Clara didn't fall asleep until almost one o'clock, and then it wasn't because her mind had stopped torturing her but because her body demanded rest and regeneration in its job of creating a new life.

Charles never did get to sleep. He tossed about until three, and then got up and sat at the living-room window, smoking cigarettes. At five, thunder sounded and rain began to fall. He went back to bed and waited for dawn.

Once, he thought of Mrs. Gorelick and her committee, and he shook his head in amazement. But then Dr. Cormond came before his eyes and he began to sweat. . . .

They left the apartment at seven-thirty, after a breakfast of coffee and cigarettes. Before they'd reached the Manhattan Bridge, Clara said, "Stop the car." Charles glanced at her, saw she was terribly pale, and pulled to the curb. She opened the door and leaned out, gagging. He leaned after her, rubbing the back of her neck with one hand, stroking her arm with the other. "Honey," he said. "Honey, please—" He said it over and over as she retched with straining, strangling sounds.

She finally stopped and leaned back in the car and wiped her mouth with a handkerchief. "Nerves," she gasped.

"Are you sure?"

She began to nod, and the nausea returned in a gut-wrenching wave. She tilted forward and vomited again. It lasted a good five minutes, and when it ended her eyes were red, cheeks white, lips quivering and almost blue.

"Christ," Charles said. "What should I do? Should I drive to the nearest doctor? Tell me, what—"

She shook her head.

"Maybe we can call it off," he said.

She looked at him.

"I mean for today," he said. "We can put it off—"

"Everything's arranged just right," she said, her voice a hoarse whisper. "This is nothing—just nerves. Nothing." But then she gurgled and jerked upright and stuck her head out of the car and retched a third time.

When she finished, she managed a weak smile. "Over," she whispered. "Better now. Let's just stay here a few minutes."

They sat in the car, and sickness of another kind swept through Charles, and he didn't know what was wrong.

"All right," she said, putting her hand on his. "I'm fine now. . . ."

Dr. Blaise Cormond let them into the house himself, but this time there was a woman sitting in his office. "My nurse," he said. "She'll assist me. And now, Mr. Maston, the fee. Cash, as I stipulated in our earlier meeting."

Charles led Clara to a leather chair and reached for his wallet. He walked to Cormond and counted six hundred dollars in fifties, twenties and tens into the doctor's outstretched hand. Cormond nodded, and smiled at Clara. "It'll be over in no time at all, dear. First I'll try to induce labor and so create a miscarriage—but don't count on it. Then I'll do the Caesarean—the hysterotomy. That will certainly work. And within a month or two, you'll be ready to utilize your husband, or anyone else—"

"Listen!" Charles shouted. "Can't you keep your mouth—"

"Charles," Clara said quickly. "Please."

He took a deep breath, nodded, and walked to her chair.

"Paternalism rears its socially acceptable head," Cormond said, smiling. He spoke to the nurse, but looked at Clara. "I believe it's the female in this case who is the truly emancipated one."

"In every case," the nurse replied. She was a tall raw-boned woman in her late forties with unnaturally black hair and a face that was attractive in a strong, mannish way. "Shall we cut the amenities and get to work?" She stood up.

Cormond made a roll of the money Charles had given him, and placed it in his trouser pocket. "Mrs. Maston?"

The nurse moved to Clara and took her arm. Clara stood up. The doctor walked to the door, opened it and said, "I suggest you take in a movie, Mr. Maston, or anything else to kill three, four hours. I'll allow you to see her in about that time—for half an hour. Tomorrow you can stay as long as you wish."

Charles nodded numbly. The nurse led Clara to the door, still holding her arm in a firm grip. There, Clara stopped, looked back at her husband and smiled.

It was a terrible failure, that smile, and it ripped at Charles as nothing ever had before. Her strength and intelligence seemed stripped from her now, and all that was left was a beautiful, pathetically helpless little girl looking at him, calling on him—

Without thinking it out, he came to a decision. "Clara," he said, "why can't we have the child?"

She shook her head, and yet resisted the nurse's tug on her arm.

"Ah," Cormond murmured, "the last gasp of bourgeois conscience." He seemed highly amused.

"We don't believe in it," Clara answered Charles. "Please don't take advantage of my fear—"

"No, it's not fear," Charles said, and his voice shook. "Maybe we don't believe in children like some people do, but I, for one, believe in this business much, much less! Look, honey, it's ugly, isn't it?"

She began to nod, and the tears spilled down her cheeks, and she was more than ever the little girl, the beautiful little girl needing something.

He felt he knew what it was she needed, and gave it to her.

"Nothing can be uglier than this. Even if the doctor were a perfect salesman, the whole concept would remain ugly— for me, at least. And it's my child too. And—listen, I think we should leave."

She was still nodding. The doctor looked at her, reached into his pocket and spoke to the nurse. "I was wrong about Mrs. Maston being emancipated."

The nurse shrugged, released Clara's arm and went back to the black leather couch. She sat down, crossed her legs and lit a cigarette.

The doctor walked to Charles and gave him the roll of bills. "There were two visits. My fee is five dollars a visit."

Charles gave him a twenty, eyes on Clara. Blaise Cormond took a ten from his wallet and put it in Charles's hand. "Now, Mr. and Mrs. Mammalian—"

"Your mother must have pissed on you," Charles said quietly. "Twice a day."

Cormond's eyes blinked rapidly and he began to reply, but his nurse's laughter cut him short. When Charles and Clara walked out of the house, Cormond was saying, "To laugh at anything so stupidly coarse . . ."

They drove a few blocks in silence, and then Charles said, "Christ, I'm glad!"

She didn't answer, and he looked at her. She was still nodding, still crying.

He pulled to the curb and took her in his arms. "I can't stop," she sobbed. "I must be turning into an idiot, but I can't stop crying. And it's not because I'm sad, or happy, or anything. I just can't stop."

He rocked her, and felt the fierce satisfaction of having stood up to something that had persecuted him for months.

"It'll be trouble," she said, pushing back from him. "Don't think it won't. We'll have to face things we hate, and deal with people we despise, and—and what about our families?"

"What about them?" he said, but he knew she was right. They'd joined the mob at last, and would have to abide by many of the mob's rules. They were vulnerable now. Isolation wouldn't be possible any longer; the wonderful isolation that had cradled them for sixteen months of marriage. And as the child grew older, they would be drawn more and more into society—the neighborhood society in which their child would live.

Charles resumed driving, and Clara looked at him, remembering her own parents, wondering what sort of father Charles would make. She was afraid.

Charles was wondering the same thing—what sort of father he would make—and he too was afraid.

Fear was to dominate their lives for days and weeks and months, and yet they soon found a bright side to the picture —they were no longer bored, or worried about being bored.

The following Monday, while reading to a class from Dickens' *Tale of Two Cities*, Clara felt one of the tiny kicks that had started two months ago. But it was as if it were happening for the very first time, and she was shocked.

Before deciding against the hysterotomy, she'd never accepted movement as a manifestation of life. What difference did such things make when the entire organism was going to be cut out and thrown away? And she hadn't mentioned it to Charles, feeling it would merely serve to make him more unhappy than he was, would have been almost obscene in its callousness.

Over the weekend, she'd been adjusting to the change in plans, the tremendous change in her life. So it was now that she first felt life.

She stopped reading in mid-sentence and breathed heavily, and then heard the class murmuring and giggling. She looked at them, and got a second tiny kick, and realized she was smiling.

"I'll let you in on a secret," she said, and closed the book. "I won't be back at school after summer vacation."

Except for a mildly disappointed murmur from a few children who had managed to make top grades with her, there was no reaction. But she didn't mind. She kept smiling, and there was a third kick from her child, and she said, "I'm going to have a baby."

A few of the girls giggled, and the boys looked down at their desks in embarrassment, and Clara told herself it wasn't the thing to discuss with a class. But she was compelled to say something more, something they might remember when they were adults and perhaps facing a situation similar to the one she and Charles had faced.

"I didn't think I'd want a baby, but now I'm very happy."

She opened her book and resumed reading. . . .

When she met Charles in the yard, she wanted to kiss him, but contented herself with taking his hand. They walked to the car and drove toward the Belt Parkway.

"Darnell finally noticed," Charles said. "He asked if you were pregnant."

"That's a coincidence," Clara murmured. "I told one of my classes today."

"Darnell congratulated—" He glanced at her. "Told one of your classes! That's nice! Tomorrow, every kid in my classes will be grinning—" He shrugged. "What the hell difference does it make?" He was edgy, irritable. "I was trying to figure out how we're going to get along on my four thousand."

"We've saved almost three thousand," Clara said, and slid over to lean against him. "I'll work out a budget."

"Okay, but you don't have to sound so damned cheerful—"
He shook his head. "I'm sorry."

She nodded, but found she wasn't hurt or angered; not even annoyed. It surprised her, this new feeling of calmness, of security. She looked at her husband and saw the dark circles under his eyes and understood that he was afraid. She also understood *why* he was afraid; sensed that he questioned his ability to play a normal male role as father. And, until just a few hours ago, she had felt the same way about herself as a mother. But not now. Life had been revealed to her, and other things had become relatively unimportant. It was as simple as that.

"I felt movement today," she said, expecting nothing from him, but savoring the words. "I've felt it before, but today it meant life. Today I *really* felt it."

He frightened her. He jerked his head around and looked at her too long and said, "No! Not really! Life? But of course —you must have felt it months ago. Of course. It moved?"

"Watch the road!"

He turned his eyes back to the highway. "You should have told me before, Clara! After all—" Then he shook his head. "No, you were right. It made no sense before. But now—" He paused. "Tell me how it felt. Exactly how it felt."

"I don't know if I can. Just a kick, inside. A gentle kick. It almost tickled—"

"Almost tickled!" he shouted, and laughed.

She laughed with him.

He stopped laughing abruptly. "I'm acting like something out of a bad movie."

"Well, this is the situation bad movies are made of," she said, and felt that it was so silly to worry about posturing and mannerisms and attitudes; about anything but the life growing inside her belly.

A grin spread over his face. "I'll have to write Mother, and Father, and Lester."

"Oh?"

"Well, the child's got to know who his father's family is, and they've got to know about him. Isn't that right?"

She nodded slowly, wondering that it was so simple now, so logical now. "Yes. And I guess I'll have to call my father."

"Sure."

"Maybe we'll even drop over?"

"If you want to."

"One visit to my Pop," Clara said, "and all those wonderful and simple solutions will fly out the window. He'll begin to talk, and we'll begin to groan. He's narrow-minded."

"He'll fit in beautifully with my folks, and especially with Brother Lester. They can all sit around and gobble with the turkeys."

For the first time, it seemed funny. They made their plans; they would visit Clara's father within the next few months, and Charles's family at the Connecticut farm as soon after the baby was born as they could manage. They would lay the ghosts of the past once and for all, and then it would be up to their families to determine any future relationship.

It made them feel wonderfully strong. They'd taken a step in conjunction with society, and the world became fully fifty per cent less hostile.

That night they played their hi-fi set too loud, and Mrs. Gorelick banged up with a broom handle. "But it's only nine-thirty," Charles said mildly, and turned down the volume.

Clara laughed. "She's got our ten-dollar donation, so she can return to being her old sweet self again."

They looked at each other, remembering how this sort of thing had bothered them before. Clara hadn't felt quite as strongly as Charles about it, but she'd wished Mrs. Gorelick in another apartment, and shared Charles's feeling that the battle-ax probably spoke of them in far from complimentary terms, utilizing their mixed marriage to best advantage.

Now it was different—Charles didn't seem to mind too much, and she didn't mind at all. And they weren't worried about being criticized or becoming the object of gossip; not after that committee call! (Though Clara had set the record straight with Mrs. Gorelick, and been surprised at the woman's so-what shrug.)

But it was more than knowing no one had been criticizing them here for their marriage. A strong purpose gripped them, and it was solving several deep-rooted problems.

It also created a few, as they'd known it would. In July, her eighth month. Clara suddenly ceased carrying small, becoming huge almost overnight—or so it seemed. Charles had taken a job as book salesman with a Manhattan department store for the summer, and Clara was on her own all day. Unable to sit in the apartment because of the heat, she did something she'd always despised in others—took a folding chair and went downstairs and sat outside. But she stayed away from the front of the house.

One of the things she disliked most about Koptic Court (and all lower- and middle-class Brooklyn neighborhoods) was its row of women, sitting on chairs and boxes out front, rocking baby carriages and knitting and chattering—chattering incessantly. Murderers' Row, Charles called it—and it was a perfect appellation. The twenty or thirty women sitting in front of Koptic Court right now were actively engaged in murdering any and all reputations, and having their own murdered by groups just a few chairs or boxes away.

The thought of being part of anything like that made Clara's stomach turn over! She went around back to the courtyard and alleyway.

The first time she did this she was left alone, except for a few children who came skating or bicycling in for brief periods of time. She read a soft-cover edition of *The Golden Ass* (the Graves translation, one of a number of classics Charles had purchased for her because of their lightness and humor), and felt a flutter of cool air every so often, and dreamed with one part of her mind of the child she would have and the things she and Charles would teach it and the wide range of choice it would be given in beliefs, approaches to history, philosophies, literature, careers, everything. She remembered what Dr. Philips (he was now her attending physician and would deliver her baby at the small hospital on Fourth Avenue) had said last week. The doctor had become a good friend, and felt that their child would be in a position to straddle several cultures.

"More than my children, more than the children of any couple of *similar* backgrounds, your child should see ways to improve society. Especially since neither of you will ever insist on a specific path. I don't mean that such a child can't run into fear and confusion, perhaps even mental problems, based on the very differences in his upbringing which will broaden his concepts. But with the right breaks—and the odds are that he'll get them—he'll probably be a liberal leader in whatever field he chooses."

"An intellectual projection of the my-boy-will-grow-up-to-be-president spiel," Charles had said, laughing. But he'd been pleased by the doctor's speech, strengthened by it.

Sitting in the alleyway, Clara wondered if the doctor actually believed what he'd said, or if he felt that a couple who'd almost destroyed their unborn child would have to be encouraged every step of the way.

But it made no difference, really, because she and Charles

had begun to think along those lines before the doctor's speech. It was logical thought; it was well within the bounds of probability.

The second day that she went into the alleyway, she was joined by two young women with baby carriages. They sat down beside her and asked personal questions and weren't at all discouraged by her cool, noninformative answers. They discussed their children, husbands and neighbors in a manner that brought all of Clara's contempt and fear back into sharp focus. She couldn't be dragged into the society of such crude, narrow-minded, acid-tongued milk cows!

When Charles returned home that evening, Clara poured out all her misery. She alternately raged against stupid hausfraus, and wept that she would soon be forced to sink to their level. "When you're at school," she wailed, "what will I do? How can I avoid those—those idiots when I'll be chained to a baby carriage?"

He had no quick, over-all solution, and admitted it. However, he calmly pointed out that they would still have their books, music, and high standards in selecting all other means of entertainment—including friends.

"You remember Wilma Kearney; taught radio writing when you first came to Laurel? Well, she lives on Ocean Parkway, and her husband Ed—algebra and geometry—spoke to me at least a dozen times in the men's smoking room last term. He said she was dying to find an intelligent friend for those long, baby-rocking afternoons. She and others like her are close enough to be visited. In time, you'll be able to choose your companions—"

Clara listened, and a few minutes later was wondering why she'd ever become so upset.

The visit to Clara's father and stepmother pointed up a problem not so easily solved, or obscured. But there too they won a victory over themselves; the visit itself being a solution in the making.

Irwin Cohen led them into the living room of the second-floor, three-room flat in which he and his wife now lived. He'd grown older, heavier since the last time Clara had seen him—almost two years. But then again, she really hadn't seen him since leaving home at the age of twenty; hadn't looked at him as someone important in her life, and so hadn't judged his physical appearance. Now she was shocked at the age which showed in his puffy cheeks and dulled eyes, in his slow walk, in his voice so changed from the strident baritone of old.

"Well, well," he said for about the fifth time, obviously nervous, obviously afraid. "It's Clara and her husband come to visit." He nodded and smiled at the stepmother, dressed for the occasion (despite the late July heat) in a stiff, dark silk dress, and silently begged her to say something that would help him along.

"Well, well," the stepmother said, and got up from the couch and stood there and looked at Clara and Charles in her good-natured way—good-natured except that her eyes returned to Charles too many times, examining his tall, lean, strange (to her prepared mind) appearance, his *goyish* appearance. "Well, so our little Clara is going to be a mother."

"A mother," Irwin Cohen echoed, his voice thick. His eyes dropped and he breathed heavily.

How old he looks, Clara thought. *Yet he can't be more than sixty—maybe fifty-eight or nine.*

"Sit down, sit down," Irwin said, remembering his role as host. "Maybe Lena should make a cold drink—"

"Not for me, thank you," Charles said, and they were the first words he'd spoken since Clara had introduced him to her father at the door and he'd mumbled, "Hello," and quickly shaken hands.

"Nor me," Clara said.

"Well," her father said.

The stepmother, Lena, sat down on the couch again. Irwin Cohen dropped down beside her, as if afraid that someone would separate him from his one and only ally. Clara chose one of the two armchairs facing the couch. Charles hesitated, and then saw a folding bridge chair against the wall. He carried it over to Clara's armchair and sat down.

"You could use the other armchair," Lena said, pointing to the corner of the room furthest from Clara. "It's more comfortable."

"He wants to sit near his wife," Irwin said quietly.

Charles cleared his throat as if to say something, but then merely nodded. He glanced at Clara, and she seemed to read surprise that the oft reviled parents were such timid, almost nondescript personalities. Where was the blatant prejudice, the narrow-mindedness, the hatred for *him?*

She too was surprised.

"How do you feel?" Lena asked her.

"Fine." Clara smiled. "Never better." And then, "Oh, my, I forgot to introduce you to my husband!"

Both Charles and Lena jumped up, and Clara had to hide

her smile. Irwin tugged Lena's arm, and she sat down again, flushing.

"Charles, this is my—my mother, Lena."

Charles mumbled his how-do-you-do, and Lena flushed even deeper at the "mother"—but with pleasure this time.

"I'm glad you came," she said, being very careful of her speech. "I want to say that it means a lot to me and Irwin. I want to say that we hope you'll visit again—with a healthy, happy child."

"Thank you," Clara murmured.

No one said anything for what seemed like a very long time. Then Irwin Cohen, perspiring freely in the ninety-degree heat, turned to Charles. "From what part of the country are you, Mr. Maston—Charles?"

"Connecticut—a farm near Washington, Connecticut."

"Imagine that," Lena said.

"It's not too unusual," Charles said, smiling to show he was joking.

But the Cohens didn't understand the joke, and both quickly began to explain, at the same time, that they knew it wasn't unusual and of course people come from farms near Washington, Connecticut, and it was really wonderful, marvelous, magnificent to come from farms near Washington, Connecticut.

"I myself love the country," Lena concluded, nodding intensely.

"As for me," Irwin Cohen said, trying hard for the casual approach, "I believe farm life—boyhood on a farm—produced this country's greatest leaders. Abe Lincoln, for instance."

Normally, Charles would have winced at that, or looked at Clara with an Oh-Gawd expression. This time he said, "I might have believed that once myself, but ever since I first met Clara I've been convinced that the only way to raise a truly intelligent human being is in a Brooklyn apartment."

It went over big. Irwin grinned, and Lena said, "Ooh, what a compliment, Clara! Your husband's a regular Continental!"

They all laughed, and relaxed a bit.

But as Irwin Cohen relaxed, he grew more himself, began to speak more freely, and his topic of conversation was reminiscences of Clara's childhood. Some of his remarks ("I didn't think you had this much of me in you; it looked like you were going—Well, anyway—") made Clara tense and angry.

They stayed from one-thirty until four, and part of that

time was spent in eating the cold-cut lunch Lena had prepared. When they said goodbye at the door, Irwin shook Charles's hand and said, "If you don't mind my being frank, when I first learned Clara had married a—a boy from outside our religion, I was afraid. But you're a fine fellow, Charles, I know you'll see that my grandchild has a good home. I'm sure that you'll send him to Hebrew school to learn a little about the Jewish religion." He held up a hand as if stopping himself, and chuckled, and said, "Time to discuss that later. You'll have to come for dinner next week—"

When they were in their car, driving home, Clara glanced at Charles. He looked washed out, exhausted, limp with heat and inner exertion. She felt exactly the same way.

"It wasn't as horrible as I thought it would be," she said, sounding him out. "I'm certainly not going to visit them next week, or any other week for quite a while, but it wasn't too bad—was it?"

He lit a cigarette. "No. But listen. That business about religious training—"

"Of course not," she said.

He exhaled smoke in a sharp jet. "My father will probably say the same thing, except that he'll be much more assured about it."

In the middle of dinner that evening, Charles suddenly put down his fork and said, "By Christ, it wasn't bad at all!"

She didn't have to ask him what he was talking about. She'd been thinking of the same thing. She'd suffered more during the visit than he had, and their roles would probably be reversed when they visited *his* family, but it wouldn't destroy them, wouldn't change their lives the way they'd thought such visits would.

They went to bed early, feeling they'd had a very full day.

The third Friday in August, at two-twenty in the morning, Clara felt she was entering labor. But since this was fully two weeks before the date Dr. Philips had told her to expect delivery, she hesitated to wake Charles who was sleeping soundly beside her. She lay in the darkness, flat on her back, hands on her mountainous stomach, waiting for another flash of the pain which had awakened her. It came, a tightening band which reached around from her back, circling her stomach, drawing tighter and tighter until she felt she would groan aloud. And then it stopped.

She had been counting to herself, trying to judge how long

the interval between pains was, and she figured it at roughly twenty minutes. When the interval became five minutes, she would have to go to the hospital. But she still didn't believe the time had actually come. There'd been an evening last week when she'd had five or six pains a few minutes apart, and told Charles, and he'd been all ready to call the doctor. Then the pains had stopped.

However, they hadn't been nearly as severe as these.

Shifting weight slowly so as not to awaken Charles, she reached over and switched on her night-table lamp. The alarm clock stood there, and she kept her head turned so that she could watch it.

The pains continued to come—fifteen minutes apart, twelve minutes apart, nine minutes apart—and at this point she began to groan.

Charles rolled over, eyes blinking dazedly, and mumbled, "Okay, honey?"

"I—yes."

"Fine." His eyes closed. "Fine."

She groaned again, and he sat bolt upright. "What is it?"

"I think it's happening," she said, gritting her teeth as an irresistible band of pain tightened around her, drawing in, drawing in. She felt she was being squeezed by giant hands, squeezed so that her very life, and the life of her child, would soon be forced from her body.

Charles leaped out of bed. "We'd—we'd better get dressed," he said. He rushed to the closet and took out the little over-night bag they'd prepared at the beginning of the month, just in case. He helped her out of bed, and she had to repeat a half-dozen times that she was capable of dressing herself before he would leave her and call Dr. Philips.

"That kid's just like his parents," the doctor mumbled sleepily. "Rebellious, unpredictable, hard to get along with. A pain in the neck. Supposed to come two weeks from—"

"Yes, yes!" Charles shouted. "Are you sure you understand? You've got to get to the hospital right away!"

"I understand. Just try to remember that you're well above the common herd and must act accordingly. *Noblesse oblige.*"

Charles made violent, strangling sounds. The doctor laughed and hung up.

After a swift, tense, but cautious ride through the black morning streets, the Mastons reached the tiny, three-story doctors' hospital. It was four-fifteen when Clara was taken into an elevator and whisked to the second-floor delivery room. By that time her pains were less than four minutes apart and Charles had been certain she was going to drop his heir onto some nonantiseptic, nonresilient surface. He was relieved to collapse into a waiting-room chair, light a cigarette, and leave the rest to Dr. Philips—whom he presumed to be upstairs.

The doctor didn't arrive until twenty minutes later, and when he popped into the waiting room, dressed in street clothes, Charles almost had a cerebral hemorrhage.

"She's been up there for hours with strangers!"

Arnold Philips shook his head sadly. "How the mighty have fallen." He then went to his patient, laughing.

Slightly more than two hours later, with the morning sun bleaching the waiting-room lights to insignificance, Dr. Philips walked up to a determinedly relaxed Charles and said, "Congratulations. You have a six-pound-three-ounce daughter. Go up and see your wife for a few minutes. Just a few minutes. She's going to be here five or six days and you'll be able to see her during afternoon and evening visiting hours."

They shook hands. The doctor went home. Charles went to the elevator and got in. The operator asked him what floor and Charles said, "Mrs. Maston's room." The operator, an elderly colored man with bald, shiny dome, sighed. "You gotta have the room number. She jest have her baby?"

Charles nodded.

"Okay. Go to the desk and ask where they put her."

Charles ran to the desk. A drowsy, middle-aged woman in a nurse's uniform checked a file of cards and shrugged. "Seems they haven't listed the room here. Guess you'll have to wait till they call it down."

"Wait?" Charles said. His voice stiffened. "You just pick up that phone and do some calling yourself and find out where she is."

"I can't—"

"If you don't, I'm going to search this place floor by floor, room by room, calling my wife's name in loud, clear, not-conducive-to-recuperation tones! Shall I demonstrate?" He took a huge breath and opened his mouth.

The nurse got on the phone. A moment later she said, "Thirty-four? Okay." She hung up and turned to Charles, but he was already back at the elevator, asking to be taken to the third floor.

The room was semi-private, as their health insurance provided. The bed on the left, however, was empty at the moment. Clara lay propped up on two pillows, paler than he'd ever seen her, but she smiled as he walked in. "What a monkey you fathered," she whispered.

He sat down beside her and they held hands and wondered what else to say and said nothing. Finally, he got up. "Doctor said only a few minutes, honey. You have to rest."

"Just as well. I feel silly as anything."

They looked at each other and smiled and felt as far from silly as possible. . . .

He didn't go to work at the department store that day. He went home and called Clara's father and then called his own family, speaking to his mother, father and brother for the first time in nearly three years. They were all delighted.

He went back to the hospital at two (visiting hours were 2:00 to 4:00 P.M., 7:00 to 8:00 P.M.) and was shocked to find the room full of people. Clara's father and stepmother were there, and so were an aunt and uncle. There were three short, dark, soft-spoken people standing around the other bed, and Charles realized that another patient had moved into the room. He kissed Clara and asked how he could see the baby. Clara told him about the viewing room, and a few minutes later he and the Cohens were staring at a bald, wrinkle-faced little lady wearing a diaper and pink-bead identification bracelet.

"Beautiful," Lena Cohen said.

"Just like Clara," Irwin Cohen said.

Charles cleared his throat, nodded, and assured himself that they all looked like plucked chickens at the beginning. . . .

He returned that evening and had Clara to himself. He was introduced to the woman in the other bed, Mrs. Anthony Gorino, and her husband, and then was finally able to sit beside his wife and discuss what he had to buy and whether or not they should start looking for a larger apartment or stay in their two-room place until the baby was six months old. The things they didn't discuss were their feelings of peace and security; the feelings they'd developed immediately after the birth.

Eight o'clock came all too soon, and the rotund, middle-aged Mrs. Gorino kissed her rotund, middle-aged husband goodbye. He departed as quietly as he had arrived, and Charles said, "I wish I could stay! There's so much—"

"Hey," Mrs. Gorino said. "Hey, Mr. Maston. Why don't you hide in the washroom? When I had my first—I got five, not counting this one—Tony wanted to stay with me. It was a different hospital—we lived in Baltimore then—but he sneaked into the bathroom and later, when all the visitors left he came out. He was wearing a white shirt—you got a white shirt—so he took off his jacket and tie and left them in the bathroom and no one even asked who he was. He must've looked like one of the workers; a porter or something."

Charles laughed, and said goodbye to Clara, and walked to the door. Then he stopped and looked back at her. She nodded. He said, "Okay, I'll try it."

There was a small washroom at the end of the corridor. He went inside, and into a booth, and sat there, smoking a cigarette. At eight-twenty, when he figured all the visitors had left, he hung his jacket and tie on the booth's door-hook and went out into the hall. It was dim and quiet. He walked into room thirty-four, and Mrs. Gorino chuckled and rolled over with her back to Clara's bed. "Be a good boy," she said. "It's too soon after the baby." She found this vastly amusing, and laughed into her pillow.

Charles stayed until ten-thirty, and would have stayed even later except that Clara admitted she was still a little weak and needed her sleep. He then went back to the washroom, put on his tie and jacket, and left the hospital without being stopped, or even noticed.

The next night, Sunday, he did the same thing, and stayed much later because Clara (and Mrs. Gorino) was feeling much stronger. He'd brought along a soft-cover book of funny stories and cartoons on the subject of having babies, and read them aloud with the help of a pencil-flashlight. Then Mrs. Gorino turned her back on them—her way of dispensing privacy.

"We're definitely going to visit the farm this winter, honey," Charles said. "My mother, father and brother begged me. It won't be so bad. Anyway, we just can't laugh them off, can we?"

"No," she said. "We can't laugh them off. And we can't laugh our little Miss Eve off either. All the ridiculous homilies about mother- and father-love have strong basis in truth, even if they do go pretty far over toward the saccharine—"

"Well, I don't know if that's it exactly. Mother and father love can be mother- and father-don't-give-a-damn, or mother- and father-hate, depending on the culture. Among the Mundugumor of the Pacific—remember Margaret Mead's book?—there's a tradition of disliking children. The parents resent having them, resent raising them, resent everything about them. So the mother-and-father-love homilies would not be true over there. And maybe we're spiritual descendants of the Mundugumor."

They laughed softly, and Mrs. Gorino said, "I don't know what you kids talk about half the time. Munga-munga of the Pacific! Who ever heard of it? Who needs it?"

Charles and Clara laughed harder, and Clara said, "Imagine being in rebellion against a society like that. We'd bravely kiss our daughter in public, smile at her in stubborn criticism of our mores, and perhaps even invite punishment by publicly avowing that we love her."

"What kinda talk is that?" Mrs. Gorino muttered sleepily. "You kids oughta have your heads examined. I never—"

The Mastons laughed, and Mrs. Gorino joined them, sensing the happiness of that laughter, the lack of cynicism and derision in it. She didn't understand Charles and Clara, but she liked them. And that was vastly significant; she wouldn't have liked them at all five or six months before.

Charles didn't leave the hospital until after twelve. This time a nurse stopped him on the ground floor and asked what he was doing there. Having no answer, he put his fingers to his lips, said, "Shhh!" and tiptoed out the front door, leaving her staring after him.

He was still laughing when he got into his car and started for home. At about twelve-thirty, he heard a dull, heavy thump of sound in the distance. For a moment he thought it was the fireworks at Coney Island, but then he realized it was Sunday, not Tuesday, and much too late. Besides, the sound was heavier than any fireworks he'd ever heard.

He didn't pursue the thought. He stopped at an all-night luncheonette and had a hamburger and iced coffee. Then he browsed through a magazine rack and bought a soft-cover book.

He got back in his car and continued home, feeling wonderfully happy, wonderfully secure.

It wasn't until he reached Thirteenth Avenue that he saw the red glow filling the sky ahead and to the left. Between Thirteenth and Fourteenth he heard the sirens and claxons. As he made his turn onto Fifteenth, he saw the fire a few blocks north and knew it was Koptic Court.

Sudden terror flooded his mind. He swung to the curb, jumped out and began to run toward the blazing house. Flames showed on the first four floors, and even as he ran, the evil, flickering light moved into the fifth floor.

Then the terror passed and he was able to remember that Clara and the baby were safe. There were books, records, clothes and other possessions in the apartment, but after all, they were insured against fire and anything lost could be replaced.

He stopped at the corner, watching two more fire trucks pull up. The street was already full of trucks and people; the clamor was deafening. But Clara and the baby were safe, and so was he.

The terror came alive again, and he couldn't understand why he should feel that way.

"Safe," he murmured. "We're safe."

But it seemed as if he and Clara were inside, burning.

He told himself he was experiencing fear for the other tenants—and yet his terror was too personal for that.

It wasn't until flames broke through the roof and the spectators cried out that he understood.

He returned to his car and got inside. He was weak and his hands trembled.

Our Father Who art in Heaven—

The words had popped into his mind. He shrugged them away. But wasn't there something fantastic about the progression of events that had saved him and his wife from that flaming horror? Wasn't there something—almost unexplainable—

He got out of the car and hurried back toward the house to see if there was anything he could do to help.

19

BONNIE ALLAN 1-J

Yipes, it was hot all that week! Mommy let her run around outside in just a pair of shorts. She played with Arlene and Little Stevie and Big Stevie (Little was four and Big was almost six) and Angela from across the street who had the big doll carriage. Gary—that bad boy—was away in the country with his mother and father, just like Bonnie had been during Daddy's vacation in July. She missed him.

Bonnie chased Big Stevie when he took her doll from Angela's carriage. She chased him and chased him, but he ran too fast. She stopped and began to cry. Little Stevie came up to her and said softly, sympathetically, "Baby, baby, stick your head in gravy." She kept crying, not even looking at him. He put his hand on her arm and said, "I'll let you play with my ball." She stopped crying and gave him a big kiss and they went back to the house, arms around each other's waists. Mommy and Little Stevie's mother laughed and Mommy said, "If I had my camera, I'd snap that!"

Later, Big Stevie gave her back her doll and she went inside for lunch. Mommy read to her from the big book of fairy tales, and she ate nicely. "I wish I had an elephant to ride on! I wouldn't even let Big Stevie touch him!"

After lunch, Mommy insisted Bonnie wear a polo shirt. "But it's hot!" Bonnie complained.

"I know, dear. We're going to Dr. Samuel's office."

"I don't wanna go!" Bonnie screamed, and burst into tears.

"But you like Dr. Samuel, Bonnie. Remember how the nurse gave you a lolly and—"

"I don't wanna get a 'jection!" Bonnie shrieked, and cried even harder.

Mommy waited until Bonnie quieted down, then said, "I'm afraid you must have another injection, baby. It's your polio booster. It'll make you healthy. And afterwards, I'll take you to the playground. . . ."

Bonnie and Mommy went to Dr. Samuel's office. They sat in the waiting room with three grownups, and then it was their turn and Bonnie began to cry. The nurse led them into the room with the desk and said, "Aw, big girls don't cry, honey. And you're a big girl."

"I am," Bonnie said, still crying, "but I don't like it here."

The doctor came through the side door leading to his treatment room and patted Bonnie on the head as he went to his desk.

"Booster shot, eh?" he said to Mommy.

"Yes."

"Allan," he murmured, searching through a file of cards. "Aha. Yes. Fine, fine." He removed the card and wrote on it, and then looked at Mommy. "By the way, I can let you have your polio shot too."

Bonnie was merely whimpering now, leaning against Mommy. She felt Mommy stiffen, and looked up. "Oh, well," Mommy said. "I really wasn't planning—"

"Big girl like you," the doctor said, grinning, "and still

afraid of a needle. In the five years I've known you, Mrs. Allan, you've tried to avoid every injection I've suggested—penicillin, polio—"

"Yes," Mommy said quickly, glancing down at Bonnie. "I'll take it. Of course."

"Of course," the doctor said, and winked at his nurse. "Take the victims to the operating room, Miss Logan."

"Very funny," Mommy said, and tried to smile.

"What's the matter, Mommy?" Bonnie asked, forgetting her own fear as she sensed her mother's. "I won't cry."

Mommy nodded, tight-lipped, and they went into the room with the white walls and white table and shiny knives in a glass case. It had a smell that made Bonnie remember sore throats and fever and all sorts of bad things. She began to cry again.

"Oh, shut up," Mommy muttered as the nurse went across the room and opened a metal box that steamed like Gramma's teakettle.

Bonnie saw the needles in the nurse's hand, and really began to wail. Mommy sat down in a chair and looked at the floor. The doctor came in. He took one needle and filled it from a little tube and said, "First the younger Allan." He took Bonnie's arm and wiped it with cotton and Bonnie shrieked at the top of her lungs. She screamed so hard she barely felt the needle enter her arm. And then it was over.

"I'll have a lollipop for you in a minute, honey," the nurse said.

Bonnie looked at her arm and wiped her tears. "I want cherry. I didn't like the lemon you gave me last time. I like cherry, or licorice, or—" The nurse patted her head and went to Mommy. The doctor stuck Mommy with a needle, and Mommy said, "Oh, God!" and turned very white and had to lean back while the nurse made her sniff a bottle.

Later, when they were walking home, Bonnie said, "Are we going to the playground, Mommy?"

"No," Mommy said, her voice weak.

"But you promised!"

"I don't feel good. I want to lie down."

Bonnie felt like crying again, but then she saw a puppy and stopped to pat it. Mommy said, "Please, Bonnie! Mommy's ill. Don't you feel like lying down after that injection?"

"Yes," Bonnie said. "It hurt me. I'll lie down and take a rest. . . ."

But she didn't. She watched TV and drank Pepsi-Cola.

Mommy lay down. Mommy stayed in bed a long time. Bonnie turned off the TV and played with her coloring book and then her dolls and then the new fire engine Gramma had bought her last week. And still Mommy lay in bed.

Bonnie went in to see her. "You feel sick, Mommy?"

"Yes, dear. My arm hurts. Doesn't your arm hurt?"

"Yes," Bonnie said, and went back to play with her toys.

Gramma came home, and then Daddy. Mommy finally got up and they all ate supper and Mommy told about the injec-, tions. Daddy started to laugh. He chewed his steak and tried to stop laughing, but it kept coming out of him in small, choking sounds. It made Bonnie laugh too.

"Thank you, Arny," Mommy said coldly. "You're very sympathetic."

Daddy made his face straight for a minute, but then he looked at Bonnie and said, voice choked, "In which arm did the doctor give you the injection, baby?"

Bonnie touched one arm, then the other, then kicked the chair leg. She couldn't remember.

"Bet Mommy remembers *hers*," Daddy said, and burst out laughing so hard he got all red in the face and had to drink water.

Mommy left the table fast and went into the living room.

Gramma, who'd been eating like a good girl, said, "Arnold, go inside there and apologize."

"Okay," Daddy said, and went in to Mommy.

"Are they fooling?" Bonnie asked, vaguely worried.

Gramma laughed and nodded and laughed some more. But she laughed so quiet Bonnie wondered about it.

After a while, Mommy and Daddy came back to the kitchen table, both smiling. "You tough little monster," Mommy said to Bonnie. "I don't know where you get your guts. Certainly not from me."

Daddy stuck out his chest and said he'd take Bonnie to Coney Island if the weather was nice this weekend.

"Yipes!" Bonnie said. "The weekend again! We just had a weekend and now there's another! We're lucky, aren't we?"

Daddy nodded and ate his steak.

Mommy nodded and ate her steak.

Gramma looked at Bonnie and said, "Yipes, we're very lucky, angel."

"Are you fooling?" Bonnie asked Gramma, because there was something funny in her voice and she'd said "Yipes."

"No," Gramma said, voice still funny. "I'm not fooling. I

think we're the luckiest family in the whole world." And
she kissed Bonnie so hard Bonnie yelled.

Bonnie stayed up late because it was so hot, and they
watched television. They watched two programs; then Daddy
said, "Bedtime. And don't start whimpering. Tonight I'm going to tell you about the ape who became king of Italy."

"Isn't she a little young to understand Mussolini?" Mommy
asked.

"Hardy-har-har," Daddy said. "That happens to be the title
of a story in the book you bought her."

It was a good story, Bonnie decided later. It wasn't scary,
and Daddy didn't skip pages like he sometimes did, and she
liked it. She fell asleep, smiling at the way Alec the Ape got
people to call him king by wearing a cape and crown.

Sunday they went to Coney Island, just like Daddy had
promised. Bonnie went on the pony ride five times, and had a
custard cone, and went on the merry-go-round. Then Daddy
took her on a grown-up ride, the whip, and held her tight
and tried to make her like it. But she was scared and sat stiff
and trembling. Later, she wouldn't go on any other rides
with him even though he asked her again and again—"Let's
try the bug, baby. Honest, you won't be scared—"

They went to another merry-go-round and she rode it
over and over and over. Daddy just sat on a bench, eating a
hot dog and looking like it didn't taste good. Mommy and
Gramma laughed at him, and Gramma said, "What's the
matter? My son is disappointed because his daughter isn't
ready for the paratroopers?"

They came home late and Bonnie was very tired and could
barely eat her supper. Mommy didn't make her finish, and
she went to bed. She fell asleep without any stories. She slept
soundly that third Sunday in August, but, like every other
tenant on the first floor who was fortunate enough to survive
it, she woke at the terrific explosion which rocked the entire
house.

She found herself on the floor. Her bed was on its side,
halfway through the floor. There was dirt all over, and smoke,
and red light coming through a hole under the bed. She felt
pain in her side, but it wasn't too bad and she didn't cry.
She wasn't really frightened; just stunned and confused.

"Mommy! Mommy!"

There seemed to be an answer, but it was far away.

"Mommy! Daddy! Gramma!"

The answer sounded again, still far away. Bonnie got up

and went to the door, falling over big pieces of wood and plaster. The door was open, like always, but there was something else in the way—a big pile of junk. She couldn't get over it, and someone was yelling on the other side.

"Daddy," she cried, and was suddenly frightened. "Daddy, I don't want to stay here!" She was shrieking now, and still no one came.

She was all alone, and terrified, and the smoke began to choke her.

The faraway voice that was like Daddy's said, "God, I can't get through!"

And another voice, like Mommy's, began to scream.

Bonnie looked around. She couldn't see anything; not even the window. The door and window were gone and the room was crazy.

She coughed as the smoke thickened, and wanted to cry, and didn't have enough breath. She sat down on the floor and coughed and coughed. . . .

20

JOE AND PAULA THECK 4-B

Summer came. Paula began dreaming of Camp Three again, and teasing the bread man again. But she stayed away from any definite plan of action—until Joe's remaining week of vacation arrived in August.

They got back from the Catskills at ten o'clock of a hot, cloudy Sunday night. "Kind of makes you wish for autumn," Joe muttered, unloading their valises from the trunk of the car. He said something else, but she was no longer listening. She was thinking that tomorrow was Monday. Joe would go to work, and she would be alone in the apartment when Walter Smith came around with his basket of bread and pastries.

"Take the two small valises," Joe said, and then turned as someone called out.

"Welcome back, Mr. and Mrs. Theck. Have a nice week?"

Joe said, "Yes, thank you, Mrs. Goldman. But the heat in the city, whew!"

"It's not the heat," Mrs. Goldman opined wisely. "It's the humidity."

Paula picked up the two valises and made herself smile as she passed Mrs. Goldman. She maintained the smile to answer the hello's and welcome-back's from a line of people—mostly women—seated on folding chairs in front of the house. The cheerful voices irritated, almost angered her. They were Jews, but they'd forgotten the horror of Hitler, the seven million dead, the hate of Germans who walked the streets of New York City and every other city in the States.

They were fools!

After unpacking, she and Joe watched television. There was a special rebroadcast of old news films of the Hungarian rebellion against the Soviet Union. It ended with scenes of planeloads of refugees arriving in the United States. "Do you know what the Hungarians did during the war?" Paula asked, turning to Joe, her face taut and pale. "Do you know?"

"No," he said.

"They were on the side of the Nazis! They were Hitler's and Mussolini's only allies in Europe; allies on their own; facists on their own. They lived under facism for fifteen years without rebelling. They killed over six hundred thousand innocent Jews. And then they come here as heroes—"

"Christ," Joe muttered. "So what good does it do to remember that now? What good does it do to eat yourself up with hate?"

"Good? It's not a matter of good! It's a matter of the truth!"

He nodded wearily. She was right, of course. That was the trouble; she was right and it made no difference because her hate was destroying them both.

Later, in bed, he moved close to her.

"Please don't," she said, and then added quickly, "It's so hot—"

He turned away. There was silence. Just when she began to think he was asleep, he said, "I only wanted to kiss you good night. You—you're making me ashamed of having feelings, Paula. I don't like it. Maybe you ought to ask yourself if you really love me."

"Joe!"

He sat up. "Well? Do you?"

"Of course I do!"

"Isn't—affection part of it? I mean, if I want to kiss you, you say you're feeling sick or want a drink or it's too hot or too cold or something, something all the time. And—and the other—physical love. Why, I've started to feel I'm an animal for wanting you!" His voice had risen, was now strong and angry. "Why should I have to feel that way? I'm normal. I want you and I want kids. Why should I go around hungry when the woman I love is my wife?"

She shook her head, not knowing what to say. He was right, and he was wrong.

"Well?" he said.

"But you're making a mountain out of a molehill, Joe." She tried to smile; found she could manage it. "Really, I'm not *that* bad."

He got out of bed and walked into the living room. The light went on. She waited. About five minutes later, the light went off and he came back to the bedroom. "Guess I acted stupid," he murmured.

"Well—" she began.

"Christ," he said, lying down. "I feel ashamed again. Why should I feel ashamed!"

He didn't expect an answer.

She didn't offer one. . . .

She'd planned to serve him a large breakfast Monday morning, but it was ten o'clock when she got up, and he was gone. He hadn't awakened her with his usual morning kiss.

She sat on the edge of the bed, rubbing at her eyes, and realized she was driving him further and further away. But there was nothing she could do about it.

Hate came first. Revenge came first. Walter Smith came first

That brought her wide awake. She showered, brushed her blond hair until it shone, and carefully applied make-up. Then she put on her silk negligee, high-heeled shoes, and a simple silver choker. . . .

He was late. She was sitting in the living room, smoking her fifth or sixth cigarette, when she heard him. She got up and walked down the foyer, noticing the way her robe flared open above her left knee.

She looked through the peephole just as he passed the door.

"Bring in a loaf of raisin bread," she said.

He started violently. His eyes went to the peephole, then swung away as someone called from down the hall.

"Got any of those sweet rolls, Hogan's?"

"Yes, ma'am," he said, moving out of the peephole's limited range of vision. "Special on 'em, in fact."

Paula opened the Yale lock and returned to the living room. She dropped into the armchair facing the foyer, crossed her legs and didn't bother checking how much of her was show-ing.

She waited. She shifted in the chair, wanting a cigarette, wanting a cold drink, wanting to get up and move. But she stayed where she was. She had to be here when he came in.

It was hot. And time passed so slowly, so damned slowly!

"Come on," she whispered, clenching her fists. "Come on, Herr Schmidt! Now is the time to make good on the bragging you must've done to your dirty German friends. Now is the time to give the contemptible Jewess a taste of Aryan mas-culinity. Now, Herr Schmidt. Now!"

The door opened. "Hogan's. I got that raisin loaf."

"Come in, Walt."

He came down the foyer, placed his basket on the table and looked at her. His eyes were bold; they traveled to her legs.

"Missed you, Paula. Did you take a vacation?"

She made her voice petulant. "Yes, six glorious days in an isolated cabin. And my husband spent most of his time fishing."

He stepped into the living room, still staring at her legs. "The guy must be nuts. If I had six days with you in an isolated cabin—" He stopped then, eyes jumping to her face to check her reaction.

She smiled and stood up. "You would probably do the same."

Now he wasn't afraid. Now he breathed faster and his hands began to tremble. "You've got a nice tan, Paula. Gee, you look wonderful. Bet you're a knockout in a bathing suit."

She widened her smile. He looked just like Freilich now. He had the same swinish flush, perspiring upper lip and feverish eyes.

"I'll have to model for you some day, Walt." She moved forward until she was only inches away from him. "You've paid me so many compliments and I haven't even offered you a drink. How about a highball, beer or Coke?"

"Coke," he said, and his voice shook. "Not allowed to touch alcohol while working. Company figures a man who goes into people's homes—"

"Might get high and kiss some pretty housewife?" she fin-ished, and started for the kitchen.

He reached out and took her arm. She stopped. He tugged her, gently, ready to let go at the slightest sign of resistance. She stood absolutely still. He tugged again, and she moved against him.

"Paula, you're beautiful. You're—" He put his arms around her waist. She turned up her face, wanting to let him kiss her on the mouth. It was part of the plan. But just before his lips reached hers, his hands began to move, and she felt his maleness through the negligee.

She expected an immediate surge of hatred—*and it didn't come.*

The absence of hate frightened her. She twisted her head aside and he kissed her neck. He must have felt a stiffening in her body because his arms loosened. She recovered quickly, pressed against him, murmured, "This is so wrong, Walt. So very wrong—" And she moved and moved until his arms tightened and his hands stroked and his lips ran feverishly across her neck and cheek and hair.

They continued that way for a few minutes, and then he parted her robe. She jerked free with a spinning motion. "No, please, Walt! I've got to think. I—I've never done—"

He was aroused. He came after her, and for a moment she thought he might have to do it now. But then he stopped. "Aw, honey, you can't keep this up. It's been months—"

"Please, Walt. You don't understand. I'm not a—a tramp. I've got to think about this. I—I just can't—"

"It'll be wonderful," he said, voice high and weak. "I promise I'll be careful. Paula, please, baby—" And he stepped forward.

She drew her robe tight. "No. I want you to go, Walt. Right now!"

"All right," he said angrily, and stalked to the foyer. "All right!"

She watched him, and refused to accept her puzzling lack of hate. She concentrated on *his* reactions. He wasn't ready yet. When he was, he'd come after her no matter what she said. Then it would be simple to destroy him.

He turned after picking up his basket, and the anger was gone from his face. "I'd like that Coke."

"Please go."

"How about the bread?"

"Please, Walt—"

He dropped a loaf on the table. "No charge," he said, and left.

As soon as the door closed behind him, the image of Freilich returned, Camp Three returned, hate returned.

She waited a second or two, breathing deeply, then walked down the foyer and locked the door. On the way back, she

picked up the loaf of bread and brought it into the kitchenette. She tore open the wrapping paper, took out a slice,
squeezed it to a pulpy lump and dropped it into the garbage
can. She did the same to every slice in the loaf, and then
went into the bathroom. She undressed, got into the shower
and scrubbed herself with a washcloth and backbrush until
her skin stung. And even then, she felt soiled. . . .

Joe came home at six. She'd spent two hours preparing his
favorite supper—sweet and sour spare-ribs, baked potatoes,
fried eggplant, chopped salad and cold beer. He ate quickly,
silently, thoroughly. When he finished, he leaned back and
loosened his belt. "Hope I'll be able to bowl after that
feast."

"I thought Wednesday was your bowling night?" she said,
busying herself with a forkful of potato.

"Yeah, but some of the guys bowl two nights a week. I was
thinking that maybe I'd try it." He patted his stomach and
tried for a jocular tone that didn't quite come off. "Got to
keep the old gut down. You feed me so well—"

She got up from the table and took her dishes into the
kitchenette. She was sure he'd follow her, ask if she minded
—and this time she'd say yes. She didn't want him out two
nights a week bowling and another night playing poker and
one night a month at a lodge meeting. And maybe there
would be bar nights and baseball nights and other nights.

But he didn't follow her, and he didn't ask if she minded.
He went into the bedroom. She began washing the dishes, feeling tears well up in her eyes. She called herself a fool, and
still wanted to run to him and cry.

When she heard him coming back, she dried her hands
and stepped into the foyer. He was dressed for bowling and
carried his ball in its leather case—her birthday gift to
him last year. She kissed him, pressed tight against him.

He said, "You don't have to do that, Paula. I know you don't
really want to."

She turned on her heel and went back to the kitchenette. He
walked out of the apartment. As soon as he reached the
elevator, he began to whistle. She stood at the sink, listening
to the happy sound. . . .

She waited up for him. It was 2:00 A.M. when he came in.

"Hi," he said.

She got off the couch without a word, went into the bedroom and lay down.

"Sorry I'm late," he called cheerfully. "We stopped for a

few beers. Man, what a lousy game I bowled tonight!" He laughed and went into the bathroom.

She turned off the lamp and stared up at the ceiling, feeling sorry for herself. Then she thought of what she was doing with Walter Smith, and feeling sorry for herself seemed out of place. She should be feeling sorry for Joe.

But when Joe came out of the bathroom, wearing pajama bottoms and a scrubbed, relaxed look, she felt only resentment. He was humming under his breath, smiling to himself. He got into bed; then said, "Oops, living-room light's still on." He bounded out of the room, turned off the lights, bounded into bed again. He settled himself comfortably on his side, back to Paula, and said, "Night, honey."

She brooded a few minutes, then whispered, "What did you do, meet some girls in that bar?"

He chuckled. "Yeah. Sure."

She brooded a while longer. "One thing is certain, you didn't worry about me being all alone here."

He rolled over to face her and said quietly, "I'm sorry if you felt lonely, Paula. I've been feeling that way myself for quite a while. Maybe I'm not as good at expressing it as you are, but when I reach for you—" He let it die there.

She'd been challenged. Now she had to go to him, give him the affection, the reassurance he needed.

But she couldn't.

It was too involved, too complex a situation right now. She hated Freilich and the Germans and what they'd done to her, and so she carried over a distaste for *all* physical love; and what she was doing with Walter Smith was an act of hate and made the affection she felt for Joe difficult to express—

Why couldn't he wait awhile; leave her alone awhile!

He did just that—left her alone. He rolled over, shutting her out.

Later, she wondered that he could be so hurt one moment and fall fast asleep the next. Perhaps all men had a basic core of callousness—

Joe Theck was not sleeping. He was just lying there, eyes closed, thinking of the war. He'd been in it, all right. He'd been in as much as any American GI could be. And he was okay; no mental scars or anything like that.

Maybe it was because he'd had such a swell childhood. Maybe it was because he hadn't stopped laughing as a kid.

Swell childhood or not, he hadn't done much laughing when he arrived at the grim, hot, isolated Texas army camp for his basic training in 1942. But neither had he cried in his beer.

He was in the infantry whether he liked it or not, so what the hell?

He wasn't a tall guy, but even at eighteen he was big—big across the shoulders; big in the biceps and chest and thigh. He had weight and muscle and a feeling that the war was necessary. He went through his first five weeks of basic in the same kind of exhausted daze as all the other guys, and then he began to wake up and look around and make friends—and a few enemies.

He never thought he'd ever make enemies. But what can you do when someone comes up to your sack, reads the name tag on your foot-locker and drawls, "Theck. What-all kind of name is that, boy? You better change it or someone's gonnah think you-all's a Jew."

That was Private Roger Thurgood Jackson Potter from Mississippi speaking. He didn't speak quite as well twenty minutes later; he didn't have as many teeth then.

Joe had gotten to his feet and glanced around the barracks. Everyone was watching; no one was interfering. "No reason for me to change my name," he'd said quietly. "I am a Jew."

"No," Potter drawled, jaw hinging open in mock astonishment. "Shit, man, no one would ever know it by that little ole nose of yourn. It's hooked so purty Ah'd swear you was part turkey. And with that mop of black hair—let's call it tight-curled—Ah'd say the other part was nigger. So you-all have to pardon me."

Two of his cracker compatriots at the other end of the barracks had laughed, and John Greer, a near-idiot from Kansas, had snickered. The rest of the trainees had remained silent.

At first, Joe had been too stunned to do or say a thing. Sure, he'd run into a few guys back in Brooklyn who made something of his being Jewish. (Sometimes during a game of ball, when tempers would flare, he too would use insulting names for his Italian, Irish or colored opponents; names he later regretted.) But never had he heard anything as deliberately, brutally, cold-bloodedly insulting as this.

Potter was in his thirties, over six feet tall, about two hundred pounds. Basic training had done him some good, but not all the meat on his bones was solid and the tire around his middle was very much in evidence. Still, he loomed over Joe, hands on hips, obviously confident of his ability to handle anything that happened.

Joe fought the red haze sweeping over him, looked Potter up and down, said in a voice weak with rage, "You lousy stump-jumping bastard. Why aren't you fighting for the Nazis?"

Potter slapped him hard, and Joe staggered sideways, almost falling over his cot, ears ringing. Potter threw two roundhouse punches and the left landed, but only on the protective shoulder Joe raised automatically.

Joe half jumped, half crawled over his sack and came around the other side into the aisle between the two rows of cots. He backed up as Potter turned to face him, and Potter said, "What's that yellow doing on your face, Ikey? Yo're supposed to be either brown or black."

For a second, Joe felt that so much hate would defeat him. Then he heard the voices calling; voices of men in his squad.

"Go on, Theck! You can take him!"

"Don't let him get away with it!"

"He's all gut, Theck; aim for it!"

"That's raht, boy! He's full of grits-'n-greens!"

It had an immediate effect. It broke the paralyzing grip of fear. But he didn't show it; he still moved backward.

The men who'd called out to him groaned. Potter's two compatriots, and the near-idiot Greer, whooped derisively. Potter contented himself with a grin and a slow, steady, menacing shuffle.

Suddenly, Joe lunged forward, pumping both fists into that soft belly. Potter grunted and sagged and then swung mightily. But Joe was already back out of range.

"C'mon, Ikey," Potter gasped. "Make believe you're white and fight!"

At that, Joe's battle plan evaporated in an upsurge of rage, and he threw away his advantage in mobility.

He cursed Potter with every foul word he knew and rushed in and swung wildly, steadily, and knew he was landing and heard the spectators shout. He also felt knuckles cut his cheeks and pound his ribs, and then he was wrestled to the floor. He managed to squirm away before Potter could bring his superior weight into play, and as he got up he belted the Mississippian flush in the mouth.

The brittle cracking of teeth was a tiny sound, but by far the most satisfying Joe had ever heard. Potter had been on his knees, about to get up, and the punch set him back on his haunches. Blood trickled through his puffing lips.

"Damn," he mumbled, and spat teeth into his hand. He looked up.

Joe was standing over him, ready to start swinging as soon as Potter made a move to rise. Potter settled further back on his heels and again said, "Damn."

"Get up, bastard," Joe said.

Potter looked at the teeth in his hand and slowly shook his head. "Some other time, boy."

"Right now, bastard," Joe said. "Right now, unless you tell me how sorry you are for what you said."

Potter shrugged. "Lookin' at these teeth, it's easy fo' me to say Ah'm sorry." He grinned wryly.

That got a laugh from the barracks. But Joe couldn't laugh. Had it been an ordinary quarrel, he'd have helped the man up, admired his ability to make a joke out of a beating, and later felt guilty about his part in it. But this was different. The hate still boiled inside him, and he wanted to go on fighting until he'd either killed or been killed.

He walked down the aisle and passed Greer's cot. The small, thin Kansan sucked his teeth and looked away. Joe wanted to kill him.

He reached the far doors, and the cots of Potter's close friends, and they looked at him. They were both medium-sized men about thirty; both Mississippians.

"What're you staring at, stump-jumpers!" Joe suddenly bellowed, whirling on them.

They got up and glanced at each other and hesitated. Then one, tight-lipped and gray of face, said, "Me first."

Joe felt a fierce exultation. A killing rage descended on him and he wanted to use something deadlier than fists.

But the others stopped it right there, shoving Joe to his own end of the barracks and holding him until he cooled off.

"Don't pick on mah friends," Potter called from where he was trying to doctor himself on his cot. "Ah tole you—we'll finish this some other time."

It was just talk; he never tried fighting Joe again. But that didn't end the trouble. Joe went to the latrine late one night and caught Greer writing, "Kill all Jews," on the wall behind the urinals. He grabbed the Kansan and shook him, but Greer refused to make any sign of resistance. Joe spun him around and kicked him as hard as he could, right through the doors. Greer fell, scrambled to his feet and ran off, shouting he would get even. Joe didn't worry about it, knowing he could handle the moron.

It was a mistake not to worry. Greer enlisted the aid of Potter's two friends, and the three followed Joe out to the latrine one night a week later. They dragged him around back and took turns slugging him in the body. It put him in the base hospital for two days, and he had no compunction about telling the provost marshal the whole story. But by then orders had come through for a bivouac and the commander wanted to make a good showing by putting every man in the field. Joe's assailants were given four days' KP.

"Anyway," the provost marshal said, "if we throw a summary at them, we'll have to do the same to you. Fighting in barracks, kicking Greer in the backside instead of reporting him to the CQ, and so on. Another thing—if they'd really wanted to hurt you, they'd have gone for your face. As it is, you've only got a sore gut and bruised ribs."

"Gee," Joe said, "I guess I ought to thank them. You do it for me, will you, Captain?"

The captain had laughed.

Joe returned to barracks in time to prepare for bivouac, and learned that his three assailants had been transferred to another company. He felt it was just as well. He had enough on his mind learning to be an effective soldier.

Later, the outfit was shipped to Michigan where they went on three weeks' maneuvers. One morning, Jackson Potter, now a Pfc attached to headquarters company (at thirty-five he'd had too much soft living to make a good combat infantryman, and they did need clerks), happened to stand behind Joe in the chow line. The first Joe knew of it was when someone tapped him on the shoulder. He turned, stared, said, "What the hell do you want?" He was in perfect condition—trained fine— and ready to take the Mississippian apart at the slightest provocation.

"Whoah, boy," Potter said. "Ah just want to tell you Ah didn't like what Greer, Crowell and Maiter did to you. Ah don't go for gangin' up on a man."

Joe kept staring at him. "Yeah?" he said. "Yeah?"

"That's right, boy." He slapped Joe on the arm. "Move up. We'll miss out on that deeelicious fried turd."

Joe moved up, and turned again. "I don't understand you," he said. "The things you called me. The way you hated—"

"Hated? Boy, how could Ah hate you? Ah didn't even know you then! Naw, just riding a Jew, that's all. Only you didn't ride well." He grinned and pointed to his mouth. Joe saw the three gold-rimmed porcelain caps. "You-all sure are sensitive. If anyone's got reason to hold a grudge, it's ole Stonewall Potter." He grinned again.

Joe was amazed. He wanted to say something about yellow-belly crackers, but instead found himself chuckling. He wondered if he would be able to take it as well as the Southerner.

"Sensitive," he said, shaking his head. "Potter, you're nuts!"

Potter's eyebrows climbed. "Why nuts, boy? Ah've handed out licks, and this time Ah got 'em. About that riding—hell, nothing personal. Ah just don't like Jews."

"How many do you know?"

Potter grinned. "You and two others. One runs a store in town back home. Got too much money and political pull for me to try anything. The other is Levy, and he's too puny to mess with."

Joe shook his head again. He didn't understand it, but somehow it no longer bothered him. As for Levy, he knew him, and pitied him. The small, thin, intelligent boy from Chicago had two years of college at nineteen, but wasn't nearly physical enough for officer's candidate school. He took a lot of guff about being Jewish, but no one knocked him around because he was low man in the outfit.

Poor Levy, Joe thought. Joe had tried getting close to him, feeling that the only two Jewish guys in the outfit should at least be friends if not buddies. But he found he had nothing in common with the Chicagoan. And besides, he wanted his friends to be good combat men since his life might some day depend on them.

They went overseas in June of 1943. During the year spent training and killing time in England, Joe had several run-ins with other GIs, but none concerned (at least directly) his being Jewish and their being something else. And he never again worried about anti-Semitism. Hell, he could take care of himself. It was the guys like Levy, or those a little tougher than Levy but not tough enough, who had a bad time. But then again, most soft or weak or meek or frightened guys had a bad time in the army. There was no helping it; there was a war on and it was just T.S. Get a crying slip from the chaplain, buddy. T.T.S. At least that's how Joe Theck dispensed with the problem.

He landed in Normandy on D-Day plus three. He fought all through France and into Germany. He was one of a group that liberated two concentration camps—but they were a few hours too late. He saw Jewish corpses stacked like cordwood, ready for the burning which he and his outfit had interrupted. He tried to stop living skeletons from crawling up and kissing his muddy GI brogans. He heard a woman sing a Yiddish lullaby to a charred rag.

He told himself he would never forget those camps. He was right, but only partly. If and when anyone spoke of Nazi brutality, he remembered and could describe what he'd seen. But otherwise he cleared his mind of the terrifying picture within six months of leaving the army. By the time he met Paula, the army itself was less a memory than a vague shadow of memory—something he knew he'd lived through but couldn't quite equate with Joe Theck. And so he was a happy guy, a healthy guy, one who didn't hold grudges, especially when there was no way of satisfying them. And hating anyone or anything for extended periods of time was completely alien to his nature.

That's why his marriage had begun to sour. That's why his love for Paula—up to now the strongest emotion he'd ever experienced—had begun to weaken. That's why he wanted to get away from her during the evenings, wanted to be with happy laughing people again—

He fell asleep and had a dream. He was walking up Sheffield Avenue to his old home. He was carrying a suitcase and whistling and feeling strangely happy and strangely sad. He knew he was going back to Mom and Dad, and that was good. He also knew Paula was lost somewhere behind him, and that was bad.

He never did get to the two-family house. He just kept walking and whistling and feeling happy and feeling sad. . . .

Paula Theck left the apartment before 10:00 A.M. every day for the next four days. She did it because she knew that if she were home when the bread man came, she would be compelled to complete her plan. There was no longer any logical reason to prolong it beyond the next meeting, or possibly two. And yet she was somehow afraid, somehow unwilling. She kept remembering the absence of hate when Walter Smith had kissed her, petted her.

She quarreled with Joe over the weekend. She was jumpy and irritable and unable to hide it. He tried to interest her in going to the movies, or to his folks, or to some friends, but she managed to defeat every suggestion. Finally, Sunday afternoon, he stalked out of the apartment, saying he was going over to Ebbets Field and see the Dodgers-Braves game. She was glad. She—she hated him! She sat in the living room with the shades drawn against the sun, thinking of Walter Smith.

She made her decision. No more running from duty. As soon as the situation shaped up right, he would pay for his crime against her people.

In the morning, she prepared herself—shower, make-up, negligee, high-heeled shoes, silver choker around her throat. Her combat uniform.

The bread man came at eleven-ten. She went to the door and looked through the peephole and saw that he was talking to Mrs. Dolberger from the apartment to Paul's left. Then Mrs. Goldman, from directly across the hall, also came out.

It was shaping up perfectly.

She opened the door, stuck out her head and said, "Hogan's. Got a raisin loaf?"

"Sure thing," he said, his voice businesslike because of the other women, but he shot her a blazing look. "I'll bring it in to you in a minute, Mrs. Theck."

"Well," Paula said, as if doubtful. "Well, all right." She smiled at her two neighbors, and Mrs. Goldman said, "Hot weather, eh, Mrs. Theck?"

"Extremely," Paula said, and closed the door, letting the snaplock operate.

She went back to the living room and lit a cigarette. She took two puffs, and then the door rattled and she killed the cigarette. She went down the foyer and said, "Who is it?" in a loud voice, hoping someone besides Walter Smith would hear it.

"Hogan's," he said, sounding surprised at the change in procedure.

She opened the door, and as he came in she saw that Mrs. Goldman and Mrs. Dolberger were still standing in the hall, holding their purchases and chatting.

The time was now! They would make perfect witnesses! They would testify that it was Walter Smith who had suggested bringing the bread into the apartment; that she'd seemed hesitant; that her door had been locked. And they would also testify that she'd screamed and they'd seen her fighting the brutal rapist.

Walter Smith walked past her. She closed the door, and this time made the snap-lock inoperative so that anyone could burst into the apartment when she screamed. Smith put his basket on the table and turned. She swayed toward him. He said, "I hope you're not mad about last time?"

She came up close. "Mad? I haven't been able to eat or sleep from thinking—" She put her arms around his neck and kissed him on the mouth. He gasped, and then she was being crushed against him. A second later, he parted her robe.

The hate didn't come. The revulsion didn't come.

She cursed herself, insisting that hate was there, had to be there.

"Soon, soon, soon," she told herself, and began backing toward the couch. It took some time to get there because he wouldn't let go of her, not even for a second. Finally, she felt her legs strike the couch, and toppled onto her back, drawing him after her.

He paused then, whispering his question. "Paula?"

She nodded.

As soon as he began fumbling with his clothing, she readied herself, sucking in a great breath for her first piercing scream.

But she couldn't scream.

She looked at him. His face was set in the same intense, determined, strained, almost-pained lines as Joe's when Joe made love to her. His lips pressed feverishly on her forehead and neck, muttering terms of endearment.

He wasn't a German! He couldn't be!

"Your name," she whispered. "Was it ever Schmidt?"

He didn't hear, or care, and she had to repeat the question three times before he answered.

"Yes," he panted. "Father's name in old country. Paula—"

"Germany?"

"Yes. Paula, please—"

She didn't hate him. She could hate the image of Freilich, she could hate Germans in the abstract, but not this man. He was a German and she didn't hate him. That's all there was to it.

She twisted suddenly, violently, and got off the couch, pulling her robe together. "I'm sorry," she said, ashamed to look at him. "It was a mistake—"

"Paula!" His voice was a sick cry. "You can't just—"

"Please leave, Walt. It would be a terrible mistake. I don't want to."

He stared. "Are you crazy?" he whispered, face red.

She didn't blame him.

"Please leave," she said. "Or must I call someone—"

He turned away from her, cursing under his breath. He arranged his clothing and grabbed his basket and left.

She spent the day trying to understand it, but she couldn't. She felt ashamed of herself for a multitude of reasons, and yet also strangely relieved.

That night, after serving Joe a roast beef dinner, she made him make love to her. She didn't feel the way she should have—but almost.

The next day, on her way out to shop, she passed the Hogan's bread man in the hall. She felt like apologizing, but that was impossible. Besides, he turned his back to her.

Wednesday, a new bread man was in the hall. She heard the strange voice and went out. She asked about Walter.

"He switched his route," the new man said. "How about a coffee ring? Got a special—"

Friday night, Joe asked if he could play poker. She said, "I promised your mother we'd drop over. All right?"

"Well, sure, honey—"

They visited his parents, and his brothers were there. They spent the evening talking. Everyone noticed the change in Paula—she laughed.

On Sunday, they drove to Jones Beach. Even though it turned cool, they stayed until almost eleven P.M., eating the remains of their picnic lunch-and-supper, lying on the sand and gazing out at the black water.

"What's happening?" Joe suddenly asked. "I mean, are you clicking back again? I can hardly believe—"

She didn't want to talk about it. "I guess I was sick. Now I'm getting better. Look out there, Joe. Lights. Is it a ship? . . ."

It was twelve thirty before they parked on Fifteenth Avenue and walked up the street, arm in arm. When they reached the deep entrance to Koptic Court, Joe glanced around and saw they were alone. He stopped and drew her close.

"It's more fun sneaking kisses," he said, and demonstrated.

After a minute she pulled away, shaking her head—but pleased. They walked toward the lobby, holding hands.

Just as they stepped through the ironwork-and-glass doors, a tremendous roar filled their ears.

Joe opened his mouth to say, "What the hell was that?" but something patted him on the head and he went to sleep.

Paula saw the tile floor rising, the stuccoed walls pushing in, the ceiling coming down. She saw Joe falling, and screamed and tried to pick him up. She screamed again as she touched his face and felt blood.

Punishment for my hate, she thought and then plunged into nothingness.

21

LUKE BROWN 1-A

The movie ended at five minutes after ten. Luke and Cora came out of the air-conditioned theater into the warm August night and headed up Fifteenth Avenue. They had a seventeen-block walk ahead of them.

"Hey," Cora complained as Luke began hurrying. "My legs can't move that fast!"

He slowed, glancing at her with some impatience. A moment later he was pulling ahead again. Cora stopped dead, placing her hands on her hips.

"First you fidget all through the movie; now you're going faster than a race horse. I declare, Luke, it's all right to work hard, but a man's got to relax once in a while too. It's Sunday. Mr. Gorman don't expect you to stay around the house, and everything's all right back there anyway."

He rubbed his face and grinned; then took her arm and tugged her into motion. "I didn't tell you about the light on the staircase, the one between the second and third floors?"

She was being pulled along quickly now. "No," she said irritably. "You didn't."

"Well, it sort of blinked once or twice when I checked it last night. I got a hunch it'll blow tonight."

"So?" she said, panting for breath.

"So!" he exclaimed, breaking stride momentarily to stare at her. "That's no way to talk, Cora. If the light blows, the staircase'll be dark in that spot. And someone might just happen to fall. And whose fault would it be then?"

She looked at him, perspiration beginning to dampen her face. Then she shook her head and smiled and hugged his arm tight against her in a sudden surge of affection. "You worrying man," she murmured softly. "You wonderful worrying man. How you ever got a son like Sammy—" She stopped then, not wanting to start him thinking along those lines. But it was too late.

"What you think happened to him?" Luke asked her. "I mean—here he ain't been at his job in the restaurant almost two weeks and I ain't heard from him at all. What you think he been doin'?"

She'd heard that question at least a dozen times in the past few days, and hadn't given him her answer. Now she decided it was time he faced the truth.

"You know what he's been doing," she said quietly. "He's been drinking and fighting. Maybe he's got himself locked up again and figured not to bother you any more."

Luke said, "Why you got to think that way? Why can't he be workin' at a better job somewhere and forgot to call us? Why can't he be—" He shrugged then. "Yeah. You right, honey. But he'd call me if he was in jail. I know it. Maybe I wouldn't help him, but he'd call me." He walked in silence a moment. "I got a feelin' he's sick or something. I got this bad feelin', this black feelin'."

She changed the subject abruptly. "Ever since Reverend Cooper gave that talk about movies, I've noticed it more and more. Like tonight. You know there wasn't one colored person in that detective story? They had parts right out on the street with lots of people walking by and it was supposed to be New York too. Yet not one colored person. And the Western—"

"Well," Luke interrupted, "they didn't have colored folks out where those cowboys used to do all that shootin'. Indians but no colored folks."

"All right. So what about the detective story?"

He shrugged. "What you want us to do—stop goin' to movies?"

"Reverend Cooper said so, didn't he? He said we should try to make ourselves felt at the boxoffice. He said if all the colored people stopped going to movies that left out colored actors, Hollywood might get to feeling we're part of this country and hire—" She paused as two white women passed by, walking in the opposite direction. "Anyway, he was right when he called it the White Fog. That's what it is. A white fog that makes us feel we're not even here. No colored people smoke cigarettes in the big magazines, or drink beer on television, or kiss and hug in the moving pictures—"

"Hush," Luke said, glancing around the street. "Seems to me Reverend Cooper ought to stick to Scripture and leave politics alone."

"Politics? That's not politics, Luke. That's just day-by-day living. We got to get ahead, better ourselves in all the ways we can, and a preacher's got to do his part too. Sometimes I

think you believe what those whites down South—" She
stopped then, seeing the way he repressed a sudden answer,
and she knew it was true—he *did* believe what those Southern-
ers said about Negroes.

She wanted to ask him right out, wanted to hear him say he
felt that he and she and Reverend Cooper and all other Negroes were inferior to whites. She wanted him to say it so
she could tell him what a damn fool he was!"

But she didn't *really* want to tell him that. And she didn't
want to hear him say anything that would hurt the love between them. He was a wonderful man, the most important
thing in her life.

Maybe he just don't know how to talk about his opinions,
she told herself. *Maybe it's just that he was born and bred in
Alabama and they kind of scared him so he can't speak his
mind even to me—*

She stopped it there, unable to go on lying to herself.
She'd lived with Luke Brown for almost seventeen years, and
yet they'd never talked about Negro-white equality; not really. It was because of Luke; because of how he felt.

It hurt her. Sure it did. But a good man was allowed some
weak spot, some wrong way.

She began talking of a sale Klein's was running on men's
clothes. She wanted Luke to get a new suit. "You'd look
real nice in a charcoal-gray flannel, Luke. Nice as that man in
the movie—"

He nodded and kept hurrying. Sure was a soft night. Trees
and bushes and gardens out in backyards pouring sweet
smells into the air. You wouldn't think the city could smell
so nice—and it seemed like the closer they got to Koptic
Court, the sweeter it got. . . .

The telephone was ringing when they reached the door to
their apartment, but it stopped before Luke could get inside
and run down the foyer to the living room. It started again
about five minutes later, as they were eating a snack of cold
cuts and potato salad. Luke answered. It was Mr. Gorman,
the landlord. He sounded unhappy.

"Listen, Luke, I got a complaint about an hour ago and
I've been trying to reach you since then. One of the tenants
called and said a drunken colored man had walked into the
elevator with him and his wife and that the drunk was singing
and laughing and the tenant's wife got frightened. Anyway,
he rode up to the sixth floor with them and stayed in the

elevator. The tenant saw him press the basement button. He says it's the same man he saw staggering into your apartment once before. Is it your son?"

Luke couldn't answer for a moment, his feelings were so violent, and so confused. First he wanted to rip Sammy apart for having compromised him this way; then he experienced rare resentment of a tenant—the one who'd been so quick to call Mr. Gorman; then he could have belted Cora for having made him go to the movies and leave the house unguarded; then he felt relief that his son was still in one piece after disappearing for two weeks; and finally he returned to his original reaction—wanting to rip Sammy apart.

"Guess it is my son," he said, voice low. "I'll get right down to the basement."

"I can't let that sort of thing go on, Luke," Mr. Gorman said angrily. "You're a good super and all that, but when you allow your son to stagger around—"

"I was at the movies, Mr. Gorman. If I'd been here, I'da tossed him out fast. You know I wouldn't 'low—"

"All I know is what my tenants tell me," Mr. Gorman interrupted. He paused a moment. "If it happens again, Luke, I'm going to have to let you go. There's nothing worse for a house than having someone like your son hanging around, sleeping in the basement—"

"I never let him sleep in the basement," Luke said, and his voice shook. "Honest." He paused. " 'Cept one time—two, three years ago."

"Oh? I got a complaint on that very thing about the time the hot-water boiler broke down. A woman on her way to the washing machines—"

Luke remembered Sammy had come out of the bin near the water boiler when the colored repairman had been there. So someone else had seen him.

"I didn't mention it to you," Mr. Gorman continued, "because I hoped it wouldn't happen again. But I can't overlook it any more."

"Yessir," Luke said, and the shaking was in his entire body now. "I'll go right down and see if anyone's there. And it won't happen—"

"Okay," Mr. Gorman said. His voice softened a bit. "I never had a better super, Luke. But that son of yours—well, I didn't bargain for him when I gave you the job."

"Yessir."

Mr. Gorman cleared his throat. "How's your wife?"

"Fine, sir."

"Give her my best." The landlord cleared his throat again. "Don't make me let you go, Luke." He hung up.

Luke turned. Cora was standing there, eyes frightened. She opened her mouth, but he walked past her with such stiff anger on his face that she said nothing. He went to the bedroom. When he came out, he was carrying his old leather belt; the thick one. He doubled it, swung it against his calloused palm three times. Cora winced at each of the sharp, cracking sounds. Luke rolled the belt and put it in his pocket.

"I hope he ain't down there," he said, rubbing his face. "I hope he's where I can't reach him." He started for the door.

"Luke!" Cora said.

He didn't stop.

"Luke, don't go till you cool off a bit!"

He went out of the apartment. . . .

It took almost half an hour before he found his son curled up in a corner of the basement storage room. He locked the door from inside with his master key and walked across the large, concrete room, pulling the belt from his pocket.

"Wake up," he said.

Sammy didn't move.

Luke hissed under his breath and brought the belt down across Sammy's side. Sammy's eyelids twitched—but that was all. Even before Luke knelt to make sure his son wasn't shamming, he could smell the alcohol.

He straightened, wondering what to do. He couldn't drag Sammy into the street and just leave him there. He had to wait until his son was conscious before thrashing him and throwing him out.

He stared down at the handsome man, and slowly his lips lost their tight, bloodless appearance, his eyes their hot anger.

So like Imogene. And Lord knows Imogene hadn't been able to stop messin' around with other men even when she'd wanted to. It was the devil in her. And Sammy was her son, blood and guts and gristle. Her son, and unable to beat the devil inside him, the devil that made him drink and fight and steal other men's women.

"What gonna happen to you, Sammy?" Luke Brown asked.

Sammy's eyelids twitched.

"You wore out. Look how the bones comin' through your cheeks, the red swallowin' up your eyes. You must've been the best-lookin' boy in all Harlem a few years ago, Sammy. Look at you now, Sammy."

He raised his hand to rub his face, and realized he was holding the belt. Quickly, as if ashamed, he rolled it up and shoved it into his pocket. Then he knelt and wiped the film of perspiration from Sammy's face with his handkerchief.

Sammy's eyelids twitched several times.

Luke turned off the light, left the storage room, and locked the door behind him. He went up to his apartment and walked into the kitchen. Cora was sitting at the table. He sat down opposite her and rubbed his face hard.

"You found him?" Cora asked.

He nodded.

"You whupped him?"

He shook his head. "He was passed out cold. How could I whup him?" He kept rubbing his face. "He must've lost fifteen, twenty pounds since I last saw him. He's gettin' sick, Cora. I gotta do somethin'."

She stared at him. "You know, before I was worried you'd hit him too hard. Now I'm mad you didn't hit him at all!"

"How could I when he was passed out?"

"That's not it! Even if he was running around down there on all fours, you'd've talked yourself out of hitting him. You can't do anything to that boy, Luke. You don't know how. You get mad for a minute, but then it passes and you're soft in his hands!"

He raised his head and seemed about to answer sharply. But then he shrugged. "Well, he's a sick—"

"He's sick, all right. And he's going to make you sick too. Won't you be a sick man, Luke, when you lose this job? Won't you!"

He got up from the table. "Let me be, woman," he muttered. "It's after eleven and I'm beat to my soul." He moved out of the kitchen.

"It's because of Imogene, isn't it?" Cora cried after him, her voice breaking. "You see her every time you look at him. You still—still got feeling for that lowdown woman!"

Luke came back to the kitchen doorway, the hurt clear on his face. "You ain't never said things like that to me before, Cora. You got no call to say them now. I'm gonna get some sleep—two, three hours. Then I'm gonna bring Sammy up here and put him in a cold shower. When he's on his feet, I'll give him a few dollars and tell him to get out."

"Sure," she said, tears welling up in her eyes, "and in another week or two he'll come back. And you won't be able to make him stop because you can't hurt him, really hurt him so he won't ever see you again. He'll keep coming back, Luke. You know it. He'll keep coming back—and he'll cost you this job. It'll kill you, Luke. It'll break—"

"It won't kill me," Luke said, voice suddenly hard. "I guess Sammy's my load to carry. I guess I got to make up my mind to that. And if I lose this job—" He rubbed his face, and his voice lost all its strength. "Well, there's others."

He washed and got into bed. Cora followed a few minutes later. They lay side by side, not speaking. Finally, Luke reached out and found her hand. "Don't let's be this way, Cora. He's a curse. He can bust up my job and everything else, but not us. Don't let him bust us up, Cora."

She began to cry, and he said, "Hey, missus, it ain't that bad."

"Luke, Luke, your wonderful job."

He couldn't stop her sobs.

"Your pride, Luke, and your living and your laughing. It's all in this job, Luke, all in this house."

There was no denying it, so he merely stroked her hair.

The lights were on in the basement storage room. Sammy Brown sat with his back against the wall, smoking a cigarette. His lips were cracked and feverish, his eyes jumpy and bloodshot, his hands shaky. But he was grinning. He rubbed his side with his left hand, proud of the way he'd played dead under that crack of the belt. Still, it was lucky Luke hadn't done it again.

"Daddy," he murmured hoarsely, "you just love your sonny boy." He smoked and grinned and wondered how much he'd be able to get this time. Five for sure. Maybe ten.

He finished his smoke, shuffled to the switch and turned out the light. Then he curled up on the floor. He knew his Daddy would come back soon. It was just a matter of waiting. . . .

Cora was fast asleep, but Luke lay on his side, staring at the wall, at patches of gray and black made by moonglow coming through the window at the other side of the bed.

He kept asking himself the same question, over and over and over. "Why can't you rid yourself of Sammy?"

Hell, he knew the boy wasn't worth a damn. And not kicking him into the gutter would cost him this job some day.

So why couldn't he drag Sammy up here in an hour or two, whup him good with the belt, and throw him out so that he'd be afraid to come back again? Why the hell couldn't he?

And it came to him.

He couldn't crush Sammy, throw him away like a used-up rag, because Sammy was Luke and every other colored man in the States. Sure, Sammy was a natural man. Sammy'd stopped trying to be white, stopped trying to be anything but what his instincts demanded he be. Sure, Sammy was what every Negro would be if he let himself go.

Luke nodded to himself, convinced of the truth of his theory. Sammy wasn't bad, just colored; and that's why he had to be given a helping hand every so often.

Sure.

He glanced quickly at Cora, afraid that she'd be awake and somehow able to read his thoughts. But she slept on.

She didn't see things his way. He wasn't sure whether she really believed in equality or was just trying to fool herself. Of course, she'd lived in New York since she was five years old, and it took Southern upbringing to make a Negro see the truth.

Luke slipped out of bed and picked up his shoes from the floor. He got his shirt and trousers from the chair near the dresser, moved into the living room and put on the lamp. He dressed slowly, wanting to give Sammy as much time as possible. It was only about twelve-thirty, but he couldn't lie in bed any more.

When he finished dressing, he paused a moment. He got a funny feeling. He'd had it once or twice before, like when he'd seen Ralph Bunche talking at that UN in the newsreels, or when he heard about colored people doing things like writing books and inventing chemicals and running big businesses. Of course, there were the colored singers, musicians and athletes, but that didn't count to Luke. It was jobs, not singing and games that tested a man. And when Cora, or a friend, or Reverend Cooper talked too much about colored people who'd done well at real jobs, Luke got a funny feeling that maybe he was wrong.

Except that he couldn't be wrong. He knew he was right, had known it ever since the day his father told him so and said, "You'll live easier, son, once you faces up to it."

He wondered why he should get the funny feeling now since no one had been talking about colored folks doing big jobs.

It made him unhappy to doubt white supremacy. It made lots of things seem too damn rotten to take—like getting twenty dollars a month less than the last super, who'd been white; like reading about them shooting colored boys in Mississippi and Florida; like all sorts of things. If everyone was equal, then a man had to stand up every day and make white folks realize it and life would get so tough—

He took a deep breath, and the feeling passed.

Hell, that just proved equality was a lot of bunk! How could colored folks live, knowing they were as good as whites and still taking what they had to take?

He rubbed his face. The hell with all that thinking. He had to get Sammy—

He was knocked over backward and the light went out and there was so much noise it stopped him from hearing any noise at all. He lay absolutely still for a moment, stunned, deafened, the floor buckling upward beneath him.

When Cora screamed, he got to his feet and went into the bedroom. The bed was tilted in a crazy way and Cora was hanging onto the side sticking up. He almost laughed—it was just so unexpected—when he saw that the other side was dipping into a hole in the floor.

He got her hand and dragged her off the bed. Before they stumbled to the door, the smell of explosive and smoke began filtering into the room. They ran through the living room, falling twice, and when they went past the kitchen they saw flames licking up through the floor about where the refrigerator had stood.

"Fire," Cora gasped. "Fire, Luke!"

He said yes, but didn't understand it.

When they opened the door and looked out, Luke went into a state of shock. The whole lobby was gone. Just gone! There was a big hole instead, and it was filled with the reddish flickering of a thousand budding flames.

"Sammy," Luke said. "Sammy's in the storage room." He stepped forward, as if to go down into that flaming pit, but Cora grabbed his arm.

"No, Luke! There's no storage room any more. There's nothing there but a hole. A hole—" She went limp. He caught her before she hit the floor.

He picked her up and saw that there was a few feet of lobby left around the north and west sides. He could hug those sides and make it to the street doors.

He began to move, thinking he would come back for Sammy.

But then he realized Cora was right. There was no storage room any more. There was no Sammy any more.

He had to step over a man and woman lying just inside the lobby. He carried Cora out through the deep entranceway and placed her on the sidewalk and looked around. A few people were sticking their heads out of windows in the house across the way, and a car had stopped in the middle of the street. Luke wanted to ask what he should do, but then he remembered the man and woman just inside the lobby. He ran back.

He grabbed them—the man's right leg in one hand, the woman's left leg in the other—and dragged them out of the lobby and all the way to the street.

There were more people around now, and he touched a tall man on the arm and said, "What'll we do?"

The man's face was white and his lips trembled. "Christ," he mumbled. "Christ, they'll all die."

Luke shook his head and started back toward the lobby. The people in his house couldn't die. They were his responsibility.

He stopped at the shattered glass doors, appalled by the huge pit, growing flames and scattered wreckage. He coughed as smoke seared his lungs, and said, "Well, gotta clean it up. Gotta get everything in order—"

He heard a voice crying; a kid's voice. There were all those apartments on the other side of the lobby, all cut off from the street doors. The people inside would have to climb out through the windows—unless the windows were blocked by fire and debris—or be helped around that blazing pit somehow. He had to get to them. He had to take them outside, out of the way, so he could start cleaning up this mess. What would Mr. Gorman think?

A terrible idea occurred to him. Maybe Sammy'd had something to do with the explosion. And whether he had or not, wouldn't Mr. Gorman tell the police about Sammy's being drunk and in the elevator and going down to the basement? And wouldn't the police blame . . .

But he didn't have time for that now; people were screaming in those cut-off apartments. And fire rose higher from the huge pit. And anyway, Sammy was gone; the beautiful little boy he'd hugged and kissed so many years ago was gone; the living image of Imogene was gone.

And even that was no longer important. His responsibility was all that mattered. He was the super and this was his house and he had to clean things up.

"God," he prayed, "help me clean up this mess."

He turned face to the wall and began clawing his way, inch by inch, around the flaming pit toward the apartments and the screams.

22

LOUIS SCHIMLER 5-F

Lou got up late that Friday morning and went to the window and looked out at the courtyard. It was sunny, but not nearly as warm as it had been yesterday. He knew it was bound to get real hot again, this being the third week in August, but the touch of coolness made him feel funny anyway. Soon it would be September, and then back to school. In just a week or so. Right after Labor Day. And it seemed to him that vacation had just started.

Not that he'd had such a great time. Heck, no. But there had been weekends at the beach with Mom and Pop and sometimes Myra—when she wasn't at a resort hotel. And two weeks up in the Catskills on Pop's vacation. And no homework. And not having to see the same old guys and girls in class and schoolyard and street.

And his skin had improved a little. Maybe it was his getting out in the sun so much. Anyway, it looked a little better. Maybe if it had been this way a month ago, Elaine would've invited him to her sweet-sixteen party.

He thought of this Sunday, and got a sudden sick feeling. Hell, he didn't care! So she hadn't invited him. He'd make up for it later, when he changed—

But the sick feeling remained. He *had* expected her to invite him, if only as a gesture of friendship, of neighborliness.

But maybe she thought he wouldn't want to go.

He shook his head and turned from the window. Gee, he'd had the blues too many times these past few months. All summer, and even before. He didn't like feeling tight and nervous and—and wanting to dig at things with his penknife.

He looked at his clothes draped over a chair, hesitated, and then got back into bed. Hell, why rush to get outside? Nothing doing anyway. Nothing interesting. He'd sleep a little more. Yeah, later he'd go down to the hobby shop on

Fourth Avenue and find a good schooner kit. Or maybe he'd
try one of those old cars. Or maybe he'd go to the movies.

He was dozing off when his mother called from outside the
door, "Lou. Lou, you up?"

"Yeah," he said, and cleared his throat. "Yeah."

She walked in. Lou was half asleep when she began talking,
but he came fully awake a moment later.

". . . I wondered what she was getting at, asking what you
were doing Sunday and all. I said right out, 'Mrs. Turner,
what are you getting at?' and she said, 'Elaine wants him to
come to her party. It's short notice—the party being day after
tomorrow—but we thought he'd like to.' Well, I wasn't going
to answer for you so I said you'd let her know today."

Lou sat bolt upright, "Mrs. Turner asked you?"

His mother nodded, watching his face closely.

"But they invited all the other guys weeks ago—" He
stopped, hoping she wouldn't think he'd been interested in the
crummy party.

"I guess they just forgot to invite you," his mother said.
"They finally remembered and Elaine was ashamed of forgetting so she sent her mother instead of coming herself."

Lou shrugged, yawned loudly and lay down. "Yeah, guess
so."

"You going?"

He faked another yawn. "Why not? Free eats."

"Good. She's a nice girl, isn't she?"

"She's okay."

His mother smiled. "Well, I'm sure you'll have fun." She
left the room.

Lou felt his heart pounding against his ribs, and told himself not to be a jerk. The way he figured it, Elaine had just
found out that one of the boys she'd invited couldn't come,
and so she'd decided to squeeze him in.

He closed his eyes, and remembered the way she'd smiled
at him that time he'd helped her with the broken bottle of
milk. Maybe she really liked him a lot and hadn't been able to
get up the nerve to ask him to the party. She might think he
didn't like her because, after all, he'd never asked her for a date
and how could she know he was waiting to change, to become
nicer-looking?

Sure, she'd been scared to ask him! It was always harder to
ask someone you liked a lot. Didn't he feel that way with
her? Didn't he find it almost impossible to go over and talk
to her when they met near the house or in school?

He got out of bed and went to the bathroom. He washed, keeping his eyes on the basin. He went back to the bedroom and dressed. Unaccountably, he began to feel jumpy, irritable, tight in the stomach.

When he came into the kitchen, Mom and Myra were having pancakes. Mom got up from the table to serve him, but he said, "I just want a glass of orange juice."

"Now, Lou," Mom said, "I insist that you—"

"Lemme alone!" he shouted. "Jeeze! All I want is juice!"

Mom was shocked for a second, and then she got angry. "Don't you shout at me I'm trying to put some flesh on your bones. If you weren't so skinny, maybe you'd—"

"Mom!" Myra said.

His mother was bad enough, but Myra was pure murder! The way she looked at Mom and shook her head was like saying:

"Of course he's skinny and ugly; that's why you mustn't talk about it."

He gulped his juice, and Mom said, "Well, anyway, he should eat more."

Myra gave Lou a sympathy-laden glance, and Lou suddenly wanted to slam his glass into her face—to hurt her, to scar her. The feeling was so strong it frightened him. He ran back to his room and slammed the door. He paced up and down awhile, and finally stopped in front of the dresser mirror. He looked at himself—a skinny, pimple-faced boy; an ugly boy.

He twisted away from the mirror. Damn Elaine Turner anyway! Who asked her to invite him to her lousy party? Who wanted to sit around with a bunch of jerks, or dance, or make stupid talk? What right did she have to—*to feel sorry for him!*

He felt something in his hand, and looked down. His penknife. He'd taken it out of his pocket and opened the blade—and hadn't known it. He wanted to dig at something, ruin something, make someone pay—

He closed the knife, put it back in his pocket and stood with bony hands clenched into white-knuckled fists. He thought and thought, and couldn't think his way around the insult, the terrible insult. *She'd invited him because she'd had a last-minute cancellation and also because she pitied him.* He was sure of it. What else could it be? Nothing else.

She pitied him.

He stood there, sweat beading his face and neck.

Suddenly, he ran from the bedroom, past his startled mother and sister, and took the staircase two steps at a time down to the second floor. He went right up to the Turners' door and pressed the bell. Elaine answered it almost immediately. She wore a housecoat and no make-up and looked more beautiful than ever to him.

"Hi," she said.

"Hi." His voice sounded a million miles away. "I'm sorry but I won't be able to come to your party Sunday."

"Oh? Well, that's too bad." She smiled.

Now he was raging. Now he wanted to say something, do something, hurt her as she'd hurt him. She didn't give a damn that he wasn't coming; if anything, she seemed pleased.

"Yeah," he said, voice high, shrill. "Since you didn't let me know in July, like you did the other guys, I made other plans."

She stared at him, a tinge of angry red creeping into her cheeks. "Sorry," she said curtly. She began to close the door.

"Anyway," he said, his body trembling, "you don't ever have to bother using me as a fill-in—"

The door swung open again. "Just to keep things straight, I never invited you to my party. It was your mother who suggested to my mother that you'd like to come, and my mother didn't know how to refuse, and so she went ahead on her own—"

"Yeah, sure," he said, and made himself laugh, and walked away, filled with horror.

His mother had asked her mother. God!

He came into the street and he wanted to kill his mother. Why couldn't she leave him alone? Why couldn't everyone leave him alone?

Some guys standing on the corner began laughing, and Lou couldn't help feeling they were laughing at him. He went past them, eyes down, and again felt the knife in his hand, blade open. He looked at the two inches of steel, and suddenly flung it into the gutter.

Silly little piece of crap! A guy couldn't do anything with it except scratch some paint. What he wanted was to show them all—his mother and father and sister and Elaine and her family and her lousy guests and the super who glared at him when he marked the elevator and all of them, the whole damned house. He wanted to make them jump out of their skins, make them yell, make them look stupid and silly —so he could laugh at and pity them. What he wanted was to to do something so big—

Like Stan Safardi dropping that load of fireworks down the incinerator of the Fourteenth-Avenue apartment house. Like that, so people would run out into the hall and yell and he could laugh his head off.

Yeah! Like that! On Sunday, when Elaine was having her party! He'd get plenty of fireworks, ten times more than Stan'd had, and he'd stuff it down the incinerator . . .

His excitement died. He couldn't get hold of even one lousy firecracker; the stuff was outlawed in New York. Stan's father had bought his in Connecticut.

"Aw," he muttered, "it wouldn't have been anything anyway."

Not like when Pop's crew blasted a foundation—

He stopped walking. Pop was on an excavation job right now, out in Queens. Lou had visited the place two or three weeks ago. He could go there again and look around. Sure. Just look around. He knew they kept explosives in a small shack—

Yeah, he'd take the subway out to Pop's job.

What did he have to lose?

And maybe he'd really be able to show them all this Sunday! Maybe he'd make such a boom it'd knock pieces off the house! By God, it might bust the incinerator and even mark up the basement and make loose pieces of plaster fall down in apartments. And wouldn't it shake up Elaine's party!

He called Mom from a drugstore phone booth. He felt like telling her plenty, but all he said was, "I'm going to visit Pop in Queens. I've got four dollars so I'll eat out."

"It might be a good idea at that. Maybe you need a little change—"

"Yeah," he said, rage thickening his voice. "And I told Elaine I'm not going to her party." He hung up.

The whole thing was so easy, he could hardly believe it. No trick at all.

He took the BMT to Times Square, and then the IRT Flushing line to Main Street, and then the bus down Kissena Boulevard to the side street and the construction job. It was a block-square, yellowish hole in the ground, and they were using steam shovels now. But a few weeks ago they'd had to blast an old foundation and a layer of rock, and they'd used dynamite.

He went to the gate in the high wooden fence, past the watchman sitting in his shack built out on the sidewalk. The old man yelled, "Hey, kid where're you going?"

"I'm Irv Schimler's son. Gotta message for him."

The old man waved him in. He walked about one hundred feet to his left around the huge pit, and saw Pop standing near a concrete-mixer down at the bottom. He kept going until he reached the explosive shack, a small, square hut made of corrugated metal, right alongside the fence. Then he went back to where Pop was, and yelled at him and waved his hand. Pop came up and they talked and the noon whistle blew. They ate together in a luncheonette a few blocks away, and then Lou said he was going to see a movie in Manhattan and wouldn't be home until after supper. Pop said he'd tell Mom, and Lou walked away.

Lou didn't go to Manhattan. He went to a double feature on Main Street, about ten blocks from Pop's job. It ended at a quarter to five, and wasn't worth seeing again, but he stayed in his seat. At seven-thirty, he left the theater, went into a candy store and bought two books of matches. He stalled around the magazine rack, and walked real slow when he got out, and didn't reach the construction site until eight-ten. It was good and dark.

He avoided passing the watchman by coming around the fence from the north, strolling casually until he reached the spot where he figured the explosives shack was located. There he stopped and made sure he was alone.

He ran into the street, turned, raced toward the fence. He leaped up, caught hold of the top, and hauled himself over.

A snap. A real snap.

He was only a few feet to the right of the corrugated metal shack. He walked up to it, looked around the mooncast construction site, saw and heard nothing. He used some of the matches he'd bought at the candy store to examine the shack's door. It was held shut with a rusty old lock. He banged the lock a dozen or so times with a rock, and it fell off.

He went inside and saw the big sign with red lettering. "DANGER—HIGH EXPLOSIVES. NO SMOKING." He used more matches to check the four wooden cases sitting on the dirt floor. One was open. He took the long, reddish-brown sticks, shoved them under his shirt until he bulged all over, and walked out. He climbed back over the fence, never giving a thought to the dynamite except as to how it got in his way and made climbing difficult.

In a garbage can on a dark side street a few blocks away, he found newspaper and wrapped the dynamite. He was sorry he hadn't thought to bring a bag, but didn't bother buying one. He made the long subway trip home without incident, holding the untidy newspaper-wrapped bundle on his lap. When he reached Koptic Court, he went around back to the courtyard and down the ramp to the basement and into the bin where Mom kept some old stuff. He put on the dim ceiling bulb, closed the bin door, and for the first time examined his haul.

He had twelve eight-inch sticks of dynamite, capped and fused.

He was disappointed. Heck, it had seemed like more— like sixteen or seventeen. But anyway, it would make a solid bang; bigger than Stan Safardi's for sure.

He found a length of cord and tied the sticks of dynamite together and rewrapped them in the newspaper. He stuck the bundle under a dusty mattress and went upstairs.

Mom asked him where he'd been, and Pop yelled a little, and Lou said, "But gee, I told Pop—"

Mom made him eat chicken and soup, even though he wasn't hungry. When he finished, he went to his room and got his love-story magazine and read until eleven-thirty. But, somehow, he couldn't seem to like any of the girls in the stories. And he kept thinking how they wouldn't be so darned uppity or sure of themselves or anything if they were scared out of their wits.

On Saturday, Pop went to work. When he got home that night, he kept talking about the thief who'd stolen twelve sticks of dynamite and how it must have been a real pro who was going to use it for blasting safes or something. "A smooth job," he said to Mom. "Real smooth. Watchman didn't see him, and he got rid of the lock without making a sound—"

Lou almost laughed. He'd banged away like mad busting that lock. The watchman was probably deaf.

Mom and Pop went visiting after supper, and Myra left for a date with Georgie Becker, so Lou had the apartment to himself. He watched TV and drank two cokes and lit up one of Pop's cigarette butts. He didn't really like smoking, but it made a guy look older, more sophisticated. Yeah, maybe he'd try inhaling next time.

At eleven-thirty he rode the elevator to the basement and made sure the dynamite was just where he'd left it. Then he went back upstairs.

He watched the Late Show on TV and didn't go to bed until 1:00 A.M.

Sunday was a nice day, clear and hot, and Pop decided on

Rockaway Beach. Myra begged off, saying she and a friend were going to see a movie. Lou went with Mom and Pop and they had a real good time. Pop horsed around with Lou, and Lou laughed and forgot to be self-conscious about his skinny body. He even forgot about the dynamite—until they got home.

It was eight-thirty when they parked the car and came around front. Music and voices sounded from the second floor, and Lou glanced up. Elaine Turner's living-room windows faced Fifteenth Avenue; her party was just getting started.

Lou's stomach tightened and he walked faster.

By the time he got to use the shower it was nine twenty, and before he'd had a bite to eat it was ten. He dressed in slacks and a sports shirt and said he was going down for a walk.

"Don't stay out late," Mom said. "You've been looking kind of worn lately—"

He almost ran down the foyer.

He went out the back way, through the courtyard, so he wouldn't have to hear Elaine's party. When he passed the ramp leading to the basement, he thought of the dynamite—but he kept going. Heck, he'd take a ride on the Sixteenth Street bus and transfer at Bay Parkway. He'd always wanted to see just how far that second bus went.

He found out. It went to Canarsie, through a section of garages, gas stations, body-and-fender shops—all closed. It was, for the most part, a grim, depressing ride.

On the way back, he was the only passenger when a guy his age got on with a pretty redhead. Lou was in back; they sat up front. They held hands and whispered together and the guy kissed the girl two or three times. They looked so happy—

He got off long before his stop. He walked almost twenty blocks, trying to shake the crying feeling. Heck, he didn't give a damn about any silly girl!

Broads. That's what Pop sometimes called them. Silly, stupid broads. Who wanted them? Who needed them?

It was almost twelve thirty when he reached the house. Because he was worrying about what Mom and Pop would say about his being out so late, he forgot to avoid the front entrance. As soon as he turned the corner, he heard the music and voices. And when he came into the deep lobby entrance, just about under Elaine's windows, there was a sudden burst of laughter—girl's laughter.

"All right!" he said aloud. "All right, you asked for it!"

He ran into the lobby and the elevator was waiting. He went down to the basement and got his package of dynamite and rode back to the lobby. He ran across the lobby to the incinerator, stepped into the closet-like room and let the door close all the way. The light went out.

"Okay, Elaine!" he said. "Laugh all you want. But in a minute you're going to be yelling your stupid head off. And then will I laugh!"

His hands trembled as he opened the chute lid and shoved the package inside. He slammed the lid shut, then opened and shut it a few more times to make sure that the package had dropped free.

"Okay," he muttered, and was suddenly frightened, and refused to admit it.

He reached for the doorknob.

Heck, it was a ball. He'd go outside and stand across the street and listen to the boom and then laugh when all the people came running out or stuck their heads through the windows. He'd laugh most when those guys at Elaine's party and Elaine herself came out yelling. Yeah, he'd laugh—

Light flashed across his eyes briefly. He didn't have time to wonder what it was. . . .

23

THE RUINS

Louis Schimler felt no pain. His destruction was too quick and complete for that. The dynamite he dropped into the incinerator blew out the entire basement and most of the lobby, and he blew out with it. It also reached and ignited the oil supply, which may or may not have added to the explosion but which definitely added to the intensity of the fire.

He'd had no idea of the destructive potential contained in his newspaper-wrapped package, and would have been amazed at the extent to which his plan to make people "yell" succeeded. By the time fire finished gutting the house, sixteen tenants were dead and forty-three injured (not counting Sammy Brown, who died a split second before Lou without ever waking from his alcohol-sodden sleep). Almost everyone had "yelled" a little, including Elaine Turner, who, with her parents and guests, escaped with minor scrapes and cuts.

Irving Schimler understood who had stolen the dynamite from the explosives shack when he later identified portions of his son's body. There was the cheap onyx ring he'd bought Lou a year ago, looking strange and terrible on the pale, waxlike hand—the hand without an arm.

Irving shook his head and wept, and then went to the hospital where his wife and daughter were being treated for shock. He just couldn't understand it. Lou had always been such a good boy. If anything, too good.

A few seconds after Louis Schimler died, Joe and Paula Theck were knocked unconscious just inside the lobby doors by pieces of falling ceiling. A few minutes after that, they were dragged to the street by Luke Brown. Within an hour, both rested in hospital beds.

Joe stayed there five weeks with a concussion and t\ broken ribs. Paula was released after twenty-four hours wit\ a small plaster patch on her forehead. She visited Joe twice a day, and each time wanted to cry her joy at his being alive.

She was oppressed by a sense of active fate, a feeling of almost excessive thankfulness. She kept thinking that if she hadn't been out all day Sunday with Joe, she'd have been in the apartment, perhaps alone, when the blast occurred. Even more than that, Joe's pausing to kiss her outside the house had prevented them from being in the center of the lobby when it was transformed into a blazing pit.

She couldn't escape the conclusion that an end of hate had saved them in one way, a rebirth of love in another.

Anyway, she and Joe were alive.

What else was important alongside that?

For the first time in her adult life, she went to a synagogue and prayed, thanking God in a trembling whisper while old men glanced at her approvingly.

At about the time Joe and Paula were beginning to stir into consciousness on the sidewalk in front of the house, Elliot Wycoff was lapsing into a coma in the courtyard. His right arm was horribly mangled; his blood formed puddles on the rough concrete and made the shoes of those trying to help him wet and sticky.

He was only moments away from death when an ambulance arrived, and might still have died if his uncle Phil hadn't run out of the courtyard to the street and pulled the intern away from a burn case. "Type O," Phil kept saying. "He once told me he had Type O blood. I remember. Type O . . ."

They gave Elliot blood plasma in the ambulance, and two hours after he arrived at the hospital surgeons decided they had to amputate. The arm was removed at a point some two inches from his shoulder, just about where his vaccination mark had been. He awoke to the fact forty-eight hours later. He screamed once, and then cried, and then just lay quietly.

A week later, he was smiling at doctors, nurses and visitors. Two weeks later, he was making plans for the future—happy plans. Hospital personnel were unanimous in stating he appeared to have made the best adjustment in the shortest time of any amputee they'd ever handled. (A staff psychiatrist was sent in to speak to him, to make sure this near-gaiety wasn't in reality a prelude to manic depression of the more ᵕt type. Elliot talked his ear off, and then sent him ᵕng with a series of jokes about analysts—"My son's ᵕnks he's a chicken. I'd take him to a psychiatrist to ᵕ, but we couldn't get along without the eggs.")

ᵕur weeks after the blast, Aunt Minnie broke down during visit. Weeping uncontrollably, and seconded in her statements by Uncle Phil, she told Elliot he'd ruined his life to save theirs.

"No, no," he protested, but they pushed on, lauding his heroism and altruism. Then they got to the point.

"You're going to be our heir, Elliot," Phil said. "We can't really repay you, but there's a nice few thousand in cash and quite a bit in blue-chip securities. We both worked until 1954, and then Minnie gave up her job . . ."

There was no way Elliot could change Phil's mind.

Minnie controlled her sobs long enough to state that she'd called Elliot's mother and told her that a trip to New York at this time was impossible. "I couldn't think of clever excuses, but I felt if she came here and saw you—this way—well, it might kill her—and it certainly wouldn't do you any good—so since she's in California why not keep it from her until you're better—"

At that point Elliot had smiled. They'd thought it was a brave-though-pathetic effort to show he was all right (reflecting the hospital staff's suspicions), but actually he was smiling because he could no longer control it. He was very, very happy. Everything was working out wonderfully.

This week had been the best of his life. It was hard to believe, but now that Mother was staying in California, every one of his problems had been solved. He was a man without a worry!

On Monday, he'd received calls from the Derrings and Slocums. Their sympathy was genuine and strong. Both families wanted him to convalesce at their homes, but despite the fact that Dorothy Slocum had visited him later in the day and sat weeping at his bedside, begging him to come to the estate, he hadn't yet made up his mind which invitation to accept.

On Tuesday, he'd had a call from the founder of the Lester Publishing Company, old Maurice himself.

"You'll always have a place with us, Wycoff. I promise you that. It's a fine thing you did for your aunt and uncle. Fine, my boy. And you haven't lost your future, your chances of advancing to executive editorial position. It's your mind the Lester Publishing Company wants, not your—" he'd cleared his throat— "arms." (Elliot had almost heard the crying violins.) Then Lester had gotten down to more prosaic matters. "By the way, your company policy insures you for three thousand dollars against the loss of a limb. And your salary will be paid until you can return to us and once again lend your fine talents to the selection of America's reading . . ."

All that, Elliot thought as his aunt sobbed and his uncle talked of eternal gratitude, *and peace of mind too*. He just had to smile!

It was the peace of mind, of course, which really made him happy. He'd licked his problem. Licked it for good. He didn't need Alex Fernol now. The blond youth had visited him only this morning—and within ten minutes had seen that Elliot was irrevocably out of his reach. Fernol had risen and said, "Goodbye, Elliot. I—I still think you're being foolish."

"Foolish?" Elliot had murmured, eyes bland. "About what, buddy?"

Fernol had left quickly.

So that was solved. And Elliot wouldn't lose the Derrings, Slocums, Sylvia Chrysler, or the respect of society. Nor would he have to fake interest in women; he finally had his excuse for not wanting to be with them. He was the bitter young man, crippled in a tragic fire, who rejected pity and preferred his own company and that of a few carefully selected friends.

No one would question that, or attempt to change it—at least not too strongly. And anyone who referred to him as a perennial guest would be reminded of the empty sleeve, or false arm, and made to feel ashamed.

He was the safe young man; safe from the contempt and revulsion he'd felt would be his no matter which way he turned.

He was the young man who'd made his peace with the world.

He smiled again, keeping his eyes on his aunt and uncle, never looking at the pinned-up pajama sleeve. Later, when they left, he would look at it. Later, he would marvel at how small a price he'd paid for a good life. . . .

Ten minutes after the explosion, Bonnie Allan sat on the floor of her sealed-off bedroom, coughing violently. The smoke thickened. She made a strangling sound, threshed about with her pajama-clad arms and legs, and fell over on her side. She lay still, breathing shallowly.

In the foyer, her father, Arnold Allan, clawed at the mountain of wood and plaster that had crashed down from the ceiling and blocked her doorway. He didn't have the slightest chance of breaking through without help, and he knew it. That's why he'd made his wife and mother crawl out the master bedroom window onto Fifteenth Avenue. "Get firemen with axes," he'd told them.

They'd run down the street, shouting for help, but the alarm hadn't yet been turned in; Luke Brown was just going back to the lobby for Joe and Paula Theck, and people were just coming out of nearby houses. There was no one to give Arnold Allan the kind of help he needed—the immediate help necessary to save Bonnie's life.

He kept clawing at the debris, and found he was fighting for breath, and then grew dizzy and fell. He lay face down, beating his fists feebly against the floor, sobbing, "Bonnie, Daddy's coming."

Bonnie didn't hear. Bonnie barely breathed. And flames began licking up around her bed.

Arnold Allan pushed himself up from the floor. The darkness was being broken by tongues of flame coming up in three or four spots between himself and the master bedroom. If he didn't get out now, he'd be trapped.

He didn't want to die.

His wife and mother needed him.

They'd need him even more with Bonnie gone—

He bellowed insanely, refusing to accept the idea that Bonnie could die. He roared obscenities, and hurled himself forward, remembering somehow the Guadalcanal beach and the men falling and the way he'd screamed his fear and hatred and kept going. He used every filthy epithet he knew, but as he rammed into what he thought was a pile of debris, he said, "Help her, God."

There was a cracking sound. Pain shot through his shoulder as he bounced backward and sat down. He felt the shoulder; nothing broken. Yet something had cracked with a dry, rotting sound.

He got up. The reddish light was much stronger, and he saw that he was off to the right of the pile of debris. He'd hit the wall between Bonnie's doorway and the room at the end of the corridor—his mother's room. It was a four- or five-foot stretch of what what should have been solid wood and plaster, and yet it had made a cracking sound, and now he could see how it was fissured. If he could go through it, he'd be in Bonnie's room—

But it was a *wall*, not a hunk of partitioning rock-wood or fiberwood or anything else weak and temporary. It was a thick, solid wall and he couldn't break it down.

He couldn't.

He hurled himself forward. He hit the wall and the cracking, rotting sound was louder. He fell back, and hit it again, and again, and again. The reddish light grew bright; flames were now licking up almost to the ceiling between him and the master bedroom—the only exit since the same crumbling outer wall that had blocked Bonnie's window had blocked his mother's and several other windows facing the courtyard.

He threw himself forward. It was a wall and he couldn't break it down. Of course not. He said it aloud: "I can't break it down, God. I can't!"

He remembered Bonnie's high, sweet voice saying, "You're a big, big man, Daddy. You're so big you reach the sky, don't you, Daddy?"

He was a big, big man.

He hit the wall. He was Samson pushing down the temple pillars. He was a mountain of a man and nothing could stop him.

"You're a *big, big man and you reach the sky*—"

He hit that wall like no human could.

He hit it twenty times in succession, and blood ran from his mashed, lacerated, broken right shoulder.

He switched to his left. He hit the wall seven more times, shrieking as bone shattered and ribs cracked and flesh tore.

"—you reach the sky, don't you, Daddy?"

He reached the sky. He hit the wall and smashed through and stumbled over his child. He picked her up and went back through the wall and staggered down the foyer. He walked through flame, shielding her, sobbing in agony, and reached the window.

He heard voices and handed Bonnie to someone and screamed as the pain became too much even for a Samson. He toppled into darkness.

The instant he awoke, he asked for her.

"Your little girl's fine," the blond, pretty nurse said as she bustled around the bed in which he was lying. He was in a hospital room. "Just a few minor cuts and bruises—"

"Don't lie to me," he said in a terrible voice.

She stepped back, face paling. He was coming out of bed— and the doctor had said: "This is one male patient that won't chase you around for a while, Anise. He's got fractured bones and burned legs and can't move—"

And here he was coming out of bed like a wild-eyed Frankenstein's monster!

She quickly raised her right hand and said, "By Holy Mother Mary, I swear your child is just down the hall, eating ice cream and feeling fine."

"I want to see," he said, but now he was convinced and the bigness went out of him and he became an ordinary man. He fell back.

He was almost asleep when Bonnie walked in between her mother and grandmother. He tried to smile, and said, "You okay, baby?"

She nodded and proudly showed him the bandages on her leg and side. "I wasn't scared, Daddy. I knew you'd take me away from that dirty smoke."

He closed his eyes. "Sure you did," he murmured, more to himself than to her. "How else could it be?"

Charles Maston didn't reach Koptic Court until almost 1:00 A.M., and then he did nothing but stare at the blazing six-story building, at the smoke and flames climbing higher and higher (eventually reaching the roof, bursting through and roaring upward in one of the greatest conflagrations Brooklyn had ever seen). Later, when he pulled himself together, he tried to help. He carried injured tenants to ambulances, comforted women and children, did whatever he could.

At 5:30 A.M., sections of the upper story began to crumble and whoever hadn't been saved was given up for dead. Police and firemen cleared the entire block, and Charles headed for a hotel.

The next day, he went to the maternity hospital and told his wife about the fire. He couldn't rid himself of the thought that he and Clara had been saved from death by a fantastic series of events involving unbelievably fortunate timing.

"Before you became pregnant," he said, "we were rarely out of the apartment on a weekend, and never out past eleven or twelve. So if things had remained the same, we would have been in bed when the explosion occurred. We might very well have burned to death like others on the sixth floor."

Clara nodded. "A woman two rooms down the hall had triplets. Can you imagine what we—"

"But really," he said, moving from the chair to the edge of her bed, "it's—well, it's amazing how everything seemed to conspire to save us. Everything! First you became pregnant and we decided to have the hysterotomy. If we'd gone through with it, we'd have been living just as we did before; we'd have been right there, in bed."

"Yes, but we didn't go through with the hysterotomy and it's all over now. Do you know that the baby finished a six-ounce bottle—"

He knew he shouldn't talk so much about it. He knew he was making her uncomfortable. But he couldn't help it. He had never been treated so well by fate, or the world, or—well, whatever it was.

"Have you considered the wonderful timing?" he said. "Have you thought of the baby coming two weeks early? If she hadn't, we'd have been in the apartment anyway. And what chance would we have had with you so heavy on your feet?"

"None," she said quietly.

"And there's more. Even with you and the baby safe here—"

"You'd have been home at the time of the blast," she concluded for him. "If Mrs. Gorino hadn't told you to hide in the bathroom, if you hadn't taken her advice and stayed late, you might be dead. I understand it all. Now what do you want me to say—that we've got to give thanks to God for a miracle?"

He stared at her, and her eyes were troubled, questioning.

"And whose God shall we thank? And when shall we start fighting over the God our baby'll thank?"

He kept staring, and his mind wouldn't function properly.

"Well, Charles, shall I say it was a miracle?"

Suddenly the whole thing slipped into proper perspective and he leaned forward and kissed her. "Miracle," he said. "Sure, a miracle that saved me and killed sixteen others. Sure. Me, Charles Maston, one of the Chosen People. By marriage."

They both laughed. They'd been lucky. And they felt their luck was only just beginning. . . .

Monday's newspapers carried a list of the dead and injured. It was a complete list, an official list, and yet it failed to include one tenant who most certainly deserved to be there. But since his wounds (his *death*, one might say) didn't show, and since he hadn't even arrived in Brooklyn until 2:30 A.M., he was understandably overlooked.

His name was Eli Weiner. He spent a horror-laden eternity searching for his wife and younger son. He rushed from one ladder to the other, from one stretcher to the other, from one fireman, policeman and tenant to the other. And all the time he kept telling his older son Dick that Rose and Teddy were all right, had to be all right. Dick nodded and wept.

At four-thirty Monday morning, Eli Weiner collapsed on the sidewalk. He'd just overheard a fireman say, "We got two from the third floor. Can't make out much except one was a woman, the other a boy. They were near the staircase. Wonder why they didn't use the fire escape . . ."

When Eli awoke, he was lying in an ambulance. It wasn't moving and he could see Fifteenth Avenue through the open doors. "Take it easy, mister," an attendant said, fillling a hypodermic. "I'm going to give you a sedative."

"That wasn't my wife and boy, was it?" Eli asked, and knew it was. Rose had always been afraid of heights. She would never go out on the fire escape with just Teddy to counsel her. So she'd tried to reach the staircase—

He passed out again, and when he woke up the attendant was giving him an injection.

"It wasn't my wife and son?" Eli whispered. "Can't you tell me it wasn't?"

The attendant said, "Just close your eyes. You need rest. You'll find out everything in a little while. Just close your eyes—"

Eli closed his eyes. He wanted to rest. He wanted to sleep and never wake up and never face the horror waiting for him.

"Rose!" he screamed. "Teddy!" He tried to get off the cot, and fell on his side as the injection took effect.

The attendant pushed him back. "Easy," he murmured. "Easy, Mr. Weiner."

Eli wanted to ask the man how he knew his name, and whether that meant he also knew the names of the woman and boy found burned to death on the third floor.

It was important that the question be settled immediately because on the answer hung his reason, his sanity. After all, if he'd been home instead of with Irene, he'd have made Rose use the fire escape and led her and Teddy to safety. And so it was his fault. And so it was he who'd burned them alive—

"Wife, son," he mumbled, and slipped away.

He came to, soon enough, in a hospital bed. He was told Rose and Teddy were dead. Dick was there, holding his hand and weeping. Eli yanked his hand away.

"Don't touch me," he said. "On the children are visited the sins of the fathers. Go away from me. Disown me. I've already killed Rose and Teddy. Go away before I kill you too. Go away. Go away. Go away—"

Dick called the nurse. She gave Eli a sedative and he slept. But he awoke, and there was another sedative, and he slept, and he awoke, and the whole thing was repeated again and again and again. Finally, he awoke strong enough to face what had happened, and that was when he became a casualty. The world was now a diabolical place; a place of Old Testament vengeance; a place of dark shadows in the corners of the new apartment he and Dick rented on Ocean Parkway.

Eli went back to his job and functioned as a member of his firm and fought a daily battle against insanity. He enlisted the aid of an expensive Manhattan psychiatrist, Dr. Lars Torrenson. He went to see Dr. Torrenson twice a week. He could barely wait for the visits, and sometimes had to telephone and beg for words of sustenance. After a while, Torrenson failed him and he tried another psychiatrist, and yet another. There were electro-shock treatments, and brief "rest periods" in a nice, private sanitarium—a place that gave you freedom when you requested it. Then he would function again; then he would fail again; then he would function again.

He never saw or heard from Irene. But he thought of her. He thought of how she'd stopped him from coming home early that terrible Sunday night; how he'd let himself be stopped. He thought of her in connection with a vengeful God and blood dripping from his hands.

Sometimes, when feeling especially weak, he couldn't tolerate the odor of broiling meat. . . .

Luke Brown was a man possessed. He didn't stop working to save his house and his tenants until dawn, and even then it was at the explicit order of an intern who bandaged his cut and burned hands and said, "Get across the street there and sit down before you fall down!" Luke wouldn't have listened (he hadn't listened when police and firemen cleared the block at five-thirty), but he was all played out, and Cora came over and pulled at his arm. They went across the street and sat down on a stoop and Luke said, "Sweet Jesus, why did this have to happen?"

"You did everything you could, Luke," Cora said.

"What'll Mr. Gorman think?"

"You—you were wonderful, Luke. No matter what he says, you were wonderful."

It was no overstatement. Luke had risked his life time and again, leading ground-floor tenants (those whose window exits had been blocked when a section of wall facing the courtyard had collapsed soon after the blast) to safety around the blazing pit. He'd gone up the staircase through what looked like a solid wall of fire to save people from the second floor. At least six firemen had already mentioned him to reporters, and the chorus of praise was gaining volume as tenants recovered from shock and began to talk about their super.

"Maybe Sammy did it," Luke said. "Maybe he fooled around with the fuel lines—"

"Police said something about the Schimler boy. Anyway, you locked Sammy in the storeroom, Luke. He couldn't—" She stopped then.

"Yeah. Locked him in. Maybe he tried to get out. Maybe he—"

"Stop trying to make yourself out to blame, Luke! Stop it! Stop it!"

He looked at her and put out a bandaged hand. "Okay, lady. Okay." But he felt the weight of guilt.

They watched firemen wetting down smoking, crumbling ruins.

"I'm sure finished here," Luke muttered a little later. "And how'll I ever get another job with this—"

Cora began to cry.

Time passed. The sky grew bright with morning. They sat on the stone steps. They didn't know where to go. Where was there to go?

And then Luke said, his voice angry, "One thing—I'd sure like my daddy to be here, to see how most of these white folks ran around and didn't help unless it was their own family and wasn't much good even then, 'cept for the firemen, and they're supposed to help. And even some of them wasn't much good. And those that was good, there was three, four colored men 'mong 'em. How can a man believe—" He shook his head and licked his lips and forgot what it was he wanted to say.

Later, he'd remember. Later, he'd begin to believe in the equality of man. Later, much later, and very slowly.

"Poor Sammy," he said, and the weariness became too much. "Let's find a place to sleep, Cora. Maybe your cousin—"

He saw them coming then. He got to his feet and brushed at his clothes and drew in a deep breath. Mr. Gorman was there, and lots of those men with notebooks, and the others with cameras. Well, he'd take whatever they dished out. He had let the house burn, and people die and get hurt, and so he deserved whatever they had in mind.

He hoped it wasn't jail. He sure hoped it wasn't jail.

"Luke," Mr. Gorman said, "for myself, for the tenants, for everyone who cares about people, I want to thank you. And I'm sorry about your son—terribly sorry." He paused. "There'll be a job for you as soon as you're ready to work. My brother has a new place in Queens—"

He wasn't sure what it all meant, but he listened to Mr. Gorman and to some reporters and to a fire inspector, and they all said nice things. Then he answered a million questions. Later, at Cora's cousin's place, he lay in a soft bed.

"Won't those white folks in Bam have a fit," Cora's cousin Lizzie was saying in the kitchen. "Won't they though! Why, Luke's a hero, and he saved white folks, and won't it look good for them to be saying colored ain't fit to ride buses and go to school with white when a colored man saved whites . . ."

Luke put the pillow over his head to shut out the happy voice. The woman was crazy! How could she be happy when he'd lost his son and the house and everything? How could she be happy that people had died?

And Mr. Gorman promising him a good job and those reporters calling him a hero. What the hell was wrong with everyone? Couldn't they see the smoking ruins of that fine house? Couldn't they smell the people who'd burned up—

He finally fell asleep. He dreamed of Sammy, and soaked his pillow with stinging tears. He eased his burden of guilt while sleeping, and when he awoke was able to sit at the table and look at the newspapers with his picture on the front pages and smile a little at all the nice things they'd written about him.

"Well," he said to Cora a few weeks later when they were inspecting the super's apartment in the new, not-yet-occupied Queens apartment house, "if this don't beat all. Imagine—this big, shiny place ours! You think the Lord's been watching over us, Cora?"

She hesitated, and then said, "Maybe, Luke. But it's you. It's what you are that's taking care of us. It's what you are that's going to take care of all our people."

He blinked at her. "Speak sense, lady."

She shook her head. "I can't. I mean, I can't make it plain. It's not a plain thing, Luke. The things in you aren't made to be spoken about plain. They're mixed up, and deep, and wonderful. They're—they're real strong, Luke. And lots of us—colored people—have got them. Maybe any time a people get stepped on, those strong things start growing. Anyway, they'll make us equal some day, Luke. You wait and see."

He grinned. "I aim to, lady. I aim to wait around a long, long time. I feel younger'n young." He pulled her to him and smacked her bottom. . . .

Months later, a thirteen-year-old boy dodged a police guard to scamper over the now-leveled ruins of Koptic Court. He found an interesting hunk of cement, and brought it home to show to his mother. "Look," he said. "It's got writing on it, see? It says 'curse.' And something else comes after it—you can make out the beginning of another letter."

The mother, a superstitious woman, made him throw it in the garbage can.

www.ingramcontent.com/pod-product-compliance
Lightning Source LLC
Chambersburg PA
CBHW021310250626
47155CB00002B/460